Sarah Ferguson, Duchess of York, is a bestselling memoirist and children's author, film producer, and has been a spokesperson for Weight Watchers and Wedgwood china. She currently campaigns for her international charity Sarah's Trust which champions children's literacy and education globally. She works on historical documentaries and films that draw on her deep interest in Victorian history. *Her Heart for a Compass* is her first novel for adults.

She is daughter-in-law of HM The Queen and former wife of Prince Andrew, Duke of York. Grandmother to August and Sienna and mother of two daughters, Princess Beatrice and Princess Eugenie. She lives in Windsor with five Norfolk terriers.

Her
Heart
for a
Compass

SARAH
FERGUSON
Duchess of York

With Marguerite Kaye

MILLS & BOON

Mills & Boon
An imprint of HarperCollins*Publishers* Ltd
1 London Bridge Street
London SE1 9GF

HarperCollins*Publishers*
1st Floor, Watermarque Building, Ringsend Road,
Dublin 4, Ireland

This edition 2022

First published in Great Britain by Mills & Boon,
an imprint of HarperCollins*Publishers* Ltd 2021
2

With thanks to Marguerite Kaye

Sarah Ferguson, Duchess of York asserts the moral right to be
identified as the author of this work.
A catalogue record for this book is
available from the British Library.

ISBN: 978-0-00-838364-0

MIX
Paper from
responsible sources
FSC® C007454
FSC
www.fsc.org

This book is produced from independently certified FSC™ paper
to ensure responsible forest management.

For more information visit: www.harpercollins.co.uk/green

Printed and Bound in the UK using 100% Renewable
Electricity at CPI Group (UK) Ltd

This book is dedicated to my beautiful girls, who have all the strength and courage of Lady Margaret. They too have followed their hearts and live life on their own terms. This book is for you, Beatrice and Eugenie, with all my love.

Chapter One

A H, THERE YOU ARE! IT'S fast approaching midnight, my dear."

Lord Rufus Ponsonby, the Earl of Killin, was considered by most to be a presentable-looking man. His tall, rather lean figure was always immaculately dressed. His aquiline profile was suitably haughty, as befitted an earl of the realm. Every aspect of him was austere, repressed, and calculated.

Lady Margaret Montagu Douglas Scott took an involuntary step back as he loomed over her. "I'm all too aware of that."

As ever, he seemed oblivious to her prickly reaction to him. "Why are you skulking in the shadows? Perhaps you are insecure about your appearance," he continued, answering his own question. "Allow me to reassure you. Your gown is neither too simple nor too ornate for the occasion. Her Grace, your mother, has excellent taste."

Surveying the man her mother had helped select to be her husband, Margaret begged to differ. "I would have preferred a turquoise gown, actually."

"All young ladies in their first Season wear white."

"Look at me," Margaret persisted, exasperated beyond words because Killin never did look at her, not properly. "Don't you think I resemble a ghost at my own betrothal party? I am, quite literally, a spectre at the feast."

"I think your tendency to be fanciful is coming to the fore."

"There are so many ruffles and swags on this gown I feel like I'm wearing a set of drapes."

His lordship, his attention on his watch, didn't notice the note of suppressed hysteria in her tone. Killin checked his gold timepiece against the ballroom clock, frowned, checked again, made a minor adjustment, then checked it one last time before snapping the case closed and returning it to his waistcoat pocket.

"We had better join your parents for the announcement," he said. "They will be getting anxious."

That little vocal tic he had, something between a cough and a snort, as if he were about to clear his throat and decided against it, made Margaret's toes curl. No-one else seemed to notice, yet every time he opened his mouth to speak she braced herself for it. "I think if anyone has a right to be anxious," she said, smiling through gritted teeth, "it should be me. My life is about to change forever, after all."

Though he smiled in return, it was a token effort that failed to be reflected in his eyes. "We are on the brink of a new life together, Lady Margaret. *I* for one am eager to embrace it."

The very notion of being embraced by him was repellent. Fortunately, in the month since their match had been arranged, he had made no attempt to do any such thing, allowing Margaret to ignore her own physical revulsion and persuade herself that she would be able to reconcile herself to marrying him. He had never tried to kiss her. If he touched her, it was merely to usher her here or there, and his hands never lingered on her. Was all that about to change? She shuddered inwardly. Was this model of propriety simply a gentleman patiently waiting until his matrimonial rights were formally endorsed? Dear heavens, even trying to imagine his lips on hers made her want to scrub her mouth with her handkerchief.

Once the formal announcement was made, there would be no going back. She would be engaged to be married to a man she loathed and who, she was utterly convinced, didn't give a damn about her. No, worse than that. The more time she spent in Killin's company, the more certain Margaret became that he actively disliked her. She had tried to believe otherwise, but she was increasingly aware of his carefully disguised disapproval of everything about her, from her manner to her weight.

The fact that he managed to keep his feelings so well hidden from everyone else was another source of irritation. Although *feelings*, Margaret reminded herself, were quite irrelevant when it came to matchmaking. Killin was set on marrying her for his own ends, and her parents were even more determined that she marry him. She had resolved to make them all happy by doing her duty, which was undoubtedly the correct course of action, so why were her wretched instincts choosing this highly inconvenient moment to rebel? Was she really going to marry this man? It seemed suddenly, terrifyingly, impossible.

"Lady Margaret! We really must join the duke and duchess. Their patience, like mine, must be wearing thin."

To speak up now, after weeks of biting her tongue, was unthinkable. And futile. Defeated and dejected, her only option was to brace herself for the inevitable. "I need a moment alone to collect my thoughts. *Please*, I beg of you," Margaret added, seeing his resistance forming. "I wish to compose myself, my lord. All eyes will be upon us, and I don't want to let you down."

More importantly, she didn't want to let Mama down. Or Papa. She didn't want to let anyone down. Not that she was planning to, but she desperately needed a moment of solitude. She had spent the entire evening being assailed by well-wishers.

To her immense relief, Killin conceded. "Very well then, if you must. But don't be long."

Without giving him a chance to change his mind, Margaret hurried away. The atmosphere in the crowded ballroom was stifling. She was so hot and flustered she couldn't think straight. The blend of expensive perfume, pomade, and perspiration made her nose twitch. She wanted to sneeze. Oh, for a lungful of pure, fresh air, or better still, for the familiar, comforting smells of the stable block back home in Dalkeith. Spider, her beloved pony, obeyed her every command unquestioningly. If only she were as well schooled. If only, as Mama opined all too often, she could be more like Victoria. Killin would probably have preferred her paragon of an older sister, too, but Victoria had been destined from the cradle to marry Lord Schomberg Kerr, the son of Mama's best friend. Victoria, the beau ideal Margaret couldn't bring herself to emulate, had been married in February, forcing Killin to settle for the Duke and Duchess of Buccleuch's second and second-best daughter.

Biddable Victoria had seemed happy to accept her fate. Margaret had endeavoured to believe Mama when she told her that she knew best, to persuade herself that her visceral dislike of the man intended for her would lessen as she came to know him. Might familiarity make him more amenable? At this moment, she simply could not believe it. Why couldn't she see Killin as others did? She had tried; no-one could fault her for lack of effort. But she had failed dismally. If only she wasn't so utterly certain that his feelings reflected hers. He wasn't in the least bit interested in her, only her family connections. Behind the suave, gentlemanly carapace Killin presented to the world lurked a decidedly cold fish. Yet no-one else seemed to realise this. Could she be wrong? In her heart, she knew she was not, but it was far too late to do anything about it.

Margaret slipped out through the French doors, her senses assaulted by the acrid stench of the Thames, for the gardens of Montagu House faced directly onto the river. Putting her hand over her nose, she edged backwards to the darkest recess of the terrace. She wouldn't linger long. She'd face the music momentarily.

Uncovering her nose, she tried inhaling through her mouth, blowing the taste of the Thames away with each exhale, like a pipe smoker using cheap tobacco, but the stench caught the back of her throat. Her skin itched under the dusting of pearl powder meant to mask her freckles. Her eyes smarted from the revolting mixture prescribed by Mama to tint her naturally auburn lashes and brows fashionably black. Though her maid Molly swore otherwise, she was convinced it consisted almost entirely of coal dust.

How much longer dare she procrastinate?

Five minutes wasn't nearly enough.

She needed five hours.

Five weeks.

Or better still, five more years.

And even then?

Her heart was racing. The cage of her enormous formal crinoline seemed to have a life of its own, despite the straps which were meant to control it. In the last few weeks, she had had little appetite for food, and Mama's constantly deployed measuring tape showed her waist had shrunk to just nineteen inches, yet she still felt breathless, as if Molly had laced her corset too tightly.

Edging farther away from the hubbub of the ballroom, she came smack up against the balustrade, snatching at it just in time to prevent herself from stumbling down the steps and into the darkened gardens. The smell from the river was overpowering, but as usual she had mislaid the fan which should have been attached to her wrist. Her hair would be frizzing in the damp air, ruining all poor Molly's hard work. What she'd give to pull every pin from her rebellious red mop and let it tumble wild and loose down her back. At least then one part of her would be free.

The notion made her laugh. Her laughter had a manic edge. Her feet took another cautious step backwards, down the first of the steps leading to the garden.

She wasn't running away.

She could not possibly run away.

She really ought to return to the ballroom and get on with it. Yet somehow she found herself at the bottom of the steps.

Inside, the orchestra struck the last chords of the waltz. She had three or four minutes at most. The dancers would be making their sedate bows and curtsies. She could picture the scene with jaw-clenching clarity. The ballroom would be a blaze of light reflected in the mirrors, for the candles in the three huge crystal chandeliers were all lit, along with the gas sconces. The crush of guests, the women in their colourful gowns and the men in their black dinner suits, would be turning to face the dais. The ladies would be plying their fans, the gentlemen dabbing discreetly at their faces with their handkerchiefs. The huge displays of roses would be starting to droop. Hers was not the only coiffure that would be starting to frizz.

Of their own accord, her feet began to back her slowly away from the house, along the path that wound its way through the garden to the wall bordering the Thames. Inside, an army of footmen garbed in formal livery, their hair moulded into a wig-like coiffure with flour-and-water paste, would be lining up under the butler's gimlet eye, ready to distribute glasses of iced champagne in anticipation of the celebratory toast to come.

The press had been speculating about the announcement for weeks. The highest born and most illustrious and influential members of society were present to witness it. Everyone who was anyone had come to Montagu House, for an invitation from the Duke of Buccleuch was second only to a royal summons. Not Princess Louise, though. Margaret's oldest friend, who counselled her to accept her fate gracefully, was chained to the queen's side at Osborne House on the Isle of Wight, and would not be present to witness her compliance.

And comply she must! Margaret willed herself to reverse her progress, to return to the ballroom, and join what amounted to a victory parade, with herself the trophy to be displayed. But she couldn't do it.

Not yet.

Not ever.

The truth brought her to an abrupt halt. From the very moment she had allowed Mama to persuade her to accept Killin's proposal, she had been deluding herself. No matter how much her parents wanted it, she could not sacrifice herself on the altar of duty by marrying a man she knew in her heart would make her miserable. She simply couldn't go through with it. Not even if it meant committing what amounted to social suicide, as it surely would.

Back in the ballroom, Mama would be standing on the dais, looking as fragrantly beautiful as ever. Beside her would be Papa, tall and ramrod-straight, his black evening clothes in stark contrast to his distinctive flame of red hair, which was almost as vibrant as Margaret's own. He would be frowning, in all likelihood impatiently consulting his watch. Victoria would be standing just behind Mama along with Kerr. And Killin would be standing at the forefront of the family group, anxious to confirm his place within the prestigious firmament of the Buccleuch dynasty.

Even as her mind raced, trying desperately to reason one last time with her rebellious instincts, Margaret's feet inexorably resumed their backwards journey.

Go back in, she urged herself. She was, almost uniquely in her nearly nineteen years on this earth, about to make her parents happy and proud. But at what cost? She would become, in the eyes of the law and society, Killin's property.

Margaret took a few more backwards steps. As long as she had the ballroom in sight, she could persuade herself that she might return there at any moment. She was keeping them waiting, that was all. Wasn't that the bride's prerogative? Though it must already be past midnight. Any moment now, Mama would send Victoria out to usher her back inside like a sheep-dog rounding up a panicked ewe.

That thought sent Margaret backwards still farther into the gloom. She tried valiantly one last time to persuade herself to do the right thing. She pictured herself on the dais, placing her hand compliantly in Killin's. He'd clear his throat before chiding her for keeping him waiting.

It was that, the thought of that incredibly annoying little habit he had and surely the most preposterous reason in history for calling off a betrothal, which decided her. If she returned to the ballroom, she knew she would be lost. Her courage would desert her, and before she knew it, the announcement would be made. On the other hand, if she stayed here hidden in the garden long enough, then her parents would have no choice but to finally put an end to her suffering. They would never forgive her, but on the bright side, neither would Killin. More importantly, if she went through with this engagement, she'd never forgive herself.

Sorry, sorry, I'm so sorry.

Repeating that one heartfelt phrase to herself over and over, Margaret hoisted up her crinoline, turned her back on the ballroom, and hurried towards the shrubs at the very edge of her father's property.

Tears streamed down her cheeks, mingling with the sooty concoction that blackened her lashes, blinding her. The scent of expensive tobacco filled her nostrils just before she collided full tilt into a man idly puffing on a cigar. She would have fallen, set off balance by the contact with his solid bulk, had he not put his arms around her to steady her. The collision overset her shattered nerves completely. Margaret screamed, flailing wildly at him, attempting to kick his shins and stubbing her slippered toes in the process.

He let her go immediately. "Lady Margaret?"

She recognised the cultured Highland lilt as belonging to Donald Cameron of Lochiel, an acquaintance of her father and some sort of diplomat. "Leave me alone. Please, forget you saw me."

Needless to say, he ignored her plea. "What in God's name are you doing out here on your own in the dark? Your engagement is about to be announced."

"I thought I'd just pop out for a smoke first," Margaret replied witheringly, well beyond any attempt to be polite.

Startled, he eyed the lit cigar in his own hand, before dropping it and stamping it out. "You're nervous and no wonder. It must be a daunting prospect, especially in front of the great and the good. Let me lend you my arm."

He spoke to her as if to a child. Lochiel was very tall and sombrely dressed, the type of man commonly referred to as handsome or distinguished. However, like most men, handsome, distinguished or otherwise, he sported a beard, and one of the most objectionable types, too, known as the Newgate frill, which framed his face like a wiry ruff. "I don't need your support," Margaret snapped. "For pity's sake, just leave me be."

For one glorious moment, she thought he was about to do as she asked. "You need a little time to compose yourself, that's all. I can understand that, but really, Lady Margaret, it will not do to keep everyone waiting indefinitely, you know."

Lochiel reached for her arm, trying to usher her towards the ballroom. "Come with me. Your parents and Killin will be—"

"No!" She pushed him violently away. Snatching up the folds of her gown, Margaret ran the last few yards to the garden gate. Heaving it open, she stumbled through, pulling it closed behind her, and fled into the night.

Chapter Two

Y OU'RE HERE AT LAST!" HER Royal Highness Princess Louise jumped to her feet as Margaret entered the room.

"Oh, Lou, it's so good to see you," Margaret said, throwing her arms around her best friend.

As usual Louise stiffened slightly, bearing the physical contact only long enough not to offend, before she gently disentangled herself. "Sit, sit, and tell me everything. How are you?"

"Never mind me, how are *you*?" Margaret untied her bonnet and yanked off her gloves, throwing them carelessly onto a chair. "Are you truly fully recovered? Let me look at you."

Louise struck a theatrical pose, turning her head from one side to the other before giving a little twirl. "See, fully mended, as good as new."

Studying her closely, Margaret was reassured to find no trace of her recent illness in Louise's enviably creamy complexion and sparkling grey-blue eyes. Her soft brown hair was as fashionably dressed as ever, with not a rebellious strand in sight, for Louise was extremely particular about her appearance. "I *wish* I had a modicum of your style. Even if I spent hours in front of the mirror, I couldn't achieve such perfection. And you're so slim. There's not a pick on you, as my Molly would put it."

"My waist and my age match perfectly since my birthday last week. Seventeen."

"A claim I could not make, unfortunately, unless I was an old maid of twenty-five."

"What you need," Louise said, "is a dose of tubercular meningitis."

"Is that what you had?"

"According to the doctor. Sick headaches is what I'd call it, but that wouldn't justify the exorbitant fee he charges. I *was* very poorly, though not sick enough to persuade the queen to leave me behind at Balmoral." Louise grimaced. "The train journey south was horrendous. They had to abandon me half-way, for I was too ill to continue, but I'm perfectly well now, I assure you."

"You certainly look it." Margaret flopped inelegantly down on the sofa. The little Scotch terrier which had been occupying the other end of the seat yapped enthusiastically and leapt onto her lap. She ran her hand along the dog's wiry coat, setting his tail wagging frantically. "What a darling. So like my own precious Lix. I do miss my dogs."

Louise pulled up a chair and set about making tea from the service which had been laid out in readiness. "That's Laddie. He's getting on a bit, so he likes to hide in here from the rest of the pack. They're too boisterous for him, poor old thing." She passed Margaret a cup of tea and a generous slice of cake. "I'm assuming you don't want to bother starting with bread and butter?"

"No, thank you." Ignoring the cake fork, Margaret took a bite. "Chocolate, my favourite."

"I know."

"Aren't you going to have even a tiny slice?"

"Not even a crumb. I have no intention of ending up like Mama. Since Papa died, she has quite literally grown in stature, and she was never exactly sylph-like to begin with."

"Oh come, Lou, in her early portraits she had a lovely figure."

"A crinoline hides a multitude of sins. The queen has no discipline when it comes to the table."

"Nor have I." Margaret rolled her eyes. "Fortunately for the sake of my many, many new dresses, I have Mama to keep me in check. At least now I'm in London you and I will be able to see more of each other."

"I hope so, though you know that the queen has first call on my time. She has become incredibly possessive of us girls since my father died, and actively discourages us from seeing our friends, never mind socialising without her. It's all a bit oppressive. Tell me, how are you finding life in the capital?"

Knowing better than to offer sympathy, Margaret did as she was bid. "Well, the smells are absolutely foul. The air itself tastes disgusting, especially when there is a fog. It's like licking a penny. And the dirt! It quite literally falls from the skies, I am forever having to wash my face and hands, and my petticoats are coated with what they call mud from the streets."

"Horses," Louise said cryptically. "Mostly."

"Everything is so brightly lit, and so noisy, too," Margaret continued. "The streets are full of people no matter the hour, and buildings everywhere seem to be in the process of being pulled down and rebuilt. I can't sleep for the noise of carriages endlessly rattling past outside, and though I've been assured that the new gas lighting in Montagu House is safe, every time it makes that funny popping noise I jump."

"Her Majesty considers gas lighting unsafe; she won't have it here at Windsor. When I asked you how you liked London, M., I meant society, for thanks to the queen's hunger for my company, I am forced to enjoy life vicariously, you know. You have made quite an impression, if the papers are to be believed."

"Honestly, you would think they would have more important topics to write about than what gown I wore to what ball, who I danced with, and whether or not my dance card was full."

"Now you have a taste of what my life has been like since childhood, living in the full glare of public scrutiny. It is why I make a point of always being perfectly turned out. One never knows who is watching."

"Well, I'm not used to it and frankly don't welcome the attention. At home in Dalkeith my only audience is a herd of cud-chewing cows."

Louise giggled. "I'm not sure the gentlemen of the press would welcome the comparison."

"Seriously, though, I have had scarce a moment to myself since I came to town. I have to change my toilette for every engagement, sometimes three or four times a day, and the Season doesn't even start properly until after Easter."

"I know you're dreading it, M., but I wish *I* could have a proper debut. I would have loved to have my own coming-out ball, but the queen refused point-blank to consider opening the ballroom at Buckingham Palace."

"Oh, Lou." Margaret reached across the table to touch her friend's hand in sympathy, thus committing two social gaffes at once. "Is there *no* sign of Her Majesty casting off her mourning?"

"Quite the contrary." Louse contemplated the thin slice of bread and butter on her plate, then decided against taking a bite, instead helping Margaret to a second piece of cake. "Almost every single day since Papa died, Mama tells us that she longs to join him. We live on tenterhooks, for almost everything we say makes her weep— honestly, Margaret, you'd think that laughing was a cardinal sin. And when the queen is not wishing she were dead, I swear she is determined to make everyone around her die of boredom. Were it not for my sculpture lessons with Mary Thornycroft, I think I would go quite mad. I feel sorry for Mama, truly I do, but she is such tedious company, and she seems quite oblivious to the fact that Lenchen and I are no longer children but young women."

"Goodness yes, your sister Helena is older than me."

"She's almost nineteen." Louise pushed her own tea-cup to one side and picked up her sketchbook, idly flicking through the pages.

14

"Last month we were invited to a fancy dress ball at Claremont. Lenchen and I were so excited, until we found out it was a *children's* ball, and Arthur was to attend with us. We made the best of it. I wore a gown in the French style from Louis Quinze. White silk looped over pink and white satin petticoats. *Naturellement*, I designed it myself."

"Naturally," Margaret agreed. "And naturally, you were the belle of the ball."

"Well, I did look rather wonderful. My hair was powdered, and I had the dress trimmed with old lace belonging to the queen which was a mistake, for seeing it brought on a fit of her megrims. 'Oh, if only my dear Albert were here to share this moment,'" Louise said, aping her mother's tone and wringing her hands.

"Stop! It is so wrong of you to make me laugh when her grief is very real."

"And it has such staying power," Louise said acerbically. "My father would be appalled to see her wear her heart on her sleeve as she does. You know how stiff and proper he always was."

Margaret shuddered. "He was terrifying. He had a way of looking straight through me, as if I was so unworthy of his attention as to be invisible."

"Better invisible than draw his ire by misbehaving."

"Which you almost never did, Lou, for even when you have been naughty, you manage to shift the blame on to someone else. Don't deny it—you know it's true."

Louise shrugged. "The trick, as I am forever telling you, is to keep a straight face and say nothing."

Margaret fed the remains of her cake to Laddie. "My father says my face is a card-sharper's delight, it is so transparent."

"It's true, M. I can always tell when my conversation is boring you."

"You are never boring!"

"No, I am endlessly fascinating and you hang on my every word, but sadly not everyone is as entertaining. I am often bored, but I never let it show. That is why the queen finds me such excellent company."

"How do you do it? Keep your thoughts from showing on your face, I mean?"

"Goodness, what a thing to ask. I don't know—it is simply something one does."

"It's not something *I* do."

"Then it's something you'd better learn to do or you are going to find yourself in trouble sooner rather than later. You don't want to get a reputation for being capricious."

"Yet that describes you perfectly."

"Ah, but nobody knows that apart from you, my dear M."

"I know I sound ungrateful, but I'm not. I am perfectly well aware of how fortunate I am. Most young women would give their eyeteeth for the opportunity I am being given, to have a whole new wardrobe of gowns and to have every moment of the day filled with engagements."

"Goodness, the duchess has been beating the duty drum hard."

"With my sister Victoria accompanying her on cymbals. The problem is, Lou, I'm not here in London to enjoy myself. I'm here to do my duty and make a good match."

"It's what we both must do, sooner rather than later. It is the price we pay for being well-born and mere females."

"Yes, but I wish I could marry later rather than sooner."

"Unlikely, however, given that you are proving to be such a hit."

"Heaven knows why! Mama is quite as perplexed as I am by my success. Perhaps it's because it's so early in the Season and there is little competition."

"Or perhaps it's because you are the Duke of Buccleuch's flame-haired daughter—"

"Second daughter."

Louise waved a dismissive hand. "I'm the queen's fourth

daughter, but in the eyes of the world all that matters is that I am a princess. Which means, of course, that if I were properly out in society I would spare you some of the press's attention, for a princess trumps a mere duke's daughter."

"You are out now, though, aren't you? You were at the ball at Marlborough House last week."

"Did you read the report of it in *The Times*? I assure you, it was every bit as dull as it sounded. It was held to celebrate Bertie and Alix's second wedding anniversary. Alix is expecting again, though of course you'd never know, for she is laced so tightly."

Margaret winced. "One can't help but wonder if it would be better *not* to squish one's unborn child for the sake of fashion."

"She wears a special corset which accommodates the baby," Louise said, dropping her voice to a conspiratorial whisper. "When she told me her happy news she was at home en déshabillé, and her interesting state was perfectly obvious. She was showing me the gown she'd had made for the anniversary ball, and I asked her how on earth she expected to get into it. So she let me see the contraption, as she called it." Louise's cheeks coloured. "It looked more like an instrument of torture than a corset."

"Why wear it then? Breeding is perfectly natural."

Louise affected a shudder. "You must not say *breeding* in polite company. Horses breed, as do farmyard animals and dogs. The populace procreate. But ladies—my dear, absolutely not. Do you know nothing?"

"Since coming to London, I've realised that my ignorance knows almost no bounds," Margaret confessed. "How does one describe it more delicately?"

"One may admit to being in an interesting condition or expecting an event—but only to one's female friends. In public, a lady must simply pretend that her unborn child doesn't exist."

"Well, I think that's preposterous, given the amount of time a married lady spends with child."

"Oh, I agree," Louise said, abandoning her affected tone. "Look at my sister Vicky. She's had four so far, in only six years. Can you imagine! It will be your sister Victoria's turn soon, now she is married. I blame the queen, you know, for setting the fashion by having nine of us."

Louise began to wander about her bedchamber, picking up and replacing the various statuettes, books, and drawing paraphernalia that covered most of the surfaces. "Now she has set the trend for inexorable grieving, and it's suffocating. She is quite determined that no-one else be allowed to extract a single drop of joy from life if she cannot."

"I hadn't realised things were so dismal."

Louise sat back down again. "I envy you your freedom."

"The only freedom I have is to disappoint my mother on a daily basis now that we are under the same roof," Margaret retorted. "If it's not my hair, it's my freckles or my figure. Or the way I enter a room—she says I burst in like a London bobby—or the fact that I can't seem to retain my fan, never mind use it properly. Did you know, Louise, that one can communicate using a fan?"

"But of course."

"Well, I didn't."

"Lenchen and I have our own secret language using cutlery," Louise said with a mischievous smile. "We use it during those eternal dinners we have to endure with the queen and her entourage. It means we can make polite, tedious conversation with the inevitably polite, boring courtier sitting next to us, and at the same time hold a completely different conversation between ourselves just by rearranging a spoon or a fork."

"No! Show me."

"Certainly not, for you would try to use it, and your face would give you away and that would be the end of that. I shall teach you something more useful. I know—I shall give you a lesson in the etiquette of curtsying."

"I was taught to curtsy at a very young age, when I was first introduced to your mother. You must have been three, for I was four and it was when I came to London for the very first time, for the state opening of the Great Exhibition."

"We were thick as thieves from the start. Prince Albert never approved of our friendship, did you know that? He thought you were a bad influence on me."

"Ha! Little did he know that it is the other way around."

"I think you will find me a positive influence and a useful fount of knowledge, when it comes to the ways of the world," Louise said primly.

"Now that I cannot argue with. I will look to you as my guide as I am dressed up and paraded about like a bit of prime blood-stock at an auction."

"Ladies and gentlemen, may I present Lady Margaret Elizabeth Louise Montagu Douglas Scott," Louise intoned. "The second daughter and sixth child of the Duke and Duchess of Buccleuch. What am I bid for this young woman, who has a large dowry and a most excellent lineage?"

"Don't forget the added bonus of a mother who has proved herself a productive brood mare."

"Margaret!" Louise's mouth quivered. "I cannot imagine the duchess ever saying anything so vulgar."

"Well, no, but I swear they have actually drawn up a list of my attributes. It is, I'll wager, a very short list, mind you, but I am equally certain that they have a corresponding list of the qualities they require any potential husband to possess. Pedigree, social standing, estates, connections, income, politics." Margaret wrinkled her nose. "All the important things. It wouldn't matter to them if my future husband was ninety years old."

"Oh no, ninety is far too old to father children. I'd say they would have set the age limit at sixty. Seventy at a push."

"Stop! There is no way on this earth I could kiss a seventy-year-old man."

"You'd have to do more than kiss him."

"Eugh!" Margaret covered her ears.

"You brought the subject up, and one must face facts. As a Montagu Douglas Scott, it is expected of you."

"But no-one seems to care that underneath I'm an actual person."

"No, but when did they ever think of either of us in that way? It's not as if it's a surprise that you must marry, is it? And there are worse fates, you know. If I don't marry, I will dwindle into eternal spinsterhood as Mama's scribe, which I am determined not to do."

"Oh no, that would be a terrible waste, for you have such an artistic talent." Margaret's face fell. "The sad fact is, though, that I have no talents to speak of."

"Then I fear you have no choice but to resign yourself to the path mapped out for you."

"I didn't expect you to be so unsympathetic."

"I'm being realistic."

"I suppose you're right. Let us have done with this depressing subject."

"Yes, let's. You are being formally presented at court in April, aren't you? I expect I'll be there in attendance with the queen as usual. Shall I wink at you as you make your curtsy?"

"Do not! I'll be bound to giggle if you do, and then I'll probably trip on my train," Margaret said, torn between laughter and horror.

"Now I feel obliged to wink, just to see if you have paid attention to a single thing I've told you today. Who has the duchess employed to take your carte-de-visite photograph? If she has not yet made the arrangements, I can recommend Mr. Jabez Hughes.

Here, take a look at this example he produced for my friend Sybil. Isn't it lovely?"

Margaret studied the little card, which showed a stern-looking young woman leaning on a pillar. "Why do they always pose in profile?"

"Everyone has a better side, and a person's face is more distinctive in profile." Louise picked up her sketchbook and a charcoal. "Look, I'll show you. Sit there with Laddie while I draw you both. In fact, let's include your ideal husband in the composition. What is he like, do you think? Describe him to me."

"Ah, there's the rub," Margaret said ruefully. "I have absolutely no idea. Someone my parents would heartily disapprove of, knowing me!"

NOTABLE DEBUTANTE TO MAKE
FIRST ROYAL COURT APPEARANCE

On Thursday, the queen will journey from Windsor to Buckingham Palace to host her fourth Reception of the London Season, at which select gathering a number of young ladies making their debut will be presented. Her Majesty will be accompanied by the Princesses Helena and Louise, and ably assisted by His Royal Highness, the Prince of Wales.

One of this year's most notable debutantes will make her first formal appearance at this Reception. The Titian-haired Lady Margaret Montagu Douglas Scott is the second daughter of the Duke of Buccleuch and Queensberry, one of the most eminent peers in the land, formerly Lord Privy Seal and currently Gold Stick for Scotland. Lady Margaret, who has been hailed as a "breath of fresh Scotch air," will be accompanied by her mother, the Duchess of Buccleuch, daughter of the Second Marquess of Bath, and former Mistress of the queen's Robes.

Readers are advised to avoid the vicinity of Buckingham Palace on Thursday if their business permits them to do so, as severe congestion of all approaches is anticipated. A strict code of dress is enforced for this most formal and exclusive occasion. Those wishing to admire the toilettes of the ladies will be able to peruse them at their leisure in next Saturday's edition which will contain as many lavish illustrations as can be accommodated between these pages.

Chapter Three

THE DAY OF MARGARET'S FORMAL presentation at court started very early when Molly roused her at some ungodly time to herald several hours of primping and titivating. First there had been her bath, a daily ritual made considerably easier in Montagu House, which had running water. Usually Margaret enjoyed this luxury, lying back with the rose-scented water washing over her, closing her eyes, and imagining she was at home in Dalkeith, but today she was not permitted to bathe alone.

Celeste, Mama's formidable French maid, was in charge, insisting that Molly apply the pumice stone vigorously to Margaret's feet while she combed oils into her hair. More emollients were rubbed into her skin when she emerged like a boiled lobster from the tub, until she glistened like an eel and her nose twitched from the warring scents, and her protests that none of this was in the least necessary since her entire person would be covered with a court dress predictably fell on deaf ears.

Draped in a cotton shift which clung to her slick body, Margaret was next placed in front of the dressing table, where the triple mirror gave her far too much insight into Celeste's machinations. The first layer applied to her face was a cold cream that Mama had insisted she use daily since coming to London in the vain hope it would fade her freckles. Though it was scented with rose water, Margaret was convinced she could smell the spermaceti, a substance taken from a poor whale's head, every time it was applied.

It had made no difference to her stubborn freckles, which meant that next Celeste dusted her face with pearl powder, and then dusted it again when Margaret sneezed violently. She lost track of the different preparations that then followed from the Celeste's mahogany box of tricks. Her brows were plucked and coloured. Her lashes and cheeks were tinted. There were drops to make her eyes sparkle, and a beeswax pomade to make her lips shine.

Her hair took an age to tame into submission, by which time her neck and shoulders were stiff and sore with the effort of keeping still and her scalp prickled with pins. Next came the trussing up in the steel-boned cage of her corset, a painful and mortifying process supervised by Mama wielding her dreaded measuring tape. Another cage was donned next in the form of her crinoline; and finally it took both Celeste and Molly to manoeuvre her into the confection of lace, silk, and satin that was her court dress, with its prescribed short puffed sleeves and low-cut neckline. The long lace train was then fixed to her shoulders, and finally the lace veil was fixed to the back of her head with a painful assortment of combs and pins, topped with the two white feathers that all unmarried ladies being presented to the queen must wear. Her long white gloves were fastened tightly, which meant, she realised with dismay, that she would be able to eat absolutely nothing until her return for fear of spotting them. The white ostrich feather fan was attached to one wrist, her simple pearl necklace and matching bracelet fixed. Then she stood for an age while Mama and Celeste inspected, adjusted, consulted, and primped and Molly watched, her smile pained. Finally, with a flourish, Mama presented her first with a lace handkerchief, and then with an enormous bouquet.

Margaret barely recognised the carefully packaged young woman staring back at her from the mirror, no doubt indistinguishable from the bevy of other debutantes to be presented that day. Even her hair managed to appear colourless. Panic made her heart beat faster, making her breathless. The whole point of this absurd, antiquated ceremony was to establish her as a member of an elite club she didn't want to join. After her presentation she would be officially, inescapably up for auction in the matrimonial mart. This wasn't the beginning of her life as an eligible young lady—it marked the end of her freedom.

"Mama . . ."

"Excellent. You look quite the part," the duchess said, unaware that this was exactly what Margaret wanted to avoid. "Now, let us go downstairs and have your likeness taken before you manage to spoil it."

She was to be captured for posterity by Mr. Jabez Hughes, as recommended by Louise. With a growing sense of unreality, Margaret watched the photographer fussing over his camera and all its associated paraphernalia on the orchestra dais of the ballroom. The spot where she was to pose was marked by a huge chalked cross, and the man had measured the distance between this and the camera equipment obsessively, several times making the most minuscule of adjustments. The backdrop consisted of several screens depicting what looked like rather tasteless dark-green curtains, and the obligatory cardboard pillar to support her supposedly fragile feminine form.

Ha! She'd like to see a man spending the day carting about a ton of crinolines and petticoats, squashed into a corset that barely let him breathe, never mind cat. Unable to rest his legs properly for fear of exposing his delicate ankles, and being forced to glide rather than totter, while keeping his head up and shoulders back at all times, he would need more than a flimsy paper pillar to lean on. One hour, never mind a day, of this would force any man to reconsider his use of the epithet *the weaker sex*!

It seemed to Margaret to take only slightly less time to have her photograph taken than it would have to have her portrait painted. It was gone twelve when she and Mama were assisted into their coach for the short drive to Buckingham Palace, ridiculously premature for a reception that did not commence until three, especially since they were forbidden entry before half past one. But in this, as in every other aspect of the day, Mama was proved right. The carriages containing that day's quota of debutantes and assorted female relatives who would present them were so numerous as to have almost stopped the traffic in the Mall. To add to the mayhem, crowds of onlookers, in a wonderful assortment of equipages from drover's carts to sporting carriages, occupied the space on either side of the main procession, their passengers peering at the debutantes as if they were animals in a zoo. Several bold pedestrians even pressed their noses against the carriage windows to get a closer look.

Margaret's relief when they finally arrived at Buckingham Palace was short-lived. Their progress through the series of hot, stifling antechambers towards the Presence Chamber was tortuous. The atmosphere was hushed, expectant, crackling with tension as mamas fussed over gowns and feathers and trains and veils, and daughters stood rigid and flushed but unable to use their fans for fear of disturbing their coiffure or dropping their wilting bouquets. When her tummy rumbled, the noise seemed like a thunder-clap, drawing the horrified attention of everyone around her.

"Margaret!" her mother hissed. "Have you no self-control?"

"It is precisely because I have exercised self-control that my tummy is complaining. I have eaten precisely nothing all day."

"For a very good reason. There are no facilities of any sort here," Mama said pointedly.

Was a debutante expected to have rigid control of her waterworks as well as her demeanour? Margaret thought better of inquiring. In truth, as the hour of her debut approached, she was fighting a very strong urge to flee. Casting a critical eye over the other debutantes confirmed that she did indeed look exactly like them. Were any of them feeling as she did? She tried to tell herself that it was simply a ceremony to be got through, but she knew it was much more significant than that.

"It is almost three," Mama said, twitching at the lace of Margaret's gown. "The Lord Chamberlain has informed me that we will be among the first to be called. I hope I don't need to remind you of the need to deliver an impeccable performance."

Like one of those dogs which jumped through burning hoops, Margaret thought. Only she was wearing her hoops. "All this effort, just so that I can curtsy to the queen, which I have done any number of times before."

"You know perfectly well that it is about much more than that."

"Before I make my entrance in this absurd outfit, I'm not out. After I've minced my way along the Presence Chamber and been kissed by Her Majesty, I am out," Margaret said, in a futile attempt to quell her nerves with sarcasm. "Does the queen have some magical powers that I am as yet unaware of?"

"Don't be so absurd. It's a rite of passage, marking your transition from carefree girl to young lady of substance. The carte-de-visite with your photograph from this morning is quite literally your passport into society. I thought you understood that."

"I do, all too horribly well." If she made some sort of faux pas, would it make the ceremony null and void? As she waited for one of the many lords in waiting to summon her into the royal presence, the rebellious little voice in her head that forever accompanied her, urged Margaret to do just that. But that would reflect badly on Mama, and in any case, she didn't really believe that failing to curtsy low enough or stepping on her train would damage her as a matrimonial prize.

A ripple of excitement coursed through the waiting throng as the two doors to the Presence Chamber were opened. The proceedings were about to commence. It was too late for anything now, save to steel herself to get through it without a hitch.

One of the lords in waiting began to organise the queue

29

according to the list he carried. "Your Grace, you have the honour of being first, at Her Majesty's behest," he said, and Margaret and Mama were ushered forward.

Despite the fact that she had been in the queen's presence countless times, Margaret felt a sheen of cold perspiration break out at the back of her neck. Her heart began to thump. At Mama's urging, she let down the train, which she had been holding carefully over her left arm, and another lord in waiting used his ceremonial wand to spread it out behind her, while another intoned her name.

"Remember what you have been practising, and all will be well," Mama whispered.

Margaret took her first step forward onto the red carpet. The large feathers on her head nodded, her veil threatened to unravel her coiffure, and her crinoline swayed from side to side. Though she had practised walking with a starched tablecloth around her shoulders many times, she still felt like a very ungainly ship in the grip of a gathering storm.

Mama had not warned her that the Presence Chamber would be so crowded. There was a sea of courtiers, the most senior of whom was the Lord Chamberlain in his full wig and gown. In addition to the numerous lords in waiting in their silk knee breeches, there were equerries and gentlemen in waiting surrounding the royal party in full regalia, their chests swathed in sashes and braid, glittering with honours and medals. Ladies-in-waiting took up more space with their feathers and crinolines, making the passageway to the dais hazardously narrow.

"More slowly," Mama hissed out of the corner of her mouth as Margaret began the short journey.

She didn't see Louise at first, for her friend was standing to one side, partly obscured by her elder sister. But as Margaret got to within a step of the dais and Mama presented her, Louise adjusted her position and wiggled her eyebrows.

Margaret bit her lip as the nervous giggle formed. Dear heavens, surely Louise would not actually wink, as she had threatened. But, no, Louise prided herself on her public poise; she would never do anything so risky.

Margaret creaked carefully into her full court curtsy, reciting the instructions in her head. Drop low enough so that her knee almost touched the ground. Hold. Count to three. Bow for three. Eyes on the ground. Keep your balance. Hold on to your bouquet. Her knees trembled, and her nose itched with the urge to sneeze. She could feel Louise's encouraging gaze on her, and Mama's, too, which gave her the will she needed to remain perfectly in control. Was she close enough to the queen? Low enough for her petite majesty to reach her cheek? Goodness, how much longer must she hold this pose?

At last, the queen bent forward and brushed her cheek with the kiss, an honour reserved for the elite few. Finally, Margaret was permitted to rise, which she did as Mama had instructed, as if a rope were attached to her head pulling her straight up.

The closing stage of the ceremony required her to pay her respects to each of the royal party. Bertie was there, though no Alix, presumably excused because of her condition. Margaret made a deep curtsy to the Prince of Wales, and then moved on. Princess Helena was next, looking very unlike the Lenchen she knew, stiff and regal in her formal gown. Margaret reached Louise and despite herself, she smiled as she curtsied. Nothing could detract from her friend's elegant beauty. The smile Louise bestowed on her as she rose from her curtsy was fleeting but warm, making Margaret glow with pride, for she had passed the test, and no-one had higher standards than Lou. Not even Mama.

"Well done."

Another of Louise's talents, her ability to speak with her mouth closed. Margaret dare not acknowledge the words, concentrating on making her way backwards out of the room, her gaze fixed towards the queen.

Another lord in waiting expertly folded her train and hung it over her left arm and the ordeal was over. Buoyed with success, Margaret beamed at her mother as soon as she had left the Presence Chamber. "I did it."

"Well done," Mama said, unconsciously echoing Louise's words. "Congratulations, you are now officially out in society."

The words made her spirits plummet. Out in society. On the market. And firmly set on a well-worn path that had only one destination. Marriage.

Chapter Four

Montagu House, London, June 1865

T HE DRAWING-ROOM WAS ONE OF Margaret's favourites in the London town house. The cornicing, the walls, and the woodwork were all painted white which, combined with the views of the garden, gave it a relaxed feel. As she hovered outside the door today, however, she didn't feel at all calm. She had been summoned and had no idea why. Bracing herself, she opened the door, only to discover to her dismay that both her parents were present.

"Sit down," Mama said, indicating one of the chairs between them.

Margaret did so, trying to smile. "This all looks rather ominous."

"No, no, I have some good news to impart. Your mother and I have identified a suitable husband for you."

Papa smiled at her encouragingly, but Margaret, for once, was lost for words. A husband had been found for her? She wondered where, exactly. Hiding in the attics? Wandering the streets desperately searching for a red-haired bride?

"Well?" Papa was looking at her expectantly. "Have you nothing to say for yourself?"

"I didn't think it would happen quite so quickly."

"To be perfectly honest," Mama said, "neither did we, but the 'Titian-haired breath of fresh Scotch air,' as the press have it, has defied the odds."

Margaret dearly wished she had not. Shocked, she stared dumbly at her parents.

"Don't you want to know who the lucky gentleman is?" Mama asked.

No, she did not, for that would make it real. But Mama and Papa were looking delighted with themselves, and it wasn't as if their purpose in bringing her to London was a secret. She pinned a smile to her face. "Who is it?"

"Come," Mama said, smiling encouragingly, "surely you must be able to guess?"

Guess! Was this some sort of bizarre parlour game? Margaret felt sick. Of the many eligible men she had been introduced to, she couldn't think of any she'd want as a husband, or even a single one who had indicated that he'd like her to be his wife. "No, I give in," she said.

"Oh, for goodness sake! It is Lord Rufus Ponsonby."

Margaret's jaw dropped. Surely she had misheard. Lord Rufus Ponsonby was that pompous man with the irritating little cough whose smile would freeze boiling water.

"Ponsonby, the Earl of Killin," her father repeated. "You'll be a countess, mistress of a castle set on the banks of Loch Tay. Of course it's a bit run-down, in need of your dowry to fix it up, and the Killin title isn't as prestigious as ours, but it's a venerable one. And as for his side of the bargain—well, it's what I would call serendipity. Our estates have lots of sheep. He has woollen mills. In more ways than one, it will be a marriage made in heaven. So, what do you say?" he concluded with a rare smile. "Haven't your mother and I done well by you?"

Horrified, knowing her feelings would be writ large across her face, Margaret prevaricated. "I had no idea he was interested."

"Why would you? He's a perfect gentleman; he wouldn't dream of fixing his intentions with you until he'd spoken to me. I'm very glad he did. Just between ourselves, he was already in our top five."

"You actually had a list?"

"Choosing your husband is the single most important decision we have to make for you as parents, and we set about it with due diligence."

Margaret tried to imagine her parents, closeted together in Papa's study, working their way through the runners and riders, but this was no laughing matter. Whether or not she and her prospective suitors shared any interests or, heaven forfend, found each other attractive or even liked each other would not have been taken into consideration.

"What does that pained expression mean? Come on, out with it."

Papa's tone was considerably less indulgent now. She braced herself. "I am so sorry, but I'm afraid I don't like Killin."

"You don't *like* him?" Papa's face was set, his expression forbidding now. "There is plenty to *like* about him, is there not, Charlotte?"

Taking her cue, Mama launched into a rhapsody about Killin and all his husbandly qualities.

Margaret couldn't argue with any of them. "It's the way he clears his throat," she exclaimed when her mother finished her encomium. "Just before he speaks, he makes this really irritating noise—"

"Margaret! You do realise that is the most preposterous—"

"I don't like him, Mama, and I'm certain he doesn't like me either. Or if he does, he's certainly done an excellent job of concealing the fact. He is so—so cold."

"You mean he does not wear his heart on his sleeve as you do. A modicum of reserve is no bad thing."

"He has vast reservoirs of it! Enough to drown me. Please, I beg you don't make me—"

"Make you! You are not some foolish heroine in a melodrama. There is no question of my *making* you do anything." Brows drawn fiercely together, Papa got to his feet. "The law of the land gives me the right to insist you marry any man of my choosing. I am not a despot, however, but a father wishing to do his best by a

daughter who should understand her duty to the family by now."
He glowered. "I have found you an eminently suitable husband,
whose family interests perfectly complement ours. What I expect
from you is compliance and gratitude, not disrespect and disobe-
dience."

"Papa! I am neither of those things."

"I beg to differ, Margaret. You are also immature and overly
dramatic. To speak so defiantly—"

"No, no, Papa, I would not dream of— I did not mean—"
Margaret broke off, tears smarting her eyes. "I am perfectly aware
that I must marry, but—"

"I am pleased to hear that." Her father cut her short. "This
betrothal has, for reasons I cannot fathom, come as a surprise to
you. You are very young for your age compared to your sister. I
will make some allowance for that, and you in turn must trust me
when I assure you that you will thank your mother and me when
you understand the many advantages of this match."

"I can already see the advantages, but—"

"As for this irrational dislike you claim, that is stuff and nonsense.
You barely know the man. I am convinced you will think very
differently when you do. Trust that your mother and I know best.
Now, if we are finished, I have other urgent business to attend to."

"Let me talk to Margaret. There is no need to detain you further,"
Mama said, accompanying him to the drawing-room door, where
they whispered together for a moment.

"Mama," Margaret exclaimed as soon as the door was closed
behind her father, "please . . ."

"No more. You have said quite enough." The duchess's pretty
mouth firmed as her expression hardened.

Margaret could almost feel the shackles being locked and bolted
into place around her heart. "But you don't understand. I haven't
explained myself properly."

"Explained what, precisely? Why you have decided to take an

obtuse aversion to a well-respected gentleman of excellent character and means? Are you setting yourself up as a superior judge of character to the duke?"

"No, but . . ."

"Or myself, perhaps? You think that I don't know you, my own daughter, well enough to judge the type of man who would best suit you as a husband? You have made your mind up without giving Killin the benefit of the doubt. The man is doing you the honour of offering for your hand, and you won't even consider his proposal. Do you think that fair?"

"No, Mama," Margaret said, mortified. "I'm sorry for my outburst."

"Very well. We will put that behind us. I trust that we now understand each other perfectly. You have approximately two hours to regain your composure and to reconcile yourself to the fact that your future husband is on his way to make his declaration as we speak. I trust you will contrive to give Killin a significantly more positive response to his proposal than the one you have treated us to."

Chapter Five

T HE GARDEN GATE HAD BARELY slammed shut behind her when Margaret heard Lochiel's alarmed voice calling her name from the other side. He would catch her easily if she tried to outrun him, and having made her bid for freedom, she was determined to hang on to it. In the ballroom her parents, their guests, and most of all the man standing on the orchestra dais waiting to claim her could go hang for now. There would be a terrible price to be paid for what she'd just done, but for the moment all she cared about was that she was free. She was absolutely not going to allow Lochiel to drag her back to face the music until she was certain she could stand resolute in the face of what would be intense pressure to recant.

Margaret had never before ventured beyond the garden gate on this side of the house. As her eyes became accustomed to the darkness, she saw that she was standing on the actual banks of the Thames. Up close, the river smelled absolutely foul. She could hear the water rushing past just a few feet away. Momentarily distracted, she inched forward, marvelling at the sheer power of the tide as it raced in from the estuary, experiencing a wild, irrational urge to jump in. She could imagine herself, buoyed by her crinoline, being carried by the river, waving at Lochiel as he stood helpless on the banks as she bobbed past. His disembodied voice called her name again, yanking her back to reality.

Her pale gown was positively glowing in the dark. She had to hide, but there was nowhere obvious. As the gate creaked open, she reached the corner of the wall marking the edge of her father's property just in time. He was *still* calling her name, for goodness sake, as he approached. She crouched down as best she could behind a bushy shrub, closed her eyes, and prayed.

Lochiel came agonisingly close to her hiding place, but he didn't spot her. Breathlessly, she waited until he made his way back to the riverfront before risking a glance. She could barely make him out, a dark figure, hesitating, unsure of which direction to take. When he finally made his choice, Margaret counted to fifty before edging out, spitting dust from her mouth. Picking up the hem of her ball gown, she fled in the opposite direction. She had no idea where she was going. She didn't care. She was alone, her whole body energized by her flight, with every step casting off the fetters of her disastrous London Season. Emboldened, she ran faster, relishing the tug of the wind in her hair, enjoying the visceral thrill of her speedy if somewhat ungainly progress.

What a sight I must be! Laughing, she pictured herself, her crinoline bouncing and swinging like a mainsail flapping in the breeze, her satin dancing slippers slipping and sliding in the mud and the slime, the pins dislodging one by one from her hair, which was unravelling from its regulated curls and flying out behind her. Back at Montagu House lay chaos, but this impetuous, grand gesture would finally force her parents to accept that she was deadly serious. Whatever happened next, she would not be marrying Lord Rufus Ponsonby.

Running at full tilt in satin slippers on ground that seemed to consist entirely of mud was hard going. Eventually forced to come to a halt, her chest heaving, Margaret sucked in air that filled her lungs with an acrid metallic tang. Above her, the sky was starless as it always was in London, for even at the height of summer, a cloud of soot from myriad chimneys cast a pall over everything. She had no idea how far she had gone, but looking over her shoulder, there was no sign of Lochiel.

Her exhilaration began to fade as she gazed around her. Impulsive grand gestures were all very well, but she'd have made her point just as effectively if she'd returned to the garden and hidden in the shrubbery, as she'd originally intended. Damn and blast the man. It was his fault that she'd run off like a spooked horse and ended up who knew where.

What was happening back in the ballroom? Would Mama and Papa still be standing on the dais while confusion reigned? Or had her pursuer returned to report her flight, forcing them to send all their guests home? They would be utterly furious with her. If they had only listened to her. No, no, that wasn't fair. She had not tried nearly forcefully enough to make herself heard. She had been too eager to please, ignoring what her instincts had been telling her from the first. They'd think her actions childish, selfish, thoughtless, undignified. They were unaware of the ongoing debate she'd been having with herself from the moment the match had been proposed, so her flight would seem like a bolt from the blue.

Her father would be cursing her. *Why is it that you are capable of thinking only of yourself!* How many times had he hurled that accusation at her? It seemed particularly unfair, given how hard she had tried to quell the rebellious little voice in her head and do as he bade her. But she had finally paid heed to that dissenting voice, and she could not regret having done so.

So what now, M.—go back and face the music? That would certainly be the sensible thing to do. Better to surrender herself than be marched back by a search party. But as she hesitated, she heard footsteps coming her way. Hurriedly, Margaret crammed herself and her crinoline into a narrow alleyway, screwing up her nose as her foot splashed in something she hoped was a puddle, even though it hadn't rained for weeks. She could hear them now, talking. Not one man, but two? Holding her breath, closing her eyes, as if that would make her invisible, her ears strained. Not talking but singing a sea shanty.

When I was a little lad
And so my mother told me,
Way, haul away, we'll haul away Joe,
That if I did not kiss a gal
My lips would grow all mouldy,
Way, haul away, we'll haul away Joe.

The men's voices were surprisingly tuneful. They staggered past her hiding place, oblivious to her presence, arms around each other's shoulders, absorbed in their drunken reverie.

As their voices faded into the gloom, she crept out. Behind her someone laughed, making her heart leap in her chest. Peering over her shoulder, she couldn't see anyone at all, but her skin prickled all the same with awareness of someone being close by, watching her. The last sparks of elation were doused by a cold trickle of fear. She was in the middle of the docks. A flight of stairs led down to the river, which was lapping near the top step, covering it in a layer of scum. Several of the barges she knew were called lighters were moored, though all seemed deserted. Behind her was a row of shuttered warehouses. Her sensitive nose twitched at the rich aroma of coffee beans and spice. Cinnamon? Nutmeg? A loose rope dangling from a winch swayed in the breeze like an empty noose on a gallows.

Cold sweat pricked her back. A small cat—she fervently hoped it was a small cat—slunk by, disappearing into the pitch-black, narrow slit of an alleyway between the warehouses. The tall, shadowy shapes of the large cranes being used on the embankment works looked sinister, like monstrous giants waiting to claim the unwary who stumbled into the deep trenches they guarded.

Margaret shivered, too late realising how vulnerable she was. Just ahead of her on the river was a suspension bridge. Below it, she could make out a light swinging from side to side as the craft it illuminated bobbed on the tide. A blur of flashing light, clanking metal, and billowing smoke rattled across at speed. A night train carrying freight or post most likely. Which meant that must be the Hungerford railway bridge. Yes, and that huge building must be the Charing Cross terminus. The more her eyes became accustomed to the dark, the more she could see. The station was glowing almost invitingly compared to the gloom surrounding her. It didn't look so very far away. From there, she could find her way onto Whitehall, to street lamps and safety.

Gathering her courage and her crinoline, Margaret hurried along as fast as her tired legs would allow. She was sure she could feel eyes monitoring her progress. A nightwatchman lifted his lamp. In its glow she caught his astonished gaze. She heard his shout, but she didn't stop. Onwards she ran, past a brightly lit riverside tavern crammed full of people, even at this hour. She heard the discordant clink of a piano. A man, who stood in the doorway inhaling the contents of a large tankard, made a drunken lunge for her, catching hold of one of the swags of her gown.

"Looking for business, my pretty?"

Panicking, Margaret tore herself free, leaving him with a handful of sarsenet and organdie. A shout went up as she ran full tilt. Footsteps followed her but quickly died away. The man had taken her for a fallen woman. In the eyes of her parents, that was probably what she was. As she swerved to avoid a huge pile of planking, her nose assailed with the scent of resin and wood shavings, she tripped over a stone and tumbled into the mud.

The murky waters of the Thames loomed terrifyingly close. Heart pounding, she scrabbled back from the edge, having narrowly avoided falling in. Perhaps it would have been better if she had. It would be a suitably pointless and ludicrous end. Would a drowned daughter be less of a headache than one who had created a scandal by running away from her own betrothal party? Almost certainly. The result of a tragic accident rather than a self-inflicted mortal blow. Mama and Papa would consider themselves better off being rid of her. They'd probably be right. Vaguely aware that she was on the verge of hysteria, unable to contemplate going back the way she had come, Margaret's only coherent thought was to reach the sanctuary of the railway terminus. Picking herself up, she plodded on through the timber-yard and into what was clearly a deserted marketplace, trampling on discarded cabbage stalks, sliding on rotting leaves, conscious that at least some of the rank odours assailing her were coming from her soiled clothes.

The terminus building was absolutely massive, but she could see no way of accessing it from the riverfront. Another freight train screeching past overhead, sparks flying, sent her stumbling backwards, muffling her scream with a gloved hand reeking of slime as the giant iron beast hurtled past, belching steam, pistons pounding. Cautiously, she began to edge her way around the walls towards, she fervently hoped, the main thoroughfare, where there were bound to be people in the environs of the station.

Her footsteps slowed. The journey back to Montagu House was no more than a few hundred yards, but away from the gloom of the riverside, she was acutely aware of her appearance. Although she was covered in mud, and she was convinced there were bits of shrub in her hair, her white silk dress with its layers of petticoats and lace and trimming was still very obviously a ball gown. Her gloves were ruined, but they were still unmistakably evening gloves. Would she be taken for a woman of the night again, one who had been involved, quite literally, in a bit of mud-slinging? Creeping stealthily onwards, keeping her eyes fixed on the treacherous cobble-stones, Margaret stumbled into a solid mass.

A loud curse rent the air. "Watch it! Ain't you got eyes in your head?" A grizzled man, who appeared to be slumped on the ground, glared up at her.

"I'm so sorry," Margaret muttered. "I didn't see you there. Excuse me."

But as she made to step around him, a hand grasped at her skirts. "Here, just a minute, miss."

In the act of trying to free herself she stopped, surprised by his accent. "You're Scottish."

"Aye, but you're safe enough—it's not infectious." She caught a glimmer of a crooked smile. "You're no Sassenach either, by the sounds of it."

He hadn't got up. Was he drunk? He didn't sound drunk. Knowing she ought to make her way homewards post-haste, she remained where she was, irrationally reassured by his accent. "No," Margaret said, "my home is near Edinburgh."

"Then what on earth are you doing here?"

A very good question. Her breathing was slowing, her panic subsiding. "I have come to London to—to visit family and friends." An answer very far from the truth, but at least it was believable.

The man chuckled softly. "I meant what are you doing *here.* This is no place for young ladies, especially not bonny ones in silk gowns."

He wasn't sitting on the cobbles, Margaret realised, but perched on some sort of makeshift wooden trolley. Oh dear lord, and his tattered trousers were pinned just above the knee. He hadn't got up because he had no legs. "I'm so sorry. I didn't realise—is there anything I can do to help you?"

"Help me?"

"Your legs, I mean . . ." She stuttered to a halt, blushing furiously. Should she have pretended not to notice? But that was preposterous.

"Lord bless you, miss, no. It might not look it to you, but I'm more than capable of looking after myself."

"I did not mean to offend, I . . ."

"Ach, you didn't, don't fret. Sure, don't us Scotsmen have a reputation for being legless six nights out of seven? I just take it a day further. That's my wee joke, you understand. So what happened to you? Had a tiff with your beau did you, run off and got lost?"

"Yes. No. I mean, I did run off." Dismayed, Margaret felt tears start in her eyes. "It's a long story."

"And you're in a bit of a state, too. Here, why don't you sit down before you fall down, and tell me all about it while you calm yourself. I'm not exactly in a hurry to go anywhere."

He stretched his hand towards her. It was grimy, but she took it gladly, sinking down beside him, touched by the simple gesture.

"You are very kind. May I ask your name?"

"It's Scott, Fraser Scott."

"Scott! What a coincidence. That is my family name."

He gave a snort of laughter. "I very much doubt we're related. My kin are from a wee village called Lochgoilhead in Argyll."

"You are very far from home, Mr. Scott."

"I've been much further afield than London. I was a soldier, Miss Scott. I lost both legs in the Crimea."

"Oh no! How dreadful. You poor man."

But Mr. Scott shook his head, patting her hand with his other filthy paw before letting her go. "It was almost ten years ago now."

The Crimean War. She dredged her mind and came up with a blank. Her sister Victoria, needless to say, had made an album about the war, including maps and clippings from *The Times*, but Margaret hadn't been in the least bit interested. "I'm so sorry," she said, with real regret. "I know next to nothing about it. Save, there is a poem, isn't there? I remember now: 'The Charge of the Light Brigade.'"

"Stupidity and needless slaughter dressed up as heroism. Lucky for me, I was a mere foot soldier, and not fit to ride with Cardigan's Cherrybum's—begging your pardon for being so vulgar, miss."

Margaret giggled. "Cherry what?"

"Bums. Their jackets were too short and their breeches were too tight, you see. They were all guts and glory. The first part, at least, was true enough."

"Mr. Scott, how is it that—forgive me for being blunt—how is it that you came to be sitting on a wooden trolley in the middle of the night?"

"As it happens I'm working. I've been keeping an eye on Percy

Wharf, which you've just passed through. If you look over, you'll see this is a fine vantage point, and no-one expects a cripple to be a lookout. I can't give chase, unless the pilferer is a tortoise with an injured foot, but I can blow my whistle if I see anything, and get the nightwatchman's attention."

"Even so, it sounds like dangerous work."

"It has its moments, but most of the would-be thieves are no more than bairns. Mudlarks, they're called, urchins who come down to the water at low tide to scavenge."

"What on earth can they possibly find in the mud?"

"Coal, mostly, lumps that have fallen overboard. They sell it on the street for a few pennies. As far as I'm concerned, that's not stealing. Though some of them are bold pieces, clambering up onto each other's shoulders to reach the decks of the barges. I've no option but to blow the whistle on them, though it pains me to do it."

"And if they are caught?"

The Scotsman shrugged. "Get off with a caution, if they're lucky enough to get a magistrate with a soft heart. At worst, a few weeks locked up, then they're straight back to work again."

"Good God, they put children in gaol?"

"Well, they have to make an example of some of them. It stops the others going to bad, so they say."

"You don't believe that?"

"It's not for me to say, but God helps those as helps themselves. Which is why I'm here trying to earn a crust."

"I'm sorry, but I think that a very poor fate for a hero who bravely served queen and country."

"It wasn't the Russkis that did for me— it was my poor eyesight." Mr. Scott snorted. "Didn't see the cannonball coming, did I? The next thing I knew, I woke up in a field hospital with two bloody stumps."

Margaret was moved to press his hand. "Oh, that's awful."

"Ach, I was so bad with the fever for a while, I didn't know my own name. That's what did for most of us that made it as far as the field hospitals, you know, the fever. No beds, no clean linen, water so foul it made you gag. I'm surprised any of us survived."

"But Miss Nightingale, didn't she put an end to such dreadful conditions?"

"Whatever she did, her good works never reached the place they laid me down to die, Miss Scott."

"Please call me Margaret. Unless you are a ghost, and frankly after all that's happened tonight, I wouldn't be in the least surprised, you clearly didn't die."

"For a while I wished I had. People said I was lucky. Do I look lucky to you? I was crippled. I'd not only lost my legs, I'd lost my livelihood, for I'd served in the Argyll and Sutherland Highlanders since I was a laddie of fourteen. Soldiering was all I knew."

"You must surely be entitled to a pension?" Margaret said indignantly.

"There are ways to claim such a thing, but—" Mr. Scott broke off, looking sheepish. "Truth is, I've never been good with my alphabet—can't write more than my name, in fact. Any road, I'd rather make my own way in life. I don't need charity. Don't shed any tears on my behalf, miss. I've a wife and three bairns waiting for me when I get home in the morning." The veteran winked. "They took my legs, but that was all."

"Oh!" Margaret blushed as she took his meaning, but she met his gaze boldly. "That must be a great comfort for you."

She was rewarded with a bark of laughter. "Oh, indeed! There now, I'm glad to see you've got your smile back, and a right bonny one it is. That's enough about me, though. Tell me, for I'm fair dying to know, what scrape have you got yourself into?"

Margaret's smile faded. "Not so much a scrape as a big black hole. I've run away from a party held to celebrate my betrothal."

Saying it aloud made her feel rather sick, but it made the army veteran laugh. "If you'd given me a hundred goes, I'd never have guessed that. What was wrong with your intended? If he had both his pins, he's already a better bet than me."

"There is nothing wrong with him," Margaret replied. "He has a castle in the Highlands. What could be more romantic? I'd have my horses and my dogs, and I wouldn't have to put up with my husband too often, for his business interests keep him in London for much of the year. You see, Mr. Scott, he is perfect husband material."

"Save you canny abide him, I'm guessing. Am I right?"

She shuddered. "That is it in a nutshell. I cannot abide him at all, though I promise you, I've tried. He disapproves of me. He thinks I talk too much, too, and that I need to learn to guard my tongue. What he really means is that I ought to say only what he thinks. He makes my skin crawl. I can't explain it any other way."

"Are they forcing you into it, lass?"

"No, no, nothing like that. I agreed. Well, I didn't disagree," Margaret said, shifting on the cobbles, for her legs had gone quite numb. "I assumed that Mama was right, that I would grow to like him." She twisted her hands together miserably. "I knew from the moment Papa named him that I wouldn't, but I allowed myself be persuaded otherwise. If only I had spoken up, I wouldn't be in this dreadful mess. And now I must face the consequences. I almost fell in the Thames back there, you know. It might have been better if I had."

"Ach, away, you don't mean that. You've your whole life ahead of you."

"I'm sorry, I'm not usually such a pathetic creature. My troubles are nothing compared to what you have endured."

"It seems to me that what you need to do is go back and face the music. We Scots have a reputation for fearlessness, and you're no different, you hear me."

Margaret mimicked a shaky salute. "I shall take inspiration from you and show courage under enemy fire."

"Your father's not your enemy, lass, no matter what you think. He'll likely be worried sick about you, and not without reason.

There's gonophs—child pickpockets—who would risk their necks to cut the lace from your petticoats, never mind the jewels you're wearing," Mr. Scott said. "London's awash with rogues and vagabonds. For all you know, I could be one of them, playing the old soldier when the truth of it is that I lost my legs—ach, I don't know, in a fall from a house I was robbing."

"You could have robbed me anytime while we've been sitting talking. I knew from the moment you spoke to me—I sensed I could trust you."

"Well, trust me on this, too. We need to get you safe home, and double-quick before your parents think you've been abducted or worse by some ne'er-do-well. Am I right?"

Though Margaret's heart sank, she could not argue with him. "Mama will be furious with me, and as for Papa—oh God, I can't begin to imagine what my father will say."

"He'll be too relieved to have you back safe to be angry with you."

"You don't understand. He has always thought me utterly selfish and rather pointless. This betrothal is the only worthwhile thing I have ever done in his eyes. He'll never forgive me."

"I'm sure it won't be as bad as you think, but any road there's no point procrastinating. Chin up, Miss Scott! Courage, lass."

His kind, heartfelt words stiffened her resolve. Margaret was struggling resolutely to her feet when Fraser Scott grabbed her arm roughly. "Run!" he hissed.

"I don't understand . . ."

"Run as if your life depends on it, miss," he urged, looking over her shoulder in alarm and grabbing a club that had been concealed behind his trolley. "Harm a hair on that lassie's head and so help me . . ." he roared.

In a blind panic Margaret picked up her skirts and prepared to flee.

"Not so fast," a male voice rasped in her ear as a pair of powerful arms enveloped her.

Chapter Six

DONALD CAMERON OF LOCHIEL RETAINED his firm hold on Lady Margaret's arm as they proceeded past Charing Cross and on to Whitehall, determined not to let her escape his clutches again. The shock of seeing her, her damp hair straggling down her back, her face streaked with mud, her gown torn and filthy, and in such dubious company, too, had made him leap to the worst of conclusions. In the confusion which followed before Lady Margaret recognised him, she had kicked him on the shin and her companion had rapped his other leg with his club. She had been quite unrepentant about both, informing him pointedly that the only person who had assaulted her was him.

Reluctantly accepting his evening cloak, she had lapsed into silence as they walked, while he did his best to keep her in the shadows, as hidden as possible from curious passers-by. "What on earth were you thinking," Donald demanded, "running off into the night like that?"

"I wasn't thinking."

"No, you most certainly were not. Good heavens, Lady Margaret, for a young woman of your station to merely venture out alone in daylight would be enough to set tongues wagging. To run off as you did, into the deserted docks in the middle of the night—you do realise your reputation would be in tatters if that became common knowledge?"

"I wasn't thinking about my reputation. In any case I suspect I no longer have one to lose. I am sure my father will have plenty to say on the subject when I get home, so I'd be obliged if you would spare me a lecture. To be honest, I don't know why you felt the need to intervene in the first place."

"Intervene!" Donald took a calming breath before speaking. "Did you expect me to stand idly by and wait for your lifeless body to be brought back on a handcart? Just how did you manage to give me the slip, by the way?"

"I hid. My point is that Mr. Scott was about to escort me back, safe and well."

"Lady Margaret, have you any idea of how naive—how dangerous—blast it, how downright stupid you have been? That man—"

"Mr. Scott is a veteran of the Crimean War."

"We only have his word for that. I hope you didn't give him any money."

"I don't have any money, and anyway I am certain Mr. Scott would not have accepted it if I had offered."

"That's as may be," Donald conceded reluctantly, "but to sit on the ground conversing with him as if you were having a picnic in Hyde Park, while your parents are likely going out of their minds with worry, it beggars belief."

"How long have I been gone?"

"An hour? No more. I was on the verge of returning to Montagu House to raise the alarm when I finally spotted you."

At this, she stopped in her tracks. "You mean you haven't actually told my parents that you saw me run off?"

"No." Donald urged her once more into motion. "I thought if I could find you and bring you back, the damage could be minimised."

"The damage could be minimised," she repeated morosely. "If by that you mean that my betrothal will go ahead, then I devoutly hope you are wrong."

"Everyone in the ballroom was expecting it. There has been speculation in the press for weeks about the announcement."

"I am heartily *sick* of being the subject of press speculation. You would do well to have a care, Lochiel; there is probably a reporter hiding behind that lamp-post eager to speculate about what we are doing out together."

"You are the daughter of the Duke of Buccleuch and the best friend of Her Majesty's most popular and, if I may say so, attractive daughter. What's more, you are perceived to be somewhat unconventional."

"'A breath of fresh Scotch air.' Hardly original or even rare, if one would but cross the border."

"Lady Margaret, the fact is that your betrothal is perceived to be a fait accompli. I cannot believe that the duke and duchess would have permitted it to have been so widely reported if there had been any doubt that you were amenable."

"Then don't believe it," Lady Margaret snapped. "Do what everyone else does, and ignore my feelings entirely."

Her manner unsettled him. He had assumed, when she ran off, that she had been overwhelmed by the occasion. It was an extremely foolish thing to do, and his only thoughts, at first, had been for her reputation and for her parents' dignity. Fear for her well-being had then taken priority, and relief had given way to anger once he had ascertained she was unharmed. Her lack of repentance puzzled him, forcing him to reconsider the situation. This was a case not of mere nerves but of genuinely heartfelt distress, which was even more of a puzzle.

"Are you seriously saying that you do not wish this marriage to go ahead? The Earl of Killin is a most respected gentleman."

"I beg you not to recite his many qualities. I am perfectly well aware of them."

"If that is the case," Donald said, struggling to keep pace with her volatile emotions, "then why humiliate the man in such a way?"

"I didn't humiliate him."

"You left him standing high and dry between your parents in

front of an audience of his peers in anticipation of the announcement of his betrothal. Short of jilting him at the altar I can think of nothing more humiliating."

"Really? How about being used as the makeweight in a deal to supply sheep for wool making?"

"Oh, come now—it's the kind of arrangement families such as yours have been making for centuries. It's the reason you are here in London, for heaven's sake."

"I know that!"

Donald looked at her helplessly. "Then why did you run away? I cannot believe your parents were forcing you into a union which was distasteful to you."

"And to Killin. He can scarcely bring himself to touch me."

"You are very young," Donald said, at a loss as to what to make of this revelation. "He probably doesn't want to alarm you by being overzealous."

Lady Margaret gave a most unladylike snort. "When I tried to explain to Mr. Scott what had happened—"

"You confided in a complete stranger!"

"And even more astonishing, he actually listened," she retorted. "You will be pleased to know that he agreed with you, Lochiel, that I should not have humiliated Killin. But he didn't try to persuade me to marry him."

"I do find Killin at times a little humourless," Donald confessed, deciding she deserved more than mere platitudes. "If he is passionate about anything, I would say it is about having his own way. He is a fiercely ambitious man—not that there's anything wrong with that."

"It's his ambition which makes him so determined to marry me."

"It is a very natural thing to wish to better oneself, and your father is a uniquely powerful ally."

"If only Killin could cut to the chase and marry Papa!"

Donald smothered a laugh. "The man's intentions are honourable, and you have spurned him in the most public manner possible. Whichever way you look at it, he did not deserve that. What's more, he was not the only injured party. What about your parents? Your running off as you did was a poor show, I'm afraid."

Lady Margaret's lip wobbled, but no tears followed. "You are quite right, a very poor show indeed. I've been blaming Mama and Papa for not listening to my objections, and I've been blaming Lord Rufus for taking advantage, but they are all simply following the rules of the game, aren't they?"

"I wouldn't call marriage a game, exactly, but if you mean they are doing what they believe is expected, and for the best, too, then yes."

"If you are right, and I cannot deny that you most probably are, then I owe my parents a huge apology." Lady Margaret sighed wearily. "And Killin, too. Though just because you're right, Lochiel," she added with a touch of defiance, "doesn't mean that I am entirely wrong. I may have gone about it ineptly, but I don't regret the fact that I have finally acted on what my instincts told me from the first. The match would make both of us miserable. Killin will now be free to look elsewhere for a bride."

Donald was not so sure. In his opinion, the Earl of Killin was far too ambitious to allow his pride to let the opportunity slip from his grasp. He was spared the tricky decision of whether or not to say so by the dismay on Lady Margaret's face as she saw the long line of carriages outside Montagu House.

"Your father must have put an early end to the festivities." He ushered her into the shadow of Admiralty House. "You can't go back through the main entrance, that's for sure."

"What do you think he'll have told people?"

"Most likely that you have been taken ill. Overcome by the occasion or some such excuse."

"He will be absolutely apoplectic." Her eyes wide, she stood rooted to the spot as she stared at the queue of carriages. "Oh God, what have I done?"

The bravado she had displayed only a moment before was a façade and in danger of crumbling as Lady Margaret surveyed the ruins of her betrothal party. She was very naive but, by heavens, she had real spirit, too, no one could doubt that. "Come now," Donald encouraged, "your parents will be so relieved to find you unharmed, they will forget to be angry."

She shrugged, but her trembling mouth betrayed her. "When you saw me and realised I was unharmed, you were furious, not relieved, and you are not even directly involved in this debacle. You have been a perfect gentleman, and I have been most ungrateful. Your seeking me out was above and beyond the call of duty as Papa's friend."

Donald winced. She obviously considered him long past his prime, while he was only just thirty, which must put Killin, who had another five years on him, in the ancient-fossil bracket to one her age. "I am sure any of your father's friends would have done the same thing."

"I am very sure most of them would have passed the chore on to a servant," Lady Margaret countered. "I am very grateful that you did not, but I must make my own way in now."

They were brave words, when she was visibly trembling with fear. Donald wished fervently that she would succeed in being heard, but his gut told him that it was far more likely she would be summarily dismissed. The life would be crushed out of her, and in a society so tightly buttoned up that sometimes he himself felt stifled, that seemed a damned shame. But there was nothing he could think of to say or do that would help. "You will be in my thoughts," he said instead. "I wish you the very best of luck."

"I'll need it," she said grimly. "I'll go round to the service door, then I can have one of the servants tell Mama I am safe, and make my way to my room by the backstairs, and wait until everyone has gone."

Keeping to the shadows as they made their way from Whitehall past the line of carriages towards the mews, Donald became more and more reluctant to abandon her. "I don't feel comfortable, leaving you alone like this."

"I won't have you embroiled. This is my mess, Lochiel. The best thing you can do is go home and leave me to it. I must bid you good night, and thank you, once more for escorting me home safely. Oh, and for the use of your cloak, too, though you'd better have it back or there will be more awkward questions for me to answer."

She unfastened the garment and handed it to him. Donald watched as she knocked on the door and heard the servant's shocked exclamation when it was opened. Then he turned away and headed for his own rooms with a heavy heart.

Chapter Seven

Y OU'VE LET ME DOWN. *You've let me down. You've let me down.*
Margaret stared sightlessly out the window of the first-class carriage, her father's words chiming mockingly in time with the rhythmic pistons of the Scotch Express, darkening her already severely chastened mood. The huge locomotive expelled enormous puffs of smoke as it powered north, giving her only fleeting glimpses of the towns and countryside they passed through. She was heading home to Dalkeith. As little as twenty-four hours ago, the prospect would have filled her with delight, but the memory of that dreadful interview with her father made the prospect of anything other than her imminent demise utterly unappealing.

If she died, it would at least lend credence to the version of events her parents had announced at last night's ball. A sudden illness that required lengthy recuperation involving fresh air and seclusion, apparently. She would prefer something quick and painless. If the train crashed—but, no, she didn't want anyone else to be harmed as a result of her folly, especially not dear Molly, sitting stoically opposite her.

You've let me down. You've let me down. You've let me down, the pistons taunted remorselessly. Margaret put her hands over her ears and bowed her head, her eyes smarting with unshed tears. Despite Lochiel's shocked reaction, until she entered the kitchen of Montagu House last night, she hadn't realised quite what a dishevelled picture she presented. Papa's austere butler had almost dropped the salver of glasses he was carrying. The stunned silence of the servants—kitchen maids, porters, chambermaids, and footmen—told its own story. And as for Molly—the look of horror on her maid's face made it clear that at the very least she thought Margaret had been ravished.

But worse was to come. She had been forced to stand before her father in her tattered dress, looking and smelling, as Molly had forthrightly informed her, as if she'd been dragged through a midden backwards. Papa wouldn't meet her eyes, fixing his gaze on the wall about a foot above her head. The way he'd spoken, the clipped tones, barely able to contain his fury, made her quake in terror.

The memory made her shudder. She had tried to stick to her resolve to explain her actions, but she had not been permitted to speak, not even to apologise or beg forgiveness, far less admit the error of her ways. He didn't want to hear her lily-livered excuses, he'd said. No amount of self-justifying waffle could explain her dereliction of duty. Having failed dismally to fulfil her only purpose in life, he considered her redundant. He may as well have placed a black cap on his head when he sentenced her to exile in Dalkeith for an indeterminate period.

When Margaret had finally been dismissed, emerging from the study emotionally flayed and reeling, Mama and Victoria were waiting outside in the hallway. Her aching heart had leapt, thinking they were preparing to plead her case, beg her father to display some mercy or simply offer some succour. But they were waiting only to reinforce her ostracized status, pointedly turning their backs on her. Mama, with her handkerchief to her nose, informed her that she stank of the gutter.

Bowing her head in shame, it was only then that Margaret noticed that having lost her reputation, her family's good name, and her bridegroom, she had also somehow mislaid her mother's bracelet along the way. The one Papa had given her to mark their own betrothal and lent especially for the occasion. Ignominy heaped upon ignominy! Could her fall from grace get any worse?

"We'll be coming in to York soon, my lady," Molly said, dragging

Margaret back to the present. "It's our only refreshment stop, so it would be sensible to take advantage of the facilities, if you take my meaning."

"Thank you, I will, but I don't want anything to eat. You and that poor footman in the corridor, dispatched all this way just to chaperone us, will need some sustenance, though."

"Jarvis has his own sandwiches. You must be hungry, for we left King's Cross at ten and it's almost two now. You had nothing for breakfast but a slice of bread, and you left half of that."

"I've lost my appetite and I don't think I'll ever regain it."

"Come now," Molly said with a forced smile, "the situation is dire but not as desperate as that, surely?" Reaching for the basket which the porter had placed in the luggage rack above her, she opened it. "Take a look at this now. Luckily there's no need for us to put ourselves at the mercy of the railway company's catering, if that's what's worrying you. It was a bit of a scrabble, for we left in such a rush that I'd hardly time to pack our portmanteaus, but Monsieur Henri very kindly put together a picnic for us. See, there's some chicken in aspic, and a big slice of that pork pie that you're so fond of."

Until now Margaret had been too shocked and shaken to cry, but this small thoughtful gesture, the first since she had returned to Montagu House last night, touched her heart. She burst into tears. "I'm so sorry, Molly. I'm completely ruined, and I have dragged you down with me."

Her maid pursed her lips, handing her a handkerchief. "There's no use in crying over spilt milk. Truth is, I never really took to London; it's far too big and noisy. I'll be glad to get home to Scotland."

"That's a sweet thing to say, whether you mean it or not." Margaret dabbed her eyes, sniffing. "I don't deserve you."

"What you don't deserve is to be treated like a criminal, in my humble opinion."

"Oh, Molly, if you could have seen Papa's face. I felt as if I was getting smaller by the second. By the time he'd finished with me, I was no bigger than a mouse, I swear."

"Even a wee mouse needs to eat, my lady. I know I'm speaking out of turn, but your father has no notion how hard you try to please him."

"He thinks I don't try nearly hard enough."

Molly clucked her tongue disapprovingly. "Och, away and boil your heid! That's nonsense."

"Boiling ma heid might knock some sense into it." The train was slowing down to pull into York station. Margaret's head ached from lack of sleep. Despite her protestations, her tummy rumbled. She smiled weakly at Molly. "Perhaps I'll have a small slice of pie. It will give me the strength to start thinking about how on earth I am going to atone for the terrible damage I've wreaked."

THE MYSTERIOUS CASE OF THE DISAPPEARING LADY M.

The Lounger at the Club, with his ear firmly to ground, is devastated to announce that London society is to be deprived of the young woman whose Titian hair and effervescent personality have been lauded in what is known in common parlance as the marriage mart. Lady M—— has abruptly departed the Capital.

Yours Truly had anticipated a most significant announcement to be made at the dinner and ball hosted by her esteemed parents, the Duke and Duchess of B—— on Wednesday night, at which a certain Lord R—— P——, a Scottish earl, was a most honoured guest. Another guest has shared with us, in the strictest confidence naturally, the surprising information that the announcement made was very far from that which everyone present eagerly awaited. Lady M—— had apparently been taken suddenly and violently ill. It must have been very sudden indeed, for she was observed dancing not half an hour earlier One might venture to suggest that one of the symptoms of her malaise was extremely chilly feet!

So indisposed is she that we understand she is currently making the long and arduous journey to her parents' home near the Scottish capital. A journey which, we most sincerely hope, does not tax her clearly fragile health further. The duke and duchess, though without question exceedingly concerned for her well-being, have chosen to remain in London, such is their confidence in their second daughter's stoicism. Of Lord R—— P——'s whereabouts, we are, alas, less certain, though it seems safe to speculate that while the lady's journey takes her north, the gentleman in question will be travelling hastily in the opposite direction.

The Lounger at the Club wishes Lady M—— a speedy recovery. If he becomes aware of any further information which might shed more light on this most unfortunate, not to say intriguing turn of events, rest assured our readers will be the very first to know.

PRINCESS LOUISE TO LADY MARGARET

Osborne House, Isle of Wight, 31 July 1865

My Very Dearest M.,

What on earth have you done!!!! Your letter arrived yesterday, but needless to say, news of your plight preceded it by some days. I knew at once there must be a scandalous reason for your sudden departure from the metropolis— a view, in case you've not seen it, that the somewhat lurid Illustrated London News *shares. Why did you not heed my warnings about the press? I told you, M., the price of fame is relentless scrutiny. The newspapers love nothing better than to knock someone from her pedestal, especially when they put her there in the first place. This tale your parents put about of a sudden illness will not be believed. (Though Her Majesty did believe it. Her many chins were shaking with disapproval at the suddenness of your departure, for you know how little my mother tolerates illness as an excuse for avoiding one's obligations.)*

What on earth possessed you to take such extreme measures as to run off? I know you had reservations about the gentleman in question, but I thought you had resigned yourself to taking him on. I cannot condone your behaviour, though I am slightly in awe of your courage. I know that a lecture from me is not what you want to hear, but I would not be your friend if I refrained. You have broken almost every rule of court life and conduct, and you will be crucified if that is discovered. It matters not a whit that you hold Killin in such distaste that you couldn't bring yourself to marry him. Were he a monster, you would still be castigated for defying your father, and Killin is not a monster.

I wish you had not been so rash! We are both of us, you and I, females who feel emotions intensely, but the difference between us is that you wear your heart on your sleeve. And that is your most heinous crime, in the eyes of the society we inhabit. You must resist the urge to let your heart steer your actions, my dearest friend. If the truth of that night were ever known (whatever it is, I know you left out a great deal of the detail in your letter!), it would be the ruin of you. What's more, it would generate a scandal that even your family would be hard put to weather. Though I am reluctant to mention it, I must point out that your behaviour affects me, too. As a princess of the realm, my own reputation must be spotless. Her Majesty's advisers would insist that I discontinue our friendship. Had you remained in London, I would have been obliged to distance myself from you. I am sorry to sound so unfeeling, but I do not make the rules; I am merely obliged to follow them.

That being said, let us adopt a more positive tone. All is not yet completely lost. If anyone knows how to play the game, it is your parents. Your exile may seem harsh, but out of sight in our flighty society is very much out of mind. The attention of the world will move on quickly to the next cause célèbre.

I wish I could be with you to prove that these difficult words are spoken from the heart, but here I am, languishing at Osborne for goodness knows how much longer, and you are at the other end of the country. I am sending you my heartfelt love and some sketches in the hope that my feeble attempts will bring you some cheer. I hope and pray I will see you soon, but the prospects are not good, for the queen is talking of a trip to Coburg in August, where there is to be an unveiling of a statue of dear Papa.

Do not despair.

Your friend now and (hopefully!) always,
Louise

LADY VICTORIA TO LADY MARGARET

London, 28 July 1865

Margaret,

    I write to you at our mother's behest. The duchess wishes to inform you that your attendance at our brother Henry's wedding at the beginning of next month will not be required. Following this event, our parents will be enjoying the shooting season with friends, and will not be visiting Dalkeith Palace. They will then spend the remainder of the parliamentary recess, including Christmas, at Drumlanrig or perhaps Boughton or Bowhill. You are to remain at Dalkeith unless the duke decrees otherwise, while our younger sister, Mary, will remain at Drumlanrig under the care of her governess.

    Margaret, I beg you to consider the impact of your indefensible actions. Our father remains furious with you, and will not countenance your name being spoken. His Grace's humiliation was witnessed not only by almost every serving peer but by all of his cronies from the Roxburghe Club. As you know, of his many public positions, it is of his presidency of this club that he is most proud. The duke blames our mother for failing to control your actions, though this seems to me unjustified, for I know from personal experience just how wilful you can be. The duchess is greatly affected by his condemnation and has kept the loss of her bracelet from him to protect herself from further criticism. Thus, Margaret, on top of everything else, you have also damaged the good relations between our parents.

    Personally, I fail to understand how you can have behaved with such an utter lack of decorum. You cannot be ignorant of the conventions and rules which govern good society, and yet you seem to have decided wilfully to break every one. Were even a small portion of the truth known, there is a real risk that the queen would ostracize us from court. That eventuality does not bear considering. It is a matter of small solace to all of us that the birth of their second child prevented the Prince and Princess of Wales from attending the ball that ill-fated night.

As to how matters stand with Killin, Mama has most graciously granted you permission to write him a conciliatory letter. I trust that you will make the most of this extremely generous concession, for it seems to me that his lordship's steady nature would be an excellent ballast to your own impetuous and capricious temperament. Look to the excellent example my own marriage provides, and have faith in our parents' stewardship. When the match with Kerr was first mooted, I confess to having had some reservations as to our suitability, but Mama assured me that affection and esteem would develop after the ceremony. With a determined effort on my part, Mama has been proved quite correct. It is with great delight that I confide in you, Sister, that I am expecting a most wonderful event in the early spring.

I expect no reply to this missive. Mama asks me to inform that she has read none of your letters, so there is no point penning more.

Your sister,
Victoria Kerr

DONALD CAMERON OF LOCHIEL
TO LADY MARGARET

London, 28 October 1865

Dear Lady Margaret,

I pray you will forgive the delay in responding to your earlier correspondence. I have been much taken up with matters of state, and in particular with the diplomatic ramifications of Lord Palmerston's death. As you doubtless know, his state funeral took place yesterday, your father being one of the many senior mourners. I was also in attendance in a minor capacity. The Times *this morning estimated that a crowd half a million strong came to our capital to pay their respects to our late prime minister. A goodly number of the mourners were veterans of the Crimean War, who credit his lordship with bringing that conflict to a close. As far as I am aware, our own Mr. Scott was not among them.*

Which brings me to the crux of this missive. I am delighted to be able to tell you that I have not only managed to track Mr. Scott down, but I have retrieved your mother's bracelet. Your logic, to suggest I return to the place where last you recall seeing it, proved absolutely sound. I am pleased to be able to reassure you that your instincts, that he is an honourable man, were also well-founded. Mr. Scott discovered the bracelet lying on the ground after I had marched you off. He kept it in the hope that you would return to reclaim it. A hero and a noble character indeed!

The clasp of the item is broken, but there are no stones missing. He was extremely relieved to know that it would be finding its way back to you, having been most concerned that its loss would, in his own words, get you into even more of a fankle than the one you were already in. I took the liberty of compensating Mr. Scott handsomely for his trouble. He asked me to pass on his very best wishes and his hope that you have resolved your matrimonial dilemma to your satisfaction. Obviously I paraphrase!

Your kindness and interest in him made a great impression on the man. If you will direct me as to what you wish me to do next, I will act upon your instructions immediately. I am acutely aware of how improper it is for me to write to you without your parents' consent or knowledge, but due reflection persuaded me that the very peculiar circumstances justify our clandestine correspondence.

It has been my pleasure to be able to perform this small service for you, Lady Margaret. My reward will be in knowing that I have provided some comfort to you in your exile. While the gratitude you express for my coming to your rescue is much appreciated, it is unnecessary. As to your apology for, in your own words, ripping up at me, that, too, is quite unnecessary. You were greatly distressed, and understandably so. Your determination to shoulder the entire blame for the episode does you enormous credit, and will, I trust, stand you in good stead with those closest to you.

It only remains for me to wish you good health and happiness, whatever the future holds for you. I trust most sincerely that in the three months which have elapsed since your departure from the metropolis, good relations have been restored with your most esteemed parents and that they are now happy to receive your letters. Sadly, without their consent, I must sacrifice the pleasure of writing to you again.

Yours with respect and sincerity,
Lochiel

Princess Louise to Lady Margaret

Windsor Castle, 4 November 1865

My very dear M.,

Vicky and Fritz finally departed this morning to go to Sandringham for the week, which left the queen most melancholy, and so she concluded that a visit to the mausoleum would be the very thing to cheer her up! I was lucky enough to be selected to accompany her. You won't be surprised to learn that paying her respects to Papa did not raise Her Majesty's spirits noticeably. Incidentally, Vicky is expecting—again! Number five, would you believe. I hear that your sister Victoria is also breeding, as you would put it. I hope she has an easier time with her first than my sister did.

I know you'll forgive me for replying tardily to your last two letters, but my time truly has hardly been my own due to my revered sister's extended visit. (Yes, I am rolling my eyes—she is so determined to demonstrate her saintliness, just like your own sister. You and I cannot possibly compete!) I shall dash off this note now and write more fully later. I have so much to tell you, M., though most of it will have to wait until we meet again, for I dare not put any of it in writing, even though I know that no-one enjoys salacious gossip more than you do—except me!

I have to say that I am concerned about your state of mind. Your last letter was frightfully serious. When you mentioned that you were determined to use your enforced idleness to read some improving material, I thought you meant digesting an etiquette manual or two— and in the process discovering all the rules which you have blithely broken! A Guide to Manners, Etiquette and Deportment of the Most Refined Society *is the kind of thing I imagined, not*

Mr. Mayhew's no doubt very worthy book, London Labour and the London Poor. *Do not imagine yourself unique in showing an interest in the less fortunate, however. I am willing to wager that another young woman of my acquaintance has read it. Lenchen's friend Lucy, who last year became Lady Frederick Cavendish, has taken up* good works *with gusto since her marriage. Amongst other things, she has been assisting at a soup-kitchen in Westminster. Would you like me to facilitate an introduction? I'm sure Lucy and the new, philanthropically minded Lady Margaret would have much to discuss.*

Have you any news at all of your potential return to the world? Surely four months is penance enough. It is only a few weeks until Xmas now, and I have already started working on my little albums for gifts—you remember, those with the pressed flowers and leaves, and my drawings opposite? Oh, M., you have no idea *how much I miss you. I am bereft of good company. No-one laughs with me as you do. Shall I use my influence and ask the queen to command the duchess to restore you to my presence? I am sorely tempted, save that my mother would be bound to take offence at my finding her company insufficient, and that would be a shame, for I have worked so hard at persuading her that I am quite her favourite!*

I have enclosed a length of silk from a bale which I chose for a morning gown. There should be enough material for one for you as well. I know that turquoise is your favourite colour, and fortunately it also suits me very well. I've taken the liberty of sketching a design for you. You are forever saying that you envy my style, so now you may adopt it! Consider it an early Christmas present. If you can find someone to make it up, you can wear it on Christmas Day which, I do most sincerely hope, will be spent in the bosom of your family. They cannot possibly leave you all alone at Dalkeith on that day of all days, can they?

I will write more very soon, I promise.

Your very best friend, always and forever,
Louise

Chapter Eight

T HE LARGE ENTRANCE HALLWAY AT Dalkeith was cold, the
marble-tiled floor missing the Christmas tree which usually
stood proudly at its centre. The banisters of the staircase were bare
of the garlands of greenery which adorned them at this time of
year, filling the hallway with the scent of pine. The table in the
grand dining room remained swathed in Holland covers. The silver
punch bowl was still locked away on a shelf in the butler's pantry.
There was no yule log burning in the hearth of the drawing-room.

Margaret had always loved Christmas at Dalkeith. The house
was filled with laughter and chatter, games and feasting. Even
Mama and Papa let their hair down a little. All her brothers and
sisters made an effort to be together for the festive season, with
their various spouses and offspring. They had gathered at
Drumlanrig this year. Mary was still there. Her eldest brother,
William; his wife, Louisa; and their two little boys had arrived
there for an extended stay last week along with her brother John
and his new wife, Cecily, and the usual collection of aunts, uncles,
and cousins who made a point of travelling to Scotland to celebrate
Christmas. Right up until yesterday, Margaret had hoped for a
last-minute invitation to join them, but nothing had been forthcoming. No letters. No gifts. No word.

Louise had been wrong for once. Her family were perfectly
capable of leaving her all alone at Dalkeith today of all days. This
morning she had attended church with the rest of the household,

sitting alone in her father's pew for the Christmas service, feeling horribly exposed by her isolation, too embarrassed to join in the hymns with her usual enthusiasm. After church was when Mama usually handed out her gifts to the village children. She had asked Mrs. Mack to act in her stead this year. The housekeeper had been clearly uncomfortable performing the task, the snub to Margaret too painfully obvious to be ignored. So much so that Margaret had denied herself her annual treat of watching the children unwrap the wooden toys and barley sugar twists before telling them one of her stories. She had written a story for Mary as usual, and sent it to Drumlanrig, but she doubted her sister would be permitted to acknowledge the gift, even if she received it.

"There you are!" The green baize door to the servants' quarters opened and Molly appeared. "What are you doing standing there like a wee lost soul?"

"I've decided to go for a walk."

"It's snowing outside. You'll freeze."

"I have my cloak and my mittens," Margaret said, "and I'm wearing my sturdiest boots. I need some fresh air."

"It'll be dinner-time soon. There's roast goose and clootie dumpling." Molly crossed the hallway to stand beside her, staring at the space where the Christmas tree should have been. "We've a tree downstairs. I spoke to Mrs. Mack. It's not right that you eat your Christmas dinner alone. We'd be delighted to have you eat with us in the servants' hall."

Touched, Margaret blinked furiously as tears started in her eyes. "Oh, Molly, that's so kind, but I couldn't."

"Why not? You'll be miserable on your own."

"Not as miserable as I'll be if I think you're going to spend the day fretting about me," Margaret said, forcing herself to smile, "especially when there is no need. I'm perfectly used to taking my dinner alone after all this time, and, anyway, you know that my presence below stairs would put a damper on the occasion."

"But—"

"No, Molly. I might pop down later for the sing-song as usual, though. I'll be fine, I promise."

"But what are you going to do with yourself in the meantime?"

"I told you, take a walk. Pay Spider a visit. Perhaps I'll build a snowman." Margaret gave her maid a brief hug, then a small push. "Go and enjoy yourself. That's an order."

Outside, the snow was falling far more thickly now, though a glance up at the sullen sky showed that it would probably clear in half an hour or so. Deciding to wait it out, she headed down the hill, by-passing the stables, for the sanctuary of the orangery.

Set on the banks of the River Esk, it was the centrepiece of the formal parterre gardens and one of Margaret's favourite spots. The circular building was neoclassical in style, with an elaborately moulded cupola roof and ornately carved columns. The boiler housed under the tiled floor, installed by Papa to heat the exotic plants and fruits grown inside, kept the place warm even on a bitter winter day like today. The multicoloured parakeets squawked a greeting as she closed the glass door gently behind her, breathing in the smell of the warm, damp earth mingled with the lush greenery of the palms. She could be in a jungle, far away in Africa or South America, save that outside snow lay thick on the ground.

Watching the Esk burble and tumble its way under the wide arch of the stone bridge, Margaret traced the path of the snowflakes as they landed gently on the windowpane before melting. This was a day like any other day, she told herself, but it wasn't true. If she wanted to torture herself, she could imagine almost to the minute what particular festive ritual or custom her family would be following at Drumlanrig. And Louise, too, at Windsor with the assembled royal family, trying to coax the queen into enjoying the day without lapsing into melancholy, a task that was beyond even Lou. Would she take Margaret's flippant advice to sneak downstairs and join in the fun in the servants' hall for a little light relief? Of all the royal children, Louise would be the most welcome, for she had that rare talent of being able to adapt herself to and charm whatever company she kept. Molly would have primed the staff to expect Margaret later, but she wasn't sure she had the heart to brave the unasked questions and awkward silences which might ensue. Christmas Day wasn't any other day. To be so very alone, so completely shunned on a day which was supposed to be joyful, when families were supposed to be united and loving, was proving difficult to bear. In bustling, crowded London, where the Season revolved around an endless whirl of tea-parties, soirées, and balls, she had often longed for some solitude. *Be careful what you wish for, M.*

Enough! Unlike the queen, she was not going to fall into a melancholy, lamenting Christmases past. What she needed, taking her cue from Mr. Scrooge, was to make sure that her Christmas future was different. She was tired of feeling that her life was suspended until further notice. She was tired of being abandoned and ignored. It was time to take matters into her own hands and act. She wanted to make amends, to prove that she had changed, that she had grown up and was ready to embrace her fate, though how she was to do that when her father decreed enforced inaction was quite a quandary.

It was becoming stiflingly hot in the orangery, so she decided to visit Spider. Outside, her footprints had already been obliterated by the snow. Wrapping her cloak more tightly around her, Margaret followed the path through the archway that led to the inner courtyard of the stable block. She could hear the whinnying of the horses coming from the boxes which lined two sides of the cobble-stoned square. One of the stable cats brushed past her legs, disappearing into the coach-house where the huge outmoded travelling coach belonging to the previous duke was stored. Margaret had never met her grandfather, who died when Papa was only twelve, but if his coach, embellished with gilt and lined with red velvet, was anything to go by, he had been a man with a very defined sense of his own importance. One summer, when Louise had been permitted pay a rare visit to Dalkeith, the pair of them foolishly tried to harness the coach up to two of the Shire horses. Fortunately they had been caught by Papa's head groom before they could do any damage either to the coach or the animals. Unfortunately, her elder sister had witnessed their escapade and felt obliged to report the heinous crime to Mama. Louise, she recalled, had put salt in Victoria's lemonade at dinner that evening, though naturally Margaret got the blame. At this moment in time, Lou would probably be getting changed for dinner at Windsor. Was she thinking of Margaret? If she was, she would be thinking she was feeling far too sorry for herself!

The fountain in the centre of the stable-yard was frozen over. A burst of raucous male laughter from the buildings opposite the clock tower, where the grooms and stable hands had their quarters, shattered the silence.

Margaret hurried towards her pony's stall. Spider whinnied a greeting, his muzzle soft on her palm. She rubbed her cheek against his flank, breathing in the familiar, comfortable equine smell. "Here you go, old boy," she whispered, fishing a carrot from her pocket. "It's not much, I know, but merry Christmas anyway." The pony whickered, making her smile. "You're very welcome."

Back outside, she followed the carriage-way as it climbed through the woodland to the crown of the hill and Montagu Bridge, built to celebrate the marriage of her great-grandfather, the third duke. There was a portrait of him by Gainsborough at Drumlanrig, which was one of her favourites, for not only did her great-grandfather have the same vivid red hair as she, he held a little dog in his arms that he was clearly very fond of.

Margaret leaned on the parapet, surveying Dalkeith Palace, standing proud on the hill across the narrow but steep valley. The bow windows of the drawing-room and, above it, the library were shuttered. The snow had stopped falling, but the steep-pitched roofs were white. It didn't look like home at all from here but unwelcoming, cold, rather forbidding. Though in the basement she could see lights glowing from the servants' hall.

She had been languishing here for five months. She could ride Spider anytime she chose, go for endless walks with the dogs, with no-one to chastise her for coming back late with muddy boots and wind-blown hair. But walking dogs and riding horses did not amount to a life lived.

Resuming her walk, she followed the sweep of the carriage-way past the house, and onwards towards the main entrance gates where St. Mary's church lay in darkness. Generations of Montagus, Douglases, and Scotts had worshipped here, all of whom had assiduously done their level best to increase the family weal. They had given up their home to King George when he paid his historic state visit to Edinburgh, decamping to a hotel in Edinburgh. More recently, they had played host to Queen Victoria and Prince Albert. They had served the county as members of Parliament. Papa served on a hundred committees, gave to a thousand charitable causes. He was responsible for the railway line into Dalkeith from Edinburgh. He had been instrumental in building bridges and roads, parochial schools, and any number of churches. *Amo*, "I Love," was the Buccleuch family motto, and as far as Papa was concerned, it meant "I Love to Serve."

She, too, would love to serve, but as a mere female, her purpose was neither practical nor philanthropic. Buccleuch women made strategic marriages, increasing their power and wealth, before breeding the next generation of dutiful progeny, raising them to do the same. That was what she'd been born to. That was her duty. Why did she find it so difficult to accept? Why couldn't she simply do as her sister had done, and her mother before her, perform her role with grace and elegance and make the best of it?

Because I'm neither graceful nor elegant! Looking down at her soaked boots, feeling the damp hem of her cloak flapping about her ankles, and knowing that her hair would be a sodden mass of rebellious curls, Margaret couldn't help but laugh at herself. Could one learn to be both? If she looked to Louise as an example rather than her sister, if she applied herself as she never had before, then surely it could be achieved. Though grace and elegance were not the issue, were they?

She walked down the main street, past the shuttered tollbooth and the busy Cross Keys Hotel, on past the Corn Exchange, shuddering involuntarily at the spot marking the site of the last public hanging there. At the railway station on the outskirts of town, which her father had steered through an Act of Parliament to construct, she huddled for shelter in the doorway of the ticket booth.

If she didn't marry at all, she was destined to become what Louise feared most, the family hausfrau, as she called it. A maiden aunt, at the beck and call of her brothers and sisters and their offspring, shunted from pillar to post as required. She would be a perpetual guest in others' homes, expected to be nothing but dutiful and grateful until the end of her days.

Exasperated, she scooped a handful of snow into a ball and hurled it across the tracks. What she wanted was to stop the questions endlessly circling around and around in her head. What she wanted was to prove to her parents that she was indeed fit for purpose, not a selfish, feckless child.

Could she play the role expected of her, as Rufus Ponsonby's wife? She could never love him, but love wasn't part of the bargain. *You must resist the urge to let your heart steer your actions.* Louise's words had stung, but she was right. Margaret should be asking herself whether she could learn to respect him, to hold him in some sort of affection. Every instinct screamed a resounding no, but look where her instincts had landed her.

Duty involved sacrifice and hard work. Her sister had successfully managed it, albeit, in Victoria's own words, *with a determined effort.* If she could find the strength of character to emulate her sister, she would be redeemed in everyone's eyes. And if she was fortunate, she would be rewarded, as Victoria was about to be, with a family of her own, even if she cringed to think how that family would come about.

If Victoria wasn't example enough, she could look to Louise. Bored senseless, deprived of her friends, denied a proper debut, forced to listen to the queen's endless lamentations and outpourings of grief, Louise did so with such grace and restraint that her mother believed she relished the task. Lou vented her feelings in her letters to Margaret, and she enjoyed her own, private little acts of rebellion, but she was otherwise a stoic.

Yes, Louise was the example she would follow. She would accept her place in the world, and she would make the best of it. She would have to wrap her heart in chains, suppress her true self in order to do so, but she *would* do it.

I can do it, Margaret told herself, as she set off back through the snow towards Dalkeith Palace. *Ex adversis dulcis. Ex adversitas felicitas.* A favourite quote of her father's. "From adversity comes strength and happiness." Something else for her to heed. As soon as she got indoors she would write to her parents, and if they didn't reply, she would write again and again until they took her seriously.

Turning in through the gates, she was surprised to see Molly rushing towards her, waving something in the air. "It's a telegram, Lady Margaret," she said, smiling. "From your father. It looks like they haven't abandoned you after all."

Margaret grabbed the envelope with a squeal of delight. It looked like opportunity had knocked sooner than she dared imagine!

Drumlanrig, 25 December 1865

NOTIFICATION OF URGENT CHANGE OF PLAN.
PREPARE TO DEPART FOR LONDON ON THE FIRST
AVAILABLE TRAIN. MAID TO ESCORT YOU. MONTAGU
HOUSE WILL BE OPENED TO RECEIVE. ON NO
ACCOUNT MAKE YOUR RETURN TO THE CAPITAL
KNOWN TO ANYONE UNTIL HER GRACE AND I ARE
ABLE TO JOIN YOU. ALL WILL BE EXPLAINED AT
THAT JUNCTURE.

BUCCLEUCH

A Cautionary Tale for Our Times

Regular readers will recall our dismay at the sudden departure of Lady M——, second daughter of the Duke and Duchess of B——, from London society back in July. The young lady was taken suddenly ill at a ball given in her honour by her esteemed parents (often acclaimed as the de facto Scottish royal family) at which a most significant announcement was anticipated.

Nothing more had been heard of Lady M—— since her retreat to one of the family homes near Edinburgh until yesterday, when a certain personage closely connected with the Duke of B——'s London household contacted us. We can now reveal the true sequence of events leading to Lady M——'s departure from the capital. Scandalous and shocking in the extreme, we cannot see how the lady in question can ever be redeemed in the eyes of society. We recount the details reluctantly, in the hope that it proves a salutary lesson to our young and still blessedly innocent female readers.

Here then, is our eyewitness account. On the night in question, Lady M—— was seen to be in perfect health. As the clock approached midnight and the announcement of her planned change of name, the lady was spotted exiting the ballroom. Contrary to the tale told at the time, she was headed not in the direction of her bedchamber, but into the garden which forms the border between the family home in Whitehall and the docklands, where the new Victoria Embankment is being built. Our eyewitness was busy dispensing the champagne toast, but some moments later as he circulated the room he heard an altercation in the grounds, the sound of a man's voice and of his young mistress's muffled response. Applying himself assiduously to his duties, he had no time to think any more of it. It was almost two hours later, as the guests were departing and the kitchens were a hive of industry clearing up, that the servants' door was thrown open and Lady M—— made a dramatic entrance, her gown torn and her hair unravelled. Shocked to the core, our eyewitness and every other person present reached the only and inevitable conclusion: Innocence had been Abused!

Lady M—— was whisked north in the company of her maid on the Scotch Express the very next morning. No word or sighting of her has there been in the five months which have elapsed since, nor is there any expectation of her return to London for at least another four months, at which time we might well anticipate an Easter present for the B—— family.

Lady M—— was born, as the adage goes, with a silver spoon in her mouth. We rightly look to such young women to set an example to those less fortunate, to provide them with a model to which they can aspire. When such persons fall from grace, they therefore fall spectacularly and completely. Though it pains us to say this, it taints all in their orbit. For her family and especially a certain Scotch earl, Lord R——, insult has been added to injury. Lady M——'s parents are part of the queen's inner circle. Lady M—— includes, amongst her intimates, the most comely of the Royal Princesses. We must assume that Her Majesty's excellent moral compass will ensure that friendship has been terminated. Our informant, his public duty discharged and suitably rewarded, has quit the service of the family.

Chapter Nine

Montagu House, London, Sunday, 31 December 1865

SIX MONTHS AND WHAT SEEMED like a lifetime ago, Margaret had stood in front of this very desk in her father's oak-panelled study, quaking in her torn ball gown. It was the last time she had seen her parents. They had arrived half an hour ago, and neither of them had greeted her, inquired after her well-being, nor even looked her directly in the eye. At least this time she was permitted to sit.

Her father pushed a copy of the *Morning Post* across the desk with the tip of his finger. "This unwanted gift arrived at Drumlanrig on Christmas Eve."

The pendulum of the case clock made a metallic clicking sound as it swung to and fro, emphasising the tense silence as she read the proffered article. The newly lit fire sparked in the grate, the damp coals causing smoke to billow into the room. Across from her, her father sat stony-faced, drumming his fingers on the blotting-pad. Reading the piece again, Margaret's stomach churned as she struggled to make sense of the vile insinuations, the way the facts had been twisted to concoct a scurrilous, vulgar story that was untrue in all but the bare bones of it.

Though she had concluded, from the tone of the telegram summoning her, that her reunion with her parents was unlikely be a joyous occasion, Margaret had worked determinedly to keep her spirits up as she waited, rehearsing and refining her apologies, her explanation for her behaviour, and most of all her heartfelt resolve to embrace her fate. Never in a hundred years had she imagined she would be confronted with this. "I don't know what to say," she said, feeling sick to the pit of her stomach, "except that it is obviously a pack of lies."

"Damned footman!" Her father hurled a brass paperweight in the form of a lion rampant at the fireplace. "Felt obliged to quit our service for the sake of his civic duty, indeed! The wretch was a sot with a taste for my burgundy! We should have had him clapped in irons when the extent of his pilfering was discovered, but instead we let him go on the understanding—as with all our staff—that he would keep his counsel about his time here. I've a good mind to have him tracked down and brought to book."

"Walter, my love, calm yourself." Mama picked up the paperweight and returned it to its rightful place, taking the chair beside Margaret. "To do so would only serve to generate yet more salacious gossip. What's done is done. We must focus our thoughts on how best to repair the damage."

Her father, however, was far from finished. "To have the Buccleuch name dragged through the mud like this is bad enough, but to add insult to injury, we received that rag in the Christmas post—from a concerned well-wisher! Ha!"

"Indeed, my dear," Mama intervened, "but really, when you think about it rationally, this nameless person has done us a favour. If we had remained unaware—"

"Little chance of that! I'm told that blasted paper sells thousands of copies. What have we come to, that our press is permitted to make such unfounded allegations? This should cost the guttersnipe editor his job."

"My dear, we agreed we would strive to remain calm. For heaven's sake, Walter, you know that would be quite the wrong approach. To engage in any way with the press is simply not done."

"Why not?" Margaret dared to ask. "Why would it be so very

wrong to contradict what amounts to libel? I don't understand why that is so beyond the pale."

Uttering an impatient oath, the duke pushed his chair back, striding over to the bookcase to pour himself a glass of his favourite Glenlivet whisky. He almost never swore. Margaret had never in her life seen him partake of strong spirits until after dinner, never mind before noon. "You explain, Charlotte, though why an explanation is needed—does the girl know nothing?"

Mama sighed. "It is not libel, Margaret, because our names are not actually printed; but even if they were, one simply cannot respond. To acknowledge that one has even read the piece grants it credibility. To defend oneself implies that there is an element of truth in what has been alleged. If you don't understand that, at least accept that those in the public eye have no other option. If only the press had not taken you so much to their hearts last year . . ."

"That isn't my fault! You asked me to endeavour to make a good impression. It's not as if I deliberately courted—"

"'A breath of fresh Scotch air,'" her father quoted bitterly. "And now you are most decidedly an ill wind that blows no-one any good."

Clasping her hands tightly together in her lap, Margaret strove for a conciliatory tone, determined to say her piece. "When I was at Dalkeith I had more than enough time to reflect on my actions, just as you hoped I would. I can see now that my behaviour was selfish, that I should have put my duty to the family before everything else, and I am determined to prove that I am capable of doing so from now on. I am quite resolved to accept Killin, if you still wish the match to proceed."

Though her mother looked gratified by this homily, her father was quite unmoved. "That horse has well and truly bolted." He slammed his empty glass down on the silver drinks tray before throwing himself back into his chair. "Killin is an eminently respectable man placed in an impossible position. If the press decides the child is his, he is a lascivious cad. If not, he is a cuckold."

"For pity's sake, there is no child! That should be obvious to even you!" Hurt and angry in equal measure, Margaret jumped to her feet, determined to be heard. "Your Grace, it has been six months since you saw me last, here in this very room. I have had ample time to reflect upon my position in this family and my future." Her father's dispassionate gaze, still pitched at a point over her shoulder, made her confidence wither, but she held firm. "If I am still required to marry Killin, I will do so willingly."

"Too little and very much too late," the duke responded icily. "While you have been languishing at Dalkeith examining your conscience, I have been expending a great deal of time and effort pouring oil on troubled waters. And until that damned footman sold his story, I was pretty sure we had weathered the storm. Despite the very public insult of your jilting him, Killin had been willing to forgive and forget, but I cannot see him taking you on after this.

"As a matter of fact," the duke continued, his voice rising, "I have no idea how I'll find any man willing to have you, let alone one of note. You've put a stain that may very well prove indelible on the family name. Can you imagine the nods and winks I will have to endure now?"

"What about the nods and winks *I* will have to endure?" Margaret interjected. "Thanks to that horrible rag, everyone in London will be fixated on my figure. For all the wrong reasons, I hasten to add."

Finally, the duke met her gaze and she wished with all her heart that he had not. His deep-set eyes, so very like her own, were like shards of ice. "You cannot possibly imagine that your feelings are of any relevance whatsoever. I leave you to deal with her as you see fit, Charlotte," he said, getting to his feet. "I will play my part in public for the sake of our family, but in private, I want nothing more to do with her, and beg you will keep her out of my sight."

The contempt in his voice was too much for Margaret. Though she tried desperately, the tears which stung her eyes leaked down her cheeks as the door slammed shut. "Why won't he listen to me? It's not my fault the footman blabbed and the newspaper chose to publish vile innuendo."

"The duke values his good name and his hard-earned reputation above all else." Sighing, her mother picked up the *Morning Post*, shredded it neatly, and threw it into the smouldering fire. "I have never in my life seen him so upset as when he read this. To have it arrive as it did, in the last post on Christmas Eve, too, when we had a houseful of guests. Have you any idea how difficult it was for us to continue with the celebrations as normal? Some of your cousins look forward to the occasion all year long, you know. Our little family traditions and ceremonies mean a great deal to everyone."

Including her! And yet she had been excluded and forced to spend a solitary and miserable Christmas alone at Dalkeith. But she was resolved not to look back, only forward. "How can we repair the damage done, Mama? Whatever it takes, I promise I will do my utmost. *Ex adversis dulcis. Ex adversitas felicitas.*"

She was rewarded with a very small smile. "There is certainly no shortage of adversity for you to take strength from. Do you mean it, when you say that you are resolved?"

"With all my heart. If it is in the family's best interests for me to marry Killin, then so be it."

"You sound as if you are about to step into the tumbrel and head for the guillotine."

"I assure you I am wholly reconciled to the situation."

He mother narrowed her eyes. "That is a significant volte-face."

"Yes, it is, but it is a genuine one."

"I don't doubt your intentions, Margaret, only your resolve. Can you truly curb this habit you have of questioning every decision your father and I take with regards your well-being, and simply heed our wishes?"

Before her exile, Margaret would have assured her mother that she could do exactly that, because she would have desperately wanted to avoid disappointing her. But the new Margaret tried very hard to think before she spoke, and was set upon trying to be scrupulously honest. "I understand where my duty lies and I am eager to discharge it. Even if it means marrying Killin." Despite her best intentions, his name made her shudder slightly. She straightened her shoulders. "If he will have me."

"I am more optimistic in that regard than the duke. I believe Killin is still willing to *consider*—and I emphasise consider—the possibility of taking you as his wife. That demonstrates great generosity of spirit on his part."

"Or a good deal of ambition. Not," Margaret amended hastily, recalling Lochiel's thoughts on the subject, "that there is anything wrong with a man wishing to better himself."

"Or with a daughter wishing to help augment her family's fortunes," her mother replied tartly. "It is because both of these aims can be satisfied that this match is such an advantageous one. All you have to do is apply yourself diligently, as Victoria did, when she married Kerr. The proof of the pudding, so to speak, is that she is now expecting an interesting event. If you put your mind to it, I am sure that you could come to care for Killin as a wife ought."

"If Victoria can do it, so can I."

Her mother studied her silently for a moment before nodding. "Very well. Once these allegations have been shown to be vindictive mischief-making I am confident that between us, you and I can bring Killin round. Provided, of course, that they *can* be demonstrated to be arrant nonsense." The duchess got to her feet and made her way to the window, which faced out onto Whitehall. "I am obliged to obtain your assurance on that."

"Mama, really! You shouldn't need to ask."

"Spare me the indignation and tell me in plain terms what happened. One cannot blame that blasted footman for drawing the conclusions he did. Anyone who saw you that night would have thought the same."

"My gown was torn when I hid in the bushes."

"Why did you feel obliged to hide in the bushes?"

Damn and blast! I can't betray Lochiel. "There were two sailors," Margaret said, grasping at this partial truth. "They were singing. I thought they sounded drunk, so I hid."

"Good heavens."

Mama continued to look out of the window. The urge to blurt out the whole truth was strong, she longed to wipe the slate clean, but trying to imagine her mother's reaction when she heard that Margaret had been exchanging confidences with Fraser Scott and was escorted home by another male guest at the ball—no. The *Morning Post* had made something vile out of the scant details it had obtained; what anyone would make of the real truth didn't bear thinking about. Anyway, she wouldn't embroil Lochiel in the debacle, not when he'd acted so nobly and gone to such lengths . . .

"Oh my goodness, I completely forgot!" With a mental apology to the man who had gone to the trouble of retrieving the bracelet and sending it express to Dalkeith, Margaret took the item from her pocket. "It was when I was hiding that I must have lost this. I took the opportunity to look for it the other day while I was awaiting your arrival. I couldn't believe my luck when I found it." She offered a silent prayer of contrition for this necessary white lie.

"My bracelet! My goodness, I thought I had lost it forever."

"The catch . . ."

"Oh, it is faulty, I know. I should have told you when I lent it to you. Thank you, Margaret. It is not a particularly valuable piece, but it is of great sentimental value to me." Tucking the bracelet into a pocket, her mother resumed her seat. "Now," she said briskly, "let us to business. First and most importantly, I must ask you to retain a dignified silence regarding the events of that evening."

"I am more than happy never to have to discuss that evening ever again."

"Good. Officially, it remains the case that you were taken suddenly ill and have been recuperating at Dalkeith. You are now fully restored to health. The first and most immediate priority is to put an end to any speculation that your innocence has been compromised. Therefore we need to show you off in public. There are not many opportunities until the Season starts, of course, but we will accept every invitation and I shall make a point of hosting a soirée myself. You will naturally be the focus of attention. Stand up and let me take a look at you."

Studying her closely, the duchess's expression lightened. "I do not have my measuring tape to hand, but it looks to me as if you have finally managed to refine both your appetite and your figure into a form more befitting a lady. However, it would do no harm to lose another inch or two. Fortunately, we have a few weeks before Parliament resumes at the start of February for you to go on a strict reducing diet as of now. In the meantime, Molly must spare no effort in lacing you up as tightly as can be managed. The next few months are critical. You may leave it up to me to make the overtures to Killin. I beg of you, Margaret, don't let us down again. A cat, however endearing, has only so many lives."

Chapter Ten

DONALD TOOK LADY MARGARET'S ARM as they set off from Montagu House.

"Thank you for being so obliging as to come to my assistance once again, Lochiel," she said. "In fact I am doubly grateful to you, not only for arranging this meeting with Mr. Scott on my behalf but for acting as my escort."

"Would an additional female chaperone not be considered appropriate?"

"Normally, yes, but on balance I decided that having Molly trail in our wake where we are going would attract unnecessary attention, which I definitely wish to avoid at all costs."

"That is a good point."

"And beside, you are all the chaperone I need," she added. "A respected diplomat and a friend of my father's to boot."

Donald grimaced. "I am younger than your father by some decades."

"Really? Perhaps it is the beard."

"You don't approve of it, then?"

Lady Margaret wrinkled her nose, making her feelings quite plain, before recovering herself. "I know that the style is the height of fashion. It certainly makes you look very dignified, which is a blessing today. I mean, not even the gutter press could put a scandalous slant on our being seen together, could they? If they saw us, which they won't, surely—we're not likely to run into a reporter from the *Morning Post* where we are going, are we?"

"I doubt it very much, but if you are at all worried . . ."

"I am permanently terrified of attracting adverse press comment, I would be a fool not to be, after what they wrote about me. Did you see it?"

"It was scurrilous. I'm sure no-one believed a word of it."

"I have become so adept at sticking to the tale of my sudden illness that I almost believe it myself. If people are still speculating, they do so out of my hearing."

She spoke lightly, but Donald, having witnessed her stoically endure the covert looks and furious whispering at various social gatherings over the last few weeks, knew that the farrago of lies and innuendo had taken a toll. "If you felt it would improve your standing with your parents, I would be more than happy to divulge the true story."

"Oh no! One of the few consolations I have is that I managed to keep you out of it. I am very glad to have the opportunity, now that we are finally alone, to thank you in person for all that you have done."

"There is absolutely no need. I am simply glad to have been of service."

"Then you are a most singular man, considering how I treated you that night. To be so obliging as to track down Mr. Scott too, which, despite your making light of it, I know must have been a most burdensome task." Lady Margaret smiled up at him. "You have my heartfelt thanks and undying gratitude."

To his horror, Donald felt his cheeks colouring. "It is Mr. Scott who is the true hero, for keeping your mother's bracelet in safe hands."

"Which is to his enormous credit, don't you think? The temptation must have been strong to sell or pawn it, for the sum raised would have been considerable, especially for a man in his situation, with a wife and family to keep. I have been thinking about our extraordinary encounter a great deal. Do you know, Lochiel, I don't think it is an exaggeration to say that meeting Mr. Scott has made me view the world in a very different light."

"Really? In what way?"

"Well, he made me see that the world I live in and the one he inhabits are vastly different, even though they exist cheek by jowl. I have been trying to remedy my ignorance through reading, but though Mr. Mayhew's descriptions of London are extremely evocative, it's not the same as experiencing it first hand, is it?"

Donald listened, bemused, as she launched into an enthusiastic summary of her research, giving him a glimpse, for the first time since her return to London, of the vibrant young woman who had taken last Season by storm. It would not do to condemn outright the actions of any parents regarding their daughter, but in his opinion, Lady Margaret had been treated harshly. Her retreat from society had been necessary, but her total estrangement from her family he thought unduly cruel. Were the duke and duchess gratified by the outcome, a now very correct young lady who made polite if guarded conversation? Certainly Killin seemed to approve. Hovering over her at every gathering, the earl had unsurprisingly decided to sacrifice pride in the pursuit of advancement.

Donald had steered them onto Parliament Street when they left Montagu House, avoiding Downing Street and next to it, on King Charles Street, the palatial new Foreign Office. Though the building was by no means complete, it was already occupied by diplomats and their staff. He had been spending a large proportion of his time there, during this sojourn from his Berlin posting, and had no desire to bump into anyone he knew, given his present company. Lady Margaret might consider him well beyond the age of acting the gallant, but his colleagues would see matters very differently. Good-natured teasing about belatedly settling into domesticity he was accustomed to, but she was the charming daughter of a very influential duke who happened to be one of the richest men in the country. He had no wish to be accused of pursuing an advantageous match, especially when the lady in question considered him a benign old gentleman.

Lady Margaret interrupted this rather depressing train of thought by tugging on his sleeve. "I meant to ask, is my outfit suitably nondescript? I am wearing my very plainest bonnet and cloak."

"The bonnet alone would be worth a week's wages in a second-hand clothing emporium."

"It is known as a slop-shop," she informed him, looking smug. "I learned that from Mr. Mayhew's book, but it was Mr. Scott who taught me my first cant words. A gonoph is a young pickpocket, you know."

"I did not, but it is a timely reminder for us to keep our wits about us."

"It's hard to believe that there is a den of iniquity nearby," Lady Margaret said, looking around her.

"You mean apart from the Houses of Parliament! When they built Victoria Street and the train station, they cleared some of the worst of the slums but, astonishing as it may sound, this area around Parliament and the Abbey is one of the most notorious in the city."

"What about the people who lived there? Where have they ended up? I shall ask Mr. Scott—he is bound to know."

Mr. Scott, the fount of all knowledge, Donald thought dryly. They were in Broad Sanctuary now, and ahead of them at the start of Victoria Street loomed the Westminster Palace Hotel. "That is Lord Raglan's statue over there," he said. "What does your Mr. Scott make of him, I wonder?"

"Not much," she replied. "He said that the Charge of the Light Brigade was sheer stupidity and needless slaughter dressed up as heroism. His words stuck in my head, and they were so very contrary to what Mr. Tennyson wrote in his poem. Since Mr. Scott was there, and Lord Tennyson was not, I know who I believe. It should be Mr. Scott, or one of his comrades, up on that plinth, not Lord Raglan."

"A radical idea."

"Ironically, Mr. Scott would agree with you. He doesn't consider himself a hero. Genuine heroes never do, do they? Mr. Scott lost both his legs fighting for our country, but instead of bemoaning his fate he got on with his life. I want to be more like Mr. Scott: roll my sleeves up and do something useful." Her face fell. "Though I have no idea what."

She seemed quite unaware that marriage would in all probability put paid to any ambitions she had. Killin wouldn't tolerate a wife who thought for herself, never mind made her own decisions. Besides, once she was married, with all the responsibilities of her husband's various households to run, and the social obligations which accompanied her new status, she would have very little time to call her own. The thought was strangely depressing, so he banished it.

Margaret eyed Lochiel doubtfully. "What have I said to make you look so sad?"

"Nothing at all." To her surprise he pressed her hand. "Stay close now; once we turn into Dean Street we are quite literally entering another world."

He was not exaggerating. As he steered her into a much narrower byway, the cobbles underfoot gave way to a mixture of mud, slime, straw, and an array of rotting vegetation. A ditch filled with sluggish grey water ran down one side, containing bobbing bits of flotsam she decided it would be prudent not to examine too closely. The air seemed to thicken, the stench from the Thames playing second fiddle to the sweet, sickly smell of decay and the stale, musty reek of unwashed bodies. Margaret tightened her grip on her escort's arm as the grimy, soot-blackened buildings on either side of them closed in. Now she understood Lochiel's initial reluctance to bring her here.

"We can turn back at any point, you know," he said, slowing, but she shook her head.

"Absolutely not. Mr. Scott is expecting me."

If Lochiel thought there was a genuine risk of harm befalling her, nothing she said would have persuaded him to bring her here. Buoyed by this, and trusting that the boots she had thankfully had the presence of mind to put on would protect her feet from the worst of what she was treading in, she sneaked incredulous glances at her surroundings.

It was as if they were walking a tight-rope strung between two worlds. On her left she could still see the clock tower of the Palace of Westminster peeking up over the Abbey. A large rectangle of green, followed by some sort of public edifice, perhaps another government department, occupied the left hand side of the thoroughfare. On the right, a warren of much lower, more-primitive buildings huddled together, as if seeking warmth and safety in numbers. Ladders and terrifyingly flimsy bridges were suspended between the roofs. The alleys between were so narrow that virtually no sunlight penetrated the gloom. Brown and grey were the predominant colours, from the sky to the buildings, the pallor of the people, and the contents of the carts that fought for space. Silent figures stood wide-eyed and staring in doorways, their clothes not much more than rags, their bare feet filthy. Though no-one approached them, almost everyone gazed with a kind of blank curiosity that Margaret found unsettling. Despite the air being filled with the calls of the costers pushing their barrows, with men hailing each other across the narrow street, coupled with raucous laughter blaring from what she assumed, from the smell, to be a gin shop, she had the strangest feeling that she and Lochiel were walking in a bubble of silence.

The next turning, away from the worst of the deprivation and what she belatedly realised must have been the rookery known as Devil's Acre, surprised her again, for the alley opened out onto a church square, and she could once again see the warehouses and wharves of the river. The houses here were terraced, small but built with something resembling a plan. On the other side of the square, the shouts and screams were of children at play in a yard in front of what she surmised was a school.

"Here we are," Lochiel said, indicating one of the tiny cottages.

"Would you mind terribly if I saw Mr. Scott on my own?" Margaret asked impulsively. "I know Mama would say it is improper, but . . ."

"I think we've gone well beyond the bounds of propriety already, don't you?" Lochiel touched her arm. "I'll wait here for you. Take as long as you need."

Chapter Eleven

THANK YOU FOR YOUR FORBEARANCE. I didn't mean to be so long, but Mr. Scott's wife insisted I take tea, and I had so many questions, and . . ."

Lochiel shook his head. "I can tell from the smile on your face that it went well."

"I feel so much better." Margaret beamed. "I know you made things right with him, but it has been weighing on my mind, how much I owe him. It mattered a great deal to be able to thank him in person. And now I owe you for helping me to do so. I am extremely grateful."

Without thinking, she put her hand on his arm, but he didn't seem to mind at all, pressing her fingers and smiling down at her. "Was he able to enlighten you regarding the displaced tenants?"

"Why, yes, and it was shocking to hear. It seems that no provision was made for them at all. How could that have been permitted?"

"The demand for new roads and railways is insatiable. Even your father could not prevent the building of the new embankment in front of Montagu House. He was heavily criticised in the press for putting his personal wishes before public need."

"Ha! Then I am not after all the first member of our family to bring the Buccleuch name into disrepute!"

"To be fair, the duke later claimed that his position had been misunderstood."

"*My* position has been misunderstood," Margaret said indignantly. "However," she continued, taking a deep breath, "that is in the past. I must remember that my father knows best. What have I said to make you smile?"

"You said it as if you were swallowing a particularly unpalatable spoonful of medicine. Your determination to be a dutiful daughter is laudable."

"I wish my father were more like Mr. Scott. No, don't laugh. I mean that he has a very enlightened attitude to female education. His little girl, Heather, is particularly bright, much more able than his two boys—his words, not mine. He has set aside the reward money you gave him to enrol her in a decent school. I have arranged to meet little Heather at a future date; I am keen to make her acquaintance. What do you say to that, Lochiel?"

"I am not in the least surprised you wish to, but please, for my peace of mind, conduct the meeting in some more salubrious location than here. Talking of which, I had best get you home."

Disappointed, Margaret gazed skywards. "It's a miracle. An actual glimpse of blue. We are very near the river here, aren't we, and just opposite Lambeth, I think, which I have read a good deal about in Mr. Mayhew's writing. I would very much like to see it for myself. Would you mind terribly, Lochiel, if we took a detour on our way back to Montagu House? It is only just after noon, and for London a positively beautiful winter's day. I feel as if I've been cooped up for months, and Mama won't be back for hours, for she has gone to call on a friend in Richmond. Please, may we take in a little more of this fascinating and unusual part of the city?"

"An epithet that could well apply to yourself, and before you take that amiss I meant it as a compliment."

"Did you? Then may I say that is the nicest thing anyone has said to me for months. What's the quickest way?"

"Your faith in my knowledge of the geography of London is touching."

"But not misplaced, I hope. Lead on, Macduff!"

"Very well, I know enough to keep us clear of danger, I reckon.

Why don't we cross the river here, then we can walk back past Lambeth Palace and Astley's Theatre, then cross back over at Westminster Bridge, if that's not too much for you? Most young women of my acquaintance require smelling-salts to walk farther than the length of themselves."

AFTER THEY CROSSED THE TOLL bridge into the Parish of Lambeth, they were quickly caught up in a steady stream of traffic.

"I can only imagine they are headed for the new station at Waterloo," Lochiel said, looking dubious.

Margaret's excitement mounted as they progressed, and the crush increased. Relying on her escort to forge a path and long past caring for the state of either her boots or the hems of her gown and petticoats, she lost herself in the spectacle. Costers with barrows piled high pushed their way through the crowds, calling out their wares as they went. Though she couldn't make out more than one word in ten, she knew from Lochiel's face that the air ought to be turning blue.

"Waterloo Road," Lochiel said, "and as I suspected, we are at the station."

"But everyone is going that way." Margaret tugged on his arm. "Look, past this theatre, the Victoria?"

"I believe they put on melodramas."

"I have been known to perform one myself occasionally," Margaret quipped. "Oh, do look, Lochiel, the whole street here is lined with food stalls. We're here now—we might as well explore it, don't you think?"

"I think I lack the resolve to deny you. You are not carrying a purse, are you?"

"Oh no, I didn't think—and now I won't be able to buy anything."

"I wasn't concerned about your ability to purchase a few cabbages, but about urchins—what did you call them, gonophs?—picking your pockets."

"Then it's fortunate I have nothing to tempt them," Margaret said, privately thinking that Lochiel was being overly cautious, for the children she could see were all respectably dressed, and most of them were in the company of their mothers.

The stench of the river and of the crowd was overlaid by more appetising aromas as they progressed along the street packed with stalls thronged with customers. Though they attracted the odd curious stare, most people were too intent on their own business to notice them, bartering, bantering, or hurrying home with their packages clutched close. Most of the shoppers were women; the market stalls, however, were run by men; but in between there were any number of boys and girls calling out their wares from barrows and baskets. Despite the fact that it was still daylight, gas lighting and grease lamps were lit to draw attention to the shops behind the stalls—a butcher, a draper, a tea merchant.

"Ripe pears, eight a penny!"

"Hot chestnuts, a penny a score!"

"Yarmouth bloaters, three for tuppence!"

"Pickling cabbages, name your price!"

A man with an open umbrella turned upside down was selling prints. A tailor, posing in the midst of a group of headless dummies, was demanding that passers-by feel the quality of the fustian jackets. A boy was bellowing out the bill for a circus, and a woman was standing on a street corner singing, while a little terrier dressed in a skirt pranced about on hind legs.

"Look, it's not only food; you can purchase virtually anything here," Margaret said as they passed a stall stacked high with china plates, beside it one bearing towers of wash-tubs and saucepans which were apparently freshly tinned, and next to that another stacked with handkerchiefs in every colour of the rainbow, and yet another with pairs of second-hand shoes and boots.

They made their way slowly from one end of the market to the other. When the stalls petered out at a crossroads at the far end,

Lochiel steered her firmly around. "It's getting late; best I get you home."

If truth be told, Margaret was tired, and very much aware that he was far less entranced by the place than she. As they retraced their steps the aroma from a stall selling roast chestnuts caught her attention. Though she had never tasted them, the smell made her mouth water. It had been an age since breakfast, which she had barely eaten anyway, for Mama's eyes were upon her and she had been nervous about meeting Mr. Scott again after all this time.

Her tummy rumbled. Letting go of her hold on Lochiel's arm, Margaret pushed her way in, ignoring his shout of alarm, for the stall was only a few feet away. Heat belched from the stove where the nuts were roasting in a brazier, the stall-holder turning them with long tongs to stop them burning.

It all happened so fast. Desperate to sample for herself whether the taste lived up to the aroma, Margaret was about to ask for tuppence worth, hoping that Lochiel would lend her the funds, when a shout of alarm made her turn, and at the same time a woman clutching what looked like a skinned rabbit barged straight into her, knocking her to her knees on the muddy cobble-stones.

No-one seemed to notice Margaret's plight as she scrabbled to get up, caught in the stampede of men, women, and children calling, "Stop, thief," after the woman. Terrified, she was about to scream when a pair of hands caught her from behind, lifting her clear of the milling crowd.

"Don't worry, you're safe now."

Expecting to hear Lochiel's distinctive Scottish tones, the cultured English voice came as a shock. Margaret whirled around as he set her down and came face-to-face with a young man of about twenty-five. Beneath his hat, hair the colour of the chestnuts she'd been drooling over flopped endearingly over his brow. He was clean-shaven, his mouth curved into a gentle smile that was reflected in his warm brown eyes.

"Reverend Beckwith, at your service."

"Reverend?" Lady Margaret exclaimed, eyeing his plain black coat and trousers.

"Fortunately, we Anglicans are permitted to reserve our cassocks for Sundays," he said. "It's not the most practical of garments."

"Ha! That's nothing, you should try wearing a—" Margaret broke off, reddening. "Gown," she substituted for crinoline. "Though I suppose a cassock is a kind of dress."

"Lady Margaret! Thank goodness you're unhurt."

"I'm perfectly fine, Lochiel. Reverend Beckwith here gallantly came to my rescue."

"You are a priest?"

"Reverend Sebastian Beckwith. Priest, parson, or rector, I answer to all, though I am more commonly known as Father Sebastian, of the Parish of St. George's. You don't look like members of my flock, if you'll forgive me saying so. Are you lost?"

"We're not lost, though you're right: we're not exactly in familiar territory." Lochiel's brow cleared and he held out his hand. "Cameron of Lochiel. How do you do?"

"And I am Lady Margaret Montagu Douglas Scott, to give me my full Sunday name. How do you do?" Margaret dropped a slight curtsy. "It was my idea that we visit Lambeth. We were intending walking back across Westminster Bridge, but then we got caught up in the crowds heading to the market. I've never tasted roast chestnuts before, and it was the lure of *that* which led me to abandon Lochiel's protection. And then that thief bowled me over. Did they catch her? The woman with the— Was it a rabbit?"

"Peggy is well-known to the stall-holders here. They're usually happy to give her any leftovers at the end of the day, for they know she's often left a bit short."

"So the rabbit was for her dinner?"

"No, most likely to be sold to pay a debt, or more accurately someone else's, knowing her husband. It's not like her to steal, though. I'll call on her later."

"She won't go to gaol, will she? I am woefully ignorant of such matters."

"I was woefully ignorant myself when I first arrived here two years ago. I was earmarked for what you might describe as a well-heeled parish in Cheltenham, but I found that a comfortable sinecure didn't sit well with me."

"And how do you find being uncomfortable instead?"

"The church provides perfectly adequate accommodation, and my widowed sister Susannah—Mrs. Elmhirst—keeps house for me." Father Sebastian's smile faded. "Compared to my parishioners, my lady, I live in the lap of luxury."

"Lady Margaret, we really should be going. I think we'd better get a hackney, if one is to be had."

"There is a stand at the station," Father Sebastian said. "The quickest way across is by Waterloo Bridge, though most people use Westminster to avoid the toll. You are going across the river, I take it?"

"Whitehall. Montagu House, to be exact," Margaret said. "If we had a boat we could be there in five minutes."

"A cab will suffice," Lochiel said firmly. "I think I can run to paying the toll. Good day to you, Father."

"Goodbye, Father," Margaret said, holding out her hand. "And thank you again for coming to my rescue. Why," she hissed, as she was shepherded away, "are you glowering, Lochiel?"

"You oughtn't to have given him your name and address."

"He's a man of the cloth, and well-connected, too, if he had a living in Cheltenham. He is obviously a man with a calling. One cannot help but admire . . ."

"Thank heavens." Lochiel hailed a passing hackney carriage, helping her in before giving directions and climbing in after her. "That was a stroke of luck. I am sure there is much to admire about the fellow, but I am still of the opinion that you should not have given him your details. He might come calling, begging for alms or whatnot, at Montagu House."

Margaret turned towards her escort, whose smile was somewhat strained. "If he does, he will not leave empty-handed. Thank you for your forbearance today, it is most appreciated."

"I wasn't bored, if that's what you're suggesting. I doubt anyone could be bored in your company."

"My father might disagree. What time is it, if you please? My boots and my gown are filthy. I don't want Mama to see me like this. I led her to believe we would be taking a stroll in the park."

"It is only just after three. We will be there in another ten minutes. Lady Margaret, I must tell you that I return to Berlin tomorrow."

"Tomorrow! Why didn't you mention that before? I have taken up almost all of your last day, when you should have been packing and saying goodbye to your friends."

"I wouldn't have missed today for the world." Lochiel cleared his throat. "Before I go, I must ask you—forgive me, I know that it is none of my business, but do you intend to marry Killin? It seems to me, you see, that your feelings for him have not changed significantly from those you confided in me that night."

"How do you know that?"

His cheeks coloured. "I should not have touched on such a personal matter."

Margaret hesitated. "I thought no-one noticed how I felt."

"You keep it very well-disguised in public."

"I am most grateful for your concern, but you need not worry. My heart may be insubordinate, but it no longer rules my head. If Killin renews his suit, then I shall accept him."

Lochiel opened his mouth to speak, then changed his mind as the carriage came to a halt. "Here we are, Montagu House," he said, looking out of the dusty window before turning back to her,

108

to her surprise catching her hands between his. "I wish you the very best for your future happiness."

"Thank you. I suspect I'm going to need it. Won't you come in?"

He shook his head. "As you pointed out, I have a great deal to do."

"When will I see you again?"

"Some months. A year or so, perhaps. I expect I'll receive my next posting direct from Berlin."

"So this is goodbye, then?"

His gloved fingers tightened around hers. "I'm afraid so. Goodbye, Lady Margaret."

"Lochiel, I hope . . ."

But the cabbie, grown bored with waiting, opened the door, cutting her short, and Lochiel let go his hold on her hand, giving her no option but to descend. "On to King Charles Street," he instructed as the door closed.

Margaret lifted a hand to wave, but Lochiel had already turned away, his thoughts presumably preoccupied with his own future prospects now that he had finally rid himself of her. She picked up her skirts and hurried to the door which the footman was holding open, anxious to change her clothes before her mother could ask her any awkward questions.

WHAT TRULY AILS LADY M.?

The Lounger at the Club, with his ear planted as firmly to the ground as ever, has a friendly word of advice for a certain, most esteemed gentleman. The Duke of B——, who is currently busy in the House of Lords supporting an Act intended to protect farmers from contracting cattle-plague, would do well to concern himself more with the well-being of a person much closer to his heart. We fear that all is not well with His Grace's second daughter. Titian-haired Lady M——, our readers may recall, left the Capital last summer on the eve of a Significant Announcement in order to recuperate from a sudden unexplained illness. The lady re-entered society some weeks ago, but while the Lounger can vouch for her seeming to be in excellent physical health, he cannot in all honesty claim the same for her spirits. Though fashionably slim, she has little to say in company and even less, alas, to make her smile.

What has become of Lady M——? Has the "illness" she rid herself of while in seclusion in Scotland come back to haunt her, along with a certain Scottish peer, who has been observed acting sentinel at almost every party she attends? Is the Earl of K—— afraid that his sought-after prize will once again be snatched from his grasp? Or are his assiduous attentions an effort to save the lady from a relapse? To prevent lightning striking twice, so to speak! The next few months will surely tell. I shall endeavour, as always, to keep you posted regarding any interesting developments.

Chapter Twelve

THE HEAT IN THE CROWDED drawing-room was stifling. Charlotte abhorred musical soirées such as this. As the latest tone-deaf young lady brought her demolition of Beethoven's "Moonlight Sonata" to an abrupt close, the duchess joined in with the round of applause. Unfortunately, relief made her, along with the rest of the audience, overenthusiastic in their acclamation. Her heart sank when the young lady resumed her seat and began to rustle through her sheets of music.

Flicking open her fan, Charlotte leaned towards her daughter, seated next to her. "I have a theory," she whispered, "that the less talent a young lady possesses, the more protracted her performance."

Margaret gave a snort of laughter. "I think it just feels that way. If it were indeed the case, I would be obliged to perform from dawn till dusk."

In fact, Margaret had a rather charming singing voice but a horror of public performance. It was ironic that Walter thought his second daughter someone perpetually seeking attention, when she was a wallflower by inclination.

"Are you feeling the heat, Mama? Shall I see if I can secure you a glass of lemonade?"

Thoughtful, too, Charlotte thought guiltily, shaking her head. "Louise was right—turquoise is your colour," she said, eyeing Margaret's new ball gown with some satisfaction. It was a deceptively simple creation worked up from the sketch made by the princess, the fabric of the skirt falling in deep pleats, lacking the swags and ruffles her daughter detested, a bertha collar of cream lace the only adornment. "Your friend has an excellent eye for what suits you."

"Thank you, Mama. Molly had to adjust it a little, for my waist is now a mere eighteen inches, the smallest it has ever been."

As was Margaret's appetite, which had all but disappeared. "I think eighteen is svelte enough," Charlotte said, adding, "Oh, dear heavens!" as, to her horror, a violinist stepped up to join the pianist.

The pair scraped and tinkled into action. Beside her, Margaret rolled her eyes, but as she leaned in to comment, her face fell and she stiffened. "Here comes Killin," she said. "Again."

Charlotte watched her daughter transform into a rigid effigy, her hands clasped tightly together, quite literally bracing herself. She could not understand this visceral reaction to the man, but it was painful to witness. As Killin manoeuvred himself carefully into the empty chair beside Margaret, Charlotte felt the girl shrink towards her. The movement was instinctive; she doubted that Margaret herself was even aware of it.

The performing duo launched into something utterly unrecognisable and she tried to catch her daughter's eye; but Margaret, her gaze fixed determinedly to the front, was no longer listening. Looking at her fixed smile and tense shoulders made Charlotte's own jaw clench in sympathy.

Killin was taking the opportunity to study his prize, his mouth pursed into a disapproving line. He had most likely read that vile piece in the *Illustrated Times*. The press really were beastly when they had some poor soul in their sights. There could be no denying that she and Walter were partly to blame for the remorseless hounding, however, though the duke would dispute that fact. Margaret's exile last year, coupled with her father's tight-lipped response when anyone asked after her health, had signalled to everyone that the Duke of Buccleuch's daughter had committed some heinous crime. Margaret *had* committed a major faux pas, but with the benefit of hindsight, their reaction had been ill-judged.

They ought to have brazened it out. At least if Margaret had remained in public view, the vilest of the allegations would have been proved demonstrably to be false.

Walter was still very set on this match, all the more so because Margaret had done her level best to thwart him. And it *was* an excellent match. There was nothing objectionable about Killin. Since Margaret's return to London at the beginning of the year, she had not once faltered in her efforts to please. Her desire to fulfil her obligations was clearly genuine, so why did she have to work so hard to embrace them? Ought a mother to ask? But what good would it do, when the die was cast? When they were married, Margaret and Killin would reach an amicable accommodation, as couples invariably did.

A final discordant screech from the violin brought the duet to a merciful close. "Well, that was most uplifting," Charlotte said, getting quickly to her feet in order to prevent another encore.

"I have not a musical ear as you do, Your Grace, and so must bow to your superior judgement," Killin said primly. "I believe that a cold collation is to be served in the dining room. If I may offer to escort you, in His Grace's absence? And your daughter, of course."

"We are much obliged," Charlotte replied, "but I notice that Margaret's flounce is torn and must be pinned. If you will excuse us, we will join you shortly."

Taking a firm hold of her daughter's arm, she headed for the ladies' retiring room.

"Mama, my gown hasn't any flounces."

"If music be the food of love, then that performance has made me bilious." The retiring room was happily empty. "I am reliably informed that after supper our hostess plans to warble her way through a selection of operatic arias. Too much of a good thing, methinks. We shall wait here while our carriage is summoned."

"But Killin is expecting to take us in to supper."

"We shall take the risk for once of disappointing him. He has been most assiduous in his attentions."

"Extremely," her daughter replied with an acid smile. "Every time I turn around, there he is, assiduously paying attention."

Charlotte stifled a laugh. "When you are married, you will likely find that he becomes considerably less assiduous."

"Oh, I do hope so."

The heartfelt words startled them both. "When you have a family," Charlotte said bracingly, "you will likely spend most of your time in the country, for fresh air is what young children need. You certainly thrived on it. I expect that Killin's business interests will keep him occupied elsewhere, so for the better part of the year, you will hardly see him."

Contrary to her hopes, Margaret was not at all reassured by this. "I have a horrible premonition that Killin's progeny will be tediously correct and rather boring."

"I doubt it, not with you as their mother. In point of fact, there is a great deal to be said for having a tediously correct and rather boring child."

"Then I will name my first daughter Victoria in the hope of guaranteeing that."

Seeing the spark of laugher in Margaret's eyes, Charlotte permitted herself a small, complicit smile.

Margaret stared down at her gown, pleating the silk of the skirt between her fingers. "Mama, you and my father do a great deal of charitable work, don't you?"

"We are both very much aware of our position in society," Charlotte replied, taken aback by the sudden change of subject. "We feel it is our duty to do what we can by serving on committees, raising funds, sponsoring causes, that kind of thing."

"I have been thinking that I would also like to do something useful. I have so much time on my hands between engagements and nothing to do with it, save kick my heels at home. I know you will say I should read an improving book or some other worthy endeavour but . . ."

"Go on," Charlotte said warily.

"There is a parson, Reverend Beckwith, who lives with his sister in Lambeth."

"How on earth did you come to meet a clergyman from Lambeth?"

"I met him through Lochiel."

Colour stained her daughter's cheeks. She wasn't lying, Charlotte was sure of it. Margaret never lied, but there was more to the affair than she was admitting. However, there was no more respectable and trustworthy man than Donald Cameron of Lochiel. "You think this parson can provide you with a useful occupation? Does he wish you to help him with his charity works?"

"Father Sebastian—that is how he is known there—hasn't actually asked for my help. His parish is near Waterloo Bridge Station, and he lives with his sister, who is a widow. I hoped that I might assist her in some practical capacity."

"Practical?" Charlotte frowned. "Are you thinking of emulating the charitable work that Lady Cavendish does, soup-kitchens and the like? It is most commendable, but hardly the kind of endeavour you should be getting embroiled in while your future is hanging in the balance. Frankly, Margaret, I am not at all sure that Killin would approve."

"I am quite certain he would not. In any case, Mama, I would rather not tag along in Lucy Cavendish's wake. She is so frightfully clever and just a little bit intimidating, if I am honest, and I don't want to be ordered about like a junior officer."

"Margaret, really! You are welcome to assist me in raising funds for one of my own favoured charities."

"No! I beg pardon, Mama, but I'd prefer to do something off my own bat. If Mrs. Elmhirst—that is Father Sebastian's sister—if she is willing to take me on, then I could go to Lambeth, not as

Lady Margaret but as plain Miss Scott, ready and willing to learn and to do whatever is needed—do you see, Mama?"

What Charlotte saw was a daughter eager to contribute, and where was the harm in that, if it helped her to cope with the restrictions that would be placed on her for the rest of her life? There was a glint of excitement in her eyes that had been absent for a long time. By the end of the year, assuming Killin came up to scratch, Margaret would be the latest in a long line of female sacrifices to the family weal. She deserved this much. And if she was in Lambeth, being useful incognito, then there would not be the additional worry of the press latching on to the story.

"Very well. If I can be assured that this Mrs. Elmhirst is a respectable person, then I see no reason to object."

"Thank you! I am certain she is, because Father Sebastian is a most respectable man. Indeed, he gave up a parish in Cheltenham to come to London and work with the poor and Lochiel says that such a post would be more than comfortable."

Margaret had met the brother but not the sister. A vague warning bell rang in Charlotte's head, but the man had Lochiel's approval, and Charlotte, herself an excellent judge of character, would take a view on Mrs. Elmhirst when she met her. It was highly likely that Margaret would quickly tire of traipsing about after the no doubt earnest and well-meaning parson and his sister, but at least she'd have had some respite from the strain she was under. And Killin would be none the wiser.

"Then it is agreed," she said. "You may send Mrs. Elmhirst a note asking her to call on me at her earliest convenience. If she passes muster, I will smooth the waters with your father."

Chapter Thirteen

LADY MARGARET I PRESUME, DO come in." Mrs. Susannah Elmhirst, a slim, fair-haired woman in her early thirties, with the same warm brown eyes as Father Sebastian, opened the door to the rectory herself. "You found us easily enough, then?"

"We came in a hackney carriage," Margaret said. "This is Molly, my maid. Thank you so much for permitting me to help out. I don't know how useful I will be, but I can promise I'll do my level best."

Mrs. Elmhirst smiled. "I was surprised when I received your note asking me to call on your mother, for you're not our usual sort of volunteer, but my brother remembered you very well. You made quite an impression on him."

"He made a lasting impression on me."

"He does tend to do that, though he divides opinion. People either love him or loathe him."

"I can't imagine why anyone would take against him."

"Certain individuals resent him hindering their efforts to make money from suffering," Mrs. Elmhirst said dryly. "Sebastian is a thorn in the side of the Board of Guardians for the Poor, too, which is where he is now, though he has promised he will be home in time to take tea with us later. I thought the best way to introduce you to the parish would be to take you on a little tour. I'm glad to see that you are dressed plainly."

"I am as eager as my mother to avoid attracting attention here. You see before you Miss Scott. Let us say I am visiting from Edinburgh, where my brother—no, my father—is a minister in

119

one of the poor parishes there, and he has sent me here on a mission to learn from your excellent example. How about that?"

"Goodness, what a fertile imagination you have. You will be a great asset to the children's storytelling group. Now," Mrs. Elmhirst continued, addressing Molly, "I think it would be best if you waited here. Our dear indispensable Esther, who is our chief cook, bottle washer, and everything else besides, will be glad of the company. If anyone calls, Esther will know what to do," she added, turning back to Margaret. "We operate an open house policy here. People come to us with problems at all hours of the day and night. Sebastian prides himself on never turning anyone away. Occasionally, some of them are even ecclesiastical matters!"

"That sounds like an excellent plan," Margaret agreed. She had been instantly drawn to Father Sebastian, with his charming smile and easy manner. His sister's smile was similar, lighting up her face and reflected in her eyes, giving her an unexpectedly endearing and rather mischievous look.

"Now, Miss Scott, are you ready for your introduction to the parish?"

"Oh yes, please, but I wish you will call me Margaret. I hope we are going to be friends."

"In that case, you must call me Susannah. Shall we?"

The rectory sat in the shadow of the church, the front step leading directly onto the street. "It was in a dreadful state of disrepair when Sebastian moved in," Susannah said, leading the way onto a series of narrow streets. "Though we have made it habitable, there is always another call on our funds which prevents us doing any more than keep it watertight. The houses generally are very cheaply built, and I'm afraid most of the landlords are reluctant to spend money fixing roofs or supplying fresh water. And damp—that is the very worst problem here. Sometimes water is literally running down the walls."

Her father, Margaret knew, owned an immense portfolio of

property, including any number of parochial houses and estate cottages, but he had factors to manage it all. She couldn't recall him ever mentioning repairs or costs, but if he had, would she have listened? "I am so horribly ignorant," she said, frowning, "but surely there are laws requiring landlords keep their properties in good repair?"

"There are regulations, but enforcing them is another matter entirely, and a fine balance has to be struck. If a property is actually deemed unfit for habitation, the tenants are made homeless, you see, and alternative accommodation is in very, very short supply. Poor Sebastian spends an enormous amount of time lobbying landlords directly, or via the vestry—that is the parish committee responsible for inspecting houses and sanitation—but with limited success. The men who sit on the committee are very often landlords themselves, and so have an interest in maintaining the status quo." Susannah smiled ruefully. "They are united in their hearty dislike of my brother. Not that Sebastian gives a fig about that."

"Aside from telling stories to children," Margaret said, rather overwhelmed, "I'm not quite sure how I can best be of assistance to you. I'm happy to try my hand at anything, but I've no practical skills or experience."

"Can you sew?"

"Plain stitching, hemming, yes, but anything more intricate—no. Mama once said that my sampler was the finest example she'd ever seen of how *not* to embroider."

"There's not much call for embroidery here, but if you are willing to help with some plain sewing, perhaps teach some of the little ones?"

"I'd love to do that. What else?"

"A good many of Sebastian's older parishioners cannot read or write, and need assistance sending and receiving correspondence. You could act as his scribe, if you don't consider that too menial a task. It would relieve some of the burden on him."

"Oh yes," Margaret said enthusiastically, imagining herself sitting opposite Father Sebastian at his desk as he dictated letters. "I can absolutely do that. What else?"

Susannah laughed. "Your mother agreed you may spend a few hours a week helping out, no more. I am sure the duchess would consider sewing or letter writing appropriate activities, but as for anything else . . ."

"Oh, please, I don't want to do only what is considered seemly. I'm not Lady Margaret here, remember? I'm Miss Scott, the practical daughter of the Reverend Scott, and used to getting my sleeves rolled up and getting *wired in* as Molly would say."

The screech of a train on the Charing Cross viaduct rattling overhead towards the river made her jump. Clouds of thick black smoke belched from its funnel, dispersing into the already murky grey pall that passed for the London sky.

"If you are truly determined to muck in," Susannah continued when the train had passed, "there are no end to the things you can do to help out. We have a mothers' club on a Wednesday. I pay house calls most days to help with whatever needs done. Some of the dwellings are not for the faint-hearted, Lady—I mean, Margaret. When one is poor, cleanliness can be a luxury."

"You mean the houses are dirty?"

"I mean the occupants smell, not to put too fine a point on it," Susannah said, grimacing. "Very few of the houses have running water. People have to queue to fill buckets, as the supply is only turned on a couple of times a week. There is a public baths, but it costs thruppence for a cold tub and sixpence for the water to be heated, which for most people here is a luxury they simply can't afford."

"I had no idea," Margaret said, too appalled to begin to imagine what the more intimate sanitary arrangements might be.

"Don't be too hard on yourself. When I first came here, I thought myself a battle-hardened follower of the drum, but there are still days when I am humbled by the deprivation I see. Here, take this," Susannah said, giving Margaret a little muslin bag tied with tartan ribbon. "I make up these little sachets for Sebastian to carry with him. It's filled with lavender. I have a tiny patch of garden at the back of the rectory where I manage to grow a few physic herbs. My nose is quite immune to smells, but poor Sebastian struggles, even after all this time."

Margaret inhaled the sweet scent of the dried lavender and immediately sneezed. If Father Sebastian didn't let his sensitive nose stop him, then she most certainly wouldn't. "You say you followed the drum? Do you mean your late husband was a military man?"

"He was indeed. Frederick's last posting was as a captain in the Light Division under Colonel Yea in the Crimean War. We had been married for five years, and most of it was spent on one campaign or another. I went with him everywhere."

"You must have been very young when you married," Margaret said, her admiration for Susannah increasing tenfold.

"I was a bride at eighteen. Our parents wanted us to wait, but Frederick was committed to his army career, and we were very much in love. All we cared about was being together. I knew nothing of the life of a military wife, and I was next to useless when it came to homemaking. Poor Frederick would come home to a fire that refused to light, a dinner that hadn't been cooked, and a wife in tears, but he never once complained. Fortunately, army wives are a tight-knit little band, and to my astonishment—and Frederick's—I eventually proved to be most adept at making do."

"You were obviously very happy," Margaret said, touched by the other woman's tender smile.

"Oh, very, right up until the end. He was—Frederick was wounded in the battle to take the Great Redan and lost a limb. It's a horribly common occurrence, when facing cannon fire.

Unfortunately, gangrene set in, and in the end, he was too weak to survive."

"You were with him?" Margaret asked, a lump in her throat.

"To the bitter end. In that sense, I was more fortunate than many other wives. Now," Susannah continued brusquely, "your nose will have informed you that is the vinegar works over there. Here we have one of the parochial schools run by our church, and just across the road another, a British school which is run by Nonconformists. Through there, you can see Nelson Square, which is a little oasis of greenery and has some of the better housing in the area, but we are headed further over to the more deprived streets."

Margaret scurried after her, her eyes wide, her ears assaulted by the clatter of barrows, carts, and horses; the screeching of the trains rattling overhead; and the rhythmic hammering from the many building sites. Her nose had grown accustomed to the smell of horse manure, which was all-pervasive in every corner of the metropolis, but it mingled here with the smoke from factories, the mud that oozed between the cobble-stones, and the sickly sweet smell of rotting vegetables in the gutters. Surreptitiously, she took another sniff of the lavender sachet.

"And here," Susannah announced, "we have the workhouse."

The huge building stood at the far end of the market where Margaret had first encountered Father Sebastian. The red brick was tarnished almost black in places, and the many windows were mean and small. An imposing gate led to an even more imposing portico.

"The size of the building, unfortunately, is testament to the extent of the need," Susannah said grimly.

Margaret shuddered. "It looks like a prison. You would have to be absolutely desperate to summon the courage to knock on that door."

"Homeless, penniless, and usually starving. Everything possible is done to discourage supplicants and to make them as miserable as possible while they are in the workhouse."

"That's barbaric!"

"Poor relief is funded from the parish rates. In impoverished parishes, such as this, there are many people in need but few ratepayers, and this heaps pressure on available funds."

"So they deliberately make desperate people miserable?"

"In order to make the alternatives more attractive," Susannah said bitterly. "Even if it means risking gaol."

Like the woman who stole the rabbit, Margaret thought. "Do women really abandon their newborn babies on the doorstep, as I've heard?"

"Tragically, they do."

"Because they can't afford to feed them?"

"That is one reason," Susannah said, looking uncomfortable. "Lady Margaret . . ."

"I am not a fragile flower to be protected from the realities of life. Please don't spare my blushes."

"If you must have it, they are more often than not women whose child has no father."

"You mean women of the night?"

"No, I don't. I mean servants who have been abused by their masters, girls who have been foolish enough to succumb to the blandishments of the chap they've been walking out with. Young women desperate to save their reputations or their livelihoods but quite unable to do so and still keep their child."

Margaret stared at the huge workhouse door. If the vile story told about her in the *Morning Post* had been true, what would have happened to her child? They would have taken it away from her, but what would have happened to it? In that moment, it didn't matter that there had never been a child. The fury that gripped her made her hands curl into fists. Looking at that door, she tried to imagine a young woman like herself creeping up under cover of darkness, clutching a screaming bundle to her chest.

"Do they leave notes? Names? Do these poor women ever know what becomes of the little ones?"

"I believe it is thought to be for the best not to maintain any ties. Each workhouse has its own method of naming the children." Susannah forced a smile. "You know, there are worse lives. There is a school attached to this workhouse that provides a basic education for both girls and boys. When they are of age to work, they are found a trade or placed into service. If they are sick, there is a dispensary. The food is nutritious if not exactly tasty—and it's a lot better than the poor fare our soldiers endure when on campaign. And talking of Christian soldiers, here comes my brother."

Father Sebastian was dressed all in black, the skirts of his coat flying out as he strode towards them, a smile lighting up his face. "Lady Margaret, welcome to our humble parish." Doffing his hat, he made a bow.

"It is a pleasure to be here, Father Sebastian. But you should know that I am to be plain Miss Scott."

"The daughter of a Scottish man of the cloth, who has come to see what examples of our good works she can take back to Edinburgh," Susannah elaborated, with a wink.

"An excellent cover story. One of your own making? Then you will be a welcome addition to Susannah's Saturday and Sunday schools."

"If I can manage to get away, then I would be delighted to attend."

To her embarrassment, Margaret felt her cheeks colour under his scrutiny. Father Sebastian was not conventionally good-looking. His mouth was too generous, his nose too decided, but he exuded a beguiling natural charm. His hair had a wave that he made no attempt to tame with the foul Macassar oil that far too many men used to sculpt their locks. Though Susannah had informed her that he was twenty-seven years old, he looked boyishly younger. And, goodness, he had the most delightful smile and a way of looking directly at one, as if he was hanging on every word. Unlike some other men she could think of, who treated her conversation merely as a convenient stopgap to allow them to formulate their next sentence.

"Well, now," he said, beaming, "has Susannah shown you enough of our little patch of God's earth? Are you ready for a cup of tea?"

"Actually, Seb, I'm going to leave you to escort Miss Scott back to the rectory," Susannah said. "I have a call to make just around the corner from here. Would you mind, Margaret?"

Would she mind! Repressing this unworthy leap of excitement, she shook her head. "The last thing I want to be is a hindrance to either of you. Unless you would prefer that I came with you?"

"Not on this occasion," Susannah answered, to Margaret's secret relief. "Mary Webb's daughter, who is only thirteen, is with child. I have yet to establish the full story, but it seems she is too far gone for them to consider any form of drastic remedy. It has taken me a while to gain her trust. I don't want to introduce her to another stranger at this point."

"Thirteen! That is two years younger than my baby sister. The man responsible should be put in gaol."

"The law deems twelve to be of age to consent. What I haven't yet been able to fathom is if the child did in fact do so. Walk back with Sebastian. I shouldn't be too far behind you."

"It is shocking but sadly not uncommon, I'm afraid," Father Sebastian said, as they watched Susannah hurry away.

"What will happen to the baby?" Margaret asked, eyeing the forbidding entrance to the workhouse. "Will it end up there?"

"Unless the grandmother passes it off as her own, which happens more often than you might imagine. But that, I'm afraid, depends on whether she can persuade her husband to go along with the deceit. In the end it will come down to what is considered the lesser of two evils. And money, of course. Everything comes down to money in the end, around here. Shall we?"

Margaret fell into step beside him. "The woman who stole the rabbit the day we met, you remember? You said that was about money."

"Peggy, like many in this parish, is struggling to keep the wolf from the door. She takes in laundry, and her husband sells flowers at the market. They've five little ones. The eldest is seven, I think—Susannah would know. The long and the short of it is, she pawned some of the laundry she'd been paid to wash, giving the cash to her husband to buy blooms, intending to redeem her bond when he sold them later that day. Sadly, her husband drank and gambled the funds away instead, so in desperation she stole the rabbit to raise the money to get the laundry out of hock and keep her job."

"That's simply awful! What happened?"

"I managed to smooth things over with the stall-holder. Fortunately, Peggy had the sense to use a legitimate pawnbroker, so she wasn't in debt to one of the sharks that feed on the unfortunate and needy."

"Susannah said you make enemies by helping people."

"You can't do the work I do without treading on a few toes. Moneylenders, shopkeepers who charge a small fortune for credit, landlords who won't make repairs, governors and vestrymen who won't spend a penny more than the bare minimum, they all like to point the finger of blame at me. But I've a thick skin, and not only am I sure I'm in the right of it," Father Sebastian said with a wry smile, "I've God on my side."

"And any right-minded decent person, too, I should hope."

He laughed, shaking his head. "You'd think so, wouldn't you, but there's scores of so-called upstanding citizens who would be happy to see the back of me."

"Did you have words with Peggy's husband?"

"Heavens, no. He'd view it as meddling in his affairs and it wouldn't be me who'd suffer the consequences."

Margaret shuddered. "Surely she won't end up in that dreadful place back there."

"A last resort, but a sadly necessary one for some. Husbands and wives are kept apart, you know, and siblings, too. We do what we can, distributing coals and food to keep people in their own homes, but the parish purse has its limits. My bishop is of the opinion that those who can't help themselves should be left to God's mercy, but what His Grace doesn't know won't harm him."

"That sounds somewhat heretical!"

"Ah no, I'm simply a practical man who believes there's more than one way to bring God into people's lives. You can't frighten people with eternal damnation if they're already living in hell, Lady Margaret, and you can't nurture the spirit if the body is starving. To me, that's just common sense. We're very grateful, Susannah and I, for your interest in our parish."

"I simply want to help," Margaret said earnestly, "even more now that I know a little of what you do. I have not much to offer, but I am willing to learn."

"Then that is all that counts, for it shows you have a good heart."

"Susannah suggested that I could help you with your parish correspondence. One thing I can do is write a neat hand."

"That is a most excellent idea. Bureaucracy is my biggest bugbear. What else has my sister suggested?"

"Teaching children sewing. Oh, and telling them stories."

"Clever Sue, to pass that task on to you. She's an eminently practical woman, my sister, and terrifyingly well-organised, but she's a bit too—let us say, restrained—to be a good storyteller. While you now, my instincts are telling me that you are the type to throw yourself into it with gusto. Am I mistaken?"

Margaret burst out laughing. "No, you are quite right. I love making up stories for children, and telling them, too, for what it's worth."

"Oh, it's worth a great deal more than some would credit. Life can be tough around here, even for little ones."

"Then anything I can do to make life easier, I will do. But I don't just want to dispense charity, Father Sebastian, I want to understand why charity is required in the first place."

"Finding the root cause and doing something to alleviate it is exactly why I am here." He smiled down at her. They had reached the rectory. She stopped to allow him to open the front door. He paused in the act of brushing past her and their eyes met. It was the strangest feeling, as if the breath had been knocked out of her. She was sure, in that moment, he felt it, too. But then he opened the door and muttered something about fetching tea, and she decided she must have imagined it after all.

Chapter Fourteen

Saturday, 17 March 1866 (Five Weeks Later)

"Aᴺᴰ ꜰʀᴏᴹ ᴛʜᴀᴛ ᴅᴀʏ ꜰᴏʀᴡᴀʀᴅ, Jenny had jam sandwiches for breakfast every morning." Margaret finished her story and smiled at the cluster of children sitting in a semicircle on the floor. There were eighteen today, three more again than on her last visit. "Now, since you have all been so very well-behaved, there are jam sandwiches for you, too, and milk, over on the table in the corner."

Scrabbling awkwardly to her feet, she made her way across the hall to join Susannah and the children's mothers, but before she could sit down, Sally Jardine thrust a squirming, wet, and very, very smelly bundle into her hands.

"Miss Scott, would you mind changing Alfie's napkin, there's a dear. Only I'm just about to have my tea."

Before she could stop herself, Margaret screwed up her nose. "Pooh."

"Yes, sorry about that. He's teething, got a bit of an upset tummy." Sally didn't look in the least bit sorry. "Course if you're too posh to get your hands dirty, I'll do it myself."

Sally knew Margaret had a sensitive nose, because Sally had taken great delight, the first time they met, in ridiculing Margaret for carrying the lavender sachet that Susannah had given her. Margaret had very nearly succumbed to tears, and Sally had noticed, of course.

Margaret knew better than to show weakness now. "Come along

131

then, Alfie," she said, deliberately snuggling him close and smiling over at Sally. "Let's see if we can make your bottom half match up to that sweet little face of yours."

Swallowing hard to prevent herself gagging, aware of the damp residue seeping into her gown, Margaret carried the baby over to the small table where Susannah kept a supply of fresh napkins and cleaning cloths. Her first attempt to change a napkin, on her first day here, had been a disaster, ending with both the child and herself in tears. Through the jeers and laughter Verity had come to her aid, gently talking her through her second attempt, earning herself a few cheers and a smattering of applause. Persistence had paid off. She was rather proficient now, and most of the women had warmed to her. Alfie, however, and his mother, were determined in their own way to challenge her. She could sense everyone watching as she gingerly removed the pins.

"Come on, Alfie, let her know who's boss," Sally called.

Desperate not to be found wanting, Margaret gritted her teeth, took shallow breaths, and proceeded to clean up the revolting mess. To her profound relief Alfie was too delighted to be pristine and dry to do anything other than coo. Handing a fresh, smiling baby back to his mother ten minutes later, she made an extravagant curtsy. A cup of strong tea was thrust into her hands, and a chair patted for her to sit on.

"I suppose you've earned that," Sally conceded, setting Alfie at her feet. "My Robert says he's never smelt the like, and he's a tosher."

Baffled, Margaret looked to Susannah for clarification. "He goes down the sewers with a fishing net looking for coins or nails to sell on," she explained.

"You know what they say," Sally chipped in irrepressibly. "Where there's muck, there's brass!"

Shuddering, Margaret took a sip of the stewed tea, bracing herself for its fierce, tarry taste. On the other side of the room, the children had finished their jam sandwiches and milk, and were playing one of their complicated ball games. Most of the mothers were either knitting or stitching as they drank their tea, their eyes on each other rather than their work. Stockings, shirts, and chemises were created at speed. Rips were repaired, holes darned, and new cuffs and collars attached. How many times, sitting through a tea with Mama's friends, had she heard the oohs and aahs of admiration for an entirely useless sampler!

"Verity couldn't make it today?"

"Her ankles have swollen up so much she can't hardly walk." Agnes tutted. "I brought her two littlest ones along, told her to put her feet up, though whether she will or not . . ."

"I have some Epsom salts," Susannah said. "Tell her to mix them with cold water and rest her feet in the solution for fifteen minutes."

"I'll tell her, but you know Verity," Agnes said. "Can't sit still for a second. I remember when she had her first, must be fifteen years ago now . . ."

"No more than thirteen, for her eldest isn't twelve yet."

"And this will be what—baby number nine?"

"Ten. Fingers crossed. She's not kept well since the last one. You must remember, she had a terrible time of it."

Margaret listened with her customary fascinated horror as the women embarked on a graphic description of the experience of giving birth. It was a popular topic, second only to the demands placed upon them by their husbands. Unlike pregnancy, which was universally abhorred, husbands split the group. Some of the women claimed discharging their marital duties was an endurance test, but a majority, to Margaret's astonishment, seemed to enjoy it.

"I make sure Robert has a good wash first, mind." Sally cackled. "You never know where he's been!"

"The problem is, we do!" Agnes retorted, and the group of women erupted with raucous laughter.

The bawdy jokes, the innuendos that mostly went straight over Margaret's head, were a revelation. She had never heard anyone talk so candidly. There were no veiled hints, no euphemisms, nor any pretence. It was liberating, for even when the women teased her ignorance, they did so mostly without malice. In the early days here, which seemed like a lifetime and not merely a month ago, her cheeks had burned constantly with embarrassment. These days, she occasionally felt bold enough to add a ribald comment of her own. It gave her a warm glow to make these tough, resilient women laugh.

"I'm afraid that we've run out of time again, ladies. Agnes, if you wait behind I'll fetch the Epsom salts."

Chairs were scraped back; mending, sewing, and knitting put away in deep pockets; and children rounded up. "I see Alfie has left his seal of approval," Sally said, pointing at the brown stain on Margaret's bodice. Leaning closer, she wrinkled her nose. "Yuck. Good luck getting that out."

Cursing under her breath, wondering if even ever-resourceful Molly would find Alfie's legacy a challenge too far, Margaret ignored the mother, smiling at the baby instead, gratified by the beaming smile she received in return. "Poor lamb, you have enough to fret about getting those teeth through. You let me worry about my dress."

"Milk will remove the smell," Agnes said, shooting Sally a dark look. "You see if it don't."

"Would you mind tidying up?" Susannah returned with her hat and basket. "I have a house call to make."

"Of course not. Is something wrong?" Margaret asked, for her friend was looking worried.

"You remember the girl I told you about the first day you were here, Mary Webb's daughter?"

"The thirteen-year-old who was expecting a baby? Oh no, Susannah, has she . . ."

"The baby was born yesterday. A boy. Early, but he seemed healthy enough. Unfortunately, he died this morning, poor little mite."

"Oh, Susannah." Tears started in Margaret's eyes. "As if that girl—she's no more than a child herself—hadn't suffered enough already."

Susannah blew her nose. "Right now, what we need to do is concentrate on the living. It was not an easy birth. I am going to see what I can do to persuade them to allow a doctor to call discreetly and examine her. If I don't see you later, I'll see you next week?"

Margaret gave her a quick hug. "Definitely."

Sebastian was late, as usual. Margaret stared out of the study window, which faced onto the street, her heart lifting when she saw his familiar figure hurrying towards her. Just before he turned into the rectory, a thick-set man dressed in an ill-fitting tweed suit jumped out in front of him, bringing him to an abrupt halt. The man had his back to her, but she could see from Sebastian's set expression that they were not exchanging pleasantries. The dispute lasted several minutes before the stranger extravagantly and deliberately spat at Sebastian's feet, pushed past him, and strode off.

"Sebastian!" she said when he entered the study. "What on earth was that all about? I saw that man—"

"Jake Briggs. He's a local debt collector. He reckons I'm bad for business."

"Because you prevent him getting his claws into decent people," Margaret exclaimed indignantly. "I thought he was going to punch you."

Sebastian grinned. "You needn't worry; he's not daft enough to do me actual harm. Doesn't want the peelers sniffing about. He feels obliged to threaten me every now and then, but I'm not going to let some thug or anyone else drive me away from here." Taking her hands between his, he smiled warmly at her. "Tell me, how were the coven today?"

"Oh, they had their moments. Sally Jardine's little boy, Alfie, has a tummy upset. So naturally she asked me to change his napkin."

"Don't judge Sally too harshly; she has not had her troubles to seek. Anyway, I'm sure you handled her admirably." Sebastian lifted her hand to his mouth, pressing a kiss to her knuckles.

The touch of his lips made her breath catch. Their eyes met, and she sensed that he, too, felt the almost irresistible urge to close the distance between them. In her other life, the world across the Thames, handshakes were fleeting, hand clasping unheard of. Sebastian's world was full of casual touches, arm brushing, helping hands, but only his touch made her skin tingle like this, made her feel like her corset was laced too tight, making it difficult to breathe.

Time and again over the last weeks, lying wide awake in the dark, replaying his every glance and word, Margaret tried to convince herself that he was simply being kind, friendly, that her growing affection for him was not returned. One could not come to care so deeply for a person in such a short time, she told herself. But it had been there from the moment their eyes had first met in the market, that tug of awareness, that breathless excitement. And it grew stronger every day. When they were apart, she could convince herself that it was one-sided, a result of her overheated imagination. But when she looked into his eyes, when their hands were tightly clasped like this, she knew beyond doubt the attraction was mutual.

And wrong. No matter how right it actually felt. Gently disentangling herself, she made her way to the desk, pulling up her own chair. "Susannah said you had a sheaf of letters for me to write."

Sebastian shrugged out of his coat and flung it over the back of his chair, leaving him in the waistcoat and shirt-sleeves he preferred to work in. His hair was ruffled—he had a habit of running his hand through it when he was thinking. "I even have a bit of good news to share, too, for once," he said, taking his seat.

"Well, don't keep me in suspense—good news is always welcome around here." Margaret sat down, leaning her elbows on the desk because Mama wasn't there to reprimand her for doing so.

"The workhouse board have finally agreed to permit Sunday visits to the infirmary."

"That's marvellous news."

"That last appeal you wrote on the matron's behalf was masterly. I reckon that was what swung the decision in our favour."

"I only highlighted the case she described to me regarding one of her patients. That poor old woman knew her time had come. To deny her daughter the chance to say goodbye because of an arcane rule is barbarous."

"Tell that to those pompous fools on the Board of Guardians. Or my bishop, for that matter." Sebastian slammed his hand down on a stack of letters. "They don't realise that people would rather suffer than ask for help, especially if they are then subjected to an interrogation or a bloody sermon. I'm sorry. My language. I shouldn't have . . ."

"Don't be." Margaret reached across the desk to touch his hand. His fingers curled around hers. There were shadows under his eyes. "The injustice of it all must be difficult to bear," she said gently.

"Many of my parishioners are no angels, but even fallen angels are still angels."

"I've never heard that expression before."

"It means there's some good in everybody."

"Why is it that we talk of the deserving poor, but no-one ever suggests there might be undeserving rich?"

"A very good question. I've a mind to pose it in my next sermon. Have I told you lately how very much Susannah and I appreciate all the help you've given us? I used to dread coming here to face the mountain of paperwork, but now I look forward to it. On the days you are here, at least."

"You work too hard."

"Unfortunately there aren't enough hours in the day, but it doesn't feel like work when you are here with me."

The warmth of his smile made her feel as if she was being heated from the inside. It made her heart flutter. It made her feel giddy. "I'm simply happy to be of service," Margaret said. *Did* he feel the same? She couldn't be imagining it, could she, the intensity of his gaze?

This time, it was he who broke the spell, dropping his gaze, sitting back in his chair. "Susannah's coterie of mothers have grown very fond of you, she tells me. I know they tease you . . ."

"Teasing is a sign that they accept me. It matters a great deal to me, to feel part of things here."

"We're lucky to have you. I know Sue considers you her friend, and I—I don't know what I'd do without you, to be honest. Even Esther and Molly have grown very close. Now," Sebastian continued brusquely, picking up a stack of papers, "to work. I've had another of my parishioners complaining about the children's hospital, I'm afraid. His little boy was in a dreadful accident, but there was no bed available, so they patched him up and sent him home. Don't worry—it looks as if he'll survive—but it shouldn't come down to a question of blind luck. The hospital is simply too small to cope with the demand and it will get worse, for we have new families moving into the area all the time. All that can be done in this case is see what help we can offer the poor lad once he's up and about again."

For the next two hours Margaret methodically worked with Sebastian through the stack of correspondence, answering queries, making cases, setting those aside which required home visits. The door-bell clanged regularly, but Esther dealt with the calls, leaving them undisturbed.

"That's the last of them for today, thank goodness." Sebastian set down his pen, rolling his shoulders. "Although I do have one personal letter to write, to my sister Selina."

"I didn't know you had another sister."

"She is married to another man of the cloth, as it happens. One rather higher up in the church hierarchy than I. It was through her husband that I obtained my living near Cheltenham."

"Your well-heeled parish. Don't you ever wish you'd remained there?"

"And married the fair Emily and had a brood of my own? Not ever."

"The fair Emily? Were you *betrothed*?"

"No, no, nothing was ever formalised," Sebastian said hastily. "She was Selina's niece by marriage. She didn't care for my choice of new parish, so that was the end of it. I couldn't marry a woman who didn't share my calling. I need someone at my side who is willing to muck in and help me improve the lives of my parishioners."

"Which is precisely what you have in Susannah."

"Indeed I do. Poor Sue. When Frederick died, he left her in somewhat straitened circumstances, and she was forced to return to live with our parents. It suited them, but not her. She was bored rigid."

"So when you were posted here, she must have been delighted."

"It's an arrangement that suits us both. She's a practical woman with absolutely no sense of smell." He winked. "I couldn't ask for more."

The bell clanged again, and Margaret checked her watch, giving a little exclamation of dismay. "I must go. I have a dinner to attend and then a soirée. Very boring," she added, embarrassed to have mentioned either engagement, "but I will have to change my clothes."

"Yes? You look perfectly fine to me," Sebastian said.

Her gown was one of her oldest and decidedly past its best. What was more, with its long sleeves and high collar, it was clearly *not* an evening gown. Sebastian never commented on her clothes. He rarely paid her any sort of compliment about her appearance and that was one of the things she liked about him.

"I'm not going to a pie shop, Sebastian, I'm going to dinner with one of my mother's oldest friends. If I turned up in an outdated day dress smelling vaguely of Alfie's napkin, she would be extremely offended."

"In that case we'd better get rid of the ink on your face, too."

He came round to her side of the desk, dabbing the tip of her nose with his handkerchief. "It tickles," Margaret said, wrinkling her nose.

"Hold still—there's another spot just here."

Sebastian leaned in to dab at her cheek. She could smell the ink on his fingers, the sandalwood of his soap, the slightly musty wool of his waistcoat. His fingers fluttered down over the side of her face, down her throat to rest on her shoulder.

"Margaret."

His voice sounded odd. Daring to meet his eyes, she knew with utter certainty that her doubts about his feelings were misplaced. "Sebastian." Her voice was no more than a whisper. She had no idea what to do. If she moved she would break the spell.

For a long moment they stood together, gazes locked. Time seemed to stop, along with her breath, until he gave a soft sigh, and she lifted her face and surrendered her lips to his. She could feel his breath on her cheek, fast and shallow, sense his nerves were stretched as taut as hers. The taste of him, the softness of his mouth, the roughness of the cheek she lifted her hand to caress, the terrified delight of being so intimate with him, shocked her. Then tentatively, he moved his mouth on hers and she followed his lead, and her shock gave way to pleasure.

The clang of the front door-bell made them leap apart. Dazed, they stared at each other. "Good God," Sebastian said, his cheeks colouring. "I'm sorry! That was very wrong of me."

"Please don't apologise. I was just as culpable," Margaret said, freeing her hands.

"It won't happen again, I swear. The last thing I wish is to scare you off. You are doing so much good here, I would hate to jeopardise that."

Ought she to have been frightened? Should she now be having a fit of the vapours? What she certainly, definitely should not be doing was wishing that he would kiss her again. "Let's just pretend it didn't happen," Margaret said, knowing that was what she ought to say, even if it was likely to prove impossible.

But Sebastian cast her a grateful look. "Thank you. You are an angel."

A soft tap at the door precluded her refuting this claim. "Begging your pardon, Father," Esther said, "but Mrs. Powers is desperate for a word. Says it's a matter of life or death."

Chapter Fifteen

THE DRAWING-ROOM OF MARLBOROUGH HOUSE was a vast space littered with gilded chairs, sofas, and chaise-longues. Artful clusters of tables were strewn with albums, Sèvres figures, and enamelled snuff-boxes. The potted palms were so tall they almost brushed the ornately corniced ceilings. The upholstery was embroidered with gold thread, the windows draped with thick velvet. Margaret and her mother had been invited by Alexandra, Princess of Wales, to take informal tea with the queen, who would be accompanied, as always, by Louise.

"You are the only guests," Alix informed them when they arrived. "Lady Margaret, you are to take tea with Louise separately. Her Majesty is eager to hear the details of your sister's lying-in from your mother. You did bring Lady Kerr's letter with you, Duchess?"

"I have it here," Mama said, holding up her reticule. "It is unusually frank and quite unfit for the ears of any unmarried woman. I commend your idea of seating Margaret and Louise separately."

"Talking of seating," Alix said, frowning at the elaborately laid tea-table, "I am not sure where to place Her Majesty. The day is cold and I have had the fire lit, but as you know the queen does not like the room to be too hot."

"Oh no, she cannot abide the direct heat. I suggest you place her here," Mama said, pointing, "and then if you have the table moved over there, you can take that seat, and I shall risk being lightly toasted by the fire."

"Thank you, an excellent plan."

Margaret watched, fascinated, as Alix summoned several footmen to carefully dismantle the elaborately laid tea-table, move it, and then replace everything, a process that took several minutes. Her Majesty's place was marked by not one but two tea-cups and saucers, for it was her habit to pour her tea from one cup to another until it was adequately cooled.

"My goodness, are you sure we are the only guests?" Margaret asked, her eyes wide at the volume and variety of food being set out.

"Signor Francatelli always excels himself when the queen comes to tea," Alix informed her with a prim smile. "He was Her Majesty's chief cook for a couple of years, and though it was back in the forties, when she was just married, he insists that no-one understands her palate as he does."

"He certainly panders to her sweet tooth." The bread and butter, sandwiches, and ices would be served when Her Majesty arrived, though Margaret couldn't see where they would fit on the table. Several bonbon dishes in the shape of scantily clad Greek goddesses holding up urns were set at carefully measured intervals. The salted almonds were at the greatest distance from the queen's place, while the pralines and sugared almonds were closest. Italian macaroons were stacked in a pyramid, while the Naples and champagne biscuits were set out on a plate like a mosaic. The queen's favourite chocolate sponge was three tiers high, but there was also a rich plum cake, a plain sponge, a selection of pastries, and another elaborate concoction with icing as delicate as lace.

"Here she is," Alix said, though Margaret had heard no announcement.

"At least you will have the opportunity to enjoy your tea with

Louise," Mama whispered as the three women arranged themselves into a welcoming party. "I find I have barely finished my first sandwich by the time our monarch has finished her tea."

As ever, Margaret was surprised by the queen's diminutive stature as she made her curtsy to the rotund, frowning figure garbed in black. Her Majesty nodded a vague greeting, but she had one eye on the tea-table and the other on Mama.

"You brought the letter, Duchess?"

"Indeed, ma'am, I have it here."

"If you will take this seat, ma'am," Alix said, rushing forward.

"I don't want to be too near the fire. This room is hot." Shedding several shawls and mantles, which were caught adroitly by the Princess of Wales, Her Majesty took her seat, and Mama waved Margaret away.

Louise, needing no further urging, grabbed her by the hand and pulled her to the far corner of the room. "Thank heavens for your sister's timely delivery. Now we can have a proper gossip. I take it," she added belatedly, "that all went well with the birth?"

"Oh yes." Margaret took her seat at the smaller but only slightly less laden tea-table. "I have never seen Mama so relieved as when she received the letter yesterday morning. When my father said that Kerr would be disappointed not to have had the son he was hoping for, she drew him such a look. They have called the little girl Cecil, after Kerr's mother and his sister who died, sadly, the day before my new niece was born."

"Good grief, what a tragic coincidence. Was she having a baby, too?"

"She was a nun, Lou, so I doubt it. Thank you. No cream for me. I try to stick to lemon these days."

Louise poured the tea. "As you know, my sister Vicky is expecting her fifth, while Alice is already having her third, and she's been married less than four years. It seems to be raining babies. Do help yourself to cake. Signor Francatelli makes the most fabulous coffee and walnut log. Good enough to tempt even me to sample a crumb or two."

"No, thank you, I'm not hungry."

"That has never stopped you before."

"The press monitor my figure even more strictly than Mama. It has rather curtailed my appetite for cake."

"Oh goodness, I'm so sorry. Don't look so stricken, M. But it's all ancient history now, isn't it?"

"Provided I don't put another foot wrong. Sometimes I feel like one of those poor little insects trapped between two slides under a microscope, you know?"

Louise chuckled. "I know the feeling, wriggling under intense scrutiny! *Are* you coping, M.? You certainly look very well, and that gown is most becoming; though if you don't mind a little hint, less is more when it comes to lace."

"I agree, but Mama would not countenance my wearing anything plainer to come to tea with the queen."

"And your hair, too," Louise persisted, "the epitome of a well-behaved coiffure with not a single wilful curl. Most impressive. I congratulate you."

"Never mind how I look." Margaret pushed her tea-cup to one side and pulled her chair closer. "I have something to tell you."

Louise also pushed her cup to one side, her smile fading abruptly. "Do not say you have been foolish again? You have worked so hard to re-establish yourself, and *I* have so enjoyed having your company. I pray you have done nothing to deprive me of it."

"I have been making secret forays to Lambeth."

"Lambeth! If it is to visit the Archbishop of Canterbury at Lambeth Palace, then I fail to see how anyone could dare find fault with that."

"You are on the right lines, but about half a mile and a world away." Margaret reached across the table for her friend's hand but stopped midway when Louise shrank away. "There is no need to start distancing yourself. Mama knows all about it—well, some of it. It is my reward for my exemplary behaviour; though when she agreed, I don't think she had any notion my visits would prove so life-changing. To be honest, I didn't either but—oh, it has been! In the last five weeks I have learned so much, experienced so much, I am a different person entirely."

"Five weeks, and you have said nothing to me."

"Don't you dare take offence. What I'm about to tell you, I've told not another soul. If you will pour me another cup of tea and cut me just a tiny sliver of cake, I will reveal all."

To her relief, Louise smiled, albeit reluctantly, and reached for the tea-pot. "Go on, then."

"AND THERE YOU HAVE IT," Margaret concluded, sometime later, her tea cold and her cake untouched. "I'm sorry. I've not let you get a word in."

"My goodness, M., but you are a dark horse. I had not an inkling of any of this. To think that you have been spending every spare minute rubbing shoulders with heaven knows who and catching heaven knows what—" Louise broke off, shaking her head. "I sincerely hope that you douse yourself in vinegar when you return home. And the smells! You have a nose like a blood-hound, too. How do you cope?"

"At first I carried a lavender sachet around. Susannah makes them for Sebastian—Father Sebastian, that is. But I barely notice now."

"It is all so very extreme. If you must do good, couldn't you have contented yourself with—oh, I don't know, knitting stockings for the poor?"

"It's not about doing good, Louise. It's about learning what real life is like. It's about being part of something and feeling useful. The women there take me at face value. They tease me for my unworldliness, and they laugh at me for my ignorance, but I don't mind at all. They are rough and vulgar, but they are kind, too. I feel valued there, more than I do at home, frankly."

"I'm astonished," Louise said, "that you prefer a den of iniquity to Montagu House."

"It's not a den of iniquity! There is a great deal of industry in the parish. There's a gasworks, pottery works, any number of breweries, and a vinegar works, too, but it is very poorly paid work; and people marry young there, so they tend to have large families. It is a hard-working community of decent people struggling to survive."

"So says the saintly Father Sebastian, I presume?"

Margaret stiffened at her mocking tone. "Sebastian is dedicated and extremely hard-working. He listens to people, Lou, and he doesn't judge or preach. He doesn't wear a halo; he simply tries to make the small corner of the world he inhabits a better place. I think he is truly admirable."

Aware that her defence of Sebastian had been rather too impassioned, Margaret made a pretence of drinking her cold tea. She had said far too much already. Dear as she may be to Louise, her friend made no bones about the fact that she valued her reputation above everything. Besides, the kiss she and Sebastian had shared last week was their secret, too precious for her to disclose to anyone, not even Louise.

She had given up trying to regret that kiss. When she lay awake at night, the memory of the giddy feeling, the rush of blood to her head, the soft pressure of Sebastian's lips on hers made her want to swoon. It would be beyond shocking of her to kiss him again, but she couldn't stop imagining that either. Did he lie awake thinking of kissing her? Did he think about her when she wasn't with him, wonder where she was, what she was doing? Or when she left Lambeth, did she cease to exist for him?

"You look positively moonstruck," Louise said. "What on earth are you thinking about?"

"Nothing. Oh, I nearly forgot," Margaret said, feeling a flush creep up her throat. Anxious to head off any awkward questions, she reached under the table for her reticule. "I brought you a small gift. Here."

Louise took the pencil drawing, her brows rising in surprise as she studied the scene. "It is by an amateur hand, but it is really rather accomplished."

"That is a self-portrait of Billy and his dog, Muffin. Here is another he did, of me."

"Goodness, he's captured your likeness very well," Louise said, diverted as Margaret had hoped she would be.

"I thought I might purchase a selection to send as Christmas presents. Billy would be grateful for the custom."

"It's a little early to be thinking of Christmas, but they would make rather nice gifts. Who is the artist?"

"A young boy, no more than twelve or thirteen. He sells his sketches at the market. No-one knows where he lives or whether he has a family."

"Not even your Father Sebastian?"

"He is not *my* Father Sebastian. He is very much his own man, and his sister Susannah is very independent of spirit, too. If I could have a tenth of her strength of purpose, I would be a significantly better person."

"You are certainly a very changed person. What does Killin make of your philanthropic endeavours?"

"He doesn't know. It's none of his business what I do with my free time."

"Yet."

Margaret's mouth went dry. She was not officially betrothed to Killin; therefore his opinion was irrelevant. *And if you say that often enough, M., you might eventually believe it!*

"That's quite enough about me," she said firmly. "Tell me your news. Mama showed me the piece in *The Times* praising the bust you made of Lady Jane. You must be very pleased."

Louise, always happy to talk about her artistic endeavours, beamed. "It is the first piece I have completed without an ounce of help. I confess, I am very proud of it. It has been discussed widely in the press, so Lady Jane tells me."

"How flattering."

"One must not pay any attention when one is lauded in the press, any more than when one is being castigated." Meeting Margaret's gaze, she laughed. "Yes, I *was* flattered, and so, too, was the queen. I think she is finally taking me seriously as an artist, M. Tomorrow we are to visit Baron Marochetti's studio."

"How exciting."

Louise chuckled. "Well *I* think so. I have such hopes now that the queen will listen to Mrs. Thorneycroft's pleas for me to have some formal training."

"Does that mean Her Majesty has no plans to marry you off next? You are turned eighteen now, and . . ."

"Good heavens, no. Mama will need me to act as her scribe when Lenchen is married, and, though that is something I dread, at least it will allow me some time to myself, while a husband would demand all of it. Besides, there is dear Leo to be cared for. I have news on that front, too."

"Oh no, poor Leopold—has he been ill again?"

"Quite the contrary. He is in excellent spirits. My brother has a new governor." Louise leaned even closer. "Lieutenant Walter Stirling of the Horse Artillery. A most handsome young man, and the most good-natured of fellows. Leo adores him."

"By the sound of it, Leo is not the only one who adores him," Margaret said, completely taken aback.

To her further astonishment, her friend blushed. "I confess, I find him most attractive."

"Louise!"

"I know, I know, it is a bit rich after all my advice to you, but I swear, M., I've never felt so *alive* as when I am in Lieutenant

Stirling's company. He has the sweetest smile, it makes me quite dizzy; and when he stands next to me, my heart simply pounds. I know, it sounds so *extreme* and so unlike me, and I barely know the man. Oh, M., do you think I could be developing a *passion*?"

Without waiting for an answer, which was as well because Margaret was speechless, Louise continued breathlessly. "*He* has said not one word regarding his feelings, naturally—he is such a gentleman but I know he senses it, too. You won't understand, but there is a—a connection when we look into each other's eyes. Oh, M., your face! You are thinking that your sensible friend sounds utterly foolish."

I'm thinking that I know exactly how you feel, Margaret thought, before saying, "I think you must listen to your own advice. You are a royal princess; your reputation must be spotless."

"It is, and shall remain so."

"If you ensure that this attraction doesn't develop any further. For heaven's sake, what would Her Majesty say if she knew you had set your cap at a mere lieutenant?"

"From past experience, she would pack him off to the ends of the earth and confine me to my room until I had learned my lesson. My sister Lenchen had an affaire de coeur," Louise clarified in answer to Margaret's baffled look. "When she was about fifteen or sixteen, Helena fell in love with the librarian. I have no intentions of repeating her mistakes, however, and absolutely no desire to be the cause of Lieutenant Stirling losing his post. I am perfectly capable of keeping my feelings to myself. And I know my secret is safe with you."

"But what will you do about it? You cannot possibly think you have any sort of future with Leopold's governor?"

"Of course not." Louise's expression softened once again. "Right at this moment, M., I'm not interested in the future. I *long* to feel his embrace. Are you shocked?"

Shocked, but on the other hand secretly reassured to discover that her friend was mortal, and that she was not alone in experiencing such longings. Not that she would say so to Louise. "Compared to what I have been regaled with in Lambeth, that is tame," Margaret couldn't resist teasing. "If you had informed me that you longed to feel some other part of him, then I might have been shocked."

"*Margaret!* What on earth—my goodness, do the women actually discuss such intimacies in front of you?"

"They take great delight in doing so. You would not believe how well-informed I am in matters pertaining to the bedchamber and its consequences."

"Really?" Eyes wide, Louise leaned closer. "Do tell."

"Certainly not."

"That is positively cruel of you. I shall have to discover for myself what you mean, then."

"Lou, you don't mean that," Margaret said, brought abruptly back down to earth. A kiss was one thing, but to contemplate more than that would not only be very wrong, it would be courting danger. "You won't do anything silly, will you?"

But her friend treated her to a sphinx-like smile. "Lieutenant Stirling is to accompany us to Osborne in April. We shall be *incarcerated* there, in our own little world. Just like you and your little surrogate family in Lambeth. I intend to make the most of it while I can."

"What do you mean, make the most of it?"

But Louise simply widened her eyes and shrugged. "I am not sure how long the queen plans to remain at Osborne, though of course we'll be back for Lenchen's wedding in July. I am not supposed to tell you yet, but even as we speak, my mother is informing your mother that you have been chosen to be one of the eight bridesmaids."

"No!"

"You should be delighted—it is the ultimate seal of approval.

It means that you are fully restored to society's good graces, M. Of course you will have to pay for it by wearing a dreadful gown because Helena has appalling taste in clothes as well as in bride-grooms. Have you seen a photograph of Prince Christian? He has many good qualities, I am sure, not least his being amenable to making Windsor his home, but he is hardly the handsomest of men. He is prematurely bald, for one thing."

"Oh no, Lou," Margaret said, suppressing a giggle, "it would be kinder to say that he has an extremely high forehead."

"So high that it looks as if his hair has migrated south to his chin," Louise quipped, adding, "Oh dear, it looks as if the queen is getting ready to leave."

"Already!" Margaret jumped to her feet. "Lenchen's wedding is more than two months away. Surely I will see you before that."

"I will do my best, but you know what my mother is like. Once she is installed in Osborne she has to be prised out like a winkle. When my sister's wedding is out of the way, you would be well advised to start preparing yourself for your own."

"Don't say that. Killin has not yet renewed his suit."

"Not yet." Louise drew her into a rare, brief embrace. "But provided you continue to behave yourself, he undoubtedly will."

A Second Chance for a Second-Season Deb

A ball was held last Saturday hosted by the Duke and Duchess of Buccleuch at their Westminster residence to mark the reopening of Parliament after the Easter recess. Though it was one of several society events held on that particular evening, it was noted that the ballroom of Montagu House was packed to capacity. Such is the prestige of the Buccleuch name, it would be easier to name the illustrious members of the Ton who did *not* attend. Alas, though we have it on excellent authority that Their Royal Highnesses Princess Helena and Princess Louise were invited, both remain at Her Majesty the queen's side at Osborne House on the Isle of Wight.

As always, the Duchess of Buccleuch was most elegantly attired in a ball gown of silver and grey silk with a scalloped hemline, trimmed with silver lace. Her daughter, Lady Margaret Montagu Douglas Scott, wore a gown of apple-green satin with an overdress of cream crêpe trimmed with green ribbons, in stark contrast to the demure hues that marked her first, truncated Season. Despite assurances that she is fully restored to health after her prolonged sojourn in Scotland, the Duke of Buccleuch's formerly exuberant second daughter's temperament is notably subdued this Season. Indeed, she now more closely resembles her more restrained and circumspect elder sister, Lady Victoria Kerr. A lasting legacy of the illness which brought her previous Season to a premature end, perhaps?

Lady Margaret's return to society initially received a muted response, but her dance card was much sought after at the Buccleuch ball. A certain Scottish earl, who has been observed paying close attention to the lady for the second year running, was rewarded with a march. Could it be that the announcement we were deprived of last July has merely been postponed, and not cancelled? Will the earl's persistence bear fruit? (And is that fruit ready to be plucked?)

We eagerly await developments in what is turning into a riveting saga.

Chapter Sixteen

May 1866

T HE HACKNEY JOLTED ITS WAY onto the bridge and Margaret, as always, felt as if she was crossing the border between one world and another. Since the Easter break, her time in Lambeth had been constrained by the daily influx of invitations arriving at Montagu House, to picnics and garden parties, dinners, balls, and soirées. Derby Day and Ascot Week were now looming. Rushing from one engagement to the next in a flutter of silk and lace and ribbons, she had become adept at smiling and making small talk while her mind and her heart were on the other side of the Thames.

She had not seen Louise since their tea at Marlborough House, and her friend's letters since then had been sporadic, little more than brief notes containing nothing of a personal nature. Louise could be fickle, making a person feel as if they were the centre of her world before snubbing them completely for no apparent reason, but Margaret knew better than to imagine she was the latest victim. Louise was preoccupied by something. Or someone.

As you are yourself, M., and not only by one person but two. In truth, she was happy to leave Louise to fend for herself for the time being. Margaret had pressing issues of her own to deal with.

The familiar feeling of impending doom settled over her like a dark cloud. Killin made a point of asking her to dance at least once at every ball. It was nearly always a march, rarely a galop, which was far too undignified for him, and thankfully it was never a waltz or a polka, which would require him to put his arm around her. His proprietorial air ensured she had no other suitors, the one positive Margaret clung to as she endured his company. His continuous surveillance of her every time they met made her feel like a criminal whose claim to have reformed the judge didn't quite believe. And yet, he persisted. The only thing constant about him was his determination to get his own way. It was but a matter of time before he claimed her.

And then there was Sebastian. The man she loved, and who she was almost certain loved her in return, even though they had stuck to their resolution never to mention, far less repeat, that one blissful kiss. Their feelings for each other were acknowledged silently every time their eyes met or their hands brushed. Their love could never flourish given the harsh reality of their respective circumstances, but that didn't stop Margaret from imagining how it might. She spent half her nights lost in an unhinged, romantic fantasy of being with him forever, and the remainder trying to reconcile herself to the marriage which she feared would be announced within a few short weeks. She desperately wanted to live up to the expectations she had worked so hard to cultivate since the start of the year. If she reneged on her betrothal again, she would never be forgiven, and rightly so.

Not that she was planning to renege, she truly wasn't. In her heart, she knew it was wrong to marry one man while she was in love with another, but she had resolved, back at Dalkeith on Christmas Day, to steel herself to do her duty. So her feelings for Sebastian, no matter how deep they ran, were irrelevant. She was set on a path to marry Killin, and that was what she was going to do. Lenchen's wedding was to be held on the fifth of July. By the end of that month at the very latest, she would be betrothed to Killin. Her new life as the Countess of Killin was fast approaching.

No, it was hurtling towards her at breakneck speed!

The cab slowed to a halt, and as Molly jumped down to pay the fare Margaret's heart lifted. Instead of bemoaning what she would come to miss, she would follow Louise's example and concentrate on making the most of what she had, while she still had it.

"Margaret, it's so good to see you." Sebastian rose from his chair as she entered the study, a smile lighting up his face.

Her heart skipped a beat at the sight of him as always. He hesitated before sitting back down again, deciding against taking her hands in greeting, and as usual she tried not to be disappointed. They settled down into their letter-writing routine, but today neither of them seemed able to concentrate. Looking up from the sentence she was composing for about the fourth time, she found Sebastian's gaze fixed on her, a frown furrowing his normally untroubled countenance.

Margaret set down her pen. "Is something wrong?"

"No. Yes." Sebastian jumped to his feet and seized her hand. "I have tried, Margaret, but I cannot stop thinking about our kiss. It changed everything for me, but if you don't feel the same, say the word and I swear I will never mention it again."

Taken aback, it didn't occur to her to prevaricate. "I can't forget it either, though heaven knows I have tried."

His fingers tightened around hers. "As have I, but to no avail. Surely it cannot be wrong to give voice to what is in my heart. I love you so much, Margaret."

The words which she had secretly, guiltily longed to hear made her forget everything else. A wild, soaring joy ripped through her. "I love you, too, Sebastian, so very much."

"Margaret!" He pulled her to her feet and into his arms. "Oh, my darling."

Their lips met in the sweetest kiss that was just as she had remembered, and yet utterly different. As he pulled her closer, she twined her arms around his neck, and he fastened his lips to hers again, coaxing her mouth open into a very different kiss. The intimacy shocked her; her reaction shocked her even more. His tongue touched hers and she broke away, breathless and utterly confused. Was this what passion felt like? It was over-whelming and slightly terrifying, and yet at the same time, she wanted more.

Sebastian looked unfamiliar, his eyes dark, heavy-lidded, colour slashing his cheeks. "I apologise," he said, his voice gruff. "I did not mean to— I allowed my feelings to get the better of me. Forgive me." He raked a hand through his hair, smiling raggedly. "It will be difficult, but I will try to exercise more restraint until we are in a position to marry."

"Marry!" Margaret plummeted abruptly back down to earth. "We can't get married."

"Of course we will marry." Sebastian clasped her hand to his chest. "My dear Margaret, you cannot have imagined I would have kissed you in such a manner unless my intentions were honourable."

She had never properly considered the situation from his perspective at all, being so preoccupied with her own. "I am so very sorry, Sebastian, but I can't marry you."

"Why on earth not, if you love me, as you say? Is it because our stations in life are so radically different?"

"It's not that. I don't give a fig about that."

"Then what is it?" His smile faded. "Don't you want to marry me?"

If only she had explained her situation earlier. "It's what I want more than anything, but it's simply not possible. My parents would never give their consent."

"When they grasp the depth of our feelings—"

"Feelings have no relevance in my parents' world." The difference between that world and Sebastian's was a chasm he had no concept of. "Marriage is about wealth, connections, status."

"And I possess none of those attributes," Sebastian said wryly.

"Very well, if they will not give their consent, then we will simply have to wait until you are of age."

"That is almost a year and a half away."

"I would wait twice as long if I had to," he said, kissing her hand. "I do not lack occupation. If it must be so, the time will pass in the blink of an eye."

For him, but what about her? Didn't he understand that she would be consigned to solitary confinement for the duration? No, how could he, when she had never explained the reality of her situation! Gathering her courage in both hands, Margaret prepared to enlighten him. "We never discuss my family."

"That's because I am only interested in you, not them."

"I know." She lifted his hand to her cheek. "That is one of the wonderful things about you, but I can't discard them like an old pair of shoes."

"Indeed, and I'm not asking you to do any such thing."

"No, but the shoe would be on the other foot, so to speak. What I mean is, they would discard me. You see, as far as my father is concerned, my only purpose in life is to make a good match."

"And a lowly Anglican priest won't pass muster, is that what you are saying?"

Imagining what her father would make of Sebastian made Margaret shudder. "My father has already selected the Earl of Killin as a suitable husband for me."

"You are already engaged!" Sebastian dropped her hand.

"The betrothal has not been formalised. It was almost announced last year, but—"

"Last year!"

"But I ran off before it could be. It caused a terrible scandal that I am only now recovering from."

"I don't understand. Are you telling me that your parents are trying to force you into a marriage against your will? That would indeed be a scandal."

"No, it's not like that. They are not forcing me. I want to marry him. At least I *want* to want to marry him." She broke off, realising how ridiculous she sounded.

"Are you or are you not betrothed to another man?"

"No," she whispered, scarlet with mortification, "but it is generally understood that I will be, before the end of the summer."

"Look at me, Margaret," Sebastian said gently. "If you don't want to marry this man, you have only to stand firm in your resolve until you are of age, and then *we* can be married, with or without their blessing."

"If only it were that simple."

"If you love me . . ."

"I do, how can you doubt it?" A sob caught in her throat. "I am absolutely miserable every single moment I'm not with you. I wish we could be together always."

Sebastian wrapped his arms around her waist, pulling her tightly up against him. "And we can be, if we want it enough."

Torn, she pressed herself closer, closing her eyes, wanting to lose herself in their perfect little idyll, to forget all about the real world and everyone in it. The familiar scent of him and the heat of his body was making her senses whirl. "I love you," she said, willing it to be enough. "I love you," she said again, an incantation against reality.

"Then that is all that matters, isn't it? There are hurdles to be overcome, I realise that," he said. "Obstacles to be removed. We may have to wait, but I am willing to wait forever for you. Do I take too much for granted, expect too much? It would be a very different life that you would lead here in Lambeth, not without its challenges and short on comfort."

"How could I be anything other than happy, if I was with you?"

"Then it's settled. You will be my wife."

He truly believed it was possible. He had no idea what he was asking of her, but if Sebastian believed in her, and in the power of love, then why couldn't she? "I can't," Margaret said, though even to her own ears, she sounded ambivalent. "I want to, more than anything, but wanting is not enough. My parents—"

"Must come to understand that your first duty is not to them but to yourself. What will make you happy, Margaret? Marriage to some man you have admitted you cannot love, playing the lady of the manor and dispensing jam at Christmas? Or a new life in Lambeth by my side, genuinely doing good, making a real difference?"

"You know the answer to that question," Margaret said, knowing full well that it was the wrong question. Sebastian made it sound so simple and so wildly attractive. He loved her. He had chosen her as the woman he wanted by his side for the rest of his life. She loved him, too, but there were more pitfalls than he could possibly imagine. And yet, when he looked at her like that, she believed it just might be possible.

He pulled her back into his arms and kissed her tenderly. "We will find a way."

She wanted to prove that she could do whatever it took to be with him. She wanted to believe that love could conquer all. Even her father.

"I know, it's overwhelming," Sebastian said, misreading her hesitation. "I never dared dream until today."

Nor had she, but now there was an irresistible flicker of hope. Instead of telling herself it was impossible, could she turn her mind to how to make it possible? "If my parents discovered my feelings for you, they would have me sent away."

"Then keep your feelings hidden from them. Though it goes against the grain and all that I teach to encourage deceit, in this instance I think it is justified."

"There is still the matter of Killin."

Sebastian frowned. "A simple refusal will suffice, surely. No man will wish to marry an unwilling bride unless he is a scoundrel."

Was it possible to discourage Killin? She sincerely doubted it. But if she wanted to marry Sebastian, which she did, desperately, surely she could find a way of ridding herself of him? If only she had not worked so hard to make herself amenable. Good grief, was she really considering Sebastian's proposal? Her head was spinning.

"You look unconvinced, Margaret," he said. "If you would rather we took the bull by the horns and declared our love publicly, I will speak to your father forthwith."

"No! Good God, no. That would be the worst thing you could do. We must not do anything rash."

"You're right: there is no point in acting with unseemly haste. After all, we have the rest of our lives to look forward to."

Did they? She couldn't believe it could happen, but when he smiled at her, with such love and tenderness, she wanted to. Then he pulled her into his arms again, kissing her with no trace of the flaring passion that had so excited and terrified her. And when he let her go, Margaret couldn't decide whether she was relieved or disappointed.

Princess Louise to Lady Margaret

Windsor Castle, 6 June 1866

My very dearest M.,

My profound apologies for the delay in answering your letter, which was waiting for me when I returned from a short visit to Cliveden with the queen. I have to confess to losing sleep over a particular worry of my own, but the contents of your letter guaranteed that I did not sleep a wink!!!!

I had assumed from the very brief *notes you have been sending that all was proceeding to plan with you, but once again I discover that my dearest and oldest friend has been keeping a shocking secret from me. You ask my opinion, but I don't know where to begin, nor do I truly believe you need any advice. You cannot marry a lowly priest, M., you must know that. It would be the end of your life as you know it, and would inevitably precipitate the end of our friendship, too. Surely you cannot seriously be contemplating this? Your visits to Lambeth were your reward for your* exemplary *behaviour. Your own words, M., I clearly remember them. And how do you return the duchess's trust in you? By falling in love with a priest. A priest!!!! I still cannot believe it.*

Margaret (yes, matters are so serious that I must address you by your full name), you have worked so hard to restore yourself to the good graces of your parents. I truly believed that you were ready to embrace your future as the Countess of Killin with a clear head and a determined heart. Your resolve must not waver now. The consequences simply don't bear contemplating. Your plan to turn the cold shoulder on your original suitor is bound to backfire. Aside from the fact that a young woman who blows hot and then cold gets herself a certain reputation, I cannot believe that it will forestall the proposal you have worked so hard to earn, and now claim to be dreading. Steel yourself, forget the priest, and marry the earl. It is your destiny.

And now I must reluctantly turn to my own concerns. Oh, M., I feel such a hypocrite telling you to quash your more tender feelings while I—I pray you make sure no-one sees this—while I have foolishly indulged mine. I dare not say any more. I fervently hope every day that my fears will prove unfounded. Perhaps by the time you receive this missive, all will be well. I must believe that, for I dare not even imagine what will happen otherwise.

We leave for Balmoral on the thirteenth, and the queen is as ever most demanding of my time. In the circumstances, I must play the attentive daughter even more assiduously than ever, so I doubt we will meet before Lenchen's wedding, by which time I hope that both our dilemmas are resolved satisfactorily. Your betrothal will have been settled, and I will have no need to contemplate a country retreat. Thus will our friendship and our reputations be preserved.

Oh, M., what foolish creatures we are when we fall in love. Is there anything more wonderful? Or so catastrophic, when it goes awry? You know better than to reply to this letter. I wish I could see you, even if it was only for half an hour. If I sound stoic, if I sound strong, then do not be fooled. You know me better than anyone. I have never needed your loyal support and wise counsel more. And yet I cannot have it, and so must soldier on alone, as you must, too.

Until we meet again, in happier times! With my best love always,
Louise

Chapter Seventeen

M ARGARET CURLED UP ON THE window seat of her
bedchamber. Outside, the church bells pealed for Sunday
service. Louise would be at Balmoral now. Her friend's latest epistle
had stated cryptically that there was no material change in her
situation.

Unlike her own. At last night's ball, Killin had informed her
that he would be calling on her father immediately after the royal
wedding to discuss the announcement of their betrothal. Her
attempts to dissuade him in the month since Sebastian had declared
himself had been to no avail. If she wasn't careful, she could well
end up betrothed to two men at once. Would it be pistols at dawn
for the right to her hand?

Oh dear lord, but this situation she'd got herself into was not
remotely funny. What was she going to do? Leaning her hot cheek
against the windowpane, she closed her eyes and tried to calm
herself. First things first. She could not marry Killin. In the quag-
mire that was her life at the moment, that at least was clear-cut.
If she had not met Sebastian, she may indeed have forced herself
to go through with it, but it would have been a huge mistake. She
had to face up to the fact that she was incapable of living a life
of dutiful misery. If that made her an errant, ungrateful daughter,
so be it.

Her relief at finally having arrived at that conclusion was,
however, very short-lived. Refusing Killin was one thing. Accepting

Sebastian was quite another. The ever-present band of pain tightened around her head. She loved him. He loved her. It ought to be a straightforward decision, but it was not. A world well lost to love was a seductive vision, but Sebastian wasn't the one who was going to have to bear the burden. That would be borne by her and her alone, and it would be a formidable undertaking. *His* life wouldn't change much at all, but *hers* would change irrevocably. Louise's letter had forced her to confront what she had known from the first. If she chose Sebastian, the price would be complete estrangement from everyone else, all her family and every one of her friends. His world would become hers. She would be leaving her old life behind forever. Her family would never utter her name, save in a scandalised whisper. She'd have to read about Montagu marriages and births and even deaths in the press. Her exile in Dalkeith had given her a taste of what it would be like. Only this time, it would be a life sentence with no hope of reprieve.

She couldn't do it. The price was simply too high. Did that mean she didn't love him enough? Perhaps, but it made no difference. Marriage to Sebastian would be, albeit in a very different way, as impossible as marriage to Killin. This simple, clear thought had the solid feel of a fundamental truth. Margaret stared, dazed, out of the window, wondering that the view remained unchanged when she felt as if the world had shifted on its axis.

The church bells stopped ringing. The duke would be working in his study. Her father was the key to unlocking the tangle she had got herself into. She had to persuade him that he must reject Killin's request for her hand in marriage. Once that that particular sword of Damocles was no longer hanging over her head, she could buy herself time to find a way to let Sebastian down gently.

She would have to stand her ground with the duke for the first time in her life. She'd have to persuade her father that she was not, once again, procrastinating, but had made a grown-up, carefully thought through decision and that she was entitled to have a say in her own future.

Could she do that? She had to, otherwise she may as well resign herself to doing his bidding. Terrified but determined, she rang the bell to summon Molly and prepared to confront the lion in his den.

DRESSED IN A DEMURE MORNING gown of pale blue muslin, Margaret hesitated outside the door of her father's study. It was almost exactly a year since she had been hauled over the coals in this very room prior to her exile, and six months since her second lambasting on her return from Dalkeith. How immature and naive she had been. This time she had to be calm, logical, coherent. Knocking on the door, she entered without waiting for permission.

"Margaret!" Her father was seated at his desk, pen in hand, an account book open on the blotter in front of him. "What do you want? I'm extremely busy."

"Good morning, Your Grace. May I?"

As she took a seat in front of the desk, the duke continued to stare down at his accounts. "Well?"

"Killin informed me that he intends to call on you after Princess Helena's wedding."

"Ah!" The pen was set down. The frown disappeared. "I hope you appreciate how fortunate you are to be given a second chance. Killin . . ."

As her father launched into a familiar-sounding litany of Killin's many attributes, Margaret stopped listening. The duke's hair was receding, she noted. He had combed it forward in an effort to disguise the fact, but the effect was to make it look as if he was wearing a hat. His mutton-chop whiskers were no longer bright red but ginger tinged with grey. His eyebrows were wildly curling and untidy, in need of a trim, and there were hairs sprouting from his nostrils. He was not omniscient and he wasn't infallible. He was merely a man set in his ways who must be persuaded to view his recalcitrant daughter in a fresh light.

"Your Grace!" Margaret felt sick. Her hands were shaking. She laced them tightly together, digging her nails into her palms. "I have come to inform you that I am not going to marry Killin," she said firmly. "I have tried. You cannot fault me for lack of effort, but I simply cannot persuade myself that we are suited. I cannot sacrifice myself to a marriage that would make me and, I am convinced, my husband, too, quite miserable. I know this is the last thing you want to hear, but it's far better that you hear it now than later."

Forcing herself to look into her father's eyes, however, she quailed. A long, fraught silence followed. While her calves itched with the urge to flee, a tic in her father's cheek made his whiskers twitch. Hopefully, his silence meant he was digesting what she had said. It meant he had listened, she told herself, which was a start.

"How dare you."

She flinched but refused to drop her gaze. "I am entitled to have a say in this matter, you must see that."

"What I see is that you have done a *damned* fine job of deceiving me and your mother into believing you had reformed."

"I have *tried* to do what is expected of me, but I do not want—"

"How many times, miss, do I have to remind you that your wishes are completely and utterly irrelevant? All this little speech of yours has proved to me is that you are what you have always been. Utterly selfish, completely insubordinate, and determined to do your best to ruin the reputation of our family."

"Father! That is not fair. I want—"

"Hold your tongue," he snapped, his face pinched with anger. "How dare you interrupt me! You have said far too much already, and none of it is news to me. You cannot like Killin. You would not make him happy. How many times must I endure this self-serving refrain!"

"I assure you this time it is different. Before . . ." Her voice wobbled. *Calm, M.* "I freely admit that I did not give the match due consideration when it was first mooted. I put my feelings first without taking anything else into account. However, I have been desperately trying for the last six months to allay my reservations, to persuade myself to do what is expected of me. I have concluded I simply cannot."

"You simply won't, you mean. I thought I made it clear after the last time that there was but one lesson I required you to learn: know your place."

"I am your daughter, not your chattel." Frustration made her reckless. "My opinion is every bit as valuable as yours in this regard, if not more. Marrying Killin would be a huge mistake. I won't do it."

For a long moment their gazes met. Momentarily, she thought she saw a tiny hint of admiration in his eyes, but it was quickly quelled. "Who has put the notion into your head that your opinion carries any weight with me?"

"I am perfectly capable of thinking for myself."

"No, someone has been doing your thinking for you." The duke drummed his fingers on the blotter. "These charity visits you have been making. To Lambeth, isn't it?"

"My mother authorised those trips."

"I am aware of that." Her father smiled coldly. "I didn't object because I believed them to be innocuous. Now, I wonder if I was mistaken."

"The time I have spent in Lambeth has been extremely educational. Father Sebastian and his sister Mrs. Elmhirst are very pleased with the assistance I have been giving them. I would even go so far as to say that I have been useful."

Her father was eyeing her as if she were a wriggling grub he had uncovered by lifting a stone. Digging her nails into her palms, Margaret forced herself to continue. "I have been helping people in a very practical way. It is Father Sebastian's belief that one cannot nurture the spirit if the body is starving."

"If I wanted a sermon on charity, I would have attended church this morning."

"Seb— Father Sebastian and his sister don't believe in dispensing charity but in finding the root cause of suffering and doing something to alleviate it. I have learned a great deal about real life from working with them. Enough to understand that I have a good deal more to learn. In that sense, you are right in saying that Lambeth has influenced my thinking."

"In which case, your visits to Lambeth must cease forthwith."

"Cease?" Her jaw almost dropped at this unexpected turn in the conversation. "But why?"

"Because I say so. Because I will not have my daughter roaming about Lambeth under the influence of a renegade priest. Because I shudder to think what Killin would make of it if he knew."

"He doesn't know. There is no reason for him to know. What Killin thinks is neither here nor there. I go to Lambeth because I would like to make a difference to the world around me. I thought you'd appreciate that, at least. Isn't it what you yourself strive to do?"

"You dare to equate your feeble attempts with my charitable endeavours?"

"No! But I dare to suggest that there are more worthwhile endeavours than being the wife of a man who doesn't actually care about me at all."

"And there we have it." Her father smiled thinly. "This wasn't ever about philanthropy, was it, Margaret? It was all about you, as usual."

Frustrated and furious, and most of all deeply hurt, Margaret struggled not to cry. He had no interest in her feelings or her wishes. She was his daughter, but he didn't love her. He never had and he never would. Getting to her feet, her legs shaking, she was set only on making as dignified an exit as she could muster. "Excuse me, Your Grace."

"Sit down. I'm not done with you yet."

Trembling, she remained standing. "Perhaps not, but I am done with you. There is nothing more to be said. I am not pointless, but this discussion is."

The duke eyed her with cold fury. "Father Sebastian Beckwith, do I have the name right?"

"Why do you ask?"

"Lambeth. He will come under the jurisdiction of the Archbishop of Canterbury, Charles Longley. It so happens I am reasonably well acquainted with him."

"What has that to do with anything?"

"From what you've told me, the archbishop will not need much persuading to clip the man's wings a little."

"Clip his wings?"

"An Anglican priest, filling your head with nonsense, encouraging you to defy your elders and betters, to wilfully flout rules. Clearly he believes the teachings of the Bible don't apply to him. Longley will bring him down a peg or two, get him to toe the line."

"No! No, that is not fair! Father Sebastian's methods may be unorthodox but they bear fruit. The people of Lambeth need him just as he is."

But the duke tapped his pen on the blotter, regarding her with infuriating calm. "That is as may be. What they certainly don't need is you. The best and only way you can demonstrate *your* usefulness is by marrying Killin."

In the folds of her gown, her fists were clenched. She willed her tears to remain unshed. "For the last time, I am not marrying Killin."

"You will cease your visits to Lambeth, and you will marry Killin before this year is out. Do. You. Understand?"

Clearly. Horribly. Painfully. "I understand that nothing I say will make a difference," she threw at him, "but I'm not marrying Killin. Not now, not ever."

Sick to her stomach, Margaret fled.

Chapter Eighteen

THE SUNDAY STREETS WERE EERILY quiet on the familiar route to Lambeth. Molly's protests about this sudden trip had melted in the face of Margaret's stony-faced determination. Her father would doubtless put her unexplained absence down to a childish tantrum *if* he actually inquired about her whereabouts, which was highly unlikely. What her mother would make of her behaviour she had no idea, nor could she care right now. Given the outcome of the conversation she had just had with her father, she needed to speak to Sebastian without delay.

The best and only way you can demonstrate your usefulness is by marrying Killin. The duke's words rang in her ears as the hackney carriage rattled over the cobble-stones. She had spent her life trying to please her father. She had twisted and turned herself inside out trying to be the daughter he wanted. When he appeared cruel, she'd convinced herself he knew better than she. When he was cold, she'd told herself she hadn't earned his affection. When he told her she was pointless and selfish, she had tried to change. She *had* changed, but it hadn't made any difference. He didn't love her. He wasn't even fond of her. If he hated her, at least she would have provoked an emotion, but he had swatted her away like an annoyingly persistent insect. He was completely indifferent to the turmoil his cruel words had created, and the hurt. He was heartless. But she was not. There was no time now for her to gently persuade Sebastian that the idea of their marrying was an impossible dream; she had to act immediately before her father threatened that which was most precious to his heart: his Lambeth vocation.

This morning she had been worried about becoming betrothed to two men at once. By the end of today, she would cut herself loose from both. Amongst the seething swell of emotions, a tiny flicker of relief glowed. Though the duke had forced her hand in terms of the timing, she had already made the decision to tell Sebastian she could not marry him. It was the right thing to do, and would spare them both in the process. Dear heavens, if her father could use his connections to force Sebastian to *toe the line* simply for encouraging her to speak up for herself, he'd likely have him banished to a mission in Africa if he dared to marry her.

Trembling, Margaret descended from the cab as it came to a halt outside the rectory, gathering together the tattered remnants of her courage. Whatever became of her now, she was determined not to be the cause of Sebastian's downfall. It was time to shatter his romantic illusions.

"LADY MARGARET! AND MOLLY, OF course." Esther held open the door, ushering them in. "What a lovely surprise. We were not expecting you today. Mrs. Elmhirst is out at the children's hospital, but Father Sebastian is in his study preparing for evensong. Shall I bring you some tea?"

"No, thank you."

Aware of Esther and Molly exchanging a significant look, Margaret was too intent on the coming interview to wonder what it might mean. She had failed to win her father over, but she was determined not to fail here. She would persuade Sebastian that his future plans could not include her.

He was seated behind his desk, his shirt-sleeves rolled up, his coat thrown over the back of the chair. The sunlight streaming in through the window created gold highlights in his chestnut-coloured hair which was, as ever, tousled from his habit of raking his hands through it.

"Margaret!" Throwing down his pen, he bounded across the

room to meet her. "How lovely. I wasn't expecting you." But as she turned her face, so that his kiss landed not on her lips but her cheek, his smile faded. "What's the matter? You're as white as a sheet. Are you ill?"

Margaret pulled off her bonnet and gloves, taking her customary seat opposite him. "I know it's your busiest day, and I'm very sorry to have arrived like this without any notice, but I have something pressing to tell you."

"That sounds rather ominous."

"Yes." There was no way to soften the blow. "I can't marry you."

"I know you can't marry me *now*, but as we agreed, I'm willing to wait . . ."

"Sebastian, I can't marry you. Not now. Not ever. I'm so sorry."

"I don't understand. What has happened to change your mind?"

He made to get up, but she shook her head, waving him back to his seat. To mention her discussion with her father would only muddy the waters. It had brought matters to a head, but her decision had already been made. "The only reason my parents brought me to London is to make a good match."

"And our union would be considered a very poor substitute," he agreed ruefully. "I understand that, which is why we agreed to wait until you are of age and can do as you please."

She had never actually agreed to marry him. She had hoped, and she had dreamed, but she had never said yes. But nor had she said no, nor even once confessed her growing doubts, and she felt guilty about that. Margaret clasped her hands more tightly together. Now was the time to make the situation crystal clear. "If I married you, my father would never forgive me."

"Surely you exaggerate. He will bluster, it is a trait of men such as he, and he may shun you for a while, for the sake of his pride, but you are his daughter. He'll come round; he won't disown you completely."

"He will, and will also insist my mother, sisters, and brothers follow suit. I have been hiding my head in the sand too long. No amount of waiting will change the fact that our marriage would not be tolerated."

"But if we presented it as a fait accompli . . ."

"I would be dead to them," Margaret said. "Forever."

Sebastian looked appalled. "I knew there would be an outcry, but—" He broke off, shaking his head. "No, I cannot believe they would be so cruel."

"I am afraid you must. I am so sorry to break it to you so suddenly and without warning, but I cannot in all conscience allow you to believe that we have any hope of a future together."

"So you are being cruel to be kind, is that what you are saying?" he said, with a short, harsh laugh.

"I am trying to spare us both inevitable disappointment and the pain that would accompany it," Margaret said in a small voice.

"Oh no, that was unfair of me. You did not deserve. . . ." Sebastian swore softly under his breath, then coloured. "I beg your pardon. If what you say is true, then my head has been in the clouds."

"And mine, too. But not anymore."

"I don't know what to say."

"There is nothing more to be said."

As she bit back a sob, he pushed his chair back, pulling her into his arms. Resting her cheek on his shoulder, she closed her eyes, drinking in the familiar scent of him, surrendering to the comfort of his soothing hand on her hair.

"Is there really no hope?" he asked.

She lifted her head to meet his sorrowful gaze. It would be cruel to tell him about her father's threats, and unnecessary now, for even in his question there was a kernel of acceptance. Deep down, had he, too, had doubts? she wondered. That, too, was now irrelevant. "I'm sorry."

His arms tightened around her. "What will I do without you?"

He sounded so unlike himself, so utterly shaken to the core. Margaret tightened her arms around him. "I'm so sorry. I'm so very sorry."

She felt him take a ragged breath before setting her at arm's length. "Was it wrong of me to dare to fall in love with you?"

"It was wrong of me, to allow us both to dream. I love you, but in my heart I have always known that we had no future, no matter how much I wanted to believe it. I am truly sorry to have to tell you like this. I know I should have told you sooner."

"You tried to tell me from the first, but I didn't want to listen."

His hair had fallen over his brow. She ached to smooth it back. "I shall miss you terribly."

"And I will miss you, more than I can say."

"And Susannah, too. Will you say goodbye to her for me?"

Sebastian nodded, biting his lip hard. Her heart felt as if it was being squeezed, seeing the effort he was making to control himself. Two steps, and she would be in his arms once again. One last embrace, one last kiss to remember him by, was all she wanted.

He leaned in, his mouth hovering over hers, but then changed his mind, pressing a feather-light kiss on her forehead instead before turning away. "Go now, I beg you. Goodbye, Margaret, and God bless you and keep you safe."

Chapter Nineteen

"MY DECISION HAS BEEN TAKEN neither lightly or rashly. I have considered the matter very carefully. Your daughter has a simple choice. You will explain that choice to her, and when you have been informed of her decision, I will act accordingly."

Charlotte recognised, from the set of her husband's mouth, the clipped tone which he so rarely used with her, that to protest was futile. "I had no idea that Margaret intended to speak to you yesterday."

"I have never in my life been addressed in such a manner." Walter snapped the pen he had been holding in two. "Frankly, I doubt you will be able to persuade her to see sense. She was defiant to the bitter end. However, I am not a tyrant, regardless of what she thinks. I will grant her this one last opportunity to do the right thing. If she rejects it, she must face the consequences."

"But, Walter . . ."

"No. I don't ever want to see her again. I won't even tolerate her presence in the same country as me." The duke got to his feet. "Let us not allow our daughter to come between us, Charlotte. We will maintain a united front as we always do. If you will excuse me, I have a meeting in the Lords to prepare for. I will expect a decision one way or the other when I return."

There was nothing for it but to bid her husband good morning and to quit his study. What on earth had possessed Margaret to rush into such an interview? It didn't help that she herself had been absent, having decided to spend the day with Lady Cecil Kerr after attending mass. When she returned, she'd thought little of finding Walter's message, saying that he was dining at his club, since it wasn't exactly unheard of, and Margaret's excuse of a sick headache was so common these days that she'd felt no need to check on her.

What difference would it have made? Recalling Walter's stern face and implacable tone, she was forced to accept that the damage was done. Her husband had all but admitted defeat in the matter of Killin, and Walter had been firmly, from the first, set on the match. Margaret must have been very determined indeed to defy him. Wearily, with a horrible sense of foreboding, Charlotte decided that there was no point in postponing the inevitable.

"Mama!" Margaret, still in her dressing gown, leapt up from the window seat as Charlotte entered her bedchamber. "I am sorry I am not yet dressed, I have the headache."

"I am not surprised. I have just come from a very unpleasant interview with your father."

What little colour there was in her daughter's face drained away. "Did he tell you that I am not going to marry Killin?"

"You made that very plain, apparently. Come here and let me have a good look at you." Charlotte tilted her daughter's face up, pursing her lips at the dark rings around her red-rimmed eyes, the greyish pallor of her complexion.

"Is he still furious?"

"On the contrary. I am afraid the duke is quite calm and completely set upon resolving your fate one way or another." Charlotte ushered her daughter to the sofa by the empty hearth, seating herself on a chair facing her. Damn Walter, for leaving it to her to implement his heartless edict.

Across from her, Margaret sat with her mouth set. "I am sorry, Mama, but if my father has tasked you with persuading me to change my mind, then you are wasting your time."

Knowing precisely what this stance would mean, Charlotte quailed inwardly. "What on earth possessed you to bring matters to a head in this way? You have spent the last six months trying to convince Killin you *are* willing to marry him."

"*And* to convince myself to do so."

"Yes, that, too," Charlotte acknowledged. "So I must ask again, why now?"

Across from her, Margaret was studiously avoiding her gaze.

"Your father seems to think that Mrs. Elmhirst and her brother have something to do with it," she persisted.

"He blames Sebastian for filling my head with nonsense. He threatened to speak to the Archbishop of Canterbury to *bring him down a peg or two*, to use his phrase."

This was news! What else had Walter omitted from his account of the conversation?

"I couldn't let him do that." A tear trickled down Margaret's cheek. "So I went to see Sebastian one last time. I took Molly with me. She tried to stop me, but I was determined. You mustn't blame her. Please don't tell my father."

"I promise that nothing we discuss will go any further, if you will tell me the truth." Charlotte waited, but her daughter simply stared at her, chewing on her bottom lip. "Very well, then. I will tell you what I think, for it seems obvious to me, if not to His Grace. Father Sebastian is the reason you are suddenly so dead-set against marrying Killin, isn't he? He hasn't influenced your thinking but your heart. Is that not so?"

Margaret's lip trembled.

"You believe you are in love with this man," Charlotte persisted gently. "Am I right?"

Another tear tracked down her daughter's cheek. "I won't let my father ruin him."

"Your father doesn't suspect your true feelings, and I promise I won't tell him. *Are* you in love with this priest?"

For a long moment, Margaret stared at her, wide-eyed before bursting into tears. Dismayed, Charlotte moved to sit beside her, putting an awkward arm around her. Her worst fears, from reading between the lines of what her husband had relayed to her, were confirmed. There was no point now in trying to persuade her daughter to marry Killin. Curse Walter and his ultimatums!

Finally, Margaret's sobs dissolved into hiccups and she lifted her head. "I've made your gown damp."

"Never mind that." Charlotte handed over her handkerchief. "Do you feel up to telling me a little more about what has transpired between you and this man?"

"What is the point, now that it's over? I love him and he loves me and he asked me to marry him but I told him yesterday that it was simply not possible and we were deluding ourselves." Margaret scrubbed at her eyes. "Sebastian finally accepted that my father would never relent under any circumstances, so I didn't need to warn him that if we married, the duke would most likely have us banished to some foreign mission, which he would, wouldn't he?"

Charlotte made no attempt to deny it, shrugging helplessly.

"I thought so. Sebastian would be distraught if he was removed from Lambeth. I would never be able to forgive myself if I was the cause of that transpiring."

This was said without a trace of self-pity, nor indeed any sign of conscious martyrdom. Charlotte eyed her daughter with new respect. "That is very selfless of you."

Margaret began to twist the sodden handkerchief around her fingers. "I had already decided that I couldn't marry Sebastian prior to speaking to the duke yesterday. I planned to let him down gently over time."

"But your father's threats forced you to act precipitately, is that it?" Charlotte's heart sank further. "Oh, my dear, I cannot condone your behaviour, but I find it difficult to condemn it."

"My father has no such problem."

Charlotte braced herself for what was to come. "No, I am afraid he does not."

"He doesn't love me. He doesn't even care about me. He made that very clear yesterday."

And he had made it equally clear this morning. Walter didn't value his second daughter at all, though Charlotte was beginning to think her vastly underestimated. Her heart ached, knowing what lay in store for Margaret, and rebelled at the unenviable task her husband had allotted her, but decades of dutiful obedience weighed heavily. "I am sorry," she began helplessly.

Despite her best efforts, something of her feelings must have shown in her face. "Am I to be sent away again?" Margaret asked.

"I am afraid so."

"May I ask when?"

"Immediately after the royal wedding."

"After! But that is weeks away, and we are due to attend any number of balls and parties between now and then. Does my father intend to torture me as well as punish me? I would much prefer to go now, if I must. And what about Killin?"

"Your father will deal with Killin."

"But how? When? If he tells him, and I am forced to remain in society, can you imagine the snubs? I'll be branded a jilt."

"I am sure that Killin will behave like a gentleman," Charlotte said, with little conviction. "You cannot be branded a jilt, for no announcement has been made. Killin has his dignity to protect . . ."

"He'll make a point of snubbing me. Mama, please, don't ask me to endure that on top of everything else." Margaret clutched at her. "Please, if I must be sent away, I'd rather it was now."

"I'm sorry." Charlotte forced herself to disentangle her hand. "The list of bridesmaids has been published. You are privileged to be among them. You must ensure that your behaviour is above reproach over the next few weeks. We cannot possibly risk offending Her Majesty by removing you before your duties at the wedding are executed."

"And after the wedding, where am I to go? Back to Dalkeith?"

Charlotte drew a deep breath. "I have no idea where you will reside. I'm afraid your father has left that decision with me. Margaret, I have to tell you that he has washed his hands of you. Completely and permanently. He will not have you in his home—in any of his homes."

I don't ever want to see her again. I won't even tolerate her presence in the same country as me. It would be too cruel to repeat those words. "There will be no reprieve, and you understand—" Her voice broke. She took a deep breath. "You understand that what the duke decrees, I must implement. All I can do is attempt to soften the blow."

"How?"

"My dear, I don't know yet, but I'll think of something."

"*Ex adversis dulcis. Ex adversitas felicitas,*" Margaret said with a sad little smile.

"From adversity comes strength and happiness." Ironically, it was one of Walter's favourite quotes. "I pray there is some truth in that."

"I do, too, Mama. I'm very much aware that I have sorely tested your loyalty and I am deeply sorry to have caused you upset."

Margaret's voice trembled, but she held herself together with remarkable dignity. Tears sprang into Charlotte's eyes that she made no attempt to hide as she pulled Margaret into a fierce embrace. "You are my daughter, and you always will be. Wherever you end up, whatever happens, you must never forget that."

Susannah Elmhirst to Lady Margaret

The Rectory, Lambeth, 20 June 1866

My very dear Margaret,

I trust you will forgive the informality of my method of address, but I cannot think of you in any other way. I have been trying to compose this letter since Sunday, when I arrived home to find my brother in a distraught state, but have found myself struggling to find the right words. Sebastian disclosed the gist of the painful conversation you had. I confess I had guessed how matters stood between you, though I had no idea that he had been so foolish gone so far as to declare himself. My brother, while in some ways very practical and worldly, has a romantic streak, and no idea of the expectations your family will have invested in you. I confess, I was surprised to hear that you had allowed his hopes to flourish. For what it's worth, and difficult though it must have been, I think you made the right decision, for both your sakes.

Sebastian has thrown himself into his parish duties. I know you well enough, Margaret, to surmise that his well-being will be your first concern. Rest assured that I will take care of him as I always do. He had no idea what your own plans were. Whatever they are, I hope one day we will meet again. It has been a privilege and a pleasure to know you.

This has been such a difficult letter to write. If there is anything I can do for you, now or in the future, please do not hesitate to ask. I consider you a friend, and will miss you greatly.

With my very best wishes for the future,
Susannah Elmhirst

REFORM OR REBELLION?

Two days ago, the Whigs' proposed amendments to the Reform Bill were voted down, causing Earl Russell's government to fall. We make no secret of our objections to the Bill, which would have extended the franchise well beyond those who, in our humble opinion, are best placed to exercise it. Members of the Reform League do not agree with our stance, however, and, we are reliably informed, intend to organise a number of protests in the Capital this summer.

Has this spirit of rebellion sprung up in certain members of the weaker sex, we wonder? Could the Duke of B——, a loyal Tory and staunch opponent of Reform, have been nurturing a rebel in his own household? The long-anticipated alliance between His Grace's second daughter, Lady M—— and a certain Scottish earl appears to have foundered. The Earl of K——, who had been paying diligent attention to the lady, has been conspicuous by his absence from her side at social gatherings of late. We have it on the best of authority that, while the gentleman and the duke were of one accord, unfortunately the lady demurred. We recommend that you oppose reform closer to home, Your Grace, and set an example to all in these turbulent times. Long-established tradition and authority must be upheld.

Chapter Twenty

I F YOU DON'T REGAIN YOUR APPETITE SOON, you're liable to be blown away by the first puff of wind," Molly said, making some last-minute adjustments to the bodice of Margaret's bridesmaid's gown. "Here, let's see how this looks."

Margaret stood listlessly while she was draped first in the various layers of white glacé, then white tulle, followed by silver. Pink roses, forget-me-nots, and white heather were used in abundance to trim the elaborate creation. More of the same had been formed into a wreath for her hair to support the long tulle veil. Molly surveyed her work with a critical eye, making a few final tweaks before nodding. "You'll do."

"Thank you." Margaret threw her arms around her maid. "Oh, Molly, I don't know what I'm going to do without you."

"Never mind me." Molly sniffed, dabbing fiercely at her cheeks, "I'll be fine. I've a wee stash of savings, and Her Grace has been most generous." She began to pack up Margaret's dressing case. "I haven't the heart to work for another lady, to tell you the truth—it just wouldn't be the same. A cottage in the country is what I have in mind, doing a bit of sewing to keep the wolf from the door."

"Goodness! Won't you be lonely? You're so used to being around people."

"Well now, as a matter of fact, I won't be on my own." Molly continued to fuss with the brushes and bottles. "As it turns out,

Esther has been hankering for a bit of a change, too. If we pool our resources, we'll be quite comfortable."

"You're going to set up home with Esther! But that's wonderful," Margaret said, highly relieved, if somewhat astonished. "Why are you blushing?"

Molly opened her mouth to say something, then changed her mind. "It's what we want, Esther and I, and it's nobody else's business but ours."

"Yes, of course, absolutely," Margaret said, slightly baffled, "though I can't imagine why anyone would question it."

"No, I'm sure you can't, bless you," Molly said. "Never mind Esther and me for now, my lady. I'm going to speak my mind, since it's my last day in His Grace's employ. You were very wrong to get yourself into a fankle with Father Sebastian, but you got yourself out of it before it was too late. I know how sorely you've taken it, and Esther says Father Sebastian has been a bit of a wee soul, but it was the right thing to do, and I hope you'll both realise that in time."

"I already do. It would have been a big mistake for both of us. But my father doesn't know about Sebastian's proposal, Molly. The reason I'm being sent away is because I won't marry Killin."

"Well, then, I think His Grace is treating you disgracefully," Molly exclaimed. "I know better than most how hard you tried."

"And yet I failed, and now I am being punished." She would not cry, not when this was likely the last time she would see Molly. Margaret managed a grim little smile. "Mama has arranged for me to go to Ireland. I am to stay with Lady Powerscourt, who is married to the son of Mama's friend Lady Londonderry, by her first marriage. It will be quite a change."

"It will that." Molly pursed her lips. "You're tougher than you look, my lady, you remember that. Every cloud, as they say. If I've learned one thing, it's that you have to take your happiness where you find it."

"I shall try very hard to bear that in mind. I hope that you and Esther will be very happy." Margaret kissed Molly's cheek. "You deserve it."

"Away with you now, and mind you don't crush that dress. It's five minutes to twelve, and we're under strict instructions to have you all assembled in the corridor outside the queen's apartments by noon." Molly pinned a smile to her face. "I won't say goodbye, for I pray our paths will cross again at some point."

With a stifled sob, Molly pulled her apron up over her face. Margaret pressed the gold locket that was her parting gift into her maid's hands and fled. Though her eyes burned, she willed them to remain dry. There would be time enough for tears. She would not permit anyone to witness her distress, especially not her father, waiting with the rest of the honoured guests downstairs in the White Drawing-Room. She intended to see this last torturous duty through to the bitter end with dignity.

Making her way to join the other bridesmaids, Margaret was assailed by the memories of happier times at Windsor in the company of Louise. Her tinkling laughter seemed to echo along the corridors. How many of those so-called informal dinners had Margaret endured, forced to sit next to the most tedious of the queen's courtiers because she had been the last to enter the dining room, lacking Louise's nerve to rush ahead of the company and claim the best seat, the most entertaining company? How many hours had the pair of them spent huddled together in Louise's apartments, giggling over court gossip, exchanging girlish confidences or simply enjoying each other's company, Margaret lolling on a settee with a dog, while Louise sketched? One encounter blurred into another, and now there would be no more.

Shaking off her melancholy, Margaret pinned her formal smile to her face as she joined the wedding party. Princess Helena was to be escorted up the aisle of the Private Chapel at Windsor flanked by the queen on one side and the Prince of Wales on the other. It could not be said that Lenchen's toilette flattered her somewhat dumpy figure, Margaret thought as she waited with the other bridesmaids for the lengthy procession to assemble. The white satin wedding dress trimmed with copious amounts of Honiton lace, adorned with orange blossom and myrtle, made the bride look like a dessert made of whipped cream and spun sugar. On top of which, she looked as if she had been sprinkled with diamonds and opals, and her train was so long that there was a real danger it might tip her backwards. The princess herself, though, radiated happiness, making no attempt to hide her eagerness to embrace married life.

The heralds and equerries, marshals and chamberlains were first to lead the procession to the chapel. Then followed the senior royals from both families, including Louise, looking very pale, but as stylishly dressed as ever. Margaret readied herself for her friend to wink surreptitiously at her, or at the very least raise a suggestive eyebrow, but she was very much her royal highness today, and gave no sign that she had even noticed her. Louise's letters from Balmoral had been so mundane that it was obvious her correspondence was being monitored. Today would be their last chance to speak face-to-face, perhaps for many years. Margaret prayed that her friend had better news to deliver than she did.

The foreign dignitaries were now summoned, including the King and Queen of Belgium, followed by yet more ladies and gentlemen of the bedchamber in a bewildering array. Next were the gentlemen of the queen's household, including Louise's precious Lieutenant Stirling, resplendent in his dress uniform, so upstanding and correct it was nigh on impossible to imagine him behaving scandalously. Could the affaire simply have been a figment of her friend's overactive imagination, an elaborate joke generated by her admittedly quirky sense of humour? But Louise's despair in that one, frank letter had seemed so real.

The bridegroom had his own procession of notables to precede him. Prince Christian of Schleswig-Holstein-Sonderburg-Augustenburg was shorter than his name. Middle-aged, balding, and bewhiskered, he was a very unlikely beau for the energetic Lenchen, but according to Louise, the princess was very happy with her mother's choice of future husband. The couple were to make their home at Frogmore Cottage, right on Her Majesty's doorstep, which would allow Helena to continue to serve as the queen's scribe, so Louise was also very happy to welcome Prince Christian into the family.

Finally, when Margaret wondered if the little chapel could possibly hold any more people, Her Majesty and the Prince of Wales stepped forward to lead Lenchen to the altar, and Margaret and the other bridesmaids, followed by stragglers of minor royal household members, finally filed into the chapel to the strains of Handel's march from *Scipio*.

The pews of the quirky, oddly shaped chapel were crammed full, with yet more guests and dignitaries packed into the small balcony above, and standing in the porch by the doorway. Sun streamed in through the tall blue and gold stained-glass windows above the altar, adding to the already stifling heat. Margaret's nose twitched at warring scents of perfume, sweat, dust, beeswax, and orange blossoms, but with a heroic effort she managed to suppress a sneeze.

The Archbishop of Canterbury performed the ceremony. Charles Longley did not look in the least like Sebastian's nemesis. Square-faced, clean-shaven, and bald, he had the appearance of one of Mr. Dickens's more genial characters. She could not imagine him hauling Sebastian over the coals, never mind dispatching him to Africa. Which reminded her that it was she who was to be cast into the wilderness.

As the queen rose to give her daughter away, and Lenchen smiled shyly up at her bridegroom, Margaret's eyes strayed to the assembled guests, seeking out her parents. Her mother's head was bowed, as if in prayer, but her father's face was set, his gaze fixed firmly on the couple at the altar. He had not spoken a word to her since that frightful final confrontation. If she was dining at home, he ate at his club. On the rare occasions when he had been forced to attend a function in her company, he had travelled in a separate carriage. If he did happen to enter a room where she was present, he looked straight through her.

After today, she would be eradicated from the family history. In years to come, when the wedding photographs were being studied by Lenchen's grandchildren, she would be a forgotten, peripheral figure. "Oh, that was a friend of Louise's," Lenchen might say. "I have no idea what became of her."

Today, as far as her father was concerned, was Margaret's last day on earth. She would see it through without breaking down. She had not once done so in his presence, nor come close to begging for a reprieve. Her dignity was all she had, and she would cling to it come what may.

The final blessing was administered. Princess Helena and Prince Christian were now man and wife. At least she had been spared Killin, Margaret reminded herself. And if her father was to consign her to history as the daughter-who-never-was, didn't that give her carte blanche to suit herself?

Courage, M.! As a march struck up, Margaret picked up the bride's train, and prepared to discharge what might be her final duty in society.

LATER, AT THE RECEPTION, MARGARET grabbed Louise by the arm. "Finally! I was beginning to think you were avoiding me."

Louise's pretty mouth pursed. "Come with me." Casting a glance over her shoulder, she led them over to the window, pulling the curtain over a little to conceal them. "The fact is, I am not supposed to be fraternising with you. The queen has only tolerated your presence as Helena's attendant because she doesn't want any bad publicity associated with the wedding, which might arise, were she to drop you at this late stage."

Margaret had guessed as much, for the other bridesmaids had been pointedly distant with her, but it was like a slap in the face to have it confirmed. "It was that piece in the *Morning Post,* I suppose."

Louise sighed. "Amongst other things."

"I wish the press would leave me alone."

"Then you should stop providing them with ammunition. The queen was furious when it was brought to her attention—and don't look at me like that, M., it wasn't my doing. You *know* what these blasted courtiers who surround her are like—they seem to positively relish delivering bad news. Is it true?"

"That I'm not going to marry Killin? Yes, it is true."

"I sincerely hope you are not now about to inform me that you are instead going to marry the priest."

"No, I'm not. You were right, I was living in a fool's paradise even thinking that I might."

"Then why on earth have you spurned Killin? I wish you had not, Margaret, for now I don't even have you to turn to."

"You can always turn to me, Lou."

"At the moment, it's more important than ever that my reputation is spotless and you, I am sorry to say, are currently tarnished goods."

"Louise!"

But her friend shrugged petulantly. "There are too many eyes upon me to risk any contact with you. Perhaps in time, but not now. I must go."

"Don't you *dare* leave without telling me how you are."

"Faring better than you, by the looks of it." Louise narrowed her eyes. "Underneath that rouge you are dreadfully pale. And you are as slender as a willow. It doesn't suit you at all."

"Never mind my figure," Margaret snapped, hurt and exasperated. "I have been so worried about you, and your letters from Balmoral, if you could call them such, said next to nothing. Please, tell me how you are, honestly? I have been so worried about you."

For a moment she thought that Louise would brush her away, but then her shoulders slumped. "With good reason, I fear."

Shocked, Margaret immediately forgot her own cares. No wonder Louise was brittle and waspish. "Dear God, do you mean . . ."

"Don't say it aloud," Louise hissed, looking over her shoulder. "Do not even think it. I could still be wrong. I know next to nothing of such matters."

"You look as well as ever," Margaret said uncertainly, for she knew that looks could be deceiving. "How do you feel?"

"I exist in a constant state of terror lest my mother find out," Louise said, looking close to tears. "I have to keep it from her at all costs."

A hope born of desperation if ever there was one, Margaret thought, for the queen was bound to find out. "And what of Lieutenant Stirling? You said that you were in love with him."

Louise shuddered. "If I was, it was a very fleeting infatuation and long over now. I am like my brother Bertie in temperament. A voluptuary, and a fickle one at that—which is *very* like Bertie, now I come to think of it."

"Louise! For heaven's sake."

"Oh, don't be such a prude. Are you saying it is different for you and your priest? Is he terribly proper?"

"Not terribly," Margaret retorted, stung, "but he did exercise restraint."

"Meaning that I did not?"

"Stop sniping at me just to make yourself feel better and tell me what in heaven's name you are going to do."

"I really don't know. What I absolutely must not do is cry."

Louise dabbed furiously at her eyes. "I shall get through it somehow. Her Majesty will never forgive me, but she won't risk any sort of public scandal. I will tell you something, M. For the first time in my life, I am glad that my father is not alive."

If her own mother was a widow, Margaret wondered, would *her* fate be different? No, no, that was a dreadful way to think. "Before you go, Lou . . ."

"I must get back to the queen. What is it? Out with it, you have that look, as if you are bracing yourself to tell me something awful. I hope you have not been as lax as I have. The queen can't disown me, but your father is perfectly capable of doing just that. After all, he's done it before."

Margaret laughed bitterly. "And he's doing it again. I'm being sent away for good. As far away as possible, as far as he is concerned."

Louise's eyes widened. "So he found out about the priest?"

"No, no, it has nothing to do with Sebastian—at least not directly. It's because I told him I won't marry Killin."

"I still don't understand why you will not, when you've been girding your loins to do just that for the last six months. So, you are to be sent back to Dalkeith again, are you?"

"No, Powerscourt in Ireland, actually!" Margaret said, stung by her friend's selfishness and lack of sympathy.

"Goodness, your father really is coming down hard on you. In that case I'm not at all sure I'll be able to risk even writing to you. When are you going?"

"Tonight, as soon as Lenchen and her prince depart."

"But they are leaving any minute now!" A tear escaped Louise's eye, but she wiped it viciously away. "Very well then, I must cope as best as I can without you."

"I'll be with you in spirit. And you'll be with me, too, won't you?"

"Yes. Of course." But Louise was already straightening her back and looking over her shoulder. "You must swear not to breathe a word of what I told you to anyone. Do you promise?"

"You shouldn't have to ask," Margaret said sadly. "Of course I promise."

"Good," Louise said briskly, patting her hair. "I'm afraid we are obliged to look out for ourselves from now on, you and I."

"I will miss you, Lou. Whatever happens, I will always be your best and true friend."

Louise brushed her cheek with the briefest of kisses. "Let us not prolong this, my dear, I can't bear sad goodbyes. Good luck, Margaret."

"Good luck, Lou." But she was speaking to thin air. The curtain flicked behind her friend, and she was gone, leaving Margaret alone.

Chapter Twenty-One

THE NEXT TWENTY-FOUR HOURS FLEW past in a blur. As soon as the royal newly-weds departed, Margaret, with her mother's assistance, changed out of her bridesmaid's dress and into her newly purchased travelling garb. Mama was brusque and businesslike up until the moment arrived for her to take her leave. There were no tender words of farewell, only a long, protracted embrace.

"No tears," Mama said, pressing a small leather pouch into her hand, her own eyes swimming. "Be brave, Margaret."

And then her mother fled, a handkerchief pressed to her face. The leather pouch contained a miniature portrait of Lix, Margaret's favourite terrier. There was barely time for her to kiss the protective glass, before she was shepherded into the waiting carriage and on to Windsor station. Waiting for her there were a rather earnest-looking maid and a manservant, who had travelled all the way from Ireland to escort her back. At Euston Station the trio boarded the London and North Western Railway service bound for Holyhead.

They arrived at the port too late to catch the night mail boat, and so were obliged to spend the night at the Royal Hotel. Lying awake in the cramped, unfamiliar room, staring blankly at the ceiling, Margaret felt numb, too tired to sleep, drained of all emotion. Only a few hours ago she had been a bridesmaid at the royal wedding. Her participation would be extensively reported in the press in the coming days, her photograph pasted into the commemorative album, perhaps by Queen Victoria herself. Would she ever see Mama again, or Louise? How long would she remain in exile at Powerscourt, the grand Irish estate belonging to Mervyn Wingfield, the seventh viscount, and Mama's friend Lady Londonderry's son? What would Lady Powerscourt, his wife, make of her? What would she make of Lady Powerscourt? Would she be expected to earn her keep, perhaps as a lady's companion? As the hours ticked by and the noise of the awakening docks filtered in through the open window, she couldn't even bring herself to speculate.

Very early the next morning, after reluctantly eating the bread and butter and drinking the weak tea which was delivered to her door by a harried chambermaid, Margaret dressed herself for the first time in her adult life without any help. She fumbled with the many tapes, strings and ribbons, her various petticoats and her crinoline, poking herself with the buttonhook, tying knots where there should be neat bows. Her dress and matching paletot were tobacco brown. Bundling her hair under the drab straw bonnet, she carefully avoided looking at her ghostlike reflection in the mirror. The dark circles Molly had so carefully disguised with powder yesterday would be even more evident today, giving her deep-set eyes a sunken, cadaverous look.

Sean, the taciturn Irish manservant, had gone ahead to see to the baggage. Making her way with Breda Murphy, the Irish maid, Margaret was roused from her lethargy by the hustle and bustle. They were to sail for Kingstown on the City of Dublin Steam Packet Company Paddle Steamer, RMS *Munster*. Passing through the Admiralty Arch onto the pier, they joined a throng of people making their way towards the huge steamship, already belching black smoke from her funnels.

Organised chaos reigned at the dockside. The cargo was being hoisted aboard in nets. Crates stood stacked on the quay beside trunks of leather and tin, portmanteaus, tea-chests, and sacks of mail. The noise of the ship's engines turning, of the stevedores shouting, of children shouting and wailing, of mothers calling anxiously and fathers grumbling made Margaret want to cover her ears. The black, sulphurous smoke tickled her nose, but the stench from the crowds of unwashed bodies, rather than make her retch, reminded her of Lambeth, bringing such a gust of longing as to stop her in her tracks. The crowd surged around her, and Breda urged her towards the gangplank reserved for first-class passengers. Clutching her carpet-bag which contained her jewellery box, her precious miniature of Lix, and a few necessities, Margaret boarded the steamship.

Immediately upon setting foot on the deck, her travelling companion's face took on a greenish hue. "I'm very sorry, my lady, but I'm not so good on the water," Breda confessed. "It was the same on the way over. If you don't mind, I'll see you safely to your cabin, and then I'll find somewhere to sit out the crossing in the fresh air."

Looking at her properly, Margaret saw that she was much younger than she had assumed. Cursing her own self-absorption, she took her by the arm. "You look dreadful. Let's get you to the cabin and make you comfortable, and I will find somewhere else to pass the journey."

"Oh no, my lady, I'm supposed to look after you and see you safely back. If you were accosted . . ."

"That's highly unlikely in first class, don't you think?" Margaret said, tightening her grip as Breda staggered. "Is this the cabin? In you go. Shall I have water fetched for you, or tea? Here, let me take your cloak. And here is a basin, just in case."

Breda sank onto the bunk. "I really shouldn't, my lady. Lady Powerscourt . . ."

"Will never know. It will be our little secret." Backing out of the cabin, guiltily relieved to be alone, Margaret closed the door softly behind her.

RMS *Munster,* which would take five hours to cross the Irish Sea, offered its first-class patrons a choice of opulent saloons in which to relax and chat with fellow passengers, but Margaret had no desire to do either. Noting that all the sofas, chairs, and tables were bolted to the floor, which did not bode well for poor Breda, she returned to the deck. Chairs with warm blankets had been set out at intervals, though most of the passengers were standing in family groups, making their farewells, or waving at those still on the dock.

A low wooden guardrail separated the first-class passengers from the other, more significantly crowded decks. She found a space at the ship's rail to watch the last of the passengers come aboard via the gangplanks, including an elderly priest in a dusty black cassock.

On the quay, a group of four balladeers were singing to entertain the crowds. One of the quartet stepped forward and launched into a plaintive song that squeezed her heart.

For Annachie Gordon he's bonnie and he's rough,
He'd entice any woman that ever he saw;
He'd entice any woman and so he has done me;
Oh, I never will forget me love Annachie.

The words were slightly different from "Lord Saltoun and Auchanachie," the Scots ballad that Molly used to sing to her, but the tune and the theme of the song were the same. Margaret listened intently to the all-too-prescient tale of a young girl, Jeannie, who is to be married off to the wealthy Lord Saltoun. Alas, poor Jeannie is in love with the highly unsuitable Annachie Gordon, and refuses the man her father has chosen for her.

As the ballad drew to its heart-wrenching close with Jeannie dying on her wedding day, a huge blast from the ship's horn rent the air. A cheer went up from the passengers and those on the

204

quay waving them off. Pennies rained down on the singers, who launched into a rousing anthem that sounded vaguely rebellious. Handkerchiefs were raised. Children were hoisted onto their father's shoulders to wave. The ropes that tethered the steamship to the quay began to strain before they were untied from the bollards and thrown adroitly to the waiting crew on the fore and aft decks. And with a second loud blast from her horn and a huge billow of black smoke, the RMS *Munster* began to edge her way out of the protective arm of Holyhead Harbour headed for Kingstown, near Dublin.

Margaret clung to the railings, ignoring the tears which mingled with soot from the funnels, stinging her eyes. It was her first sea voyage and, though Ireland was part of the United Kingdom, she felt as if she were travelling abroad. Under different circumstances she would have been excited beyond belief, but instead she felt numb, her only emotion a vague sense of dread about what lay ahead when she landed.

Powerscourt was located just south of Dublin. Lady Londonderry's son had inherited it when he was a child and had devoted much of his adult life to restoring and enhancing the massive house and gardens, according to Mama. He had married Lady Julia Coke two years ago, but spent most of his time abroad, leaving his young wife alone to come to terms with her new position. Lady Julia was twenty-two, just over two years older than Margaret. Lady Londonderry, Mama had confided, had for some months been concerned that her daughter-in-law was feeling neglected and rather lonely. Unable to deter her son from travelling, she had leapt at Mama's suggestion that Margaret provide her with some much-needed company. Or so Mama claimed.

Margaret wasn't convinced. If she was an abandoned bride stuck on a vast estate in a foreign country, would she welcome a complete stranger into her home? There was no guarantee they would be compatible. Yet it could have been so much worse, she supposed, reading between the lines of all Mama had *not* said in the weeks since her father's ultimatum. If it had been left to the duke, she could have ended up in Timbuctoo.

The breeze which had been ruffling her skirts and tugging her hair free from its loose chignon became a stiff gust of wind as the steamship reached the open sea. Clutching her hat to her head, Margaret watched as the mainland disappeared from sight, and the waters churning below turned from green to iron-grey. If she cast herself into the briny depths, her father would be spared the embarrassment of having to explain her absence away. She would be remembered not as the black sheep but as the tragically drowned daughter.

An echo from the past made her reconsider. Almost a year ago, she had thought the exact same thing regarding the Thames when fleeing from her betrothal ball. Back then, she'd still believed her father cared for her, that his actions were motivated by a genuine desire to do his best by her. His behaviour since had proved her misguided. It was time that she started trying to learn not to care about him. A lifetime of subservience, of trying to please, would be a difficult habit to break, but she had all the time in the world to manage it.

The salty air stung her cheeks. The wind made her eyes stream. She would survive this. She was, in Molly's words, tougher than she looked. And it was time, as Louise had pointed out, for her to look out for herself. A gust of wind tugged at her hat, snatching it from her head and sending it tumbling into the seething waves below. Her hair unfurled like a scarlet flag, wild curls whipping across her face. The sun peeked through a break in the grey, lowering clouds overhead. Her spirits lifted. She had no idea what lay ahead, but it couldn't be worse than the mess she had left behind. For the first time in a while, Margaret smiled, taking pleasure in simply being alive.

But as the steamer berthed in Kingstown, her optimism gave way to trepidation. The crowded harbour-side; the flags which fluttered along the long, covered walkway that led from the quay to the custom house; the calls from the crew to the dockside; and the crush of people pushing and shoving in their eagerness to disembark made her feel as if she was physically shrinking. RMS *Munster* was one of two steamships berthed in the large harbour. A traditional sailing ship was docked over on the other side. Countless little boats filled the gaps between, bobbing at anchor.

Her knees shook as she descended the gangplank and set foot on Irish soil for the first time. She was happy to defer to the much-refreshed Breda, who ushered her safely through the throng and found a quiet place for her to wait while their luggage was collected, leaving Margaret to clutch her carpet-bag close and try not to surrender to panic. Almost all the voices around her were Irish, from thick brogues to a soft lilt that reminded her a little of Molly. Though most spoke English, she caught the occasional phrase that she presumed was the Gaelic language, lyrical and oddly comforting.

Lady Powerscourt had sent her landau to meet them. The elegant, beautifully sprung carriage was painted yellow and trimmed with gold. Under normal circumstances, Margaret would have been charmed by the perfectly matched team of four bays harnessed to the traces, but seeing the Powerscourt crest emblazoned on the doors reminded her that she was about to embark on a life in an unfamiliar house with a complete stranger for company.

What if Lady Powerscourt took an instant dislike to her? Even if she did not, Margaret would be at the mercy of her hostess's goodwill, an uninvited guest who would be expected to entertain, to smile and make pleasant small talk, no matter how she felt. Tolerated, but not wanted.

"Sean will follow us with the luggage," Breda said, ushering Margaret into the forward-facing seat and arranging herself opposite. "It's ten miles to Powerscourt, over the border in County Wicklow. We'll be there in plenty of time for tea, my lady. I'm right sorry to have abandoned you on the steamship. I hope you took no harm?"

"None, I promise. I'm terribly sorry, Breda, I must have appeared dreadfully rude. I've barely spoken a word to you. Tell me about yourself—have you worked at Powerscourt for long?"

"Two years, my lady." Breda smiled tentatively. "I was one of the staff brought in when his lordship married."

"And are you a local girl?"

"Ah no, not at all. My family are from County Mayo, which is in the west, though we've been in Dublin sixteen years now."

"Have you a large family?"

Breda shrugged. "I've five sisters and three brothers, last count. I'm the eldest."

"I am number six of seven," Margaret said, ignoring the thought that none of her siblings would own to her now. "Do you like working at Powerscourt, Breda?"

"Oh yes, it's grand. Lady Powerscourt is young and pretty, like yourself, though she keeps herself to herself, as they say. A bit shy of company. Not that we have much. His lordship has not been home since he lost his brother back in February."

"Goodness, how tragic. Is Lady Powerscourt in mourning, then?"

"She's put off her blacks, but she doesn't entertain. It will be just the two of you, I reckon, for much of the time."

Which, Margaret thought, would be more than acceptable if Lady Powerscourt didn't take her in dislike, and torture if she did.

"This road is known as the Scalp," Breda informed Margaret some few miles later. "It passes through the Wicklow Mountains. I was terrified the first time I made the journey."

Looking out of the window, Margaret could understand why. Huge granite boulders protruded from the steep sides of the chasm, some of them leaning at such precarious angles that they looked as if they might crash to the ground at any moment. It was a relief when they reached a small village with a large square clock tower at its centre.

"Enniskerry," Breda said, as the road began to rise steeply. "That's St. Patrick's church on the left. It won't be long now, till we reach Powerscourt."

Almost as soon as she finished speaking, the carriage began to slow, and a huge pair of gates came into view. It was too late for Margaret to worry about her tangled hair and lack of bonnet, for the gates were already being opened and the landau drove through, providing her with her first glimpse of her new home.

The classical Palladian façade of Powerscourt House was clad in grey granite. Three storeys high, it had a balustraded roof and central pediment featuring what was presumably the Wingfield family crest, and what looked like a carved eagle. Beneath the pediment, five busts peered imperiously out of the five round windows. The main house was book-ended by two low-terraced service wings, each with a circular sweep of wall terminating in an obelisk, though the towers with their copper cupolas peeping out from behind each wing hinted at a very different, hidden aspect.

"You get no sense of how grand it is from this approach," Breda confirmed. "It looks like a foreign palace from the other side, where all the gardens are being landscaped."

The door of the landau was opened by a liveried footman, the steps folded down, and Margaret's travelling companion disembarked. "Here is her ladyship to greet you." Breda smiled tentatively up at her. "I hope you enjoy your stay here, my lady."

"Thank you for your company," Margaret replied, but the maid, having dropped a quick curtsy, was already hurrying away.

Gathering her skirts and the tapes of her crinoline, Margaret pasted a smile to her face and descended from the carriage, only to be almost bowled over by a huge hound which came lolloping forwards and with a joyful bark threw itself at her, its massive front paws on her chest. Laughing, she staggered, pulling off her gloves to caress the beautiful animal's head. The hound's fur was dark grey flecked with white, the tips of its ears a much darker colour. "Well, that was quite a welcome," Margaret said. The dog whimpered, licking her fingertips, its graceful, feathered tail wagging furiously.

"Sorry, her manners are atrocious. She was meant to say a polite hello, not knock you over like a skittle. How do you do, Lady Margaret?"

Lady Powerscourt was wearing a day dress of dove grey with pagoda sleeves, the bodice cut away over a white lace blouson with a high lace collar. She was slim and delicately pretty, with big brown eyes and chestnut hair worn in an elegantly braided chignon. "Welcome to Powerscourt."

Her smile was rather frosty. Margaret scrambled to her feet to make her curtsy. "Lady Powerscourt. I am very much obliged to you for having me to stay."

"Since you are to make your home with us for the time being, I think it would be best if you called me Julia. And this is Aoife."

"Eeefa?"

"Eva, is the closest in English. She is named for the warrior princess of Irish legend. Aoife, however, is the gentlest of hounds. Your mother told me that you are very fond of dogs."

"Did she? I am, and Aoife is a very beautiful creature."

"I can see she's taken to you, too. She will dog your every footstep, if you will forgive the pun, but please don't feel obliged to put up with her."

"Oh no, I'm delighted to have her company. And yours, too, Lady Julia—Julia. I hope I will not prove too much of an inconvenience."

"This is a very large house with any number of rooms. I am

sure we won't get under each other's feet. Come in, and I will show you to your bedchamber, and then we will take tea."

Margaret followed her hostess, her heart sinking in the face of this rather tepid welcome. The reception hall was a vast square space with double arcades on each side. The cornicing was bright unadulterated white, as were the walls. The simplicity would have been dazzling, were it not for the massive stags' heads which were mounted at intervals, their widespread antlers almost reaching the cornicing, giving the room a very Gothic feel.

"There are twenty-eight," Julia said dryly, seeing Margaret's expression. "My husband collects them. I believe these are mostly from Germany. There are a great many more in the other rooms, too, herds of them. As you will discover if he ever returns home, deer, both alive and stuffed, are something of an obsession with him. Don't worry though—your bedchamber is mercifully free of them."

Julia led the way up a wide staircase to the first floor, then a second, white-painted staircase to the next floor. "I've given you one of the turret rooms since it has the best view. It has been very recently decorated, but if you'd prefer something more traditional, I can show you the Pink Room or the Ivy Room or even the Tent Room, though the bed there is so large I fear you would be lost in it."

"I am sure this will be perfect."

Margaret stepped into a room that was semicircular and flooded with light from three arched windows. The half panelling was painted a soft cream, giving way to cream wallpaper with a gold trellised design. A modern bed was positioned on the central wall facing the windows, which were hung with cream and gold damask, the chaise-longue at the foot of the bed upholstered in the same fabric. A pretty marquetry desk stood by the window, on which a bowl of white and yellow freesias were letting off their delicate scent, while a larger display of mixed white blooms sat in the empty hearth.

"Oh, but it's lovely," she said. To her delight, a window seat spanned the whole length of the embrasure. Margaret treaded over the soft rugs, which were scattered over the polished boards, to the window, where she got her first glimpse of Powerscourt's gardens. "Oh, my goodness!"

An amphitheatre with a series of wide terraces was cut into the steeply sloping ground. At the centre, the foundations of a stone staircase were being laid, sweeping down to a pond. The grass terraces were a brilliant emerald green under the grey-blue of the sky, their manicured perfection enhanced by the series of raised flower-beds laid out at regular intervals. The pond was framed by newly planted trees, the sensual, natural movement of the water in direct contrast to the regimented order of the raking terraces. Beyond the glinting blue of the pond the eye was drawn to the pale outline of the Wicklow Mountains, the purple-blue hues of a conical hill, and above it all the sky scattered with puffy clouds.

"That is Sugar Loaf Mountain," Julia said, joining her.

"What an absolutely spectacular view. It is simply breath-taking."

"The garden is very much a work in progress, but, I agree, it is a wonderful vista. Your mother also mentioned that you love the outdoors. Please treat the grounds as if they were your own. It was the late viscount and his gardener who dreamed up most of what you see before you. Mervyn, my husband, is determined to see his father's vision fully realised. He's in Bavaria at present. I track his progress by the crates of purchases which arrive every month or so. There are a stack of them now, waiting on his return."

"Bavaria! Wouldn't you have liked to accompany him?"

The question, which seemed perfectly natural to Margaret, was clearly not a welcome one. "My husband prefers to devote his time while abroad to enhancing his collection."

As opposed to devoting his time to his wife of only two years? Poor Julia. Then again, perhaps she preferred to be alone, in which case she must be ecstatic to have had Margaret foisted upon her. "When do you expect him home?" she asked, rather at a loss.

Julia shrugged. "In September or October at the latest. I presume you are aware that he lost his brother in February?"

"Please accept my condolences."

"Thank you. To be honest, I hardly knew Maurice, but Mervyn was very fond of him and took his loss badly. I hope when he comes home he will be over the worst of his grief."

Margaret was feeling more uncomfortable by the minute. "I am sorry to have been foisted on you at such an awkward time."

"My mother-in-law, Lady Londonderry, believes I am in need of female company."

"I expect you'd have preferred to choose your own company, all the same."

Julia frowned, fussing with one of the large tassels that tied back the curtains. "My sister Anne, who is next to me in age, does not wish to interrupt her London Season. Gertrude, my next sister, was married in April, and Mary, my next, is planning to make her debut. Besides, she's five years younger than me. You, I believe, are twenty, so we are more of age."

"I'll be twenty in October."

"Lady Londonderry speaks highly of the duchess, your mother."

Which begged the question of what Lady Londonderry had said about her. Margaret braced herself. "I don't know if you are aware of my circumstances, but—"

"I know nothing," Julia interrupted, abandoning the tassel, "save that you are in need of a period of rustication. Pray do not feel the need to elaborate. I am happy to oblige Lady Londonderry, and hope you will feel at home here. Apparently you are a keen horsewoman. Please feel free to make use of the stables."

"You are very kind," Margaret said, mortified to find her eyes smarting.

"Your bags will be sent up as soon as they arrive, and I'll have

213

some hot water brought straightaway. If there's anything else you need, you only have to ask. The bell is by the fireplace. Now, I'll leave you to get settled, and we'll have tea in half an hour, if that suits? Don't worry about getting lost, I'll come back and fetch you. There's chocolate cake. A favourite of yours, I believe."

The door closed behind her with a soft click. Margaret unbuttoned her paletot and sat down on the window seat, opening the casement to inhale the sweet, lush scent of the gardens. Powerscourt was beautiful. Thanks to Mama, she had a dog and horses for company, and she was free to walk these lovely grounds, but the one thing she wasn't free to do was leave. Her prison was a luxurious one, but it was still a prison. And Julia? Margaret's instincts told her that there was more to her hostess than a very natural reserve, but at this moment, she had no energy to conjure up some empathy. She had never felt so alone. What she wanted more than anything in the world right now was to lie on that comfortable-looking bed and pull the covers over her head, shutting out the world.

A tap on the door forced her to abandon that tempting thought.

"Your hot water, my lady."

"Breda!"

"I'm to be your maid, my lady, if you are happy to have me?"

"More than happy," Margaret replied. A friendly face. And chocolate cake for tea. That was a great deal more than she had any right to expect under the circumstances.

CHARLOTTE, DUCHESS OF BUCCLEUCH, TO LADY MARGARET

Drumlanrig Castle, 12 August 1866

My dear Margaret,

It is the Glorious Twelfth, but as you can see from my address I have eschewed grouse-shooting this year. Your father has once again accepted the Duke of Sutherland's invitation to Dunrobin Castle, but I find myself rather disinclined to socialise at present.

I have your sister Mary with me for company. We have been spending time walking in the grounds getting to know each other a little better. A strange phrase to use regarding one's daughter, perhaps, but long overdue as far as I am concerned. Mary lacks your impetuousness, but neither has she Victoria's reserve. After long consideration I decided to explain your situation to her—though not, I hasten to add, anything concerning Lambeth! In doing so I have contradicted your father's instructions, but I find myself quite unable to ignore Mary's questions. She begged my leave to write to you herself. I reluctantly refused. While your father did not expressly forbid communication, I have no doubt that is what he intended. It would be wrong of me to encourage my youngest daughter to follow the example set by her elder sister, in disobeying her father's wishes. As for myself, however, I have learned, Margaret, that a mother has a duty to her daughters which can sometimes subvert her duty to her husband. I intend to continue our correspondence if it pleases you.

I will remain at Drumlanrig at least until September, and hope *that you will write to me here. You are much missed, Margaret. I pray you do not forget that.*

Mama

P.S. Please tell Lady Powerscourt that I am much obliged for her recommendation that I order some table linen from Mr. Ferguson's factory in Banbridge. The quality of the sample you sent is superb.

Chapter Twenty-Two

I N THE WEEKS SINCE HER arrival, Margaret tried to put all that had happened behind her, to recapture the spirit of optimism she'd felt on the voyage, but every day dragged painfully, like walking uphill on soft sand, leaving her drained and defeated. Julia made polite conversation at mealtimes, accepting her listless assistance with such mundane tasks as sorting linen, but otherwise making no demands on her. Margaret was perfectly aware that she should be making more of an effort to become acquainted with her hostess. She was being a very poor companion, but Julia seemed in no rush for company, content to maintain her distance whether through tact or a natural reserve. In Margaret's present maudlin state of mind, she was happy to follow her lead.

She ate too much of the cake Julia served up with tea every day, and made no attempt to resist the puddings, which were served at dinner, or the hot milk Breda brought to her room before bed with bread and honey, comforting food that reminded her of the nursery, though it never filled the aching void inside her.

By day, she took to roaming Powerscourt's extensive gardens and the deer park beyond, with only Aoife for company. Her hair curled wildly, her face was becoming freckled, her skin tanned. With no need any longer to conform to the rules set down by society for a young lady, she had, shockingly, cast off her crinoline. It was enormously liberating to be free of this article of clothing. At times, when she knew she was safe from observation, Margaret even dispensed with her shoes and stockings to wander barefoot, digging her toes into the velvet-soft lawns, perching on the side of either Juggy's Pond or the Green Pond to dip her toes in the cool waters. She had twice visited the stables, but the familiar smells of hay and horseflesh made her yearn for Dalkeith and her own beloved pony, Spider. She hadn't the heart to ride another horse—it felt almost disloyal. She would never again hear the wind whistle through the stands of trees that bordered the River Esk as she walked her dogs, and she would never again taste Mrs. Mac's peerless clootie dumplings or enjoy the fragrant smell of the peat burning in the kitchen range. If only she could turn the clock back to those innocent days and begin again. She would make a better fist of it the second time around. Would she though?

Mama's letter had arrived at breakfast time, her first and only correspondence since she came to Powerscourt over a month ago. Margaret had read it while perched on the wrought iron seat on the topmost tier of the Italian garden. The duchess's words should have provided her with some comfort, but instead the letter shattered the fragile hold she had on her self-control. Her stay here was not an interlude. Her period of exile stretched endlessly in front of her.

Sorrow and regret welled up inside her. The distant trundling of a wheelbarrow reminded her that the gardeners would be here to start work any moment. Jumping to her feet, Margaret hurried towards the seclusion offered by the walled garden, barely noticing that Aoife was bounding after her.

The Bamberg gate, which marked the entrance, had been one of the present viscount's many contributions to the estate. Originally designed for a cathedral in the German town for which it was named, it was a beautiful affair made of wrought iron painted black and gold. The central panels were fashioned to give the illusion that one was about to step into an aisle bordered by twisted pillars, covered by a domed, starred roof. Today, however, instead of marvelling at the ironwork, or lingering to drink in the scents from the nearby rose garden, Margaret simply pushed the gate open and stepped inside. Loneliness, like a heavy, suffocating blanket, was wrapping itself around her. Sensing her mood, Aoife whimpered.

The lavender border, which had been one of Julia's innovations, was in full bloom. The fragrance released as the skirts of Margaret's gown lightly brushed against them made her feel slightly giddy. Though this was primarily a working kitchen garden it was still a creation of great beauty, with symmetrical beds separated by grass so carefully trimmed Margaret sometimes imagined the gardeners must use nail scissors rather than scythes. The fruit bushes on the south-facing wall were beautifully espaliered, the herbs planted out like a floral bouquet. Fresh earth, new-mown grass, and the contented drone of bees ought to have been soporific, but by the time she passed the little fountain at the convergence of the paths, making for the sheltered bench on the farthest wall, tears were already tracking down her cheeks.

She sank onto the bench, crushed by the enormity of all that had passed in the last weeks and months. She had read somewhere that a drowning person saw their life pass before them just before they perished. Hers played backwards in her head now, as if she were rifling through a series of pictures in a photograph album: standing on deck with her hair blowing in the wind as her homeland receded; posing with the other bridesmaids at the royal wedding; saying goodbye to Mama and Louise; saying goodbye to Molly; parting ways with Sebastian; the confrontation with her father; Sebastian proposing; her first meeting with him way back in February; her return to London at the start of the year and her resolution then to marry Killin. All of that, in the space of just over six months.

Dropping her face into her hands, she surrendered to her grief, letting her tears trickle through her fingers, making no attempt to quiet her sobs. She cried for the loss of her friendship with Susannah and the camaraderie of the days spent with the Lambeth ladies. She cried for the pain and the worry she had caused Mama, and the rift she had created between her parents. She cried for Louise, her best friend, who had retreated into silence at a time when they needed each other more than anything. She cried for the loss of her sisters, whom she had never really known or appreciated, and now would not. She cried for Sebastian, whose face was already growing hazy in her memory and who seemed now more like a figment of her imagination than the man she had once dreamed of marrying.

But most of all she cried because she had never felt so completely alone and so utterly wretched. She had spent her life trying to mould herself into the unquestioning daughter her father wanted her to be. Having failed to meekly obey and having compounded her felony by challenging his decisions, she was going to have to come to terms with the fact that nothing would alter his jaundiced opinion of her.

Mama, however, was another matter. Mama had been forced to write to her own daughter in secret, flouting her husband's authority, and for that, too, Margaret was responsible. She was racked with guilt, thinking of how often she had questioned Mama's love over the years without realizing that she was also a victim of dutiful obedience.

You are much missed, Mama had written. *I pray you do not forget that.*

Her head was thumping. Rubbing her eyes with her sleeve, Margaret gave herself a shake. Rather than continually berating herself over the mistakes she had made, what she needed to do was learn from them. Easier said than done, but it wasn't as if she was short on time! Aoife whined, licking her salty fingers before giving a sharp, welcoming bark. With a sinking heart, Margaret spied Julia coming towards her.

"Am I disturbing you? I was hoping that your letter brought good news." Julia's small smile faltered as she neared. "Oh dear."

To Margaret's dismay, she seemed not to have run out of tears, for a fresh reservoir began to roll down her face. "Sorry," she said, scrubbing frantically at her cheeks. "I don't seem to have a hand-kerchief."

"Here." Julia produced one from her pocket and sat down on the bench by her side.

"My letter was from Mama. She has decided to write to me, even though it is against my father's wishes, and . . ."

"There, take your time," Julia said, patting her hand awkwardly.

Margaret drew a shaky breath. "I've been an appalling guest, and you've been very patient with me. I was supposed to be keeping you company."

"There is nothing worse than being forced to keep someone company when all you want is to be left alone to wallow in misery," Julia said.

Margaret laughed weakly. "Was it so obvious?"

"Yes," Julia replied simply. "I worried that you might think me indifferent, but I did not wish you to feel obliged to confide in me. If you want to talk now, though, I am happy to listen. Though only if you choose to."

Margaret blew her nose. "I don't want to take up your valuable time."

"Time," Julia said with a wry smile, "is one asset I have in abundance."

"So there you have it," Margaret concluded. "I am dead to my father, and I have no idea when I'll ever see Mama or any of my family again." The relief of unburdening herself was already giving way to doubt about the wisdom of her confession. "I am afraid I have shocked you."

"I won't lie," Julia said, "I am shocked. I had suspected it was a doomed love affair which brought you here, but I did not for one second imagine a secret betrothal to a parish priest. It's a romantic notion, but only within the pages of a novel."

Margaret shifted uncomfortably on the bench. "I never *truly* believed we could marry, but it took my father's threats to force me to put an end to the dream that we might."

Julia opened her mouth to speak, then closed it again.

"What is it? Please, I want you to be frank with me."

"Very well then. In all honesty, I think you have behaved very foolishly, but the situation is not nearly as bleak as you imagine it to be."

"I fail to see how it could get much worse. I'm very grateful that you took me in, but I don't have the means to leave, and nowhere to go even if I had."

"Your father is understandably angry with you. You have publicly flouted his authority not once but twice. But you are far too valuable an asset to be written off completely. You're not even twenty years old, Margaret. Your mother sounds like a very sensible woman. She'll find a way to bring you back into the fold, I guarantee it."

"And then my father will find someone else to marry me off to."

"Naturally, it is his duty as your father. Would you prefer he did not? You would become the spinster aunt then, little better than a glorified servant."

"I won't marry simply to please him."

Julia frowned. "Then do it to please your mother. Think how relieved she would be to have you established. You would be able to forge the new relationship with her that you claim to want."

"I do want to, very much."

"Then bear in mind that it will be impossible if your father continues to disown you." Julia got to her feet. "It's a trifle cold sitting here. Shall we stroll down to the Green Pond?"

"So what you're saying, in a nutshell, is that you think everyone would be happy if I married, except me."

Julia drew her a level look as she opened the gate that led to the Green Pond. "Why are you so sure that marriage will make you miserable?"

They reached the edge of the pond. Margaret stared down at the water, where a shoal of tiny fish darted among the reeds. "What would you do, if you found yourself in my situation?"

"Is your situation any different from that of every other young women of our class? We are raised with the sole purpose of making a good marriage. The only choice we have is whether or not to make the best of it, or not marry at all, which is hardly a palatable option. You are fortunate to be the Duke of Buccleuch's daughter—"

"That is highly debatable!"

"And to have a dowry to match your lineage," Julia finished coolly, disposing herself with her usual quiet elegance on the wooden bench. "When Wingfield offered for me, I was not exactly enthusiastic. My husband is rather staid, his manner reserved, and it doesn't help that he sports a very long beard, which makes him look a great deal older than his years."

Margaret wrinkled her nose. "If we must spend hours every day pinning up our hair and lacing ourselves into corsets and crinolines, I don't see why men can't spend a few minutes every day shaving."

"It is the fashion for a man to sport a beard, just as it is the fashion for a woman to wear a crinoline."

"Then I must be extremely unfashionable," Margaret retorted, "for I like neither."

"What you like or don't like is entirely beside the point," Julia said, sighing impatiently. "If you are asking for my advice, then I suggest that you do as I have, and make the best of it. Despite my initial reservations about Wingfield, I came to see that it was an excellent match. My mother approved of him, and my father was particularly pleased with the connection. Like my husband, my father is rather obsessed with restoring the family seat to its former glory and as we speak is furiously planting trees. But what mattered most to me was that Wingfield provided me with the opportunity to have a family of my own. It is what I have always wanted, and Wingfield needs an heir. Thus, we have a joint ambition, even if we have little else in common."

"So you think I was wrong to reject Killin? Even though I could not, to use an old friend's words, abide him?"

"I think you could have overcome your initial distaste for him if you had put your mind to it. I think that if—or rather when—

another gentleman offers his hand in marriage, you would be wise to consider it seriously, whether you *like* him or not."

"You make it sound so cold. As if marriage is a commercial transaction."

"In essence, that's exactly what it is, and a lifetime's commitment, too. A similar background, a satisfactory financial arrangement, and the support of one's family make it more likely to succeed, but without the will to do so, it is bound to founder."

"You don't think that love has any role to play?"

"I believe that respect is vital. I expect in time I will come to care for Wingfield, as the father of my children."

And yet there was no child, nor any prospect of one while her husband trailed around the Continent spending a fortune on antiques and antlers, Margaret thought sadly.

"I can see what you are thinking," Julia said, getting to her feet, "but life is what you make it."

Margaret smiled. "That sounds like something Molly, my former maid, would say."

"It is one of my mother's mottos, too, and her most valuable advice to me. She also says that patience is a virtue, and that all things come to those who wait. I hope she is right on that score."

"You have only been married two years," Margaret said tentatively.

But Julia shook her head, turning away. "We had better get back—it looks like it is about to rain. I actually sought you out to tell you that I, too, had a letter this morning, from my husband. He will be home at the beginning of October. He asks after you and says he is looking forward to making your acquaintance."

"Does he plan to remain here long?"

"He generally goes deer stalking in Scotland towards the end of the year, but he made no mention of that. Perhaps your presence will persuade him to prolong his stay. With luck," Julia added, with a twisted smile, "I will be the beneficiary."

Balmoral Castle, 30 September 1866

Dear Margaret,

This will perforce be no more than a brief scrawl, for I am about to head to Dunkeld with the queen to visit the Duchess of Athol. I have been much occupied since the wedding. We travelled to Osborne with Lenchen and her new husband straight after the celebrations. The happy couple had only just left for the Continent when Lieutenant Stirling also departed the Isle of Wight—for good. He has been replaced by a Mr. Legg. A poor substitute indeed!

In August I attended the queen in Balmoral for the usual family gathering which even included Bertie, much to Her Majesty's delight. There was a ball at Abergeldie where I wore the most delicious new gown, and then Lenchen and her prince returned from their wedding trip looking suitably content. The queen will host a ball in their honour later this month, when Her Majesty and I return from Dunkeld. I have designed my own gown for that prestigious occasion—and made an excellent fist of it, if I do say so myself.

I am summoned! My days are not my own now that Lenchen is married, but I find my new role as Her Majesty's scribe bearable. Alas, it leaves very little time for my sculpting and no time at all for my own correspondence.

Louise

P.S. Leo not only has a new governor in Mr. Legg, but a new tutor, too. The Reverend Duckworth is a most charming man.

Chapter Twenty-Three

October 1866

THE DAY WAS CONSIDERABLY ADVANCED when Margaret headed back to Powerscourt with Aoife dutifully padding along in her wake. She had walked farther than she had originally intended, tempted by the warm autumn sunshine to wander out to the deer park which Julia's husband had established as a home for his rare Japanese sika breed.

She had read Louise's letter several times now and still could not decide how to interpret it. Was her friend so concerned that her correspondence was being monitored by the queen's over-vigilant courtiers that she couldn't comment on the concerns which had been at the forefront of her mind when they last met? Or was it simply the missive of a young, flighty woman with nothing more to worry about than party dresses and handsome new tutors, and no time for absent friends who had fallen from grace?

Louise was always at her most brittle and superficial when she was most unhappy. Margaret's instincts told her that all was not well. She longed for the chance to speak to her, to comfort her, even if she had no sage advice to offer. But that would be impossible for the foreseeable future, and there was nothing to be gained by writing a letter that might not even be read or, worse, fall into the wrong hands. Whether their friendship would ever be rekindled was a question for the future. For now, their paths were heading in very different directions. Ha! If going round in ever-decreasing circles could be called a direction.

Her steps slowed, her booted feet kicking up the mulch of dried leaves and soft Irish soil of the woodland floor. She was sick of her endless, purposeless daily wandering. She had been at Powerscourt for three months now. The days trickled past, one much like another, like grains of sand in a bottomless hour-glass, as she sank more and more into a lethargic acceptance of her fate. Even the press seemed to have forgotten all about her—for Louise would surely have mentioned it, if there had been any adverse comment. She had taken to avoiding her reflection, fearing seeing a dumpy ugly duckling staring back at her, one who looked as if she had swallowed her own crinoline.

Kicking up another heap of leaves, she caught one as it fluttered down like a crinkly, mottled butterfly. Was she to pay for her refusal to do what was expected of her with a lifetime of listless inertia? She crumpled the leaf and dropped it onto the ground.

"No, I will not!" she shouted aloud, the sound reverberating through the trees. The time had come for her to take Julia's advice and make the best of things. She was going to forgive herself for her mistakes and stop lamenting what might have been. Tomorrow was her twentieth birthday. As a gift to herself she would finally take up Julia's offer to borrow a horse and go for a ride. Why should she continue to deny herself one of the great pleasures of her life!

Viscount Powerscourt was due home imminently. For the last two weeks, Julia had been a whirlwind of activity, preparing the house and gardens for her husband's arrival. It was almost as if she thought that by proving to be the perfect chatelaine she would be rewarded with a child. Margaret hoped fervently that she got what she wished for. Julia's situation was heartbreaking, though she endured it stoically; and whenever Margaret tried to raise the subject, she demurred. It must have cost her very dear to mention it in the first place.

Poor Julia was another person that Margaret was powerless to help. Though it might be a good idea, now she considered it, to make herself scarce while she and her husband tried to remedy their childless state. The very notion of playing gooseberry—no! In fact, the viscount's arrival would be the perfect excuse for her to explore the country that was currently her home. Dublin was supposed to be beautiful, and then there was the seaside town of Bray nearby. As long as she took Breda with her, it would be perfectly in order. It was a very small step, but at least she was finally looking forward.

Entering the house through one of the side doors, Margaret was about to take the backstairs to her bedchamber with the intentions of sprucing herself up, when Aoife gave a loud, joyful bark and galloped for the main staircase. Exasperated and laughing, she gave chase all the way up to the first floor, where the dog, to her horror, bounded into the main saloon.

This was Powerscourt's largest and most formal room. It had been used to entertain George the Fourth when he visited Ireland after his coronation, and was therefore considered sacrosanct. The armchair covered in red velvet, made specifically for His Majesty and known as the Throne, still stood in pride of place. Julia said the ornate saloon with its classical pillars and arched balcony made her feel as if she was visiting an art gallery, and Margaret couldn't disagree. A series of niches boasted scenes painted by Wingfield's apparently loathed younger brother, Lewis, who was, among other things, an artist. Full-size statues of semi-naked Greek and Roman goddesses stood sentinel between the pillars. In the far corner, incongruously, was a depiction of Lady Londonderry, the current viscount's mother, whose presence was also marked by the large ebony sofa in the saloon, the coverings of which she had embroidered with Egyptian designs while on a sailing trip with her husband on the family cutter, according to the family mythology—of which there was a great deal.

Julia, whose only sewing ambition was one day to embroider a christening robe, never used this room, but today she was taking

229

tea with a gentleman. It was not hard to deduce, from Aoife's furiously wagging tail, that he was Lord Powerscourt, arrived two days early. His luxuriant beard covered most of his face and some of his shirt front, so bushy as to appear part of a stage costume. Suddenly remembering her dishevelled state, Margaret was on the point of retreat when Julia spotted her.

"Margaret, as you can see, my husband has arrived home earlier than expected. Come and meet him. Mervyn, this is Lady Margaret Montagu Douglas Scott. Margaret, my husband."

"How do you do, Lord Powerscourt?" Mortified, for her hair was hanging down her back and her gown was mud-spattered, Margaret dropped a curtsy.

Lord Powerscourt's eyebrows were as bushy as his beard, yet his hair, which had receded though not yet entirely retreated from his head, sat in soft curls, like a baby's. He had a good nose, neither delicate nor forceful, and his brown eyes reminded her of a spaniel. "It's very good to meet you, Lady Margaret. I am indebted to you for keeping my wife company."

"It has been a pleasure, my lord," Margaret replied, feeling guiltily undeserving of any praise in that regard.

"Well now, sit down and join us."

"Margaret will wish to get changed, won't you, Margaret?"

"Oh, yes." Responding to Julia's plea, she started backing away. "I can't sit here caked in mud."

"Nonsense," Lord Powerscourt exclaimed, "a sod of good Irish soil never hurt anybody."

"But you will wish to catch up with Lady Julia, after being apart for so long."

"There's nothing urgent, is there?" Lord Powerscourt said. Then, when Julia shrugged defeatedly, he turned back to Margaret, indicating the chair next to him. "Please sit down. Your father owns many estates, I believe. I would value your opinion on my own humble abode."

Susannah Elmhirst to Lady Margaret

The Rectory, Lambeth, 28 October 1866

Dear Lady Margaret,

I obtained your forwarding address from Her Grace, your mother, who reluctantly granted me permission to write to you, with certain caveats, which I am sure I need not spell out. I understand your stay at Powerscourt is likely to be a lengthy one. I hope that you are in good health and spirits, and able to make the most of the fresh country air— how I envy you that!

I have not written until now because I believed that a clean break would be best for all concerned, most particularly you. Be assured, though, that you are often in my thoughts. I write now in the hope that time has healed the scars and that you are able to take comfort from knowing that life in Lambeth goes on as usual, with all its highs and lows.

There have been a few changes in our household since you last visited us. My brother was finally persuaded to approach the bishop about a curate, and to his astonishment, the bishop agreed. Mr. Glass is young but extremely enthusiastic, and his presence has greatly cheered Sebastian. I, however, am still missing dear Esther, whom I have not been able to replace. As a result I am forced to spend a great deal more of my time on household management than I would like, especially now that I have two men to run after! Esther and Molly seem very happy in their new life together, and that is something not to be sneezed at, as the saying goes. Sebastian says we are all equal in the eyes of God, which is typical of him.

Our ladies continue to meet, and your name comes up in conversation every now and then. The children in particular miss your stories, and are scathing, in the way only children can be, of my feeble attempts to replace you. We had a cholera outbreak during the summer which put a great strain on the infirmary as you can imagine. I am sorry to have to inform you that Sally lost her little Alfie to it. It is a cruel and indiscriminate disease.

It is Sunday afternoon, and ~~I can hear my brother making those harrumphing noises that tell me his sermon is not going well~~ Sebastian is preparing for evensong. He will be expecting the kitchen fairy to have prepared tea before then, so I must end now and go and assume her duties!

I pray you find contentment and fulfilment in the fullness of time. God bless you, Lady Margaret.

With kindest regards,
Susannah Elmhirst

Powerscourt, County Wicklow, 2 November 1866

Dearest Susannah,

Thank you for your kind letter, which I assure you warmed my heart to read. I will not insult you by pretending that the last few months have been sunshine and roses, but there are fresh buds of hope which I trust will bloom. (The natural beauty of my surroundings has not only been a tonic, it seems to have pollinated my letter writing!) My own dear Molly has written confirming how happy she is in her new life, which is another great comfort to me, though I am saddened to hear that Esther's departure has forced you into the kitchen, when your time could more usefully be spent easing the domestic woes of women. But alas! I cannot deny that we live in a man's world.

I was touched to hear that the children ask after me, and sorry, if somewhat amused, to hear that your storytelling skills have been derided. I have dashed off a little tale for you to tell them in the hope of sparing your blushes further, which you may happily claim as your own. It is called "The House in the Middle of the Wood." I have left it to the children to provide the ending, something which I discovered they take much pleasure in doing. If my small contribution is a success, then I would be delighted to write more and send them to you.

I will not ask you to pass on my best wishes to your brother, though he has them regardless, and will, as you do, always occupy a special place in my heart.

> *Your friend,*
> *Margaret*

Chapter Twenty-Four

Viscount Powerscourt had been home for three weeks now, and Margaret had as yet failed to effect her planned escape. She had mooted the notion several times, and though Julia had been enthusiastic, the viscount had effectively vetoed any trip, preferring instead to bestow on Margaret the benefit of his wisdom.

These delights had included a master class on the difficulties of cross-breeding Japanese sambur deer with German roe deer, and the problems of keeping Sardinian mouflon sheep, accustomed to their dry and rocky native terrain, healthy in the damp Irish climate. Margaret had been treated to several lectures on the origin of the myriad stags' heads which adorned the walls of the viscount's abode, and had now heard his favourite anecdote, of how his father had nearly accidentally drowned King George at the waterfall, at least three times. She had inspected his latest acquisitions and feigned interest in his plans for creating a fountain in Juggy's Pond and the technical obstacles to be overcome in doing so. Which was riveting compared to the subject of ornamental trees and their planting and drainage.

Night after night, Lord Powerscourt proudly described his plans for remodelling his farms; draining his fields; rebuilding his house; and peppering his lands with bridges, gates, and roads. There was no doubting his enthusiasm, his genuine regard for his tenants, his pride in his estates, or even the scope of his vision for his various improvements. But his prodigious ability to make the most interesting subject bottom-numbingly tedious, combined with his utter lack of humour, made his company an endurance test. Last night, in despair, Margaret had suggested that it might be a good idea to move the whole of County Wicklow slightly to the east. Though Julia had let out a snort of laughter, quickly muffled, her husband, after looking slightly perplexed, had patiently explained at great length just why the county borders could not be adjusted willy-nilly without a political outcry.

Lord Powerscourt could speak, without seeming to stop for breath, for an hour at a time. He would ask for an opinion, and then provide it himself, at great length. On the rare occasions when Margaret had observed Julia persisting in positing an alternative view, he listened patiently and then ignored what she had said. He was never rude, never overtly condescending, but he had an earnest air about him that put Margaret's hackles up. He had several times commented on the serendipity of Margaret's stay providing Julia with company, not seeming to imagine that she might prefer her husband's.

Would this have been what marriage to Killin would have been like? Were all the men her father would consider marriageable cast from the same mould? And were women any less uniform? Reluctantly, Margaret had concluded that she and Julia would never be close. Julia's reserve was almost impossible to penetrate. Though she knew, from their single heart-to-heart, that Julia had feelings, she almost never betrayed them. She reminded Margaret of Victoria, which made her wonder if her sister's outward compliance and stoic forbearance hid a more emotional, and therefore much more interesting, person. It might well be so, but now Margaret would never know. One thing she *had* concluded, from her forced close observation of Julia's marriage, was that she could never bring herself to replicate it. Witnessing Julia's polite suffering while her husband relentlessly held forth made her scream silently with frustration. *Speak up*, Margaret wanted to shout. *Remind him that you actually have a voice!* She knew now with utter certainty that she had been absolutely right to reject Killin.

On just one occasion had the viscount's volubility deserted him.

A chance mention of his deceased brother, Maurice, had set his beard trembling and had him first scrubbing furiously at his eyes, then clenching his fists. "A good man," he muttered. "An officer decorated by the queen herself, by God. A real man, unlike that— that frivolous *fop!*"

"Lewis," Julia had explained as her husband stormed out of the room. "My husband held Maurice in such high esteem, his younger brother is bound to suffer in comparison. That Lewis is so very determined to be different doesn't help."

"Different in what way?"

Julia pursed her lips. "He has a penchant for low company and no respect for either the Wingfield name or his elder brother. Fortunately, the feeling is mutual. We rarely see him."

Margaret pondered the paradox of a viscount who loathed his current heir but took a very lax approach to the task of replacing him with a son of his own. She could see no evidence of intimacy in the everyday behaviour of the married couple. Wingfield held the door open for his wife, he held her chair out at dinner, but that seemed to be the extent of their contact. A more physical dimension must exist behind the closed doors of Julia's bedchamber, Margaret thought as she studied the pair of them over the breakfast table, but her toes curled trying to imagine what form it might take. Would the viscount have himself announced by his valet? Would he ask for Julia's permission in advance, in writing? Would he initiate proceedings with a kiss or simply proceed to—ah, but, no, she was putting herself off her coddled eggs.

"What is it, Margaret? Are you choking on something?"

She pushed her half-eaten plate of food aside. "No, not at all. I was wondering, Julia, if I might borrow the carriage to visit Dublin tomorrow, or the next day."

"Dublin? What is there to see in Dublin . . . ?"

"Margaret has been cooped up here for three months now, my dear," Julia intervened. "I think a change of scenery would do her the world of good. I could accompany you, Margaret. We could take tea, and—"

"I've a consignment arriving from Germany tomorrow, of new stags' heads," Lord Powerscourt said. "They are very delicate as they are made from papier mâché. I purchased them from Count Arco-Zinneberg, where they form part of his collection at his house in the Wittelsbacherplatz in Munich. I shall need your assistance in positioning them, Julia. The entrance hall is the obvious choice, but I was thinking . . ."

"Naturally I would be delighted to assist you," Julia said with a pained expression. "I will order the carriage for first thing tomorrow, Margaret. Take Breda with you, spend the day seeing the sights, and take tea. I had better remain here."

"Indeed," Lord Powerscourt said. "There's far too much to be done here. I've a lot of lost time to make up for."

"You have," Julia agreed. "You have indeed."

THE FOLLOWING MORNING, MARGARET DRESSED with care in a day dress of copper silk patterned with a geometric border in contrasting chocolate brown. The combination was most unusual for an unmarried young lady, but it had been her choice, and Mama had indulged her. The bodice had a white lace collar and cuffs, and fastened with a row of tiny jet buttons. A matching paletot jacket with a short front and a long tail, a small hat with a very wide bow on her carefully braided coiffure, which Breda had taken an age over, completed the ensemble. With her full quota of corset, crinoline, and petticoats and a pair of kid gloves in hand, Margaret was finally ready to face the outside world.

Though before she did, she must face the mirror. The first surprise was that the ensemble fitted. Breda had not laced her as tightly as Molly, and doubtless she would have failed Mama's measuring tape test. She was curvaceous rather than willowy, but she decided she preferred that. What was more, the effect had been achieved without any effort on her part. Over the last few weeks, her cravings for cake and pudding had disappeared. She enjoyed her food but was content with an elegant sufficiency.

The next surprise was her face. The features were still hers, the deep-set blue eyes, the straight Montagu nose, the mouth which was slightly too generous to be fashionable, yet the woman she saw reflected back at her was virtually a stranger. She looked older than her twenty years. There was a determined tilt to her chin, a wariness in her expression. Her skin was tanned and freckled; her brows were their natural dark-auburn, as were her lashes. Was it the copper of her gown that made her hair look like the colour of burnished autumn leaves and not the gingery-red she had always thought it? A tiny furrow had been etched into her forehead, testament to her sleepless nights and permanently dark mood, no doubt. She tried to smooth it away, but it was obviously a new fixture. This was Margaret au naturel, and she decided that she rather approved of this new incarnation. She essayed a smile. "What do you think?" she asked, turning to Breda and twirling around, making her crinoline bounce and herself laugh.

"You look so different," the maid said. "Pretty, but not in the usual way. It's the smile that transforms you, my lady, if you don't mind my saying so. It's very good to see."

"I show too many teeth when I smile, my mama says. 'A little more demure, Margaret,' she was forever telling me."

"Well, far be it for me to contradict a duchess, but I think it's a lovely smile with just the right amount of teeth," Breda said. "A real smile, if you know what I mean."

"I do, actually." Margaret pulled on her gloves. "Now, fetch your hat, Breda, and I'll see you downstairs in five minutes. Dublin awaits us."

THE POWERSCOURT LANDAU SET THEM down on Grafton Street, which Breda informed her was Dublin's main shopping district.

Beneath black awnings glass-fronted shops, displaying gloves, hats, and fine china, sat beneath tall Georgian buildings. Well-dressed shoppers thronged the clean-swept pavements; smart carriages and dray-carts fought for space on the broad cobbled street.

"Don't you want to make some purchases, my lady?"

"Perhaps later. I see there is a bookshop over there. For now I'd like to stroll, if you don't mind, and get my bearings a little. Lord Powerscourt has furnished me with an itinerary. He tells me that I must be sure to see the old parliament building and Trinity College, especially the Book of Kells."

"The Book of Kells, my lady? Isn't that just some oul book written by a monk?"

"That's one way to describe a historically important manuscript." Margaret laughed, seeing Breda's face. "Don't worry. I am no more disposed than you are to spend this lovely autumn day poring over a dusty book."

"May I take a look at what his lordship has written," Breda said, "then I'll know what direction we are to take. For the love of God," she added, pursing her lips, "he has a terrible spidery scrawl. Why is it that the better educated a person is, the worse his writing is? My brother Padraig can write in a better hand, and he's had but three years of school. We'll go this way, my lady, past St. Stephen's Green towards Merrion Square."

Turning away from Grafton Street, a few steps took them to an impressively wide boulevard, and Margaret got her first glimpse of the true splendour of Georgian Dublin. The iron railings of a pretty park were on one side, where four open carriages sat waiting for custom. On the other side, the red brick and sandstone frontage of the Shelbourne Hotel dominated, with a liveried doorman kept constantly occupied by the stream of carriages. Margaret had imagined a cityscape similar to the New Town in Edinburgh, but the frontages of the houses here were red brick rather than sandstone, the buildings themselves, with their flat roofs and pretty porticos with shallow steps and fanlights above the glossily painted doors, less uniform and to her eyes more appealing. Georgian town houses faced onto all four sides of the pretty Merrion Square. Peering over the railings into the private gardens, nursemaids could be seen pushing baby carriages along the meandering paths, and well-dressed children scampered on the grass playing with hoops and balls.

"It's lovely here," Breda said, "but walk a bit farther on to the canal, and it's a different story. Leinster House, which is on his lordship's list, is just down here, though I'm not sure why he mentioned it."

"It is by the same architect who redesigned Powerscourt," Margaret informed her. "Apparently there are many similar features. That must be it over there." She paused to gaze at the Palladian style mansion from the edge of its extensive gardens, trying to summon an appropriate sense of deference, but instead found herself mildly irritated, for by following the viscount's itinerary she was allowing him to dominate their precious day away.

"Trinity is next," Breda said, setting out stoically.

The college was lovely, gracious grey granite buildings looking out over more swathes of green, with gowned undergraduates rushing about clutching books; but as Margaret and Breda emerged at College Green opposite the bank which was once the parliament building, Margaret had had enough, though they had completed only a fraction of the viscount's tour. "I think I'll visit the bookshop now, and then it will be time for tea at the Shelbourne," she said firmly.

"Would you mind, my lady, if I took the opportunity to visit my mammy while you are taking tea?" Breda asked. "It's not far, and I'd be back in two shakes of a lamb's tail. I wouldn't ask, only she's a bit poorly at the moment."

"Goodness me, of course you must go. You should have said sooner, Breda, rather than traipsing about after me."

"Well I couldn't leave you on your own in a strange city. I'll come with you to the bookshop and on to the Shelbourne, and then—"

"You will do no such thing. You will go straight from here to your mother's and I will come with you."

"Oh no, my lady, it's a rough oul area, I wouldn't dream . . ."

"I have probably seen worse, when I did voluntary work in the Lambeth district of London, so lead on, unless you think your mother is too ill for uninvited visitors."

"Mammy will be delighted to meet you, for I've told her all about you in my letters. If you are absolutely sure, my lady, it's just across the river."

AS THEY APPROACHED THE RIVERFRONT, the Georgian buildings wore an air of neglect, the streets becoming shabbier and the people a little more grubby. The ground-floor shops sold second-hand clothes and boots, and every third frontage seemed to be a tavern. Margaret became conscious that people were studying her, but she was accustomed to brazening that out, and Breda's fierce defiant glare was acting as an excellent deterrent.

On the corner of the street leading to the bridge sat a little flower girl. Barefoot and filthy, she was unkempt, with knotted brown hair and huge brown eyes. Her tentative smile tugged at Margaret's heart. "What have you for sale?" she asked.

The girl tilted her basket, which contained a few slightly limp pink roses. "Perfect," Margaret said, fishing in her pocket for a shilling. "Is that enough?"

"That would buy the basket, too," Breda cautioned, but Margaret shushed her, taking the flowers and handing over the shilling. The little girl stared at the coin for a moment, as if she was afraid it wasn't real, then grabbed her basket and fled.

"They will be lucky to last more than a couple of days," Breda pointed out, eyeing the roses disparagingly.

"But they have a sweet perfume, and I couldn't go empty-handed to your mother's. I know perfectly well I paid over the odds," Margaret added, "but the little girl doesn't know I know, and now she can go home and tell her mama how clever she was."

"You have a good heart," Breda said, shaking her head. "Mammy will appreciate them anyways."

The River Liffey ran brown and sluggish, and Dublin city's heritage as a flourishing Georgian capital was obvious in the elegant expanse of the Custom House with its distinctive high-domed cupola on the opposite bank. Across the Carlisle Bridge was Sackville Street, another wide boulevard lined with elegant shops, a department store, and several hotels. Farther on, however, as they passed the post office, and the Nelson Pillar, into Upper Sackville Street, the surroundings became shabbier.

"Tuck your watch out of sight, my lady—oh, I see you have already done so."

"And my purse is safe in my petticoat pocket. I told you— I'm used to areas such as this."

Breda stepped a little closer to her. "I always think those houses must have been very grand when they were first built, but even when we came here from Mayo, which was almost twenty years ago now, they were in a bad way. We turn here, my lady."

A young boy, clinging to the bare back of a wild-maned grey horse, came riding at full tilt down the street they now entered. One step in from the main thoroughfare heralded a considerably more dilapidated world. It wasn't only that the cobbles were obscured by the filth running down the centre of the street, or the boarded-up windows or the missing slates making gaping holes in the shallow roofs. It was the stench of poverty, of unwashed bodies, filthy clothes, stagnant water, damp plaster, and rotting wood.

"Mind your skirts, my lady. Sorry about the smell." Breda was wrinkling her nose. "I never used to notice it when I was growing up here. Mammy does her best to keep the house clean, but it's hard work at the best of times."

"Please, don't worry about it. I understand perfectly how

difficult it is without a fresh supply of water. What is wrong with your mama, Breda?"

"The same thing that's ailed her nine times before, only she's getting far too old for it. I had a new baby brother two weeks ago. She thought she was past all that, for my youngest brother is now six years old, and it would have been better if she had been, for something went wrong when her time came. Agnes, who is my third sister, had to take her to the Rotunda—that's the lying-in hospital just a few steps from here. They thought the little one wasn't going to make it. He's very sickly yet, and Mammy has had the priest round to baptise him as a precaution."

"Oh, Breda, I wish you had told me. If there is anything she needs . . ."

"What she needs is to have my father let her alone," Breda said tartly. "If you'll forgive the plain speaking, my lady. She's forty-four years old, and doesn't need an extra mouth to feed. To be perfectly honest, and God forgive me for saying so, it might have been better if the little mite hadn't survived, and—ah no, I don't mean that. I only hope this time it is her last. Mind your step now, for we have to cross here. And there is Cillian, if I'm not mistaken. My youngest brother. He should be at school, the little scallywag."

Breda stomped over to where a cluster of urchins, some barefoot, others wearing outsize boots, were playing a game of marbles. The smallest but cleanest, presumably Cillian, stood up at her approach, throwing his arms around his sister's waist; and Margaret laughed, for his winsome smile immediately dissipated Breda's frown as she crossed to join them.

"It's this house here," Breda said, "first floor. There's only Mammy, for Agnes had to go back to work yesterday at the biscuit factory over in the Liberties, and the boys all work near there at the brewery, where my father is employed. My other sisters are in service like me, in a big house in County Kildare. That just leaves Padraig, who is at school, and the little one, too, of course."

"Baby Liam. He cries all the time," Cillian informed them solemnly. "And so does Mammy."

Breda pressed a penny into her young brother's hand. "Away and buy yourself a barley sugar now. And it's back to school tomorrow or else." Breda's smile faded as she got to her feet. "Mammy cried like a watering spout for a month after Cillian was born too. Come on then, my lady. Let's go in and see if we can cheer her up."

TWO HOURS LATER, THEIR MISSION ACCOMPLISHED, they found themselves at the Shelbourne Hotel. The foyer of the hotel was as opulent as its frontage promised, with highly polished marble floors, gilded cornicing, marble pilasters, and a series of arches leading to the public rooms. It could not have been more of a contrast to the three cramped rooms in which Breda's family lived across the Liffey.

"I am Lady Margaret Montagu Douglas Scott, a guest of Lord Powerscourt," she informed the maître d'hôtel who greeted them. "I believe the carriage is stabled here? I would like to take tea, and then have the carriage sent round in perhaps an hour?"

"Certainly, my lady. Your maid may wait in the foyer."

"Miss Murphy will take refreshments with me." Margaret almost laughed, for it was difficult to tell whether Breda or the maître d'hôtel was the more scandalised. Margaret threw the man an imperious glance worthy of her mother, which resulted in them being led into a large salon decorated in gold and cream, facing a garden, and placed at a round table in the window.

"My goodness, you didn't half put him in his place," Breda whispered, casting a harried glance over her shoulder, "but it's not seemly for me to be here."

"You must be hungry, surely."

"Growing up in our house we were never anything else, but . . ."

"I have no desire to take tea alone. Lady Julia assures me that the Shelbourne does the best afternoon tea in Dublin. And look," she added as the platters began to arrive, "I think she was right."

There were smoked salmon and watercress sandwiches on soft white bread, and egg mayonnaise with cress on Irish soda bread. Buttermilk scones with cream and strawberry jam, and sticky gingerbread. There were delicate apple and blackberry pastries with Chantilly cream, and choux pastry éclairs glazed with chocolate. And there was tea, fragrant in the delicate Belleek porcelain teapot, served with lemon slices or milk.

"I can't believe this spread is for just the two of us," Breda said, her eyes on stalks.

It struck Margaret that it did seem an obscene amount of food, given where they had just come from. "Do you visit your mama often?" Margaret asked, serving them both a selection of sandwiches and pouring the tea.

"Once a month, on my day off if I can, and I write every week."

"Can all of you read and write?"

"Yes, for Mammy made sure of it, and gave us all lessons even before any of us went to school. I remember we had a few books when I was learning, but they're long gone, and she's had to try to teach Cillian using newspapers, which is probably why he's not doing so well. Mammy wanted to be a teacher, and had started working in the village school back in Mayo, but then she met my pa, and he'd no sooner looked at her sideways, to hear her tell the tale, than she was expecting me."

"What a shame—oh, I don't mean that she had you, I am very glad she did, but . . ."

"Ah, well, not long after that the famine came, and the village school closed and that's when my father brought us all to Dublin." Breda finished her salmon sandwich, and Margaret helped her to a scone. "Thank you, my lady. Mammy was talking of teaching again, when Cillian was a bit older, but my father did not approve and now he has given her Liam to take care of, so that's that."

Mrs. Murphy's skin had been ashen, that of a malnourished woman who has lost far too much blood bringing her child into the world. After ten children, she looked considerably older than her forty-four years, and had barely had the energy to hold the mug of tea Breda had made her. "I believe fried liver is good for building up one's strength after a difficult birth," Margaret said, recalling Susannah's advice to a new mother.

"Don't worry. Agnes will see to that, and make sure Mammy has plenty strong porter to drink, which one of my brothers will bring back from the brewery." Breda cut her scone in two and took a delicate bite. "You are full of surprises, my lady. I thought Mammy was going to fall off her chair when you changed Liam's dirty napkin."

Margaret laughed. "It was positively fragrant compared to some I've encountered."

"You'll be doing the nursemaid out of work, when you have your own babes."

"Perhaps. What about you? Do you intend to get married?"

"I'm in no rush. I'd have to give up earning money if I took on a husband." Breda took a sip of tea, her brow furrowed. "God's honest truth, though, is that I've no wish to end up like Mammy. I know the church teaches us that children are a blessing, but if I bide my time before I take the plunge, I'm thinking I'll be less blessed but maybe happier." Breda winced. "Sorry, that sounds selfish."

"It sounds an eminently sensible approach to me. Have you finished?"

"It seems a crying shame to leave so much food, but I don't think I'll be fit to eat again for days."

"I have an idea," Margaret said, summoning the waiter. "Please have all of this wrapped up and put in a hamper, and supplement it with whatever you think necessary to feed—how many will be home tonight, Breda, including your father?"

"Eight, but you can't—"

"Eight people," Margaret said to the waiter. "Eight very hungry people."

"I am afraid the Shelbourne does not provide picnic hampers, Lady Margaret."

"I'm sure that can be remedied," Margaret said, for the second time that day adopting her mother's most imperious tone.

"I will speak to the manager; it may be possible," the waiter said doubtfully.

"I am certain that it will be. Miss Murphy here will provide you with the directions. If you will have the Powerscourt carriage brought round now, I would be much obliged."

"*My lady!*" Breda watched the waiter's retreating back with a mixture of glee and horror. "You shouldn't have."

"Do you think your mother will be insulted?"

"No, Mammy will be over the moon. Never look a gift horse and all that."

Margaret got to her feet and handed over her purse. "Here, I'll leave you to settle the bill, please, and do so without trying to barter it down. I will see you in the carriage. Will the groom mind waiting on Grafton Street for me, do you think? I would still like to visit the bookshop. I want to buy your brother a storybook. One with lots of pictures to capture his interest that your mama can read to him."

"That would be very generous of you, my lady, and thoughtful, too. Thank you."

"I wish I could do more for your mother, but I suspect your father would call it charity and take umbrage."

Breda laughed. "You've got his measure, all right. I bet you wrap your own father round your little finger."

Margaret laughed. "If you only knew the half of it," she said wryly.

Berlin, 1 January 1867

Dear Lady Margaret,

I wonder if you are surprised to hear from me, or whether your host has alerted you to my intention to write? As you will no doubt be aware by now, for I understand you have been in Ireland since last summer, Lord Powerscourt is an avid collector of antiquities, and is in the habit of enlisting Her Majesty's embassy staff to assist in the acquisition process. I have been of service to him several times—as you know from personal experience, I can be an accomplished detective when the occasion demands it! However, it was only when discussing his latest project (yet more stags' heads, the man is obsessed!), that I discovered you were paying Lady Powerscourt an extended visit. I obtained his permission to write to you, deeming it unnecessary to seek additional authorisation from the duke, your father, since the viscount is, in effect, acting in loco parentis.

I read an excellent account in The Times *of your appearance as bridesmaid to Princess Helena, but did not read the announcement which you had assured me, when last we met, was imminent. In fact, there has been no mention of you at all in the press since August, as far as I have been able to ascertain. When I returned to London for a brief visit in October, I took the opportunity to call at Montagu House in order to pay my respects and to inquire after you. I was informed by the duke that you were out of town and not expected back. His manner did not encourage me to question him further.*

I hope this letter finds you well at the beginning of the New Year.

If it would please you to respond with an update on your well-being, it would be very much appreciated. As you can see from my address, I remain in Berlin, though I am expecting imminently to be transferred to Rome, but a letter to either embassy will find me.

With very best wishes,
Lochiel

Powerscourt, County Wicklow, 13 January 1867

Dear Lochiel,

What a lovely surprise it was to receive your letter. While Lord and Lady Powerscourt have been inordinately accommodating, I confess it was a real treat to hear from a familiar face, so to speak. Your mention of his lordship as a connoisseur of all things cervine amused me greatly. Powerscourt is a shrine to his obsession, with deceased deer festooning the walls and the park awash with live ones. If he could dress himself entirely in deer-hide he would, and you will not be surprised to learn that his favourite dinner is venison pie, which we are obliged to have every Saturday.

I can assure you that I am in excellent health and good spirits. You remain as tactful as ever but I, as you know, prefer plain dealing. I refused to marry Killin for many reasons which I will not dwell on. My father refused to accept my decision. As a consequence I was cast out into the wilderness, and for a while, I will admit, was in despair. But despair is such a draining emotion, and remorse can only be sustained while one believes oneself entirely to blame. I regret many things, not least my misguided attempts to bow to my father's will, but my intentions were always pure. Since the duke will never forgive me, I have decided to forgive myself. What will you make of this confession? I wonder. I am tempted to score it out, but will let it stand. If we are to be ~~correspondents~~ friends, then let us be true and honest ones.

You do not ask me how I occupy myself, but I will tell you, for I think you will approve. I have been helping out at the Enniskerry village school, and at the school for infants, which is nearby, both being largely funded by Lord Powerscourt. His grandfather built the school—not, I hasten to add, with his own hands. I am not an actual teacher, of course, but act as assistant to Mr. and Mrs. Doherty, who are the schoolmaster and -mistress. I do a great deal of wiping of noses and drying of tears. I help those who are a little behind with their arithmetic and their handwriting. Oh yes, and I tell stories, Lochiel—but then you know that! I am writing them down and collating them in a little book. There! You are the first and only person I have dared to trust with that secret. Another in our list of shared confidences. The stories are modest efforts, but the children here like them, and I am informed by Susannah Elmhirst, who tells them to the Lambeth children, that they are popular there, too.

Goodness, how I have run on, and all you wanted to know was whether I was alive and well or not! I hope it will not embarrass you when I tell you that your concern made me shed a little tear. If it pleases you to continue our correspondence, I would be delighted to do so. If my loquacity (isn't that a wonderful word!) has frightened you off, I will understand. If it has not, I would love to hear some tales of your time on the Continent. Being away from England has made me realise that there is a big world out there. Now I really must stop wittering on!

> Yours most sincerely and with very best wishes,
> Lady Margaret

Chapter Twenty-Five

March 1867

As Margaret, astride her favourite chestnut mare, headed out through the main gates of the estate, Pennygael was champing at the bit. "You can have your head in a moment," she said, keeping a tight rein. "Patience, girl."

The day was overcast with what in Scotland would be called a smur of rain, and Breda would call a tear of mist coming in from the bog, but Margaret's spirits were in direct contrast to the lowering sky. Heading through the deer park in the direction of the famous Powerscourt waterfall, she relaxed her grip on the reins and Pennygael's stride lengthened. The ground was soft, the mare's hooves drummed a muffled, rhythmic beat as Margaret leaned in, the wind catching at her hair and the skirts of her riding habit. The sweet scent of damp bracken and mulched leaves filled her nose, mingling with the smell of leather and horse sweat. A hawthorn hedge loomed, but Pennygael soared over it, her grey fetlocks just brushing the top, galloping on without missing a beat, slowing reluctantly only as the viscount's newly planted woods loomed into view.

At the waterfall Margaret dismounted, leaving the horse to drink, while she took her favourite seat on a rock by the pool. The water was grey blue today, the weed on the boulders glinting brown and gold, mimicking the colours of the surrounding heavily wooded hills. The cascade pounded down a sheer rock escarpment, the central flume a powerful torrent of white water with many smaller rivulets tumbling over the jagged rocks on either side. A huge cloud of mist hung in the air and a thunderous roar drowned out all other sounds. This was by far her favourite place on the estate. The exhilarating power of the falls, the contrasting tranquillity of the pool, and the ever-changing beauty of the forested slopes never failed to entrance her, or to lift her spirits.

She could not claim to be happy, but she was busy, and that was enough. She had found a niche here at Powerscourt, and a purpose, which was so much more than she'd ever imagined possible. She had stopped railing at her exiled state, stopped questioning the rights and the wrongs of it, stopped asking herself when and how it would end, or if it ever would. Was that burying her head in the sand? Perhaps. But what was the alternative when she was powerless to influence the outcome? Unlike so many she had encountered, she was safe and well-fed, with a roof over her head. She was resolved to be patient, and in the meantime to continue to follow Julia's lead in making the best of her lot.

IT WAS A SATURDAY, so the school was closed. Lord Powerscourt had left yesterday for London and the sale rooms, which meant that Margaret could safely ensconce herself in the octagon library and scribble away at her stories without fear of interruption. Julia would probably be indoors, too, working on her chair covers, since the weather had deteriorated markedly by the time Margaret stabled Pennygael. What his lordship insisted on referring to as Lady Powerscourt's sitting room was one of the few stag-free chambers. Instead, two pairs of large and particularly ugly Sèvres pug dogs squatting on gold cushions sat on opposite ends of the mantelpiece, gazing out belligerently at all comers. When Margaret entered, Julia was sitting at the window beside her embroidery frame, the canvas for her latest work-in-progress chair cover stretched taut, the coloured wools laid out in a row on top of her sewing box.

"I thought I'd find you here," Margaret said. The Berlin work cover on the frame was embroidered in a trellis pattern of diamond shapes in muted tones, with a violet, scallop-like flower in the centre of each. "This is so pretty. And the colours are very restful. How many have you completed so far?"

"This is only the third. I have another twenty-one to make. My legacy to Powerscourt," Julia said. "Most likely my only one."

Her tone was morose. Looking at her more closely, Margaret saw that her eyes were red-rimmed. "What is the matter?" she asked, sitting down on the sofa beside her and taking her hand.

"The usual. Another month, and still no sign of me being with child, and now Wingfield has gone off to London and heaven knows when he'll be back." A tear trickled down Julia's cheek. Snatching her hand back, she found her handkerchief and dabbed her eyes. "We have been married for three years come April, and I have signally failed to find myself in an interesting condition. The matter wasn't so urgent while Maurice was alive, but now he is gone, and Mervyn is becoming increasingly agitated at the thought of Lewis inheriting." Julia sighed wearily. "Wingfield married me to produce an heir. It is the one thing he required of me, and I have let him down."

"It takes two people to make a child, Julia, and Lord Powerscourt was away from home for six months."

"He has been home since October. Four months! You'd think that would be time enough. The truth is, even when he is here he pays more attention to his collections," Julia said bitterly. "His gardens are flourishing, his precious deer are breeding, but his wife is barren."

"You don't know that!" Margaret exclaimed, appalled. But as she slid a glance at Julia, sitting rigidly erect, gazing blankly out of the window where the rain was falling so heavily it all but obliterated the view, Margaret struggled to think of any practical advice to offer. The matter was so delicate, and Julia so very reserved.

Yet she was obviously wretched; something had to be said. "When he is at home, does he— what I mean is, does your husband come to your bed?"

Julia's cheeks flooded with colour. "Yes."

"And does he . . ." Margaret flinched. Her own cheeks were blazing. "Does he perform the act? Adequately, I mean?" she asked, realising as she did so that she wasn't at all sure what she meant.

"I think so," Julia whispered, keeping her gaze fixed on the window. "As far as I am aware, he does what is necessary, but to no avail. Every month I have to endure the embarrassment of my maid removing the evidence of my failure, knowing that the bad news will be all over the servants' hall in five minutes."

"Oh, Julia . . ."

"And it's not only the servants. The whole county are watching and waiting. When Wingfield brought me here as his bride, Margaret, there were such celebrations, and I was so filled with hope. He was more conscientious then, when we were first married, but I think my continued failure to conceive has put him off." Julia shuddered. "It is mortifying. I shouldn't be discussing this with you. You are not even married."

"You must talk to someone. Couldn't you write to your mama?"

"And say what, exactly? She has had twelve children; nine of us survived. She won't understand. She'll tell me to be patient, to wait, but I'm sick to death of waiting. I want a child! What am I to do?"

"I don't know," Margaret said, feeling utterly helpless in the face of such raw pain and anger. "Have you consulted a doctor?"

Julia recoiled. "It is bad enough exposing myself to my husband."

"Then have you a married friend you could consult?"

"I could not."

"Well, what about a midwife?" Margaret suggested, acutely aware that she had reached the limit of her own knowledge.

But Julia shrank still farther away from her. "Can you imagine the gossip, if it were known I had done so? If Wingfield found out, he would be furious."

"I can't help but think that if you discussed the matter with him—"

"No!" Julia covered her face with her hands. "My husband is clearly not one of those men who relish the—the intimate side of married life." Tears seeped through her fingers. "But he does at least try to do his marital duty. Forget I said that. It would be wrong of me to imply that the fault was somehow his."

"I'm sorry," Margaret said. "I'm being worse than useless."

Julia sniffed, tucking her handkerchief away. "Please don't apologise. I was at a low ebb, but I should not have discussed such a very personal subject with you. You are an unmarried young lady—it is not a fit topic for your ears." Julia picked up her needle and selected a strand of lilac wool. "I appreciate your sympathy and your willingness to hear me out, but I'm afraid there are some things which cannot be fixed, no matter how much you want them to be."

"You're not a failure, Julia. You mustn't think that."

"No? It's how the world views a childless woman."

There was no disputing this. No matter how unjust, it was the truth. "You don't need to pretend that it doesn't matter, though. You shouldn't bottle it all up."

"I am not the weeping and wailing sort," Julia said primly, pulling her embroidery frame towards her. "I have never seen the point in bemoaning my fate. It doesn't make me feel any better, for there is nothing I can do save wait for my husband to return, and hope that when he does, fate will look more kindly upon me. When you are married, you will understand."

Margaret sighed. "Speaking for myself, I think there are more than enough children in the world anyway. I would rather do what I can to help those already here than add to the numbers."

"What an odd way you have of looking at things."

"I am aware of that," Margaret said, grimacing, "but I am coming to the conclusion I can't look at it any other way."

"You are enjoying working at the school, aren't you?"

"I adore it. You should come with me one day. They are always in need of another pair of hands, and you might—"

"No," Julia said flatly. "I know you're thinking it might take my mind off things, but it would simply make me more conscious that I have no child of my own."

"Oh, Julia."

"I pray you will not pity me. If you feel that Mr. and Mrs. Doherty require more help, why not take Breda with you? Didn't you tell me that her mother had aspirations to be a schoolmistress? I would happily excuse her from some of her duties, if it does not inconvenience you."

"Really? That is a marvellous idea. Breda will be thrilled."

"Now if you don't mind, I need to concentrate on my Berlin work. It requires very intricate stitching and any mistake requires laborious unpicking."

"Then I'll leave you to it."

But as she prepared to rise, Julia stayed her. "I know that what you say is right. There are too many children in this world, and far too many of them are unwanted, too. I take my hat off to you."

"It's a modest enough contribution, but I love it."

"I know. But one day, when you are married, you'll understand that it's simply no substitute. It's not only that I wish to give Wingfield an heir, I want a child of my own. A child who will love me, and whom I can love back. That's all I want, Margaret, a child of my own to love. Is it too much to ask?"

A lump rose in Margaret's throat. "No, it shouldn't be too much to ask," she said in a small voice. But as she left the room she couldn't help thinking sadly that it was too much to expect.

Vienna, 14 April 1867

Dear Margaret,

 You will perhaps be surprised to hear from me after all this time. Mama has been keeping me abreast of your progress by sending me copies of all your letters to her. Can you believe me when I tell you that it gives me great pleasure to read them? Perhaps you are asking yourself why, then, I have not written to you myself? The short answer is that Kerr forbad it. This does not reflect his opinion of your behaviour but his belief that we should honour our father's edict.

 And so what has changed? Life, and almost death, is responsible. Are you raising those questioning brows of yours and thinking, how unlike Victoria to be melodramatic? You are right, but I do not exaggerate. My son, Walter William Schomberg Kerr, Earl of Ancram (what a mouthful for such a little scrap of a baby!) was delivered just over two weeks ago. He was early and his journey into the world was not only unexpected but extremely protracted and painful for both of us. For several days afterwards the pair of us had a very fragile hold on life. Thankfully, we are both now much more robust, but confronting one's possible demise makes one reassess one's priorities somewhat. Hovering on the edge of one world, I resolved to write to you if I was spared, no matter what Kerr thought. As it turned out, he did not argue with me at all—though I cannot say whether this was due to relief that I survived or gratitude for my having produced his much longed-for heir. A mixture of both, I suspect. What matters is that he consented, and so I am free to write to you at last, and am determined to take a leaf from your book and speak more candidly.

You have always thought that Mama preferred me to you. Second daughter, second best, to borrow one of your phrases. I will tell you now, Margaret, that I have often resented the burden of being held up as a model and envied you the freedom to rebel—though I wish you had not *rebelled in quite such a flamboyant manner. And since I am* fessing up, *to use yet another of your inimitable turns of phrase, I envy you your ease with people, your ability to mix with anyone and everyone. We have not been close, there is no denying that, but I hope that through our correspondence we can forge a new, sisterly bond. It is asking a great deal, I know, but you have a generous heart and I am confident you will indulge me by trying.*

Little Cecil had her first birthday in February. I enclose a sketch of her. I look forward to her becoming acquainted with her aunt Margaret at some point, though I am not sure, in all honesty, that I have grounds for optimism. Instead, I pray you will treat this letter as a fresh start between us, and write back.

With love,
Your sister,
Victoria

DONALD CAMERON OF LOCHIEL
TO LADY MARGARET

Paris, 24 April 1867

Dear Margaret,

Forgive this hasty scrawl, but I have just finished reading your compendium of children's tales and wanted to tell you how much I enjoyed them. I took the liberty of reading the one about the flower girl to my hostess's daughter, Emily, who is nine. I must confess that I expected some sort of benevolent lady to appear in your story just at the right time to purchase the fur-lined boots the child dreamed of, but I was informed in no uncertain terms by my audience that this would have been far too unlikely! The wicked aunt was, in her opinion, much more believable.

I went up significantly in her estimation when I told Emily that the story had been written by a friend of mine. You simply must have these published; they deserve to be read more widely. I do agree with you that they should be illustrated and, alas, I am forced also to agree with you that your own drawings—well, let us say they do not do your words justice!

My host is calling me. We are to visit the great exhibition. I will write more fully when I return, for I know you will be anxious to hear all the details. Rest assured, I shall make a point of seeking out the strangest and most outlandish exhibits for your delectation and delight.

With very best wishes as always,
Donald

LADY MARGARET TO DONALD CAMERON
OF LOCHIEL

Powerscourt, County Wicklow, 1 June 1867

Dear Donald,

It is five months to the day since you first wrote to me in exile here. I counted the number of letters which have passed between us since and the total is rather astonishing. Isn't it odd, to become so well acquainted with a person and yet to have no prospect of furthering that acquaintance in person? No, do not fear I am becoming maudlin, only wistful, my dear friend—is it too presumptuous of me to call you that?

Breda, who was my maid, is now teaching at Enniskerry School which is set to join the national school system once Lord Powerscourt has made the requested improvements the board require for entry. Mr. Doherty is to be retained as schoolmaster, thankfully, and Breda has been promised some formal training, much to her mother's joy—I think I told you that Mrs. Murphy was a schoolmistress before she was married? I am not sure whether all this upheaval will mean that my days at the school are numbered, but I have been assured my services remain most welcome at the infants' school.

It is at this point in my letters that I usually tell you that life at Powerscourt otherwise continues as usual, but that is not so! We are to have a rare visitor! Mr. Lewis Strange Wingfield, black sheep, bad penny, fop, as his elder brother variously refers to him, is to grace us with his (hopefully colourful) presence. He comes to us at a time when Lord Powerscourt is guaranteed to be absent. His lordship is once again abroad on one of his buying trips, so be warned, Donald, your services may yet be requested in the quest for a particularly elusive stag's head.

Julia is much put-out at having to play the hostess to this renegade youngest son and has warned me several times to beware of him. She has failed to enlighten me as to why I should be cautious of cultivating him, merely pursing her lips and informing me that he is "the antithesis of what the son of a viscount should be." You will not be surprised to know that this intrigues me greatly. I have hopes that Mr. Lewis Strange Wingfield will live up to his middle name (in the interesting *sense of the word, and not the* odd *sense, needless to say). If he does, I shall make the most of his company—and ignore Julia's qualms about my reputation suffering for, as you well know, I cannot lose what I do not have!*

There, now I have most likely alarmed you thoroughly, but you must not fret, I have not reached the grand old age of almost twenty-one without being able to take care of myself.

Margaret

Chapter Twenty-Six

June 1867

MARGARET HAD REMAINED BEHIND AS usual to help put the classroom to rights before leaving the infant school to head back to Powerscourt. A young man was leaning nonchalantly against the wall of the playground when she emerged, but he straightened up when he saw her, making a flourishing bow.

"Lady Margaret Scott, I presume?"

She knew immediately who he must be. "The very same," she said, dropping a small curtsy. "The Honourable Lewis Strange Wingfield, I presume? Lord Powerscourt's youngest brother. We have been expecting you."

"Please, I beg of you, drop the honourable. My title is neither welcome nor particularly accurate. I am considered the theatrical youngest brother, a description I much prefer. Now, it has been a long-held ambition of mine to walk a teacher home from school, rather than the other way round. May I have the honour?" He offered his arm, but seeing her hesitation immediately withdrew it. "Ah, I see my reputation precedes me."

"I prefer to make my own mind up about people," Margaret said. "Having said that, you must admit this is an unconventional way to be introduced. I'm not sure Julia would approve. Does she even know you are here?"

"Julia doesn't approve of me, full stop. However, she did, admittedly most reluctantly, divulge your whereabouts once I had assured her I would be on my very best behaviour."

Margaret bit back a laugh. "I have been trying to discover from her why I should be wary of you, but to no avail."

"Come—my brother must have said something. Did he call me a fop?"

"He did. And Julia said that you are not what you ought to be," she risked.

Lewis gave a snort of laughter. "That, I will admit freely, is perfectly true. Though the same thing, I understand, could be said of you, if you don't mind my saying so. But I can see from your expression that you do. Ought I not to have mentioned it?"

Margaret put her hand to her heated cheeks, shaking her head. "What have you heard about me?"

"Enough to whet my appetite."

She eyed him narrowly, her amusement tempered with wariness. "Are you always so—so forthright with people you have just met?"

"No, only those who interest me. I am the epitome of Victorian reserve and good manners with bores."

She couldn't help it—Margaret gave a peal of laughter. "I am flattered," she said, tucking her hand into his arm.

"And I am vastly relieved. I have high hopes of you, Lady Margaret. I do hate to be disappointed, but I am aware—as my brother will attest—that I am not everyone's cup of tea. Talking of which, I am thirsty after my walk. Shall we take some refreshment at the Leicester Arms before we return to Powerscourt?"

"A cup of tea would be most welcome, Mr. Wingfield."

"Lewis, please, since I am quite determined we are to be friends, and I was rather thinking of a glass of strong porter."

"I can't go into a tavern and sup ale!"

"No? Well then, go and sit down by the river and I'll bring a jug out. There's a lovely spot. . . ."

"I know it. You go and purchase our ale, then, and I will see you there."

It was five minutes later when he emerged, and Margaret had

266

settled herself on the sunny riverbank. Lewis was twenty-five, she knew, but she would have guessed at something closer to her own age. His dark-brown hair was worn long, parted in the centre, waving down over his ears. Like his elder brother's, his hairline was already receding to reveal a high, smooth forehead. His jaw was smooth, too, with no trace of a beard. He was not handsome, his nose being rather too big, his mouth rather small, but he had an infectious smile and a gleam of mischief in his eyes that Margaret found vastly appealing. Though his slim figure was soberly dressed, his red necktie hinted at a tendency towards ostentation, and there was, in the way he carried himself, something of the feline grace of a ballet dancer.

"Well, do I pass muster?" he asked, settling himself beside her and pouring them both a glass of the dark beer. "You were positively drinking me in, my dear."

"You are nothing like your brother," she answered, somewhat taken aback.

"I'll take that as a compliment. I have what is known as a thespian bent." He touched his glass to hers. "Slainté, as they say here. Good health." He took a long draught and smacked his lips theatrically. "I always know I'm in Ireland when I taste that."

Margaret took a sip, nodding approvingly. "It *is* rather good."

"You're something of an expert, are you?"

"Oh, I wouldn't say that, but I've had the occasional glass in Dublin."

Lewis leaned back on his elbow, smiling over at her. "Have you, now? My mama told me that you were 'a bit out of the ordinary way,' and since that is how I view myself, I reckoned we would be bound to like each other."

Elizabeth, Lady Londonderry, was one of her mother's closest friends, which was why Margaret was here with Julia. She had lost her first husband, Viscount Powerscourt, when her three boys were very young. Though it was said that her second marriage was a love match, it, too, ended tragically when her husband, the Marquess of Londonderry was confined to a lunatic asylum, effectively making a widow of her for the second time. Like Victoria's mama-in-law, Lady Cecil, Marchioness of Lothian, and Mama herself, Lady Londonderry had converted to the Roman Catholic religion in middle age. She was an established beauty and a woman of fearsome intellect, and Margaret had always found her rather intimidating.

"What else has Lady Londonderry said about me?" she asked Lewis, frowning.

"You must not worry that she has been spreading gossip. My mother is *most* discreet. She said only that you have a most decided mind of your own. Since I pride myself on sharing that trait, too . . ." Lewis made an expansive gesture. "She also told me last year, when I was first considering a visit, to leave you be."

"And you have done so for almost a year, but now your curiosity has got the better of you, is that it?"

He shrugged. "If you must know, I needed a change of air."

"There is nothing like the fresh Irish air for healing the spirit," Margaret said, half teasing. "I myself am testament to that." She waited for Lewis to elucidate, but he was frowning down at his hands, looking slightly uncomfortable. "Whatever the reason for your visit," she said, "I am glad you are here."

She earned herself a relieved smile for this. His reluctance to confide made her warm to him. He was not as shallow as she had first thought. She finished her porter, shaking her head when he made to top up her glass. "I like it, but more than one makes me feel sick."

"Waste not, want not," Lewis said, emptying the jug into his own glass. "In any case, we had better make our way back soon. I don't want to upset Julia on my first day here by being late for dinner."

"Tell me a little about yourself first. I know next to nothing about you, save that you are an artist. You painted those lovely panels in the saloon, didn't you?"

"In happier days, when Maurice was still alive and Mervyn did not live in fear of my inheriting. In the last few years, I have been many things, an artist, an actor, and an attendant in a lunatic asylum. I worked in a prison, too, as a warder. For a short while only, you understand."

"Good heavens, why?"

Lewis shrugged. "The same reason that I pretended to be a pauper and begged a bed in a workhouse or dressed up in petticoats to play an elderly spinster in a burlesque. For the fun of it. Because I get bored easily, I suppose. Mostly because I would rather be almost anyone than the heir to the great Powerscourt estates." He grimaced. "Now that really is the most tedious role I can imagine— unless one imagines actually being Lord Powerscourt."

"Do you mean that? Truly?"

"Truly, honest to God and cross my heart," Lewis said, suiting action to words. "I dread the very idea of having to walk in my brother's shoes. I do wish Julia would hurry up and produce an heir."

"Don't say it like that," Margaret said sharply. "No-one wants a child more than Julia."

"Save my brother," Lewis continued in the same flippant tone, quite unrepentant. "Mervyn would do anything rather than see me inherit. It does beg the question, doesn't it, why he spends so much of his time away from Wicklow. You'd think that after all the effort he has put into the house and gardens, he might strain a sinew to produce a son to inherit them."

"Lewis!"

"Oh, have I shocked you?"

"You have, and I am aware it was quite deliberate on your part."

He laughed, getting languidly to his feet, and holding out his hand to help her up. "I think I'm going to enjoy my brief stay."

"Bray," Lewis informed Margaret five days later, "is not nearly so fashionable as Brighton. It is a quaint little seaside town with a charming promenade, but has not much to offer by way of diversion."

They were seated together in Julia's landau with the top down, for the day was fine and the sun shining. Margaret dragged her eyes away from the view of the River Dargle, which the road had been following for much of the short drive, to smile at him. "I don't need diversion when I have you."

"If only the critics agreed with you, but they can be so cutting. Do you know, after my debut performance in a burlesque, they said that my 'idiotic dance in petticoats might stand for something in a competitive examination for admission into the Earlswood Asylum.' Why does one only remember the bad reviews?"

"Have there been any good ones to recall?"

"A few. A very few, actually. My Roderigo was fairly well-received, but when one treads the boards with Mrs. Kendal and Ira Aldridge, one cannot help but shine. I don't suppose you happened to see that particular production of *Othello*? It was on at the Haymarket a couple of years ago. August, I think it was."

"A month after I was sent off to Dalkeith," Margaret said, grimacing.

"Ah yes, after you fled the ball at midnight, just like Cinderella in the pantomime. I have not had the pleasure of appearing in it, which is a pity, as I do have a fine pair of calves for a pair of breeches." Lewis raised his leg to be admired. "Actually I have decided to bring down the curtain on my acting career, so to speak."

"Why?"

"Alas, I am never going to be an Edmund Kean. In any event, I am a bit of a butterfly, always flitting from one endeavour to the next. Now here we are arrived in Bray. I have asked the charming coachman to drop us off at the promenade, where we can take a stroll and enjoy the fresh air. What do you say?"

"An excellent idea. I can smell the sea already."

The River Dargle widened as they neared the harbour, and the air became distinctively briny. The nondescript little main street gave way to much more imposing buildings as the landau came to a halt on the wide promenade upon which were located several very grand hotels. A long sweep of neat gardens with a bandstand in the centre was bustling with visitors, some clustered in deck chairs, others conversing in groups. The promenade itself ran in a long straight line next to the shore, where the waves pounded up the steep strand, spraying the unwary. Margaret clutched at her hat, for the breeze had got up, and closed her eyes, tilting her face towards the sun. The sound of the sea, the swoop and cry of gulls, and the smell of salt and sand, and something indefinable that was the seaside reminded her of the sands at Portobello near Edinburgh.

She opened her eyes to smile at Lewis. "Do you think we might go for a paddle?"

He shuddered. "Aside from the fact that the water is freezing, I have no desire whatever to roll my trousers up and totter about on those pebbles trying to keep my balance. It is a most undignified prospect. I sincerely hope you are jesting."

"I expect I am," Margaret said, looking longingly at the sea.

"You will be telling me next that you wish to hire a bathing-machine."

"Do they have them here? Can one hire a bathing costume, too?"

"Dear heavens, I have no idea." Lewis took her arm, and they set off along the strand. "Those are the Wicklow Mountains you can see to the south. The walk to Bray Head should take us half an hour or so each way. Then we shall have earned our tea."

The sea breeze ruffled her hair, which was already escaping from her hat, and it made her crinoline sway in her wake. "If the wind catches me the wrong way, I shall take off into the air. I wish that women could wear trousers."

Lewis chuckled. "Only on the stage, alas."

"Are you serious about giving up acting?"

"I am almost never serious about anything."

"Lewis!"

"Oh, I don't know," he said off-handedly. "I find learning lines that others have written somewhat tedious. I by far prefer to create my own characters."

"Such as Ned Smith, the cabman's friend, the character you adopt when carousing in rough taverns. If, of course, you weren't teasing me."

"No, it's true enough. I am rather fond of Ned, though Ned is too fond of the drink, which is why the cabbies are fond of him. He overtips when he is in his cups."

"What will you do, if you give up the stage?"

"I said I would give up acting, not the theatre. I might try my hand at stage adaptations or directing and I will continue with my reviews, for the meantime. I write as Whyte Tyghe, for the *Globe*, you know."

"I didn't know that. Honestly, Lewis, I can hardly keep up with your many alter egos."

"I lose track of them myself sometimes. Perhaps I shall write a book about my travels to Algeria."

"Good heavens! You are a traveller, too?"

"Everyone should see the world, including you, dear Margaret."

"I would, if I had the means. Would I like Algeria?"

He shook his head decisively. "You must go to a country where your being a female is not a barrier. America, for example. My friend Ira—the actor, you know—he is an American. It is the land of the free, he tells me, though I am not precisely sure I know what that means."

"What would I do in America?" Margaret asked doubtfully. "I don't know anyone there."

"But that is the whole point about travel, whether to America or Algeria or Timbuctoo."

"I nearly went there once," Margaret said, laughing at Lewis's bewildered expression. "Ignore me, do carry on."

"As I was saying, the point about going abroad—and I don't mean Europe, that is too close to home. The point is, Margaret, that you *don't* know anyone and more importantly, no-one knows you. You have no past, and the future is yours to write. I thought of going to America myself actually, and of acting on Broadway which is where all the theatres are, so Ira tells me, but now I have given up that career."

"Perhaps you will become an explorer. Like Dr. Livingstone."

"And disappear forever? Mervyn would like that."

"I still don't understand why your brother dislikes you so much. *I* like you very much."

Lewis pressed her hand. "Because, like me, you are a maverick, though being a female, you are forced to disguise it more." He was silent for a few moments, and when they reached Bray Head, turned towards the sea, leaning on the spray-damp railing of the promenade. "It's not so much what I do that makes Mervyn dislike me, it's the fact that I won't settle to anything. He thinks I'm capricious, and he's probably right, but I don't see anything wrong with that."

"You like to test yourself, that's all."

"Ah, Margaret, you have a generous soul."

"Your brother is worried that if you inherit Powerscourt, you will not be interested enough to maintain it—is that it?"

Lewis shrugged. "I suppose, and I expect he is right about that, too."

"Do you like him?"

"Do you know, I don't think I've ever asked myself that question. Not particularly, is the answer. Mervyn is extremely worthy. But so *very* boring. I mean, deer, honestly? Shall we change the subject?" Lewis took her arm again, and they began to retrace their steps. "What does Julia make of our friendship?"

"Julia doesn't judge."

"Don't bristle. I admire Julia, I'll have you know. I admire anyone who puts up with my brother."

"She is reserved, but just because she doesn't wear her heart on her sleeve doesn't mean she is cold. And she's been very good to me, Lewis. *I* don't know what she thinks of our friendship. I don't even know what *I* think of it. Will it last beyond this visit?"

"You mean, will I forget all about you when I am gone from here? Out of sight, out of mind? No, I am generally thought to be a loyal friend, though the chances of my paying another visit here are low. I don't like to stay where I am not welcome. Mervyn would never deny me my right to come to Powerscourt, but he much prefers if I don't. And Julia—oh, poor Julia, I am afraid I am a constant reminder of her failure to produce an heir."

"Don't say that," Margaret snapped. "It is not Julia's fault that she has not yet had a child."

"Don't bite my head off. As it happens, I agree with you that it is in all likelihood *not* Julia's fault."

"What do you mean by that, Lewis?"

He opened his mouth to answer her, then clearly changed his mind. "Shall we see if they serve tea at the Turkish baths? I had planned to take you to the International Hotel, but I heard that the baths have reopened as some sort of assembly rooms. When they were first built, the staff wore scarlet dressing gowns and Turkish slippers. It would be fun if they still did. What do you think, Margaret?"

She thought his attempt to distract her glaringly obvious. What was it he had decided against telling her about Lord Powerscourt? But though Lewis had a vicious streak, and though there was clearly no love lost between the two brothers, he had refrained. She respected him for that. "It sounds fun," Margaret answered. "Will I be permitted to smoke a Turkish pipe?"

He pressed her arm, smiling down warmly at her. "Back in the day, one could loll about on velvet divans and smoke. I was never there in its heyday, but I'm told there were fountains and palm trees and domed ceilings set with glass stars. Let us hope the new owners have not stripped it of all its ambiance."

"And let us hope they serve tea. The sea air has made me very hungry."

A WEEK LATER, MARGARET WAS ensconced in the octagon library, at the desk which she had claimed for her own. The door to the room was decorated to look like one of the bookshelves, complete with imitation books. *The Key to Paradise* was the tome covering the lock, hinting at a sense of humour, which ruled out the current viscount being responsible. She was staring into space when it opened, and Lewis entered.

"I thought I'd find you here. I came to tell you that I've decided to leave tomorrow."

"Tomorrow! That's rather sudden, isn't it? You've been here for less than a fortnight."

He began to pull books at random from the shelves, pursing his lips at each one before replacing it. "Mervyn is due back soon."

"Not until next week. Can't you stay a few more days?"

"My mind is made up. I won't risk being here if he decides to arrive early. Does Julia always turn the house upside down and inside out when her husband is due home?"

"She likes everything to be perfect. Is there anything wrong with that?"

"No, I suppose not. What are you doing? Are you working on that little book of stories?" He pulled the notebook from her and began to flick through it. "I agree with your friend Lochiel: you should have them published, they are quite out of the ordinary. And, of course, your name on the cover will ensure that they will receive lots of attention in the press."

Margaret shuddered. "One of the best things about being here is that the press have forgotten all about me. I have absolutely no desire whatsoever to have my name in the newspapers again, for any reason."

"Understandable, though I think you could use it to your advantage if you wished." He rifled through the pages, frowning. "You need illustrations to go with these. I could dash them off for you."

"Oh, would you?"

"I could, but they would be too good. Now, don't give me one of your haughty looks, I mean that the stories have a childlike quality to them. They need drawings in a similar vein. Perhaps one of your star pupils?" Lewis set the book down again. "Just a thought. Come for a walk with me, will you? I want to talk to you."

"That sounds very serious."

He quirked an eyebrow. "I do have a serious side; I simply keep it well hidden. Come on, let's get out into the sunshine or the rain—I have no idea what the weather is doing. Let's stick to the gardens as a precaution. I am in the mood for a little introspection."

"I really will miss you," Margaret said, a few moments later as they walked arm-in-arm through the walled garden. "Have you decided what you are going to do when you get back to London—assuming that London is your destination?"

"For the moment. I have itchy feet, the one trait I share with Mervyn. I am thinking I might voyage to China."

"China! Good heavens."

"Or perhaps not. Perhaps I'll get married, if I can find a female who understands me as you do, my dear."

"If this is the prelude to a proposal, Lewis, I should warn you—"

He burst into a peal of laughter. "You deserve better than me, Margaret, and I need someone—oh, I need someone like Julia. A nice understanding woman who will make no demands and who will be waiting patiently for me when I come home from my travels. No," he added, patting her hand, "don't subject me to one of your reprimands. I admire Julia, I really do, but I did not ask you to come for a walk with me to talk about Julia or even myself, believe it or not. Let us talk about you. What are *you* going to do when I am gone?"

"It will be very dull here without you. I shall carry on at the school, I suppose."

"But they have Breda now, don't they?"

"They will still need me at the school for story time."

"When you publish your book, the children will be able to read the stories for themselves."

"That's a lovely thought. I wish that I could give every child a copy, but books are so expensive unless I—oh my goodness, you have just given me the most wonderful idea. Lewis Strange Wingfield, I do believe you are a genius."

He preened. "I know. What was my wonderful idea exactly?"

"I could have the stories published as chap-books—you know, like the lesson books they have in the school. They are very cheap to make." Margaret's smile faded. "Though probably not cheap enough. I don't really have any money."

"Speak to Julia. I know for a fact that Mervyn gives her an allowance for charitable purposes. I would think your books qualify."

"I didn't know that. Do you think she will help me?"

"I am sure she will be delighted to. She's not very happy, is she? She covers it up well, but her smile is sometimes quite pained."

"All she wants is a baby. It seems so tragic that people like Breda's mother get more children than they can cope with, while people like Julia . . ."

"Perhaps this time when my brother is home he will—they will—oh, you know. I hope they do resolve the matter. Aside from my not wanting to inherit Powerscourt, it would be wrong."

"In what way?"

Lewis paused to open the gate that led to the Green Pond. "I was only two when the Sixth Viscount died, and my mother married Londonderry two years later—or Castlereagh, as he was then. But there is a rumour, a persistent rumour, that my mother and he were lovers before she was widowed. That I am not a Wingfield at all, but Londonderry's bastard."

"Lewis! That is shocking!"

"Is it?" He frowned down at the pond, then shrugged, heading for the path once more. "The man whose name I bear died when I was an infant. The man whose blood in all likelihood runs in my veins has been locked up in an asylum for the last five years. Which would I choose as my father? Does it change who I am?"

Lewis led the way to a wooden bench. "Sit with me a moment, Margaret, I'm going to be that rare thing for me, deadly serious. You are wasting away here. I know you are busy making yourself useful—and though Julia doesn't say much, she appreciates your company—but don't you think you've been hiding away long enough? There is a big world beyond Powerscourt's gates."

"I know there is, and I would love to see it, but how? I have no means to support myself . . ."

"Never mind that for now. Do you agree or not?"

"Yes, I do. I admire Julia, but I could never be like her. Every time I try to do what is expected of me, I fail."

"Then stop trying. That is my advice to you."

She laughed. "Is it really that simple? I don't want to do what someone else tells me, I want to please myself. I *know* that is a frightfully selfish thing to say. . . ."

"It is music to my ears. If you don't stand up for who you are, then no-one else will."

"I've never thought of it that way."

"And here endeth the lesson. Be yourself, Margaret. You are different. Find a way to embrace that."

"But how?"

"Now that, I'm afraid, I can't help you with. We each need to follow our own path. I have chosen mine; you must forge your own. What is stopping you from leaving here?"

"Who, you mean. My father."

"There you are, then; that is the obstacle you must overcome."

"That is easier said than done."

"I never said it would be easy. I do believe it's starting to rain. Come on." Lewis pulled her to her feet, shaking his head at the tears which filled her eyes. "What are those for?"

"Embrace being different. No-one has ever said that to me before. I will try, though I don't know how."

He kissed her cheek. "You'll find a way. As I said, it won't be easy. There will be tears, and times when you will ask yourself, is it worth it? But take it from one who knows. Ultimately, it is."

The Rectory, Lambeth, 26 July 1867

Dear Lady Margaret,

What a lovely surprise to hear from you after all this time, and for such an unexpected and exciting reason. Yes, Billy does still sell his drawings at the market and, yes, he still has Muffin with him and of course he remembers you. When I asked him if he would be interested in doing some drawings to illustrate your stories, I thought he would burst with pride. He can't read, as you suspected, but I have arranged for Verity's little girl Nellie to read the stories to him. In fact, they began this morning, working at a table in the church hall. The money you sent was more than enough for pencils, paints, and paper. I have given Billy an advance of a quarter of the fee you so generously offer, and will take the precaution of paying him the rest over a number of weeks.

I hope you will excuse me if I take the liberty of saying that you sound in much better spirits, and I am both glad and relieved if that is the case. All is well here. I have finally managed to recruit someone to help with the housework, thank goodness. And as for my brother— time is a great healer.

I look forward very much to seeing your work and Billy's drawings in print. A chap-book is an excellent idea. I am sure we will be able to find the funds to buy some as Christmas gifts from the parish if it is published by then. I will send you the first of Billy's artistic endeavours very soon.

> *With very best wishes,*
> *Susannah Elmhirst*

Donald Cameron of Lochiel
to Lady Margaret

Rome, 28 August 1867

Dear Margaret,

What times we live in! I know you are not much interested in politics, but the passing of the Second Reform Act is such a momentous event, I felt I must mention it. The number of people who can vote in the next election will be more than doubled—and, yes, I know that they are all men, for Mr. Mill's amendment to include the female sex failed dismally, but still it represents significant progress. At the risk of sounding like the rather staid gentleman you once assumed me to be, I find myself increasingly drawn to the idea of taking a more active role in politics, and am contemplating standing as a member of Parliament. At the grand old age of thirty-two, I have a hankering to end my sojourn on the Continent and return home to settle down.

My home is the Achnacarry Estate in Invernesshire, near the little village of Spean Bridge, and just north of the town of Fort William. The land is rugged, with some fine woods, and the castle itself sits low on the terrain, not far from Loch Arkaig, where I am thinking of building a new pier to allow a steamer to berth. The lands were forfeited after the '45 was lost at Culloden, for my family fought for the Young Pretender. It was my grandfather and my namesake who had them restored, and who laid the foundations of the "New Achnacarry." Alas, he was profligate, and when he died he left my father with a half-finished home and a mountain of debts. My father completed the house but continued the tradition of spending beyond his means, which is why I have had to make my own way in life. But I have prospered, enough to turn my mind to improving the estate and making a home of it. The castle is in the Scots baronial style. I think you would like it, Margaret. I know that I would very much like to show it to you one day.

With regard to your latest letter, I am delighted to learn that Lady Julia has been so forthcoming with the charitable funds for your children's book. As to your decision to write to your father—we promised always to be honest with each other, did we not? While I admire the sentiment that lies behind the approach, I confess that I think you are acting prematurely. I assumed that you were content at Powerscourt. I know that Lewis Wingfield's visit gave you pause for thought, but Mervyn considers his brother to be a somewhat erratic and unreliable character. Is he the reason you are suddenly impatient for change? What would be the harm in waiting until October, for example, when you come of age? Writing directly to the duke, and not through the intermediary of your mother, also seems unnecessarily risky.

I will say no more on this for the present. Do not take this mild censure amiss, I beg of you. Please believe that I have, above all, your interests at heart. You say that you are indifferent to your father, but I fear you will discover, in his rejection or his silence, that you are mistaken. I know how deeply hurt you have been by his actions in the past. I only wish to spare you being hurt further.

> With very best wishes always,
> Donald

Chapter Twenty-Seven

Thursday, 10 October 1867

M ARGARET SAT IN THE WINDOW seat of her bedchamber, her birthday letters spread out in front of her. Mama, Victoria, and Mary had all written to congratulate her on her coming of age.

There was nothing from Louise. Margaret had braced herself for this, for the two brief, bland missives she had written to Louise had remained unanswered or may never have been read. All the same, the continuing silence hurt. She and Louise had marked so many milestones in each other's lives, she could not believe Louise had forgotten this one. Unless the fears she had expressed at Helena's wedding had been realised? What exactly had she been afraid of? Frowning as she tried to recall the conversation, Margaret began to doubt her own assumptions. Had Louise been exaggerating the situation, or even made it up entirely, wishing in a perverse way to trump Margaret's romance with one of her own? Despite the fact that she was younger, she always liked to think of herself as the more worldly, the more sophisticated of the two of them.

Whatever the truth, Margaret would in all likelihood never know. All she did know from Mama, was that Louise was still keeping the queen constant company both in public and in private. She had been at the State Opening of Parliament in February. In May, she was one of the godparents to Bertie and Alix's daughter, her new niece bearing her own name. And in August she and the queen had visited Floors Castle, where Margaret's father had been one of the guests, though Mama had not been present. If there had been any hint of scandal, surely Louise would, like Margaret, have been hidden from public scrutiny? Then again, perhaps she had learned from Margaret's painful lesson that to do so would heighten speculation to fever pitch.

Margaret sighed impatiently. Wherever Louise was, whatever her state of mind, she wasn't thinking of her former friend on this, her birthday. Nor, it seemed, was Donald, which did surprise her, though it could be that his letter was still in the post. By far the biggest surprise, however, was the letter from her father.

She stared incredulously at the single sheet of paper bearing the Buccleuch crest. She had given up hope of receiving a reply to the proposal she had sent her father back in August. She had agonised for weeks over the precise wording. Donald had cautioned her not to expect a response, and as the weeks passed, she had reconciled herself to having failed. The urge to write again had been strong, but she had nothing to add to what she had already said, and she would not weaken her case by pleading. She had resisted the temptation to ask Mama for the duke's reaction, warning her in advance that she had written and going so far as to ask her not to intervene.

Margaret read the letter again to make sure she had not misunderstood, but the contents, written in her father's familiar scrawl, were unambiguous. *I have carefully considered your proposal, and have reluctantly decided to accede to your request.*

Her father had granted her wish to live independently, awarding her the full settlement she requested, the equivalent of the dowry which he would no longer be required to offer. She would be able to live well, to travel without scrimping, and she would certainly not be required to hide away in a little cottage subsisting on bacon fat and dry bread. There were strict terms and conditions attached, of course. Wherever she chose to live, it could not be in England or Scotland or, as he put it in his usual grandiose terms, *on the same sovereign soil as any of my residences*. Any hint of a public scandal, and her annuity would be instantly revoked. The duke had finally accepted that she would never do his bidding, acknowledging her right to choose a different life for herself, but he would continue to judge her.

Let him! His opinion of her no longer mattered. She was free. Standing in front of the mirror, Margaret watched a slow smile spread across her face. Today she was twenty one years old, and she really had come of age. Her gift to herself was to wipe the slate clean. She was going to take Lewis's advice and start being herself.

The question was, what sort of life did she envisage? And just as important, where? The obvious choice was to travel to the Continent. There was a big world, as Lewis had said, beyond Powerscourt's gates. She could visit the canals of Venice, the boulevards of Paris, the Acropolis, the Colosseum. Though Lewis had actually suggested that she travel further afield, to America perhaps. The shared language was an attraction, but it seemed too big a first step to seriously contemplate.

Ought she to contemplate it nevertheless? Was crossing the Channel too tentative a step? Her father's reach was long, the tentacles of her family connections extensive. On the Continent she would still be Lady Margaret Montagu Douglas Scott, the second daughter of the Duke of Buccleuch, with her scandalous history trailing behind her in a cloud of half-remembered gossip. Eyebrows would be raised at her purposeless meanderings without family or a husband in tow. Which raised another question: Who would accompany her, for she couldn't travel on her own. She would have to find a chaperone of some description for the sake of propriety.

But there was no need to make such a momentous decision rashly or on a whim. She had only just discovered she was a woman of independent means. There was time enough to think about what that meant.

Margaret gave a little skip of delight. She would tell Julia her news later, but the sun was coming out for the first time in days, and Pennygael was overdue an outing. Hurrying to her wardrobe, unbuttoning her gown as she did, she pulled out her riding habit and began to change.

As she jammed her hat onto her head and swept the long skirt of her riding habit over her arm, there was a tap on her bedchamber door. "You're wanted in the morning room, Lady Margaret," the maid informed her.

It would most likely be something to do with the school. With her husband once again absent, Julia had started taking a much more active interest. Now that Enniskerry had been accepted into the national school system, she was overseeing all the necessary work to ensure that it would be the best equipped in the system. A gift to each child of a copy of Margaret's stories was one of Julia's aims, and so she had been harrying the printer into producing the first proofs as soon as he had received the last of Billy's illustrations. Perhaps the volume had arrived!

Margaret hurried to the morning room, only to stop short in the doorway. The sole occupant of the room was a tall man with his back to her, gazing out the window. Thinking the maid must have been mistaken, she was about to leave when he turned and smiled. "Good morning, Margaret."

She stared blankly at the stranger who was crossing the room towards her. He was tall and well-built, plainly dressed, clean-shaven, and rather handsome. He looked oddly familiar. "Donald? Good heavens, is it really you? Oh my goodness, I barely recognised you without the beard."

"Does it really make such a difference?" he asked, smiling.

"Yes, it really does." He had a decidedly square jaw, which had been completely obscured before, and there was a dimple in his chin. He wore his hair shorter than she recalled, neatly and most unfashionably trimmed around his ears without any side-whiskers. "You are *much* improved," Margaret said. Realising that this was a rather a back-handed compliment, she hastily added, "I mean transformed."

Donald laughed, taking her hands in his. "As refreshingly candid as ever. No need to ask if you are well. I can see you are glowing with health. I thought I would surprise you, and congratulate you on your coming of age in person."

His smile made her feel oddly breathless. This was the man who had been her regular correspondent for almost a year now. A man she called her dear friend, in whom she confided, who she thought she had come to know well, but whom she had not thought to actually meet in person. Seeing him in this new, attractive guise unsettled her.

"When I had no letter from you," Margaret said, "I thought you had forgotten."

"Never! Happy birthday, Margaret." He lifted her hand to his lips and kissed her fingertips.

Blushing wildly, she snatched her hand away. "It's so strange," she said, her thoughts jangling. "I have come to know you so well from your letters, but I feel almost shy seeing you in person. No, don't take that amiss. I'm delighted to see you. Does Julia know you are here?"

"No. I wanted to surprise you."

"You have certainly succeeded. Are you planning to stay?"

"That very much depends on you."

What did he mean? She didn't want to ask, for she had the feeling that it would change everything between them and she had no idea how she felt about that. First the letter from her father, and now this. "I was just about to go out riding," Margaret said. "Will you join me?"

"An excellent idea. It's a lovely day, and I am sure that Wingfield won't mind my borrowing one of his mounts. The fresh air will clear my head. Then we can talk."

DONALD, ASTRIDE A STRAPPING GREY, slowed from a gallop to a canter as they entered the woodland. He rode well, handling the stallion with a quiet mastery without being showy about it. Beside him, Margaret's surprised delight at his sudden appearance out of the blue had given way to a definite apprehension. This was Donald, her friend, she reminded herself, but he didn't *look* like the man she imagined when she read his letters. It wasn't only the loss of the beard; it was his smile, she decided, which had not been the chaste smile of an old friend. And the way he had kissed her hand. More perturbingly the effect that kiss had had on her senses.

As they neared the waterfall she slanted him another glance, only to find that he was doing the same. Their gazes met and the world tilted and realigned itself, for in that brief moment there was no mistaking what had passed between them.

Donald dismounted. Nervously, Margaret slid off Pennygael, who led the way to the pool, the grey following her. The fresh-fallen leaves were gold, chestnut, and burnished amber underfoot. The sun glinted down on the cascade, making diamonds of the curtain of water as it crashed into the pool. "Isn't it entrancing?" she asked, joining him.

"Breath-taking," he agreed, turning towards her. "But I personally prefer this view."

She read his intention clearly in his eyes as he reached for her, and she made no attempt to evade him as he pulled her into his arms. He was going to kiss her, and she wanted him to. Alarm bells were clanging, but only faintly as she tilted her face to his. He smelled of shaving soap and wet wool, and his coat was damp with the spray from the waterfall. She lifted her hand to his cheek and felt his sharp intake of breath at her touch.

"Margaret," he said, his voice both rough and gentle at the same time.

The roaring of the waterfall became a roaring in her ears as their lips met. There was no slow, tender preliminary to this kiss, only a clamouring need. Donald's arms tightened around her, and heat flooded her body as she clung to him, urging him to deepen the kiss, though he needed little encouragement, muttering her name and pulling her closer. They kissed. Deep, starving kisses, adult kisses, their tongues tangling, hands clutching and clinging. Only as they stumbled, precariously close to the edge of the pool, did they stop, coming shakily to their senses.

Donald swore under his breath, an odd smile on his face. "I had intended the kiss to follow the speech, not the other way around."

Too late, far too late, Margaret realised what he meant. No matter what she felt for him, no matter that she had already made her feelings very clear, she wasn't ready for that. "Donald . . ."

"No, please, let me speak." He clasped her hands in his, smiling at her so tenderly she caught her breath. "It must be obvious to you how I feel about you, but I know how much you like plain dealing. I love you. There you have it."

Her fingers tightened involuntarily in his. There was no doubting his sincerity, nor any point in denying her own feelings, but it would be wrong. She had no idea how she knew this, but she did. She dare not speak, lest the words he was so patently desperate to hear escape her mouth.

"You look surprised," Donald prompted when she remained silent. "Surely you must have been aware of the growing affection in my letters? Ever since that fateful night, when I found you conversing with Mr. Scott, I have been drawn to you. Love has crept up on me slowly, as we became firm friends through our correspondence. I have never sought love, or a wife, but now that I've found you, I know you are my journey's end. Will you marry me, Margaret, and be my companion in life?"

She had never in her life longed to say yes more. Yes, she loved him. Yes, she would marry him. Yes, she would share his life. But

the words stuck in her throat. She couldn't breathe. "I'm so sorry."
As his tender smile faltered, she almost changed her mind, but
she had learned many lessons in the last two years. She could not
risk having her entire future decided by one passionate kiss.
Carefully, Margaret disengaged her hands.

"I don't understand," Donald said. "Have I misjudged your
feelings?"

"No. Yes. It's not that I don't—though I hadn't realised until
now."

"You need time. I thought I had prepared the ground, but I see
now I have been too opaque. This is a momentous decision, I will
not rush you."

It was so tempting to agree, to delay the inevitable, but she
had learned the hard way to trust her instincts. She had only
just obtained her independence. She could not immediately
surrender it. She wanted to do what Lewis had urged her to
do: to become herself, whatever that might entail. She wanted
to make her own mistakes, to live without having to accommodate someone else's wishes. Given that, she couldn't in all
conscience agree to marry Donald. It would be dishonest and
cruel, and she loved him too much to do that. Though she would
have to cause him pain.

"I'm sorry, Donald." Was she really doing this? She gazed at
him, the man she had only just fallen in love with, knowing that
she might be throwing away her one and only chance for happiness. "I'm sorry," she said again, and there was a steely resolution
in her tone that made his smile fade. "I don't need time to consider.
I simply can't marry you."

He did not speak for a moment, and when he did, his tone was
gruff. "May I ask why?"

It would be so much easier if he would be furious with her, or
even blame her just a little. But then he wouldn't be Donald, and
she wouldn't find this so heartbreakingly difficult. No matter what

it cost her, she owed him the truth. "Until today, I've thought of you only as a very dear friend, and one of the few people—perhaps even the only one—who has always accepted me as I am."

"Why would I change you? I love you as you are."

"With all my numerous imperfections." Margaret swallowed the lump in her throat.

"Which are far outweighed by your many, many excellent qualities."

She knew he meant it. Donald never said anything he didn't mean, and once again she was swayed. But it would be *wrong*. "Before I met you I thought I lacked any admirable qualities, but thanks to you, my dear friend, I know that to be untrue. You like me, warts and all, and have given me the encouragement and the confidence to believe in myself. I owe you a great deal. I trust your judgement more than anyone's save my own. Whenever I am in a quandary I ask myself, what would Donald think?" Margaret drew a shaky breath, for she knew now what she had to say, and knew that it would put an end to everything between them. "And now you honour me by asking me to be so much more than a friend and I am so very tempted, because though I had no idea until we—until today that my feelings for you are real and run deep. But I am not ready to be a wife, far less a mother. In all honesty, I've no idea whether I will ever be ready. I am so very, very sorry."

Still he said nothing. Margaret took another steadying breath, acutely aware of his hurt, confused gaze. "I had a letter from my father this morning." Briefly, she explained the terms of her annuity. "So you see, I now have the means to live my own life, to make my own decisions without having to consult anyone else. I've never had that privilege before. I've never been free. If I agreed to marry you . . ."

"You think that marriage to me would enslave you?"

"No!" She made to touch his arm, but he jerked away. "Of course not, but I would be your wife, Donald, and as your wife I would inevitably be changed. I couldn't simply be me; I would be part of something else."

"You would be one half of us. Isn't that the best of both worlds?"

Her mother would think so. Most women would think so. It would be the safe solution, the conventionally acceptable one, undoubtedly an attractive one, but that was not enough. "I know you can't understand. I struggle to explain it myself, but it would be the wrong choice for me, Donald. I cannot marry you."

"Would your answer have been different had your father's letter not arrived this morning? No, don't answer that. I don't want you to marry me because I'm your best option. I want you to marry me because . . ." He shook his head despondently. "Oh, what's the use? I won't beg. May I ask what you plan to do now that you are no longer obliged to remain here?"

It came to her then that she had to remove herself far from temptation for both their sakes. She had to make her decision irrevocable. "I'm considering going to America."

"America! What the devil! Why? Who do you know there?"

"Not a soul. That's the whole point."

"Can you honestly be thinking of embarking on a journey to the other side of the world to a country you know nothing about in order to be, what—anonymous?"

"No-one will be able to tell me what to do and when. They won't make their minds up about me before they meet me. I won't be *stifled* by expectations."

"You have no idea what such a drastic upheaval would entail. The practicalities of it for one thing. Where would you stay? Dear God, Margaret, what you are suggesting is terrifying. If you must travel, why not go to the Continent and take the Grand Tour like everyone else?"

"It's not far enough away from you, from my family, from the world I know and which thinks it knows me. I know it won't be easy, I know that I might fail spectacularly, but I will regret not having the courage of my convictions if I don't try."

"So you must go to America," Donald said with a twisted smile. "A new world fit for a new Margaret, is that it?"

Finally, at this evidence of his understanding, a tear escaped her. She nodded. "Whatever that means. I'm so sorry."

"Not as sorry as I am. I wish you all the luck in the world. You will need it." He stooped to pick up his hat. "If you will excuse me, I will ride back alone."

"Donald . . ."

"Don't say you're sorry again. I'm not prepared to settle for second best either." He pulled her to him, hugging her tightly, briefly, then let her go. "Goodbye, Margaret."

She watched him in stricken silence as he mounted the grey stallion and rode off, before her legs gave way and she slumped to the ground. If she had glanced up, she would have seen him pull up to look back with a wistful expression, but instead she dropped her head into her hands. She had just made either the best or the worst decision of her entire life.

Chapter Twenty-Eight

TWO HOURS LATER, AN EMOTIONALLY drained Margaret was waylaid before she could reach the sanctity of her bedroom. "What on earth is going on?" Julia demanded, guiding her into her sitting room. "First Lochiel turns up completely out of the blue, and the pair of you go off together before I have the opportunity to ask if he intends to spend the night. Then he returns alone and informs me he is going straight back to Dublin and not even staying for your birthday dinner. He was very abrupt, almost rude, and I thought—"

"Donald proposed," Margaret said baldly, sitting down wearily on one of the chairs by the window. "And I turned him down." A lump rose in her throat as she recalled the stricken look on his face when he left, but she swallowed hard. "He said he loves me, and I think I might love him, too, but I cannot, Julia. I can't marry him."

"Good heavens, whyever not? Admittedly he is not the man your father chose for you, but he is eminently respectable and an excellent catch. You surely cannot be worried that the duke would object to the match?"

"I don't want or need my father's approval," Margaret snapped. "Sorry," she added, immediately contrite, "I am, as you will have surmised, a little overwrought. I was not expecting . . ." She spread her hands helplessly.

"Has there been no hint in his letters of Lochiel's intentions?"

"If there were, I missed them."

"You need time to adjust, that is all. I am sure he thought it a wildly romantic gesture to come here unannounced and propose on your birthday, but it would have been far better if he had adopted a more conventional approach. Doubtless that is what he will do, when his pride has recovered a little."

"It is not his pride but his heart I have wounded. If you are imagining that he will enlist my father's help in persuading me to accept his suit, you are much mistaken. Donald knows me far better than that." Margaret's lip trembled. "His coming here today, his *wildly romantic gesture*, as you put it, was exactly the kind of proposal I would have wanted. If only I could have accepted it." A stray tear escaped, but she scrubbed it away. "But I *could* not."

Julia frowned. "I don't understand. If he really does understand you so well . . ."

"He does! He knows me better than I do myself at times."

"Do you know how rare a quality that is in a man? And yet you have refused him?"

"Yes!"

"Is it that you don't return his feelings?"

"No. I didn't know that I had those sort of feelings for him until today but . . ." Margaret dropped her head into her hands. Julia was making her doubt herself. Ought she to have agreed? But no, no, no, it still felt completely wrong. She lifted her head. "I am simply not ready to be married, Julia, and I told him so. What's more, thanks to my father, I don't need to marry. I had a letter from him today. Wait here, I will get it."

Thinking that it would explain far better than she could, Margaret quickly retrieved the letter from her bedroom, then handed it over, watching anxiously as Julia perused it. But when she reached the end, there was no clearing of her brow, only a deepening of her frown. "I find this shocking in its calculated coldness."

"The point is I'm free. I am now of independent means."

"The duke is paying you off. This is the equivalent of a—a

divorce settlement between you and your family," Julia said, her hands shaking as she folded the letter back up and handed it over. "Your father is disowning you. If you accept his terms, you will never see your mother or any of your sisters and brothers again."

Which of course Margaret understood, though having Julia articulate it made it sickeningly real. "But if I do not accept, I must remain here in limbo, quite powerless."

"I would be happy for you to remain here, but Lochiel has offered you an alternative."

"I won't marry Donald simply to escape my father's clutches."

"You have admitted that you love him. He has declared his love for you. Even more importantly, Margaret, you are true friends," Julia said earnestly. "Do you have any notion how unusual that is, between a husband and wife? Lochiel has *everything* you could want in a husband. As his wife, you would be re-established in society, accepted back into the family fold, and you'd have the chance to create your own family, too. That is so much more than most women can dream of, yet you . . ." She stared at her, shaking her head. "What more can you possibly want?"

"I don't know," Margaret replied wretchedly, knowing that she had already been offered a great deal more than Julia herself had. "I don't want more. I want—I want something different. I know how fortunate I am to have received such an offer. When Donald proposed I was sorely tempted, of course I was, but I knew it would be a mistake."

"A mistake! To do what every woman aspires to, to marry and hopefully raise a family? I simply don't understand you. Do you realise what you are throwing away?"

"I know it must seem perverse to you. I can't explain it, I simply know that it would be wrong for me."

"And what of Lochiel?" There were spots of colour in Julia's cheeks. "How did you explain your rejection to the poor man who has come all this way to lay his heart at your feet?"

"Don't! I pray you, don't make me feel any worse than I already do. I told him that I was not ready to be a wife."

"And so he is to wait patiently until you are ready, then?"

"No! I don't know if I will ever be ready. I made that clear. I would never be so cruel as to hold out the prospect of false hope, and especially not to Donald. I told him that I must learn to be myself, and now I have the means . . ."

"So you are accepting your father's thirty pieces of silver?"

Margaret jumped to her feet, leaning her forehead against the cool windowpane as the raindrops rolled down the outside. "That's unfair! I am already estranged from my family, Julia. I am already forced to accept that I may never see Mama—" Her voice broke. She cleared her throat. "I have had no expectations of seeing my family again since I arrived here. The settlement my father offers doesn't make that situation any worse, but it does offer me the freedom to live my own life, without being dependent upon anyone or, more importantly, responsible to anyone. I can be myself. Whatever that means." She smiled grimly. "I intend to find out."

"How?"

"I'm going to America."

Julia's jaw dropped. "Please tell me you are jesting."

Margaret resumed her seat. "I'm deadly serious, actually."

"Is this Lewis's doing? Did he put this ridiculous notion into your head?"

"No, not really. Well, I suppose he sowed the seed with his talk of his own travels."

"For the love of God, Margaret, if you must travel, why not do what everyone else does, and tour round Europe?"

"That is what Donald suggested."

"Lochiel is a very sensible man."

"But I don't want to be sensible." Despite all she had been through, the hurt she had caused Donald, a bubble of excitement began to form, quelling her doubts. She had been right to refuse him. And America—yes, that, too, was the right choice of destination. "I need to be somewhere no-one knows me. A place where I can be myself, without the weight of expectation my life entails. Do you see?"

"No, I don't," Julia said tartly, looking quite baffled. "Who will protect you from danger? Who will introduce you to society? Where will you live? Dear heavens, even the journey—those transatlantic liners sink all the time. It is also so far away. Half a world away, in fact. If anything happened . . ."

"That's the whole point: I will have no choice but to stand on my own two feet."

"No, Margaret, you are being wholly irresponsible. When you have considered the matter more rationally—"

"I don't want to be rational, Julia." Margaret leapt to her feet again, smiling, spreading her arms. "I am the black sheep of the family, the outcast. Why on earth would I be sensible?"

"I think you have lost your senses."

"No, I haven't, I promise." She took Julia's hands in hers. "You have been so good to me, and so kind. Don't be angry with me, please. Can you not try to understand—"

Julia snatched her hands away. "Think of the ramifications of what you are proposing, Margaret. It seems to me that you are deliberately choosing the most unconventional option, simply to thumb your nose at the duke."

"My father may choose to interpret it that way, but I can no more dictate his thoughts than he can mine."

"You are truly set on it, then?"

"Yes." There was that fizz of excitement inside her again. The future beckoned enticingly for the first time in many months. The prospect of facing the unknown was terrifying, but it was also irresistible. "Yes," Margaret said firmly. "I truly am set on it."

Julia sighed, getting to her feet. "Very well, then. I suppose we must turn our thoughts to the practicalities. You will need a travelling companion for a start. You may call it serendipity if you like, but I had a letter the other day from my aunt Marion. She is not really my aunt—she is a friend of my mother's who was widowed a couple of years ago now. She has no children, and her diplomat husband left her rather badly off. She is forced to live in genteel poverty in Twickenham but has spent most of her life in rather more exotic locations. If you were to offer to pay her return fare and take her on as a companion for a few months until you are settled, I am fairly certain she would leap at the opportunity. You need more than a companion, you need someone well-travelled and worldly wise, and Aunt Marion is most certainly that."

"Do you think we will get on?"

Julia permitted herself a small smile. "In addition to being extremely practical, she is very outspoken and rather eccentric. I think the pair of you will get along very well indeed."

Montagu House, London, 14 November 1867

Dearest Margaret,

I am at a loss to know how to respond to your last letter, which set my emotions in turmoil. A situation from which I am not yet recovered, I hasten to add.

Naturally I was aware of the settlement the duke was offering you, though I was not privy to the precise terms, nor did he consult me regarding them. I hoped his acceding to your wish to be independent indicated a softening in his attitude towards you, and was encouraged enough to raise the possibility of my visiting you at Powerscourt. The duke made it very clear that there is no prospect of this. Against my better judgement I attempted to persuade him to change his mind. Not only did my appeal fall on stony ground, I fear it aroused his suspicions, for he challenged me on the subject of our correspondence. I could not tell a blatant lie.

The duke was outraged and ordered me to cease all contact forthwith. My dear daughter, though it breaks my heart to write this, for the foreseeable future I must ask you to confine your correspondence to your eldest sister. Victoria will give me your news, and will relay back my own. You have fought too hard for your independence for me to risk it being withdrawn. I pray you understand, and pray, too, that this is a temporary situation though how it is to be resolved, Lord knows.

Margaret, your decision to make a new home in America fills me with terror and admiration in equal measure. That you signally fail to explain your reasons makes me smile. Your heart has always been your true guide, and you have finally recognised this. For that I commend you, but why, oh why must your instincts compel you to embrace danger? Your letter is full of optimism, when you have every reason to feel trepidation. You confess to fear, but at the same time you dismiss it. I cannot decide whether this is brave or foolish.

~~*If something happened to you while you are so far away, beyond reach*~~
~~*As your mother, I must always live in fear for your safety*~~

The travelling companion proposed by Lady Julia will, I trust, afford you some protection and provide good counsel. I do hope that you will take pleasure in each other's company, too, and become friends as well as companions.

It is ironic that our estrangement has brought us to a mutual understanding, as Mother and Daughter, through our letters, do you not agree? Your father will never understand you, but I do. Therefore, no matter my own reservations about your decision, my fear for your wellbeing, and my fervent desire to hold you and to keep you safe, what I must do, what you need most from me, is to let you go with my blessing and very best wishes. A mother's love is enduring, and it is strong. It knows no boundaries and can stretch as easily across the Atlantic as the Irish Sea. Your courage will be tested, Margaret. There will be times when you feel quite alone, when you will be forced to make difficult decisions; and no doubt there will be occasions when your judgement, and your resolve, falter. At those points, remember that you have my love, that I hold you in my heart, and that I am with you in spirit.

I have but one request to make of you, and do so only after much painful soul searching. Your father has specified that your allowance will be discontinued in the event of your being the cause of fresh scandal. You have assured me, and I don't doubt you believe it, that there is no reason to fear that occurring. Your intentions are always pure, but the outcome of your actions at times— You do understand, my dear, what I am saying? For your own sake, but for mine, too, I beg you to have a care not to rock this precariously balanced boat.

I have said more than enough. I confess I have never written a letter

such as this. No-one who knows me would believe me capable of such
an emotional missive, but I assure you it comes from the heart, and
every sentiment expressed is deeply felt.

You are in my prayers every night.

With much love,
Mama

P.S. I enclose a copy of a book, The Englishwoman in America, *written*
by a Miss Isabella Bird, which you may find enlightening. When I
discovered that Miss Bird's travels were funded by her father, I could
not resist purchasing it, though I fear you will find it more moralising
than informative.

Princess Louise to Lady Margaret

Osborne House, Isle of Wight, 20 December 1867

Dear Margaret,

Since we arrived at Osborne a few days ago, I have had some precious time to myself, for the queen is much occupied with the furor following the Fenian bombing at Clerkenwell and her ministers' concerns for her personal safety. The Irish republicans' plot to kidnap her from Balmoral was foiled, but we are now told they were also plotting to assassinate her, and attempts are currently being made to apprehend the American conspirators aboard their ship as they cross the Atlantic. I mention this, obviously, because of your letter, which I received just before we left Windsor, though I have only now found the time to read it. Having heard nothing from you for many months, I was astonished to learn that you, too, are planning to traverse the Atlantic, abandoning your friends and family for the New World. And so I, who had previously considered myself one of your oldest and dearest friends, must finally relinquish any hope of ever seeing you again.

Our parting, at Helena's wedding a year past July, was difficult for me to bear. Your exile could have been avoided had you honoured your parents' wishes and heeded my advice and agreed to the long-anticipated betrothal, but you chose not to do so. Our resultant separation has weighed heavily on me. You were aware of my own extremely awkward situation, and yet elected to place yourself in a position where you could provide me with no comfort. Though I naturally made little of this, in my efforts to spare your feelings, I was forced to endure a period of prolonged suffering while you established yourself in Ireland, leaving me bereft of a confidant.

Relations since then between myself and Her Majesty have been fraught. I was forced to continue in her service in the public eye in order to quell suspicion. However, despite having succeeded beyond her expectations, my credit with her remains very low, her esteem for me in tatters.

At this time, when I am more in need of a good, loyal friend *than ever, I hear the news of your emigration! I will not burden you with the pain this news has inflicted upon me. Instead, I will wish you well in your new life, Margaret. I hope you enjoy the freedom which you have extracted from your family, and make* new friends *to replace those you leave behind. Indeed, it seems you have already begun to do so, in the form of the travelling companion of late arrived at Powerscourt. I need have no fears that* you *will be lonely.*

Meanwhile I will continue to serve my country, to smile graciously when I feel least like doing so, and to bear the burdens of my station without complaint. The stiff upper lip, *which you have so often mocked, is not a feature, I am told, of American society, where the heart is worn openly on the sleeve. That should suit you very well.*

You must not be thinking that this is a plea for you to remain, or even to concern yourself with my suffering. I will, as I always do, endure with grace and elegance, and look after myself. I have an excellent example of fortitude in my mother to follow. I will not disappoint her expectations, nor will I disappoint myself.

I trust you will not regret your decision.

~~Oh, M., I miss you.~~

> *Bon voyage, M.*
> *Louise*

A TALL TALE ABOUT SETTING SAIL?

Tall Tales and Wagging Tails is a book of children's stories recently published in Dublin. You might ask what possible interest the Lounger at the Club has in such a frivolous tome. The answer is that it was written by none other than Lady M——, second daughter of the Duke of B——, though naturally her name is not on the title page. Lady M——, who was last sighted serving as bridesmaid at the Royal Wedding a year past in July, has since been determinedly rusticating in Ireland. This is her second *confinement* from society. Could it be for the same reason as the first? Idle speculation on my part, nothing more—or is it? You decide, Dear Reader, but I ask you, does a leopard change its spots?

I am now reliably informed that the young woman has decided to abandon her homeland altogether and will set sail for America before the end of the year, in which country she intends to settle. In a society which has no aristocratic pedigree nor any blue blood, such tarnished goods as Lady M—— will doubtless be welcomed. In the so-called Land of the Free, a young lady with a penchant for snubbing the well-established rules of good conduct and a reputation for setting a determinedly poor example will find her spiritual home. We wish Lady M—— bon voyage, and our American cousins the best of luck.

Chapter Twenty-Nine

Queenstown, Ireland, Friday, 27 December 1867

THERE HAD BEEN TIME FOR only the briefest of farewells before Margaret set off in the Powerscourt travelling coach for Kingsbridge Station in Dublin in the early hours. With the horses stamping their feet in the icy predawn and Aunt Marion consulting her omnipresent list and checking off the baggage, there was time only for Breda to press a St. Christopher medal into Margaret's hands and for Julia to fuss over the blankets and foot warmers. No time for tears, thank goodness, nor any time to contemplate the fact that she and Julia might never see each other again. Merely one last brief, fierce hug, and then they were on their way.

The train journey from Dublin to Cork, where the station was reached through a tunnel almost a mile long, passed in a blur. Here she and Aunt Marion boarded the train to the port of Queenstown, a scenic route that hugged the banks of Lough Mahon, allowing Margaret to stare out at the view, though her thoughts were elsewhere, to those she was leaving behind, perhaps forever.

Mama's last, precious letter had been the source of tears, sleepless nights, and much soul-searching. It was impossible not to regret the fact that they had always been at odds and to wish that they had grown closer sooner. Though if she had followed the path her parents had chosen for her, she and Mama may never have grown close at all. Their new relationship was the product of adversity, of strife and suffering, of separation and endurance; and the same could well be said for her relationship with Victoria, perhaps even Mary. Even now, as the train ate up the miles, knowing she was in her mother's thoughts and prayers gave Margaret some comfort.

Louise was another matter entirely. Louise was truly lost to her now, perhaps forever. Her letter had deliberately set out to wound; but as ever with Lou, Margaret knew she lashed out at those she cared for most when she was feeling vulnerable. It was not the first time Louise had rewritten history to put herself in the right, or at least in a better light. The jibes and accusations she made were the weapons she used to deflect from her own short-comings—not that she would ever admit to having any! As to what had transpired in the last eighteen months, it was impossible to be definitive from her veiled hints, though Margaret could hazard a guess, and her heart ached with sympathy. To admit to frailty or needing love and support were beyond Lou. Like Julia, she was determined to lock her feelings down and to endure. Margaret could not help her, and any offer would be rejected. Would Louise even read her brief reply, assuring her of her continuing love and friendship? She could hope, though she wasn't convinced.

From Donald, Margaret had heard nothing, nor had she expected to. She did not regret turning down his proposal, but, oh, how deeply she regretted losing his friendship. The temptation to write, to confide in him her fears and hopes for this new phase in her life, to set out her tentative plans for his consideration, had been almost irresistible as the weeks since her birthday flew past, but doing so would have been cruel and selfish, and she loved him too much to hurt him further or to give him false hope.

Julia, once it became clear Margaret was not to be dissuaded, had generously thrown herself into making arrangements for the journey. She could neither understand nor approve of a decision which was so completely contrary to her own careful choices and her fervent desire for a family, but she had demonstrated a shrewd understanding of Margaret's nature by suggesting Aunt Marion as her travelling companion.

As the train began its slow approach towards Queenstown harbour, Margaret smiled to herself as she studied the woman opposite her, who was frowning over her notebook, where a list of tasks was being methodically ticked off. Mrs. Marion Scrymgeour, or Aunt Marion, as she insisted upon being addressed, was in her mid-fifties and neatly but plainly garbed in a tweed jacket and skirt with a high-collared blouse. The skirt had two large, concealed pockets, and the blouse was a revolting shade of tobacco-brown, her preferred colour for travelling garb. *It conceals the grime even the most fastidious of traveller must inevitably accumulate, and it repels the heat in warmer climes,* she had informed Margaret, eyeing her own choice of dove grey with a disapproving frown.

Aunt Marion's arrival at Powerscourt just under two weeks ago had been preceded by a barrage of letters containing detailed instructions which Julia and Margaret had diligently and most gratefully followed, covering everything from the most robust and commodious style of travelling trunk; the essential contents of a medical case, a dressing case, and a carpet-bag; to the itinerary for the journey and the travel papers which would be required. Though Julia was minded to question Aunt Marion's assertion that the department stores in New York were reputed to be the best in the world and could supply all their needs when they arrived, Margaret was relieved to be spared the necessity of purchasing a new wardrobe. For herself, she could not imagine why a small flask of brandy, strong smelling-salts, a bottle of eau de toilette, and full set of clean undergarments and stockings must take up valuable room in her carpet-bag, leaving no room for her writing case or her book, but she decided to bow to Aunt Marion's vast experience.

In fact, Aunt Marion was so thorough that Margaret had begun to anticipate a rather austere schoolmistress type who regimented her day by following a strict timetable, rising at five and going to bed at eight, who drank only water and thought that cream on her gruel was an frightful extravagance. She could not have been more wrong. There had been an instant rapport between them. Aunt Marion was one of those women whose appetite for life matched her appetite for food. Originally hailing from the Scottish Borders town of Peebles, she had travelled extensively with her diplomat husband, primarily in the Far East. She had a stock of tales, the constitution of an ox, a very dry wit, a pleasing tolerance for foibles, and an abhorrence of hypocrisy. Her notebook, her embroidery frame, and a glass of champagne were her permanent companions. Eccentric and irreverent, Aunt Marion was a maverick who took everything in her stride.

"What is it that is making you smile?" she asked now, closing her notebook and tucking the little silver propelling pencil into its holder.

"If I had been asked to describe the perfect travelling companion," Margaret said, "it would have been you."

"Thank you, my dear, but we have barely set foot out of Powerscourt. You should reserve judgement until we have travelled a few more miles together."

"No, I don't need to. If I didn't owe Julia an enormous debt already for taking me in, I would be hugely obliged to her for introducing us."

"It seems to me that you have more than repaid Julia with your companionship," Aunt Marion said. "She's quite come out of her shell, what with getting embroiled in the school and what not. Of course she'll never be happy until she has a baby of her own to hold in her arms, but knowing that husband of hers—ach, I have no patience with a man who shirks his duty as he does. He should not have married her if he'd doubts about—" She broke off, pursing her lips.

"What on earth do you mean? I didn't realise you were particularly well acquainted with Lord Powerscourt."

"I have encountered him several times on his travels abroad. He embroiled Alexander, my husband, in the tracking down of a statue once. In Persia it was, in the early days of my husband's posting there. Alexander was most put-out to be asked to wield influence he did not truly possess, for he never did rise above the lower ranks in the service. His lack of blue blood was against him, and he was far too reticent to cultivate the right people, you see, but Powerscourt was most insistent. An arrogant man, I have always thought, and a very selfish one—I may say that now that poor Julia is out of earshot. I much prefer the younger brother, Lewis."

"I have met him, and like him very much," Margaret said.

"Yes, I can imagine that the two of you would have hit it off. At least with Lewis, you know where you are. He makes no pretence. Wingfield, on the other hand—he is the sort of man who should have remained a bachelor, and that is all I am prepared to say on the subject. Now, we must gather our things, Margaret, for we are about to arrive in Queenstown and the terminus is actually on the quay itself, I believe. Stand close by me, and allow me to deal with officialdom. Keep your hand on your purse and your wits about you and we will be fine."

Two hours later, Margaret stood on the deck of the Cunard line's most prestigious paddle steamer, watching the tenders bring the final passengers on board. The decks of the RMS *Scotia* were crowded with people vying for a space at the ship's rails to wave farewell, though their loved ones assembled on the quay were no more than a sea of indistinguishable faces. Smoke billowed from the two funnels at the centre of the ship, and the massive sails on the two masts were being unfurled in preparation for departure. The steamer, which had won the much-coveted Blue Riband for the fastest westbound transatlantic crossing four years before, was a luxury liner, with no steerage class, the vast majority of the passengers travelling in first class with only a few in second. All the same, as Margaret leaned on the guard-rail clutching her thick woollen cloak around her, she couldn't help thinking of the thousands of Irish poor fleeing the Great Famine in years gone by, taking their chances in the New World. Breda's uncle had been one who, with his wife and three children, had embarked at this very quay fifteen years before. Though there could be no comparison between those brave, desperate souls and herself, save the determination to make a new life for themselves, the enormity of what she was doing struck her forcibly as the last tenders emptied and the ship's engines developed a more determined rumble. She was committed now. There was no going back.

Several blasts of the ship's horn made the crowds push further towards the rails. Aunt Marion appeared by her side, miraculously bearing two glasses of champagne, handing Margaret one of them. On the quay, handkerchiefs were waved, hats were raised, tears began to fall, and the decks shuddered beneath their feet.

"I thought a bon voyage toast was in order. I expect you are feeling trepidation. It is my experience that one always feels that way at the point of departure. A natural enough emotion, when one is leaving friends and loved ones. If one did not feel it, it would mean that one had nothing and no-one to regret leaving behind."

"That is a very positive way of looking at it."

"I've no time for those who are constantly bemoaning their fate. One makes the best of the hand one is dealt."

"Julia said that to me when I first arrived in Powerscourt."

"A sensible gal, is Julia, though I am of the opinion she has a smidgen of the martyr in her. I would also have loved to have children of my own, but the Lord did not bless us. Mind you, I cannot fault Alexander for endeavour. In that department, unlike Wingfield, he was ever eager, right until the end," Aunt Marion said with a broad wink. "I see I've shocked you. The young imagine passion to be solely their province, but it's not at all. I'm fifty-five years old and far from decrepit. You should find that reassuring."

"I am sure I shall, one day," Margaret replied, blushing and laughing.

"True, true, time enough to concern yourself with that kind of thing—you've your whole life ahead of you." The ship's anchors were creaking up, and the RMS *Scotia* was rocking into motion. "There's no going back now."

"I know, and when I am not excited about that, I'm terrified."

"I won't say have no regrets, for that would be plain silly. You'll have regrets by the score, but the trick, my dear Margaret, is to continue onwards and upwards." Aunt Marion raised her glass. "A toast, my dear. Here is to pastures new."

The *Scotia*'s horn gave one final blast. "Pastures new," Margaret said, as the ship began to pick up speed at an alarming rate, and they set sail for New York. "And here is to making the most of second chances," she added quietly to herself.

Chapter Thirty

New York, January 1868

RMS *Scotia* SAILED TO NEW York under the command of Captain Judkins. One of Cunard's finest officers and a staunch upholder of ship's discipline, he ruled with a rod of iron. The captain had once legendarily threatened to clap a number of passengers from the American Deep South in irons when they not only refused to listen to a lecture given by Frederick Douglass but threatened to throw the abolitionist overboard. Captain Judkins, a taciturn man with the appearance of a distinguished politician, made no attempt to endear himself to his passengers, most of whom lived in fear of his acerbic tongue. However, he and Aunt Marion had struck up an unlikely friendship in the ten days spent at sea, as a result of which she and Margaret were invited to dine at his table almost every night and given a pride of place at the grand gala ball thrown to celebrate the New Year. It was a dubious honour, for the captain enjoyed the sound of his own voice rather too much, and his officers held him in a combination of reverence and fear, but when Aunt Marion pointed out that it ensured they had champagne on tap, Margaret could hardly demur.

The huge paddles of the *Scotia* had temporarily stopped turning in the early hours of this morning, some miles off the American coast, to allow US government officials to board. Wrapped in her thick travelling cloak, her hands in fur mittens, Margaret stood at the rails of the first-class deck as the engines started up again to complete the short final leg of their transatlantic journey up the East River to their berth in New York Harbour. The docking process was terrifyingly complex, for the river was teeming with ships, tugs, barges, and rowing boats, all jostling for position. As the engines were cut for a final time, a cacophony of voices rang out, shouting instructions from the dockside, from the barges, and from the bridge of the *Scotia*. Horns blasted, rigging creaked, gulls screeched plaintively, and the tang of salt gave way to the acrid scent of smoke that filled the leaden skies. On the decks of the other ships Margaret could see hordes of people crowded together, all straining, as she was, for their first glimpse of New York City.

Her stomach was churning like the vast ocean they had just crossed as the barges on which they would be disembarked came alongside. She couldn't believe they had actually arrived in the New World. Her mind had been in constant turmoil as they steamed at alarming speed across the Atlantic, every creak and roll of the ship, the foaming wake it left in its trail, a reminder of the distance they were travelling, of the world and the loved ones she was leaving far behind. It was easy during daytime to put her fears aside and enjoy the *Scotia*'s lavish hospitality, but at night in her cabin she had lain awake, questions and worries swarming like bees in her head. In those long, dark hours, she felt completely alone. Gazing out the porthole at the pincushion of stars in the ink-black sky, she had veered between exhilaration and the sensation of being trapped on this hulking, roiling iron vessel. Forced to forge relentlessly onwards, secretly relieved that the choice to turn back had been taken out of her hands.

Now, looking out at the emerging New York skyline, Margaret's optimism reasserted itself. She had taken a huge leap into the dark, but despite all her doubts and fears, she was still convinced it was the right move. The article in the *Illustrated Times*, which Lord Powerscourt had so kindly shown her before she left, simply confirmed her in her views. No matter what she did, no matter what her motives, at home she would always be the scandalous Lady Margaret.

As she watched the first nets containing luggage being winched down onto the barges, Aunt Marion joined her. "Good morning, my dear. Isn't this exciting?" Her eyes twinkling, she produced two glasses of champagne. "The sun must be over the yard-arm somewhere. This will be our last opportunity to sample the contents of Captain Judkins's most excellent cellar and our first chance to toast the New World."

"Good morning, America," Margaret said, smiling as she raised her glass.

"We are quite delighted to make your acquaintance," Aunt Marion added, taking a deep draught. "Now drink up, for we will be disembarking on one of those barges directly. I fear I will resemble a prize heifer being unloaded from a cattle boat."

The barge deposited them at Castle Garden pier, on the southern tip of the island of Manhattan, with Governors Island nearby. In the distance lay the green hills of Staten Island. The *Scotia* was one of many ships disembarking this morning, and the jetty was a seething mass of humanity hailing from every corner of the world, or so it seemed to Margaret. Her legs wobbled so much as she set foot on dry land that she was momentarily frozen to the spot. Her nose twitched at the smells; her ears rang with the noise. Officials were shouting instructions, waving their arms, and she panicked as the crowds surged forward.

"Stay close, my dear," Aunt Marion said with reassuring calm, grabbing her arm, casting a disapproving gaze around her at the milling throng. "It seems that Americans are true to their principle that everyone is equal from the very outset. I can see no separate process for first class. Ah well, leave this to me. Dealing with bureaucracy is one of my many talents." She frowned disapprovingly at a fellow passenger ranting at an official. "Patience and courtesy are what will see us through, so pin that enchanting smile of yours to your face, and let us have at 'em."

True to her word, Aunt Marion steered them quickly through a cursory medical examination and into the main rotunda building, a vast circular space where the noise of so many people talking in so many different languages was deafening and the stench from so many passengers who had been cooped up in steerage was overpowering.

"Take deep breaths, and you will quickly become accustomed to the smell," Aunt Marion commanded as she pushed Margaret in front of her towards the registering department.

By the time their papers and baggage had been checked, and arrangements had been made to send their luggage on to the hotel which would be their temporary home, it was late morning. Emerging on the other side of the rotunda, they found themselves in a large courtyard, where passengers, children, and baggage stood in groups, looking as dazed as Margaret now felt. Exiting through another door, they were officially disembarked and on American soil.

The Battery, as it was known, was a vast space with a few sparse trees and a great deal of traffic. Conveyances of every size and description blocked the way—carriages, carts, and pedlars' barrows. Touts proclaimed the name of the hotel or boarding-house they represented. It was here that the reunions took place. Families embraced, lovers kissed, and people laughed and cried at the same time. Babies were held up to be inspected, dogs barked, and children bounced on their toes, clinging to their mothers' skirts. Margaret smiled at one little girl who was holding an exuberant puppy on a lead, and was rewarded with a gap-toothed grin.

Aunt Marion, meanwhile, was carefully noting down the licence number of the hansom cab. "One can never be too careful," she said, ushering Margaret ahead of her. "Drivers," she added with a meaningful glance at the man who had descended from the box to assist her, "are the same the world over in my experience, always eager to charge one double the going rate if they can get away with it. We are off to the Fifth Avenue Hotel, my good man, which should be no more than a fare of seventy-five cents, if I am not mistaken."

"Spot on, unless you care to add a generous tip, lady," the man replied, winking at Margaret as he closed the folding wooden doors over their legs, before leaping up onto the box behind them and urging his horse into action.

The wind bit at their faces, for the hansom cab was only partially enclosed, but Margaret leaned forward, eager to catch her first glimpse of what she knew enough to call downtown New York. "I can't believe we're actually here. I know you are a seasoned traveller, but until we set sail, Ireland was the furthest afield I've ever been."

"There is nothing like travel for broadening one's mind." Aunt Marion grimaced. "A dreadful platitude, but true nonetheless, provided one is happy to embrace the experience, of course. You would not believe the number of people I came across in the diplomatic service who put all their efforts into recreating a little patch of England. You must know the type, for your father mingles with ambassadors and high-ranking officials. They are the ones least likely to learn the local lingo or customs. Don't get me wrong now; there were plenty others like my dear Alexander, who made every effort to adapt, but some—" She broke off, shaking her head. "Such people, I fear, gain little from their foreign travels save continual bouts of homesickness and occasional bouts of the scours."

"Well, I intend to throw myself into life here with gusto."

"I am sure you will," Aunt Marion said, patting her hand. "You will be homesick, there's no avoiding it, but the trick is not to wallow in it. And remember that you are not alone, for I am by your side."

"Thank you, Aunt Marion." Margaret leaned over, surprising her with a kiss on the cheek. "For everything. I am so glad you are here with me."

"Please, I beg you, let's dispense with the *aunt*. We are to be friends and accomplices, not guardian and ward. I am very glad to have been given the opportunity to accompany you, my dear. Since I lost Alexander, my life has been rather dull, I must confess. I, too, am eagerly anticipating pastures new, you know, even if only for a limited period, and I freely admit that I am also looking forward to enjoying a bit of luxury. I am reliably informed that our accommodation incorporates something called a vertical railroad to convey us to our rooms. I hope it is of sturdy construction. I am rather looking forward to trying it out."

New York Welcomes an
Aristocratic Arrival

The Cunard liner RMS *Scotia* docked this morning in New York Harbor, having sailed from Liverpool and Queenstown. Among several illustrious passengers on board was the Lady Margaret Montagu Douglas Scott, second daughter of the Duke of Buccleuch and Queensberry. One of Great Britain's most eminent peers and Gold Stick for Scotland, His Grace previously served Her Majesty Queen Victoria as Lord Privy Seal and was a close friend of Prince Albert. Lady Margaret's mother, the Duchess of Buccleuch, is the daughter of the Second Marquess of Bath, and former Mistress of the queen's Robes. The family's several homes and estates include Montagu House in London; Drumlanrig Castle, Bowhill, and Dalkeith Palace in Scotland; and Boughton House in Northamptonshire, England.

Lady Margaret made her debut before Her Majesty Queen Victoria in April 1865, and was one of the London Season's most fêted debutantes. She is a close friend of the most beautiful of the royal princesses, Louise, and served as a bridesmaid at the marriage of Princess Helena to Prince Christian of Schleswig-Holstein-Sonderburg-Augustenburg in July 1866. Ill health forced Lady Margaret to retire from society and take refuge at Powerscourt near Dublin, where she has been the guest of the Seventh Viscount and his wife.

Lady Margaret travels with a companion, Mrs. Marion

Scrymgeour, and is expected to make her home in the United States. She will be a most welcome addition to our homegrown aristocracy here in New York.

New York Herald, Wednesday, 8 January 1868

New York, New Start for a Duke's Daughter?

We are delighted and intrigued to note that one of the passengers who disembarked yesterday from the RMS *Scotia* was Lady Margaret Montagu Douglas Scott, the second daughter of the Duke and Duchess of Buccleuch. Lady Margaret was accompanied by Mrs. Marion Scrymgeour, about whom we can glean nothing at all, save that she is the relic of a minor British diplomat and no relation to her ladyship.

Readers who are imagining a faded, aged spinster peeress and her down-at-heel paid companion should prepare to have their expectations quite confounded. Lady Margaret is twenty-one years of age, flame haired, and perfectly proportioned, according to our source on board the *Scotia*, with a charming and unaffected manner. Not the average English Rose that the British aristocracy export, not by any stretch!

Why has this matrimonial prize been permitted to escape the Old Country? What does she hope to find here in the New World? The *New York Herald* has no time for scurrilous rumors and ancient scandal. America is the Land of Second Chances as well as the Land of Opportunity. Whatever her past misdemeanors, Lady Margaret will be welcomed with open arms into the heart of society in the Metropolis and will, we have no doubt, fast become the most sought-after guest at any and all of the current season's events.

Though the most eligible of our bachelors may balk at wooing a lady who is already their senior (and in Gotham terms on the shelf), in the event that she wishes to ally herself more closely with her adopted home, her noble birth must ensure that she has her pick of any number of wealthy widowers. The *Herald* bids Lady Margaret a wholehearted welcome, and will closely monitor her progress.

Lady Margaret is currently residing at the Fifth Avenue Hotel, where she has been allocated one of that luxurious establishment's premium suites.

Chapter Thirty-One

Wednesday, 8 January 1868

THE FIFTH AVENUE HOTEL WAS a huge white marble edifice six storeys high, made fashionable by the Prince of Wales, who had occupied the most lavish suite during his visit eight years previously. The main saloons were sumptuously decorated; every bedroom equipped with its own fireplace; and many, Margaret and Marion's suite included, even had their own bathrooms.

After the excitement of their arrival in the city, Margaret's mind was preoccupied with practical matters. How did one summon a maid? Was she to unpack her belongings herself? Dress herself? How did one order meals? Did one eat in private or in the public dining room? If a female guest sat in one of the saloons alone, did she risk being accosted? All the conventions she took for granted might not apply now she was on the other side of the Atlantic. The gulf between her old life and this new one seemed too vast to digest.

But even as she sank wearily onto the gilded sofa in their shared sitting room, Marion was at hand. "Tea is the order of the day," she said, ringing the bell by the fireplace, "and then bed for you, I think. Leave everything else to me for now—it's why I'm here. Trust me, my dear, a good night's rest, and tomorrow you will be ready for anything New York can throw at you."

And Marion had, once again, been right. Despite the fact that the pounding of *Scotia*'s paddles was replaced by the endless rattling and clopping of carriages and horses outside her window, Margaret had her first sound night's sleep in a very long time.

In their sitting room the next morning, she found Marion seated resplendent in her husband's red-and-gold Oriental dressing gown, while a waiter set out a bewildering array of covered dishes.

"I was just about to call you. I took the liberty of ordering us a light breakfast. We could eat in the dining room, of course, but apparently one cannot reserve a table for that particular repast, and I do not wish to risk having to share. I am not at my best until I've had at least one pot of coffee."

"A light breakfast?" Margaret said, eyeing the groaning table incredulously, noting that Marion slipped a coin into the waiter's hand before he left. Tipping, it seemed, was yet another custom she would need to embrace.

"I may have ordered a smidgen too much," Marion agreed, pouring her coffee, "though it's a fraction of what's available on the breakfast menu. The tea is English Breakfast. Does that suit you?"

"Very much," Margaret said, relieved to see that this one, in her view essential commodity, was served just as she liked.

"Now, let's see." Marion began to lift the lids. "Fried oysters. And this must be the codfish with cream. Kidneys—a mixture of veal and mutton, according to the menu, though they smell just like lamb to me. Fried potatoes, a plain omelette. These pancakes must be the buckwheat cakes, which means that is the corn-bread, and these two last items—well, one of them must be the fried Indian pudding and the other the hominy. How disappointing— they look like custard and porridge. Ah well, one lives and learns."

She began to help herself to a substantial selection, while Margaret took a tentative taste of the hominy before spooning out a small plateful of it. "Thank you very much for looking after me yesterday. I'm sorry I was poor company."

"Stuff and nonsense. I'm not surprised you were somewhat overwhelmed. I must say, though, you look much refreshed this morning."

"I feel much better, thank you." Margaret cut a slice of the omelette, which was light and fluffy and flavoured with parsley.

"A number of calling cards have been left for you already," Marion said, "and I am informed by the hotel concierge, a contact well worth cultivating, to expect a great deal more. It seems to be the practice here for the passenger lists of the liners to be published and for hotels to place lists of their more eminent guests in the newspapers."

"Good heavens, we are not going to be besieged by callers on our first day, are we?"

"Oh no, I don't think so, and in any case, I thought we could spend the day finding our feet, so to speak. A task that in my case is rather more of a voyage of discovery than yours," Marion said, patting her tummy. "I think I must have gained at least a stone at sea, between the ten-course luncheons and banquet dinners, to say nothing of the champagne—not that champagne counts, of course. I will be banned from using the elevator, at this rate. I am afraid I have never had your commendable restraint when it comes to food. Mind you, I've never in my life had such a svelte figure as yours. Even in my younger days, my curves were what was known as generous."

"It's strange," Margaret said, succumbing to the deliciously warm, doughy corn-bread, "but when Mama was forever wielding her measuring tape and fussing over the size of my waist, I craved cake. Yet in Ireland, where I was free to eat as much cake as I wanted, I found that I didn't want to. Perhaps that is simply my contrary nature."

"It is certainly human nature, to want what one is told one cannot have," Marion said dryly. "I'm afraid I have little patience with this fashion for tight-lacing. No wonder so many women are forever fainting away—they can't blooming well breathe. I abandoned my corset when Alexander was posted to Syria. It wasn't only the heat but the sand—I assure you, my dear, you have no notion of the havoc even a few grains of the stuff trapped between your corset and your chemise can wreak. I adopted native dress, lovely loose tunics that let the breeze circulate about one's person, and made it a dashed sight easier to let one's husband circulate about a person, too. There was something about the heat that made both Alexander and me—" She broke off with a hearty sigh. "Ah, but there's no point in dwelling on that now. What was it I was saying, about wanting what one can't have?"

"You must miss him a great deal."

"Oh, you have no idea. However, Alexander made me promise not to mourn him and to enjoy life to the full, and I try my best to do just that. It's an odd way of mourning, some might say, but it's my way."

"I think it's rather wonderful."

"Thank you, my dear. Now then," Marion said, inhaling the dregs of her coffee, "I have been busy while you have been catching up on your sleep. In my experience, the best way to get to know a city is to get the lie of the land, as they say. The charming concierge informs me that for the sum of five dollars one may hire a hansom cab and driver for the day. So if you are finished your repast, we will make hay while the sun shines which," she said, casting an eye at the window, "it seems to be trying very hard to do."

Their hotel was situated near the busy juncture with Broadway on Twenty-Third Street, with the charming small park of Madison Square nearby, no doubt a welcome oasis of green in spring. This was, according the information Marion had gleaned, at the limit of fashionable uptown when it was built about ten years previously. "Though that has all changed since," she said as their cab jolted into action. "Mrs. William Astor, who is the arbiter of New York society and whose card, I noticed, was one of those left for you, has her mansion on Thirty-Fourth Street. I must say, this way of numbering the avenues and streets is eminently practical. It will make it quite difficult to get lost, though I am told that downtown, as it is referred to, is a different matter entirely. Not a place one ventures into, apparently."

"You should not have said so, for now it is the one place in all New York I yearn to visit," Margaret quipped.

"Ha! We shall content ourselves with uptown today, and the new Central Park. Though it seems to be acceptable for a young woman to go about unescorted, there are certain areas which would be foolhardy to venture into, never mind unescorted. I know you are teasing, but you will remember, Margaret, that it will undoubtedly be as easy here as it is in London to accidentally find yourself in an unsavoury district."

"I am aware, and I was teasing. A little, anyway. Goodness, but isn't it busy, and so very different from London. The pavements look as if they have been swept clean."

"Sidewalks," Marion corrected. "And this is Fifth Avenue, where the great and the good reside."

Margaret looked about her, slightly awed by the city unfurling before her. There were two sets of tracks for the horse-drawn trams which she must remember to call streetcars, one of the many obstacles their driver faced, for despite the width of the street—*avenue!*—there were vast amounts of traffic. And throngs of people, too, all of them, it seemed to her, walking very quickly and purposefully. As the cab made its slow way north, the sidewalks gradually became less crowded, the buildings more widely spaced, interspersed with trees and several extremely well-kept churches. There was an air of permanence here that belied Marion's assertion that this part of the city had, as recently as fifteen years ago, been little more than mud, hovels, and farmland. The mansions were tall, square, and similar in proportions, the brown-stone of the façades presenting a pleasing uniform appearance.

"One of these must be Mrs. William Astor's house," Marion mused. "I would have thought it would be grander. Caroline Astor is a formidable woman, I am told, who is the gatekeeper to New York society. The husband is not fond of socialising and prefers country pursuits." She rolled her eyes. "A phrase that I have no doubt means exactly the same on this side of the Atlantic, if you take my meaning—or rather Shakespeare's. Was it Shakespeare? No, it was Donne, of course. 'The Good-Morrow.' One of Alexander's favourites of his poems.

"*'If ever any beauty I did see,*

"*'Which I desired, and got, 'twas but a dream of thee.'*

"Do you know it?"

"I don't," Margaret said, hurriedly reassessing her image of the mysterious Alexander. "Your husband sounds as if he was quite the romantic."

Marion chuckled. "Oh, how he would laugh to hear himself so described. He wasn't given to grand gestures, but what use are a bunch of roses or a diamond necklace when what one requires is a foot rub."

"I wish I could have met him."

"Ah, my dear, I am sure the pair of you would have got on swimmingly. However, if he were still with me, I would not be with you." Marion blew her nose vigorously. "Now, that is more than enough about me. What were we talking about?"

"Mrs. William Astor."

"She left her card, which is considered a great honour. If you are to immerse yourself in New York society, you will require her seal of approval."

"I think I would rather be immersed in an ice-cold bath."

"You have been out of society for some time now, have you not? No need to explain what sent you into hiding with Julia, though I am assuming it was a man, for it invariably is, with young women."

"It was, but not in the way you assume."

Marion patted her knee. "I'm not assuming anything. Let us take in the view and say no more on the subject."

Margaret nodded gratefully, and as the hansom cab continued to make its way north, she did as Marion suggested. New York was expanding at a rate that made London's growth seem positively sedentary. Only a few streets farther on from the Astor's house, the elegant façade of the avenue began to alter. There were buildings in various states of construction everywhere. Materials were stacked beside the foundations of the nascent mansions: brick and marble, slate, chimney stacks, timbers and stone, window frames and doors. Despite the freezing weather, construction seemed to be continuing apace.

An ugly stone structure which, Marion informed her, frowning down at her notebook, was a water reservoir, took up two whole blocks. One imposing edifice was clearly a cathedral in the making. At a particularly large construction which her well-informed companion said would be the new Central Park Hotel, the traffic became busier again, for several of the streetcars terminated here, and a number of the special carriages which could be hired for drives through the park stood awaiting customers.

Informing their driver, through the hatch in the roof, that she most certainly did wish him to drive into the park, Marion smiled apologetically at Margaret. "I know you would much prefer to walk, but it is a very large park, bigger by far than anything London has to offer. Hard to believe it is only a few years old, isn't it?"

"It's lovely," Margaret said, her eyes wide as their cab once more jolted into action. "It feels as if we have stumbled into another country."

Though it was the depth of winter and the branches were bare, the park was still enchanting. A large pond with a pretty arched bridge gave way to vast swathes of what would be tempting green lawns in the summer. The main carriage-way ran at an elevated level, crossing a number of arched stone bridges below which smaller paths criss-crossed, and which Margaret determined to return to explore. A lake, clearly used in summer for boating, was partially frozen. They drove past woodland, and then south again, past another pond, and a large boathouse, before the carriage drew to a halt.

"Don't want you to miss this, ladies," their driver said, through the roof hatch. "The terrace is over there. It's a short walk, but well worth the effort, I promise."

They descended one of two broad flights of steps to a natural-looking amphitheatre, where an arcade or cloister had been built beneath the carriage drive. Refreshments were served inside this rather beautiful tiled interior, but Margaret and Marion were drawn to the large round basin where a fountain played, facing the pond, with a sign cautioning would-be skaters that the ice was dangerous.

"I love to ice-skate," Margaret said, looking longingly at the partially frozen water. "There is a lochan, which freezes over most years, near Dalkeith Palace, my father's home on the outskirts of Edinburgh." She smiled, watching a little boy and girl chase each other round the fountain. "In London, one goes to the park to show off one's toilette, to see and be seen. In the Season, by late afternoon there was a positive crush of carriages."

"I expect they do something similar here."

"I hated my London Season. I felt crushed by the weight of expectation."

"To make a good match? It will be a very different experience here, if your only ambition is to establish yourself and not to find a husband. Assuming that you don't wish to do so?"

"I most certainly do not." The image of a smiling Donald flashed before her eyes. "I could have married a charming, kind, and respectable man who loved me, but I chose not to."

"May I ask why? Didn't you love him?"

"Not enough to build my world around his. Do you think that is selfish of me?"

"I think it very brave not to do what most women would."

"Julia thinks it was a mistake."

"Poor Julia. I think it more likely she envies you your confidence. Of course you are fortunate in having the means to support yourself."

"I don't think I would have married Donald, even if my father had not granted me an allowance." Margaret grimaced. "At least, I'd like to think so. I miss him so much. Though we rarely met, he was always there in the background, a rock I could rely on. I miss his wise counsel and his humour and—oh dear, that sounds very much as if I regret refusing him, but I don't."

"I find that once a decision is made, it is best left at that and not continually questioned."

"That is sound advice."

Marion chuckled. "But not so easily followed, I warn you."

"Well, I'm going to try, and I will start by making my entrance in New York society. You're quite right: it is bound to be a very different experience from London. We shall have fun!"

"We! I am not so sure I would be as sought after as you by the Mrs. William Astors of this world."

"They will be obliged to, if they desire my company. They can have both of us, or neither," Margaret said firmly. "More importantly, we need to find somewhere to live. I have no idea of the costs involved. My allowance seems like an enormous amount to me, but I have never had to run my own establishment."

"I have established any number of homes for myself and Alexander in my time. I would be delighted to help."

"And will you stay on and share it with me?" Margaret asked impulsively. "Not forever, but for more than the few months we agreed to?"

Marion did not hesitate. "I will, for the time being, and then we shall see."

"Excellent." Above them the sky had darkened. The snow fell suddenly, in a soft flurry, and laughter echoed around the park as people jumped to their feet and held their faces to the sky with childish delight. Margaret gave a little skip of excitement. "I think we are going to be very happy here."

Chapter Thirty-Two

T HE CITY OF NEW YORK boasted so many attractions it
would be easy, Margaret quickly realised, to spend the next
few months as a tourist. But since she planned to settle here, she
must do more than see the sights, she must engage with the locals.
The growing stack of calling cards on the table in her hotel suite
offered her ample opportunity to do this, though the sheer volume
of them as she laid them out like playing cards was daunting. She
was tempted to close her eyes and select one at random, but as
ever, Marion's good sense prevailed.

"When in doubt, start at the top," she advised.

So it was that three days after their arrival in the city, they set out
to pay their first call. The snow had melted, but a hard frost had set
in overnight, making the sidewalks glitter. They decided to walk the
short distance from their hotel, and set out just before noon, dressed
for the weather rather than the occasion, in thick cloaks and boots.

Mrs. William Astor occupied what Margaret now knew to call
a brown-stone at number 350 Fifth Avenue. It was a square town
house four stories high, separated from the sidewalk by a low
balustrade and a neat flight of steps leading up to a door flanked
by two pillars. This was opened by a liveried footman in an eye-
catching combination of green coat, red waistcoat, white knee
breeches, and black silk stockings.

"Good morning," Margaret said, smiling and holding out her
visiting card. "Is Mrs. Astor at home? Then you will tell her, if you
please, that Lady Margaret Montagu Douglas Scott is returning
her call."

After a moment's hesitation, they were ushered into a large marble-floored reception area where the footman took their cloaks, gloves, and hats, then bade them follow him upstairs. The plain façade of the Astor town house belied an opulent interior. Heavy tapestries hung from the walls, jostling for space with large paintings in gilded frames, most of them still lifes, doubtless Old Masters, but rather dull nonetheless. On the first floor, there were an array of busts and bronzes on plinths. There was not, Margaret noted with amusement, a single set of antlers in sight. Presumably because Julia's husband had cornered the world market.

"Lady Margaret Montagu Douglas Scott and Mrs. Scrymgeour," the footman intoned, ushering them into a large drawing-room that had the gracious proportions of the Regency era. The classical elegance was lost however, as the room was so crowded with chairs and sofas, tables cluttered with Sèvres figures, flower arrangements, and curios that it was with some difficulty that Margaret managed to prevent her crinoline from knocking anything over.

"Lady Margaret, this is a most unexpected surprise. How do you do?" The woman who got to her feet was nondescript in appearance, the kind of woman who would have been called homely were it not for her intent grey eyes and her reputation as the doyenne of New York society. Mrs. William Astor was as plain in person as the façade of her home, her severe black gown augmented only by a small lace ruffle at the neck, with none of her legendary diamonds on display.

"I am so sorry," Margaret said, eyeing the gentleman who had also got to his feet. "I didn't realise you already had company."

"Oh, Lina and I are such close friends, I don't count as company. Samuel Ward McAllister at your service, Lady Margaret."

The gentleman looked to be in his forties and like Mrs. Astor's, his dress was plain to the point of funereal. Perhaps, Margaret thought as he bowed over her hand, to compensate for his hair which, despite the Macassar oil which he had applied so copiously that she could smell it, had failed to tame the grizzled curls which looked as if they were beating a hasty retreat from his high domed forehead. His goatee and absurdly long moustaches looked as if they had been badly knitted from thin wire; and she could see, as he made a decidedly shallow bow, that Marion was trying very hard not to laugh.

"Please do sit," Mrs. Astor said. "And you, too, Samuel."

"Strictly speaking, I should leave," Mr. Ward said, resuming his seat. "But since you have, albeit inadvertently, broken the rules, Lady Margaret, I am sure you will not object to my bending them just a little further. It is the custom here," he continued in response to her blank look, "to leave a card before paying a call, but I assure you we take no offence."

"Oh, none at all," Mrs. Astor said.

"Well," Marion said rather dryly, "that is a relief."

"Mrs. Scrymgeour, isn't it? I am afraid I am not familiar with the name."

"Mrs. Scrymgeour's late husband was one of Her Majesty's diplomats," Margaret explained.

"Were you ever attached to the embassy in Paris? No? What a shame. It is a marvellous city," Mrs. Astor said. "I myself go to Paris every spring, to buy my new season's gowns. There is nowhere like it."

"I am looking forward to shopping here in New York. I have never been to a department store. I am told that in A. T. Stewart's one can buy anything from a mousetrap to a—a . . ."

"A throne," Marion quipped, as Margaret floundered, making her giggle.

Mrs. Astor's eyebrows shot up. "Ah, the famed British sense of irony. I will be more than happy to supply you with a list of the best shops if you are thinking of refreshing your wardrobe. You may mention my name."

"No-one could give you better advice than Lina in matters of lady's fashion," Mr. McAllister chimed in, "though in all other matters, you may turn to me with confidence."

"Oh, indeed," Mrs. Astor said, bestowing a warm smile upon the man who, Margaret had decided, reminded her of a supercilious newt. "Samuel is the *arbiter* of taste here in New York. In fact, I would go so far as to say that there is no-one, save myself, of course, who understands the intricacies and nuances of society more. He was just helping me finalise the supper menus for my ball. You will receive an invitation in due course, Lady Margaret. And Mrs. Scrymgeour, too."

"Lina's ball is the most exclusive event of the season. You have no idea the lengths some people will go to, to obtain an invite. A woman who shall remain nameless recently accosted me at a soirée, determined to persuade me there existed a tenuous connection between her family and a cousin of a cousin of Lina's." Mr. McAllister tittered. "Needless to say no invitation will be forthcoming. You, however, are a different matter entirely, Lady Margaret. No-one could question your lineage. All doors will be open to the daughter of the Duke of Buckley? Buckluck? Is that how it is pronounced?"

"Buccleuch," Marion corrected him. "It rhymes with *clue*, as in 'haven't a clue.'"

"I believe you were one of the bridesmaids at Princess Helena's wedding, Lady Margaret," Mr. McAllister continued, blandly ignoring this intervention.

"An honour earned through my mother."

"Ah, yes," Mrs. Astor said. "I had heard that the duchess is great friends with the queen. Is it true that Her Majesty wore black to her daughter's wedding?"

"The queen never wears anything other than black."

"Such a difficult colour for some to carry off as well as I can. Especially when they are lacking in inches. I do feel Her Majesty would be better advised to try softer tones. Grey, for example."

"Yes?" Margaret said, nonplussed. Was Mrs. Astor imagining that she would pass her suggestion on to the queen? Louise would have been tickled by this. If only Lou were here—but, no, of all things, Louise loathed pretentiousness and toadying. She would have made mincemeat of Mrs. Astor's chief courtier, for there was no doubt that was the role Mr. McAllister had allotted to himself.

"How long do you intend to grace us with your presence, Lady Margaret?" he now asked her.

"I plan to make New York my home, and Mrs. Scrymgeour's, too, for the foreseeable future."

"Really? Will you take a town house? I would be more than happy to advise you—"

"I am sure you would," Marion intervened, "but Margaret and I are looking forward to combining a little sight-seeing with house-hunting, aren't we, my dear?"

"We have acquired a guide-book. *Lloyd's Pocket Companion and Guide through New York City.* It contains a number of walks we intend to explore."

"Walks! Are you not intending to purchase your own carriage?"

"Hansom cabs are more than sufficient for our needs, and I am looking forward to riding on the streetcars," Margaret said.

"Ha, very good joke." Mr. McAllister's laugh was unconvincing. "If your guide-book was written before yesterday, it will be obsolete already, you know. When you're ready for some up-to-date advice, then I'll be happy to oblige."

"Thank you. Now, I am unsure of local conventions, but in England a morning call should not last more than half an hour, so you will excuse us."

"Very proper," Mr. McAllister agreed. "I shall tell everyone that I have had the pleasure of making your acquaintance, and Lina will, too, no doubt. I predict that you will be in danger of drowning in invitations before the week is out."

"Toad," Marion said under her breath when they had said their goodbyes and were reclaiming their cloaks.

"I rather thought newt," Margaret replied with a grim smile. "I have crossed the Atlantic to escape being dictated to. I am seriously tempted to seek out the most unfashionable address in the city, just to ensure that I am never accused of having paid heed to him."

"I know exactly how you feel, but you will not take a word of advice from me amiss, my dear, will you? Don't cut off your nose to spite your face. It requires little effort to keep a man like Mr. McAllister sweet. Snubbing him might give you fleeting satisfaction, but why make an unnecessary enemy of him? Let him have his say; that is all his vanity requires. Then you may smile and do precisely what you please."

"Dear Marion, you are so wise. And I promise, I will not ask you to live in a hovel, not even to spite Mr. McAllister."

No Barbarians at the Gate— Mrs. William Astor's Annual Extravaganza

The third Monday in January is the date Mrs. William
Astor has appropriated for her annual ball, which is fast
becoming the high point of the season. An invitation to
this society event signals that a person has been decreed
by the hostess and her so-called gatekeeper, Mr. Samuel
Ward McAllister, to have a satisfactory pedigree and to be
untainted by the stain of newly minted money. Those of
humble origin, whose wealth is attributable to commerce,
will never enter that hallowed portal. This year, a number
of those omitted from the guest list left the Metropolis in
advance of the great day in search of fresh country air,
having been advised to do so by their physicians, who had
been advised to advise them to do so! We know of at least
one prominent family who, having failed to persuade Mrs.
Astor's gatekeeper of their right to an invitation, took the
extreme measure of crossing the Atlantic to avoid the
accusation of having been snubbed.

As ever, this year's glittering occasion was attended by
the cream of New York society, with the hoi polloi being
kept at bay by the policemen drafted in to conduct the
traffic which clogged the avenue from nine in the evening.
Owing to the ladies' continuing allegiance to the crinoline,
the gentlemen perforce arrived on foot at the red-carpeted
sidewalk, while the so-called weaker sex traveled with their
maids and their metal cages in carriages.

Mr. William Astor was once again absent, apparently

enjoying the solitude of his yacht—unlike his spouse, a self-professed poor sailor, Mr. Astor prefers the high seas to High Society! All the mundane details of the great event—the various toilettes, descriptions of the glittering jewelry adorning the ladies, the order of the dance and who partnered who with what level of skill and dexterity (or lack of it!)—can be found in other newspapers. Suffice for us to say that the ladies were beautiful, the gentlemen distinguished, and the notoriously baffling (for the uninitiated) German dance was performed.

The cost of the evening must have made even the rich Mrs. William Astor's eyes water. Five hundred bottles of champagne were consumed. That is more than one per guest, assuming the hard-worked staff refrained from imbibing, at over four dollars a pop! The famed Midnight Supper consisted of hot and cold service. The menu included cold quail, tongue, and a variety of force-meats, all of which sound much more appetizing in French.

So far, nothing new from last year or the year before, you may be thinking, but you would be mistaken. Standing out from Mr. Ward McAllister's carefully vetted guest list were two Scotch women who are fast becoming the toast of the Metropolis. Mrs. Marion Scrymgeour, a widow of ample years and girth, partook of the cold *and* the hot supper with some gusto but entirely forsook the dancing. Foreign travel with her deceased spouse, a minor diplomat, has given this widow a wealth of irreverent anecdotes which she tells with a great deal of self-deprecating humor and none of the tedious boastfulness which, alas, certain more noted diplomatic wives adopt.

Mrs. Scrymgeour arrived in the city with Lady Margaret Montagu Douglas Scott, who, unlike her traveling companion, wears her twenty-one years exceedingly well.

Her noble birth and her close friendship with two of the Royal Princesses have brought her a deluge of invitations, but it is her most charming personality, her forthright manner, and her ready wit which will ensure she receives a good many more.

Lady Margaret, a woman of independent means and intentions, plans to set up her own establishment with the doughty Mrs. Scrymgeour. Widowers with thoughts of paying their compliments be warned, however. We have it from a very reliable source that neither of these ladies intend to abandon their current solitary status.

Chapter Thirty-Three

New York, March 1868

SINCE THEIR ARRIVAL IN NEW YORK, Margaret and Marion had accepted invitations to countless balls and soirées, afternoon teas and dinners. They had attended an Offenbach operetta at the magnificent, newly opened Pike's Opera House, a piano recital at Steinway Hall, and had the honour of sharing Mrs. William Astor's box at the Academy of Music for a performance of *Lucia di Lammermoor*. For two women both starved, for very different reasons, of a social life, the warmth of their reception, the generosity of their various hosts, and the sheer variety of entertainments on offer made their first few weeks in this new country a giddy delight. New York society was governed by as many unwritten rules and conventions as its London equivalent, but to Mr. McAllister's barely disguised chagrin, New Yorkers seemed inclined to be indulgent of Margaret's inadvertent breaches of the strict rules of etiquette for which he took personal responsibility.

The social whirl had left little time for the business of house-hunting, so when the manager of the Fifth Avenue Hotel had discreetly offered the ladies a discounted rate for an annual lease of the suite they occupied, Margaret thought it worth considering. That was, until he revealed the so-called bargain rate, which was considerably more than her entire annual allowance.

"And to think I believed myself wealthy," she had said to Marion, still in a state of shock.

"Seven hundred and fifty pounds a year is hardly penury," Marion had pointed out. "You could comfortably keep a family, servants, and even a small carriage for that in England."

"When you convert it into dollars, it is over five thousand, yet compared to almost everyone we have been socialising with, I am a relative pauper. I have never before had to bear the expense of my own home. It is shocking how ignorant I am of such things. As indeed Mr. McAllister is of my financial status. 'One may live fashionably and entertain in modest style for a mere fifteen to twenty thousand a year,'" Margaret mimicked.

"What I'd like to know is how much commission he earns from his various recommendations," Marion said disdainfully. "He has a friend with a conveniently empty town house, or he can put in a word at the Stevens House and obtain one of the better apartments for us. Ha! I'm sure he can, and line his pockets into the bargain."

"I could just about afford an apartment in the Stevens House, though."

"If all you wanted to do was stay in and treat a ride on the steam elevator as entertainment. No, we must look farther downtown. I am sure the rental will decrease in tandem with the street numbers."

Marion had been proved correct, but they had viewed several properties and were beginning to lose heart when the house on Washington Square became available, on a crisp, cold Monday in the middle of March.

"According to our guide-book," Margaret said, "this park was once a burial ground known as potter's field."

"Presumably the bodies have been relocated. Although they certainly would make for quiet neighbours," Marion said, as they strolled through the pleasant green space bounded with low iron railings, with a fountain and some fine trees just coming into bud.

They were to view the middle of a row of town houses bordering the northern side. Built of red brick, the elegant façades were fronted by white marble stairs leading up to an entrance with Ionic columns. "This reminds me of Merrion Square in Dublin," Margaret said as they approached it. "I think it might be the one."

"If you don't mind being surrounded by boarding-houses. This square is certainly not a fashionable address."

"Not yet. Wait until we move in, we'll set a new fashion," Margaret retorted, smiling at the real estate agent, who was waiting for them on the stoop.

"Two bedrooms, two parlours, and a bathroom for eighteen hundred dollars per annum," Marion said an hour later, having persuaded the agent that he had waxed lyrical enough and should leave them alone to discuss the matter. "We will need help to run the household."

"Two maids, provided one could double up to cook, the agent suggested would be more than sufficient. He said that would add another four hundred a year." Margaret giggled. "Listen to me! If Mama could hear me, she would be horrified."

"Nonsense. Every woman should have a solid grasp of her accounts. There is nothing like being in debt for keeping you awake at night. Alexander left me as poor as a church mouse. Foolish man, he had allowed himself to be cajoled into investing in copper mines that never produced an ounce of copper. When I found out after he died that I was pretty much penniless, I was furious—not that he'd lost all his money but that he'd kept it a secret from me. However," Marion continued, shaking her head, "there was nothing to be done about it. I could bemoan my fate and be miserable, or I could cut my cloth accordingly, and get on with the business of enjoying life."

"It's an admirable philosophy." Margaret looked out of the parlour window onto the square beyond. "Is it horribly ungrateful of me to say that I am a little bored with this constant round of parties, especially when everyone has been so kind and generous."

Marion perched on the window seat beside her. "Are you beginning to regret coming here?"

"No, I had to get away." Margaret sighed. "I want my life here to be different, and at the moment it's in danger of becoming horribly familiar. Don't get me wrong—I know how fortunate I am, and I know that most women would be thrilled to be in my position. Oh dear, I sound like a malcontent."

"You're a restless spirit, and that's a very different thing. By that I mean you are not so much interested in the destination, it's the journey you enjoy. Rather like myself."

"Is that more of your homespun philosophy?"

"If you like."

"But what does it mean?"

"Stop fretting so much about the future. What's for you, as my old mother used to say, won't go by you."

Margaret smiled. "Like this house? Do you think it's meant for us? It feels right. I know that's not a very practical reason for taking it on, but . . ."

"Oh, don't underestimate it. And as it happens I agree with you, though it will cost a pretty penny to furnish. We should take a look at the *New York Times*. There are any number of household auctions advertised in it—there are bound to be some good practical furnishings and carpets amongst the plethora of oil paintings, statuary, and mirrors."

"House clearances following a death, you mean?"

"More usually a financial demise. One can get rich quickly in this city, and lose everything even more rapidly. I'm sure we could pick up a few bargains, particularly if you crave a seven-octave pianoforte with ebony inlay. There seems to be at least one in every sale."

Margaret giggled. "Musical soirées were the bane of Mama's life. She had a theory. 'The less talent a young lady possesses,' she used to say, 'the more protracted her performance.'" An unexpected lump rose in her throat. "I miss her."

"And you know from your sister Victoria that the feeling is mutual," Marion said, patting Margaret's arm.

"Yes, but I wish that she could write to me herself."

"Keep out of trouble, and perhaps your father will relent."

"He won't, ever; and as long as I am beholden to him, Mama will not risk going against his wishes for fear he will withdraw my allowance."

"Then perhaps you should find a way *not* to be beholden to him."

Margaret stared at her in astonishment. "How will I do that?"

Marion spread her hands. "This is the Land of Opportunity, remember? You are a resourceful and charming young woman. I am sure you can find a way if you put your mind to it. In fact, perhaps we should both put our minds to it."

"That is an excellent idea," Margaret said, giving Marion a hug. "And in the meantime, we shall take a lease on this house and make my father's hush-money work for me, not him. You see, I am starting to think like an American already!"

Chapter Thirty-Four

M ARGARET HAD VISITED THE SHOPPING district known as the Ladies' Mile several times with Marion, but this was the first time she had ever ventured there on her own. It was still a novel experience for her to be out and about without an escort, and she couldn't help but feel that she was doing something scandalous. However, the throngs of shoppers she joined, disgorged from private carriages, hansom cabs, and streetcars in front of their emporium of choice, were almost all women. Some were accompanied by their maids; some were with friends; but others, like her, were alone.

The array of stores seemed to change, like the city of New York itself, at a bewildering rate. As people moved uptown, so department stores followed, with both the ladies' outfitter Lord & Taylor and the jeweller Tiffany's, known as the palace of jewels, in the process of building new premises. The pace at which New York and New Yorkers moved filled Margaret with a mixture of excitement and awe. New buildings seemed to appear overnight, every one of them more imposing than its neighbour. Her neck hurt from craning it to look upwards at the stores built of iron and glass, Crystal Palaces on a towering scale, flaunting their wares in a manner that the staid London shops would consider vulgar. The welcome they extended was very different, too. Every customer was treated identically, greeted with an enthusiasm that would appal a London shopkeeper eager to disdainfully look down his nose at those he deemed unworthy of his emporium.

At Fourteenth Street Margaret left Broadway to head over to

Sixth, and Macy's with its distinctive red star beside the name. She dallied in front of the window display, marvelling that such mundane items as sheets and towels and blankets could be made to look so attractive. One window, set out like a child's nursery complete with a large cradle and a doll's house, made her think of Julia, who had been alone at Powerscourt since Margaret left. Her last letter had been full of her plans for the gardens, which, she had written, she could at least be reasonably sure would bloom. Julia, whose linen cupboards were a hymn to domesticity, would thoroughly enjoy a shopping trip in New York. Resolving to recount it for her in detail, and mindful of how much she had to acquire on the budget she had worked out with Marion's help, Margaret entered the store.

Two hours later, she headed for A. T. Stewart's on Broadway between Ninth and Tenth Streets, just five minutes from Washington Square, to complete her shopping. Known as the Iron Palace, each of the floors and galleries of this magnificent dry goods store were filled with light from the huge windows and the glass dome which soared above the central atrium. After another extensive bout of purchasing, during which Margaret reckoned she must have walked several miles between the various departments, her feet were beginning to protest.

Pausing on the landing of the fourth floor, she looked about her and was struck by one of those strange sensations that assailed her every now and then: that she wasn't really here at all but merely dreaming. The vista before her, of the tiers of galleries, the vast ground-floor atrium, and the glass roof high above through which the grey winter sky could be seen put her in mind of an enormous theatre. The cast of thousands, almost all women, promenaded below and around her, circling the counters, viewing the goods, consulting their lists and their friends. On each gallery there were more people, a chorus of women that never stilled. And above her, in the workrooms behind the scenes, there would be more women sewing and altering clothes; there would be clerks making up accounts and delivery men packing items. The range of goods on offer was dazzling, from clothes to carpets, china and toys from all over the world. And the women themselves were from every walk of life—New Yorkers, immigrants, and tourists—each customer treated in the same way whether she was buying a box of pins or furnishing a mansion.

What would Mama think if she could see Margaret now, standing quite alone and unobserved in the midst of all this activity, this world within a world? It was liberating, to blend into the crowd, but at the same time it made her acutely aware that she was not yet one of them. Her days were filled, yet she still felt purposeless. And her feet were aching. Deciding to take a rest in the Ladies' Parlour which she had heard of but never visited, she made her way to the second floor.

The parlour was set out like a drawing-room, with clusters of chairs and sofas in groups. Most of them were occupied, and when Margaret stood uncertainly in the doorway, she found herself the unwelcome object of attention. New Yorkers did not disguise their interest when it was aroused, and though she knew they were not being rude, the women's scrutiny scraped away her thin veneer of newly acquired confidence. Fortunately an attendant came to her rescue, ushering her to a free chair with a friendly smile and informing her discreetly that the facilities were in the next room, should she need to use them.

Imagining Mama's horror at the mention of this very practical amenity made Margaret smile to herself. Across from her, a petite woman in a grey gown smiled back at her, clearly thinking the smile had been intended for her. Embarrassed, Margaret sat down and pretended to consult her shopping list, but the woman was not to be put off, and came over to join her.

"Excuse me. I hope you don't mind my interrupting, but are you by any chance Lady Margaret Scott?"

She looked to be in her late thirties or early forties and had brown hair and blue eyes the colour of Margaret's own, an open smile, and an unexpected accent. "You're English," Margaret replied in surprise.

"Originally, though I came here as a child almost thirty years ago. I am Mrs. Jane Cunningham Croly," she said, holding out her card. "And now that I've heard you speak, I know you must be Lady Margaret. I do love a Scotch accent."

"How do you do?" Margaret said, getting to her feet.

"I do very well, thank you. You're thinking I've taken a real liberty accosting you like this, I can see. I should explain that I am a journalist, better known to my readers as Jenny June. Oh no," she added, as Margaret instinctively shrank back, "I'm not a hack in search of scandal; and, though I will confess that I do write two gossip columns, they are both of them perfectly harmless, I promise."

"Is there such a thing as a harmless gossip column?"

"Oh, dear, that is the reaction of one who has been badly burned, if I'm not mistaken, but I assure you mine are really very tame. I swear I couldn't publish a fraction of the things I hear right here in this room."

"Really?"

"The Ladies' Parlour is notorious for tittle-tattle. Trust me, that little coterie over there aren't comparing the price of table linen," Mrs. Croly said. "A long day's shopping, weary feet, and a soft seat loosen the tongue. Now, please feel free to say no, but if you'd like to join my friend and me, then we'd be very pleased to have your company. That's Mary Louise Booth, who has written a history of New York and who is the editor of a magazine called *Harper's Bazar* which launched last year," she added, nodding over at the other woman.

Two female journalists, and both of them looked entirely respectable, yet Margaret hesitated. Mama would politely decline the invitation. Louise would tell her that no journalist was to be trusted. But Marion—hadn't Marion exhorted her to enjoy all that New York had to offer? And here were two women who actually made their living from writing. "Thank you," Margaret said, "I would be delighted to join you."

Mrs. Croly beamed. "Come along, then. Mary Louise," she said, as the other woman got to her feet, "this is Lady Margaret Scott. Lady Margaret, this is Miss Mary Louise Booth."

"It is a pleasure to meet you, Lady Margaret."

The woman who extended her hand was strong-featured, with a generous mouth and a rather prepossessing nose, but there was an air of quiet self-possession about her, of a woman confident in herself, that drew Margaret to her instantly. "Miss Booth, how do you do?"

Like Mrs. Croly, she laughed at the question as the three of them sat down. "I do very well, thank you."

"Lady Margaret is worried I'll write something scandalous about her," Mrs. Croly said.

"In one of Jenny June's columns? Clearly she's not familiar with them. Jane—Jenny June to her many, many readers—writes gossip of the elevating and informative kind. You know, how to climb a ladder without showing your ankles or the polite way to blow your nose in public."

"I do not!" Mrs. Croly said, laughing. "Honestly, Mary Louise, just because I'm not permitted to write on any *serious, manly* subjects doesn't mean that what I do write is pointless."

"You know I'm only teasing you," Miss Booth said, tapping Mrs. Croly's arm affectionately. "Jane here," she said, turning to Margaret, "has written a best-selling cookery book and is a past master at writing about serious subjects under the guise of feminine trivia."

"Thank you, but I won't deny that my columns for *New York World* and *The Sunday Times* and *Noah's Weekly Messenger* are frivolous. 'Parlour and Side-Walk Gossip,'" Mrs. Croly added, rolling her eyes. "Now never mind me, Lady Margaret. Is it true that you are taking a house south of Thirteenth?"

"This is not an interview, Jane," Miss Booth said sharply. "Tell us how you are enjoying New York, Lady Margaret."

"I would say it's the most exciting city I've ever visited, but since I'm not very well-travelled, that is hardly saying much."

"What appeals to you most?" Mrs. Croly asked.

"Well, this, I suppose," Margaret replied. "Shopping alone. Sitting in a parlour in a department store talking to two women with careers. None of this would have happened in London, where one must be introduced by another acquaintance, so that one never meets anyone new—or at least, one is not supposed to."

"Do I sense that you broke a few rules, Lady Margaret?" Mrs. Croly leaned forward. "Do tell."

But once again, Miss Booth intervened. "So women have more freedom in New York, you think? And yet Jane and I were just talking about how sick and tired we are of being told to be happy with our lot. Don't stretch your tiny little minds to the limit by writing about politics or science, just tell us what colour is in this season and whether the crinoline is going to give way to the bustle."

"I wish it would," Margaret said. "If ever there was a test of woman's ingenuity, it is getting in and out of a carriage in a crinoline."

"You should try riding a streetcar in one. Or perhaps you have?" Mrs. Croly said.

"Not yet, but when I do, I shall note down my thoughts and send them to you for your column," Margaret retorted.

"Ha! She has your measure, Jane."

"You know, that's not such a bad idea. Have you any writing experience, Lady Margaret? Are you a great letter writer?"

"I don't know what you mean by great. I do write home regularly . . ."

"And describe your life here? Your thoughts? What you like about New York, how it differs from London?"

"And Dublin, for my friend Julia's sake."

"Excellent! Then I have a proposition for you, Lady Margaret. How do you fancy writing a piece for me?" Mrs. Croly asked. "You can simply draft it up if you like. I can finesse it for publication."

"Actually . . ." Margaret hesitated. Would these two erudite women think her stories trivial? *You are a published author!* She could almost hear Donald urging her not to hide her light under a bushel! "Actually, I have already been published. I've written a book of children's stories. It was published in December last year—a cheap edition, which I believe has proved very popular, intended for use as a primer in schools."

"Well!" Mrs. Croly exclaimed. "That is very interesting."

"It was a charitable endeavour, privately funded, I was not paid for it."

"I wasn't paid a single cent for any of my writing when I first started out," Miss Booth said, "and I barely made enough from the first edition of my history of New York to feed myself. If you agree to write for me, then you will be paid a fair rate."

"Mary Louise, I saw her first! Lady Margaret, I reckon if you wrote a little column—'A Peeress in New York'—no, we can come up with a better title than that—then I can help you sell it. *Demorest's* would love to publish it, I'm sure. And they will also pay you."

"Lady Margaret, I can top that. I could have you published in the first-anniversary edition of *Harper's Bazar* which will be out in November this year. Your name will appear on the list of contributors along with Charles Dickens—"

"You haven't signed Dickens yet."

"I will, if I can get invited to that blasted dinner at Delmonico's."

"You know they won't let us in. No women allowed."

"Even though it is for the Press Club, and you and I are both members."

"Even though my own husband is on the board," Mrs. Croly said grimly.

"I am determined to find a way. However, I am equally determined," Miss Booth said, "to recruit Lady Margaret. What do you say? You could write me a sample column on a subject of your choosing . . ."

"I've already offered her the opportunity to do that."

"How about she does both and then everybody wins?"

The two women smiled at her expectantly. "I'm very flattered but I've never written for the press," Margaret demurred.

"As I said earlier, we would be able to pay a fee." Mrs. Croly quoted a figure that took Margaret aback. "It *is* high for a new writer, but your name will sell."

"And I can pay the same rate. That is per article," Miss Booth said.

"My name? Do you mean my real name would be printed?"

"Is that a problem?"

Her father would be furious. But her father was on the other side of the Atlantic. "Are your magazines published in England?" Two decisive shakes of the head were her answer. "Are these serious offers?"

"Very." Miss Booth took a card from her purse and handed it to her. "We've ambushed you somewhat. Why don't you think about it? Draft something and then we can talk more. There's no rush."

"And the same goes for me, though the sooner—ah no, you must take your time." Mrs. Croly also gave her a card. "We will say no more on the subject for now; you must make your own mind up."

I have already decided, Margaret wanted to say. But exciting and tempting as it was, she was determined not to rush into anything, and so she tucked the cards away in her purse, handing over two of her own before getting to her feet. "Thank you. I will be in touch."

"I do hope so." Miss Booth extended her hand again. "It was a pleasure to meet you."

"A real pleasure," Mrs. Croly said. "I hope to hear from you soon."

"You will, one way or another. But for now," Margaret said mischievously, "Jenny June may tell her readers that Lady Margaret Montagu Douglas Scott and Mrs. Scrymgeour have signed the lease on a small town house on Washington Square. And that, I promise you, is what you call an exclusive."

"SO WHAT DO YOU THINK?" Margaret said. "Should I accept their offers?"

Marion, who had never seen her so animated, resisted the urge to tell her to grab the unexpected opportunity with both hands. Margaret had pounced on Marion the moment she returned from the auction. Margaret's eyes were sparkling, her cheeks flushed, barely giving Marion a chance to ease her aching feet from her boots. "I can see you're all fired up. I take it that you want to write for them—both of them?"

"Yes, though I still can't quite believe they asked me. Do you think that people will be interested in reading what I have to say? Both ladies wish to publish me under my real name. Perhaps they fear if I write anonymously, no-one will read it."

"It's certainly true that fewer people will read it."

Margaret's face fell. "So it's only my name that interests them—is that what you mean?"

"Your name will gain you readers, but it is your writing that will keep them wanting more."

"There was talk only of one article for each."

"Miss Booth and Mrs. Croly are businesswomen. They want to taste and try before they buy, as everyone does here. If you come up with the goods, they'll bite your hand off for more."

Margaret laughed. "What an extraordinary way to put it."

"I heard someone use that phrase today," Marion said, smiling to herself at the memory.

"If my father ever found out, if he saw the family name in print, he'd be appalled and would very likely stop my allowance."

Every time Margaret mentioned that bully of a father, Marion's fists curled. He should admire his daughter, not denigrate her. If Margaret was her daughter, she'd be the proudest mother in the world. But there. "If your writing is successful, you may not need your allowance," she pointed out. "Besides, it's your name, too."

"That's true, and my father was happy enough to use it when he was trying to marry me off."

Bravo! And about time, too, Marion thought. "Precisely," she said.

"It hadn't occurred to me that I could earn my living as Mrs. Croly and Miss Booth do. Now I have started to think about it, I have all sorts of ideas. My children's stories, for example—but I'm getting ahead of myself."

"There is nothing wrong with being ambitious, my dear. I take it you've decided to wield your pen, then?"

"I think I have. I would be foolish to let this opportunity pass, don't you think? Dear Marion." Margaret kissed her cheek. "I have wittered on enough about my day and I haven't even asked you about yours. Did you enjoy the auction?"

"Actually, I don't think that sort of auction is the place for us to acquire our household goods. We don't need gilded chairs and marble-topped side tables, and we certainly don't need a seven-octave pianoforte. Yes, there was one on offer, but there was a distinct lack of good practical furniture."

"Oh dear. So it was a waste of time, then?"

"Not quite." Marion bit back a smile. "I met someone there who has promised to help us."

"Excellent. Who is she?"

"His name is Patrick Valentine. He's an Irishman. A charming and very rich Irishman, actually, though I'm not quite sure how he made his money, for all he would tell me was that he has a finger in many pies. He came over here from Cork during the Great Famine."

"Marion, are you blushing?"

"Don't be ridiculous. We fell into conversation, that is all."

"Clearly that is not all. Is he handsome?"

Marion chuckled. "In a bluff sort of way. He must be shrewd, ruthless even, to have come over on the boat with nothing but a pocketful of potatoes, as he put it, and make his fortune. He has what they call a touch of the Blarney. It's his eyes, I think; they are the kind that twinkle when he laughs. He has a shock of white hair and a moustache that is waxed at the ends. He has an infectious smile too, and such a raucous laugh it made everyone stare. Oh dear, I'm not drawing a very attractive picture, am I?"

"A very intriguing one, though. Go on. Is he tall?"

"He's certainly imposing. A big bear of a man. Not fat, but solid. The kind of man that makes even a woman of my proportions seem frail."

"I wish you wouldn't talk about yourself like that. You are not fat, you are Rubensesque. No," Margaret said, frowning at her, "don't make a joke about it as you always do. As you are forever telling *me* not to do."

"I stand corrected, my dear."

"And another thing," Margaret said, clearly warming to her task, "you talk as if you are in your dotage, which you are not. Mr. Patrick Valentine clearly doesn't think so."

"Actually, he has offered to take me shopping for bargains tomorrow. Do you mind?"

"Of course I don't mind. As a wise woman once told me, you must embrace all that New York has to offer."

"I hope you are not suggesting that might include Mr. Valentine."

"Marion!"

"Oh, don't look so shocked. I am only going shopping with the gentleman."

"Oh, well, in that case," Margaret said, looking entirely—and rightly—unconvinced, "will you please add a writing-desk to your list?"

JOURNAL OF A NOVICE NEW YORKER,
LADY MARGARET MONTAGU DOUGLAS SCOTT

Dear Diary,

Today I awoke for the first time in my newly rented town house on Washington Square. From my bedroom window I can see trees coming into bud, and just for a moment I thought myself back home in rural Scotland. But only for a moment, before the noise of the city assailed me and I knew I could be nowhere else on earth but in New York. I'm not a country bumpkin (or in local parlance, a hick), as I have experience of life in Edinburgh, London, and Dublin, but there is something *unique* about this city. This humble journal will attempt to capture the character of the Metropolis through the eyes of a newcomer.

Take this morning. New York doesn't so much awake as burst into life. I watch the residents of the neighbouring boarding-houses set out for work in their brown suits, cutting across the square to Broadway. I can hear the rumble of the streetcars they will catch and the cries of the newspaper hawkers on the corner. Even this early, the city hums and crackles with energy.

Breakfast in my new abode, however, is an oasis of calm Englishness—pots of tea and bread and butter. Do not assume from this that I am one of those people intent on diluting the experience of living here by recreating my homeland. I intend to become, as far as I can, a true New Yorker, but there are limits. I cannot take to coffee first thing, though my well-travelled and very dear companion

prefers it. She misses the banquet that was the breakfast offered by the Fifth Avenue Hotel, where we have until recently been residing, too. During our stay, she dedicatedly worked her way through the entire menu. Everything but hominy met with her approval, and I confess that I feel the same. We were assured that it was like porridge, and both being Scotswomen were predisposed to enjoy it, but it was nothing like our traditional oats. I take my porridge with cream and salt. My companion puts sugar on hers—sacrilege! I have heard tell of others who have it with stewed fruit, with honey, or even strawberries. Abomination! Does the serving of hominy arouse as much controversy? I must investigate.

I spent the morning, Diary Dear, arranging my furniture and my linens; but in the afternoon, having had a surfeit of domestic bliss, I decided to take a trip uptown in a streetcar. A first! The place I have chosen to live is positioned quite literally at a crossroads in the city. In one direction live those who can choose to work or not, and in the other direction are those who have no option. In Dublin and London the rich and the poor live cheek by jowl. I have not yet encountered this in New York, but perhaps I've not strayed far enough yet? In my experience one learns most about a place by accident. Happily I am very prone to accidents!

There is nothing like a streetcar in London, and I cannot imagine there ever will be, for the tracks would have to be laid on the roads, which are much narrower than New York's avenues, and that would cause complete chaos. Climbing aboard while wearing the full complement of fashionable skirts was a feat so difficult I almost gave up. Imagine trying to get astride a horse without the use of a mounting block, and you will be half-way there. I am sure

my technique, a combination of heaving and clambering, can be bettered with practice, but it will never achieve any vestige of elegance. However once on board and perched upon one of the well-worn seats, the journey was swift and smooth. My fellow passengers were an eclectic mix, and I discovered that being seated opposite one another on a streetcar is the one situation in New York where it is deemed ill-mannered to stare. Everyone contemplates their feet.

For my next outing I am resolved to head downtown on the stage horse car, though I have been warned that these vehicles are considerably more difficult to ascend than the streetcar. Even more exciting, I believe that the West Side Elevated Patented Railway will open in the summer. I am not precisely sure what this might be or where it may take you, but it sounds like far too alluring an experience to miss, and I shall try my best to be among one of the earliest passengers.

Travelling alone on public transport is a mundane experience for many New Yorkers, but it is a great novelty to me, and a very liberating experience. I hope that I never become blasé about it, but I resolved, while making the return journey downtown to my home—for already this house feels like home—to try to capture my impressions while they were fresh. So I sat at my new desk and opened a fresh notebook and began this little journal.

I have barely scratched the surface of New York and am curious to know more. I have a list the length of my arm of new adventures crying out to be experienced. Rest assured, I will record all my impressions, good, bad, and indifferent.

LADY MARGARET TO LADY VICTORIA KERR

Washington Square, New York, 25 July 1868

Dear Victoria,

Your letter reached me on Thursday, less than three weeks after it was posted—the wonders of modern communication methods! Please accept my elated and heart-felt felicitations on the safe delivery of little Margaret. I am honoured and absolutely thrilled to have a namesake, and hope that she proves less troublesome growing up than I was. I am enclosing a little gift for her from Tiffany's. It is only a trinket but a very pretty one, I think you will agree. One day I hope to be able to hug her myself, but for now I will entrust you with the task of giving my new niece a special kiss and cuddle from her American aunt.

You ask me to tell you honestly how I am. Though you do not say so, my instincts tell me that it is because our dearest mama is worried about me. Please reassure her. I am well. No, that is an understatement. I am more than well. I am happy here. I have been welcomed into society and never lack for invitations. In fact, I am to spend August at Mrs. William Astor's retreat in Ferncliff, which is "upstate" in a place called Rhinebeck. This invitation, I assure you, is considered a great honour and I shall be on my very best behaviour. The elusive Mr. Astor breeds horses and his stables are reputed to be second to none, so I hope to be granted the privilege of putting that boast to the test. I am also looking forward to enjoying the country air. Imagine London in the summer and then some (as we say here). Already the heat is stifling, the smells of the drains overpowering, and the plagues of flies—beyond description.

In reply to your other, less than subtle hint about my marital prospects here, let me assure you I am of the same (single) mind as I was when I arrived. If I were inclined to play surrogate to a widower's children or even mother to one of the absurdly young men—boys almost—who are considered eligible bachelors here (for society's eligible bachelors marry before they are twenty), then I could perhaps acquire a husband. Though that is not a foregone conclusion because even by New York standards I am deemed unconventional, and the renowned and esteemed Buccleuch name does not compensate for my conspicuous lack of dowry. However, I am not so inclined, Victoria. I do not say I will never marry, but at this moment in time, I am relishing every moment of learning to be myself. ~~In any case, I fear that I have already loved and lost~~

Please pass on a special hug to Mary and my best love to Mama. Write soon with all your (growing) family news, dearest sister.

With love as ever and another kiss for my little namesake,
Margaret

Washington Square, New York, 20 September 1868

Dear Julia,

I returned from my summer visit to Ferncliffe, Mrs. William Astor's country retreat in Rhinebeck two weeks ago, but it already seems like months. New York is still stifling, with not a hint of autumn—or fall, I should say. The grass in the square is scorched to hay, and the leaves on the trees drooping with dust. In fact everyone seems to droop, exhausted by the summer. Even the boarders next door leave for work in the morning with a reluctant trudge rather than their usual brisk stride.

Mouse and Bina (Mary and Davina, to you!) had the house looking pristine for our return. I cannot tell you what a godsend those sisters are—tell Breda she is an angel for recommending them. They showed every sign of being pleased to welcome Marion and me back, though they assured me that they enjoyed the free time and have been regaling me with tales of Coney Island and day trips on the Hudson Bay steamer which sound like far more fun than the sedate picnics and highly uncompetitive archery that Mrs. Astor considers entertainment. Though I really have no grounds for complaint, for I was permitted to try out one of Mr. Astor's mares, and he deemed me competent enough to grant me the use of her every day, which was a real treat.

Marion continues to enjoy the company of the exuberant Mr. Valentine. I have never before met anyone who could be described as rumbustious, but I think the word was invented just for him. You ask if he is vulgar, and the answer is that you would most certainly think so. He is never *going to make Mr. McAllister's list, that is for sure, though he once told me that if he ever did, he'd slit his own throat! I am no closer to understanding what the various endeavours are that generate his great wealth, though Marion has tried to explain it to me. She has an astonishing grasp of numbers and has even made a little money on the stock exchange here. Don't ask me what that entails; I think it is like gambling—or as Mr. Valentine puts it, having a bit of a flutter.*

You will doubtless be wondering what will become of this unlikely pair—though naturally you will refrain from asking me to speculate. I, however, being a New Yorker, have indulged my curiosity and put the question to Marion myself. She is having a fling, she tells me. Whatever that entails, it does not include marriage. I know, for I asked her that, too, and she said the most touching thing: Patrick is great company and he's a lovely man, but no one can replace my Alexander. *Where it will end, I know not, but I believe it* will *end sooner rather than later, for Marion has confessed to being homesick. Will you invite her to stay with you for a while, Julia, when next your husband is away? I think, if you don't mind my saying so, it would do you both good.*

I will end this overlong letter with some news of my own. My monthly "diary" in Demorest's Magazine *has proved so popular that they have commissioned me for another year at an increased rate, and have offered me very generous terms for three longer articles in what they call my "refreshing and lively" style. I enclose the September issue to keep safe under your pillow, since you tell me you enjoy it (oh, I do hope you are not simply being polite, dear Julia!). I am considering confessing my new career as a journalist to my sister, but have not yet decided, for fear it will put Mama in a tizzy about its offending my father. But if you had never heard of the magazine, then I cannot imagine how it would ever come to the duke's attention.*

And now I really must go, for I have some writing to do and time, as Mr. Valentine would say, consulting his solid gold fob watch, is money!

With great affection,
Margaret

P.S. You will be receiving a parcel from Macy's at some point, containing a selection of towels which are cornflower blue to match your eyes!

New Horizons by
Lady Margaret Montagu Douglas Scott

I first arrived in New York at the beginning of this year. As a young lady from an aristocratic British family, I was raised to marry well, to settle into comfortable domesticity in some venerable rural pile, and produce a brood of children to carry on the line. As such, I was not expected to have an adventurous mind, let alone a restless spirit. So why am I here? Because I possess both, and New York is the perfect place in which to nurture them. A place where I can grow and develop, much as Gotham is doing!

It was autumn, just over a year ago when I came of age and decided to start my life afresh in America. The warmth of the welcome extended to me, the friends I have made are testament to this great Metropolis and its inhabitants. Every day offers fresh possibilities, new opportunities and experiences, and I have tried to sample them all.

But a letter from home has reminded me of the loved ones I am missing, and the distance between us feels impossibly, unbearably vast. It is the fall, a year on from my momentous decision and a time for reflection and reassessment. I look out of my window at Washington Square. The dusty, lifeless, endless days and oppressive heat of summer have finally come to an end. The air is fresh now, the leaves, which provided a palette of burnished colour as they turned, have fallen dramatically after the first sharp frost. I see the people rushing purposefully once more, and my spirits lift. I have that sense, which comes so rarely to one in life, of knowing that I am in the right place at the right time.

I came here at the urging of my heart, but that is not to say the decision was easy. Social convention and the desire to please all too often quell one's inner voice. Haven't we all made the mistake of doing what is expected, or what others wish us to do, when we know, deep down, that it is wrong? I know I have, and deeply regretted it. To act in the face of fierce opposition, particularly from those we love or whose opinions we value, can amount to nothing less than a leap of faith. Having the courage of your convictions takes just that, a great deal of bravery.

One of the aims of this brand-new periodical is to advise readers how to live well in the modern world. I would not claim to be an authority on the subject; to do so would be to imply that I have ceased learning myself, and one prediction I can confidently make is that I will continue to make mistakes. But I always endeavour to learn from them, and am happy to humbly offer readers the benefit of my experience in the form of a few tenets that I use to guide my actions. I call them (rather grandiosely) my Golden Rules:

1. Be kind, even when others are not.
2. Look forward and not back. Don't let the past dictate the future.
3. When a decision is made, there is no point in regretting it.
4. Your opinion is as valid as anyone's. Don't be afraid to speak your mind.
5. Don't bemoan your fate. Take advantage of what life has to offer.

But first and foremost, above all these Golden Rules, I will continue to let my heart be my compass and let it chart my path as my New York adventure continues. Onwards!

Chapter Thirty-Five

A s a treat, Margaret and Marion cooked Christmas dinner for Mouse and Bina, serving it early to allow the two sisters to join their own family, taking with them a hamper crammed full of food and candy.

"I feel terrible abandoning you on Christmas Day. It's not too late to attend one of the parties you've been invited to, you know," Marion said, when they had finished clearing up and returned to the parlour. "Caroline Astor would probably be insulted after you'd declined her invitation, but there are any number of other hostesses who won't mind your turning up unexpectedly."

"I'm sure there are, but I'm not in the mood for socialising. Honestly, Marion, I will be perfectly happy here alone, so please enjoy your last evening with Patrick. I have you all to myself tomorrow before you leave for Ireland."

"I shall miss you terribly, my dear. I can't help feeling as if I am abandoning you."

"Don't be silly. I have had a whole year of your company, and enjoyed every moment of it, but you never intended to remain here long-term. In fact, if you had not met Patrick, you would have gone home before now, wouldn't you?"

"It's true—Patrick has been an unexpected but delightful diversion," Marion said with a wicked smile. "As I have been for him, it seems, since he has important business in California that he has been putting off for some time." Her smile faded. "And as you know, my dear, I

379

have been fretting about Julia, and was seriously considering renting a little cottage near her rather than returning to the rather tedious life I had in Twickenham, which you so kindly rescued me from."

"But now Patrick has ridden to the rescue with his ingenious proposition." Margaret reached across to pat her hand. "Just think, thanks to him you're about to embark on a whole new chapter in your life."

"I still can't believe it, to be honest," Marion said, a slow smile dawning. "Dear Patrick, he is aware how constraining my meagre funds are and would happily supplement them if I would let him, but he knows I would not accept charity."

"There is still no question of marriage, I take it? I know he could never replace Alexander, but . . ."

"Oh, it is not only that. We rub along very well, Patrick and I, but we also value our independence. It is because he understands how important that is to me that he has come up with this plan of his, which will allow me to earn a decent living and enable him to do some real good in his homeland without having to be there in person," Marion said, chuckling. "The perfect solution. Though when I think of the responsibility he has entrusted in me, I am rather daunted, to put it mildly."

"Patrick is a hard-headed businessman. He would not trust you with this venture if he didn't believe you capable."

"Oh, I know that, Margaret, but all the same, it's quite a challenge. I know nothing at all about breeding and training racehorses."

"Which is why you will be hiring experts in the field—and goodness knows, in Ireland they are all horse mad, so there will be no shortage of candidates. Anyway, Patrick is putting you in charge of this stud farm venture because, first and foremost, he trusts you. He knows you won't try to—what's his phrase, diddle the books?"

"Fiddle. Yes, he does think I have a good head for figures," Marion admitted.

"And you are an excellent judge of character, so you're not going to be taken in by any flim-flam merchants," Margaret said, in a poor imitation of Patrick's thick brogue. "And of course, there is the ace up your sleeve, to use another of his phrases: the stud farm in Egypt you visited."

"Alexander and I did get along very well with the owner, that's true, but it was a few years ago, and it's a bit of a long shot, thinking that I can persuade him to sell me any of his precious Arabian thoroughbreds. Patrick would love to be able to boast that his new stables in County Kildare were the first in Ireland to have such prized bloodstock, though of course it's essentially a charitable venture. His aim is to provide employment for young men from humble backgrounds, just like him."

"To give something back to the Old Country," Margaret said, once again failing appallingly to capture Patrick's brogue. "It's a wonderful idea. Breda's brother Brendan is horse mad. You could probably fill every position, from stable-lads to trainee jockeys, from her extended family and the Enniskerry school alone."

"I'm certainly hoping that I can persuade Julia to help in some way. She needs something to occupy her, and Kildare is not too far from Powerscourt." Marion pursed her lips. "She's invited me to stay for a few weeks since Wingfield has gone on yet another of his interminable expeditions. Lady Londonderry will be there, too. I'm looking forward to meeting her."

"And you'll make sure to ask her how Mama is, won't you?"

"Of course I shall, and will give her your gifts to pass on."

"I got rather carried away with my Christmas shopping spree, I'm afraid. You don't mind having to take a second trunk?"

"As long as I'm not expected to carry it. Margaret, are you absolutely sure you'll be happy here on your own?"

"I have Mouse and Bina to look after me here, and Jane and Mary Louise will keep me busy on the work front."

"You do understand there will be some who will be shocked by your living alone with only servants for company?"

"Please don't suggest that I employ a companion in your stead, because you are irreplaceable. Those who know me and like me for myself will remain my friends. Those who drop me because I've broken another of their rules—well then, that is their decision. I will happily weather the storm of Mr. McAllister's disapproval. Dear Marion, you really mustn't worry about me. Besides," Margaret teased, "you've made your decision—there's no point in questioning it now. You have to look forward, not back."

"Ha! Hoisted by my own petard." Marion heaved herself to her feet. "Very well. Patrick will be expecting to pop a cork or two to celebrate our last evening together. I'd better go and primp myself up a bit."

An hour later, having waved Marion, decked out in one of her finest gowns, off in a hansom cab, Margaret returned to her parlour and lit the candles on the little Christmas tree. It was decorated with baubles from Macy's that Bina and Mouse had helped her pick. The huge Christmas tree that stood in the entrance hall at Dalkeith would be hung with the wooden stars she and her sisters had made over the years. Victoria's were always gold and Mary's were silver, but Margaret had chosen to paint hers a different colour each year. Would Mama have thought of her as she hung them up, those stars in emerald and scarlet and purple? There would be new additions now, made by nieces that Margaret had never seen. She retrieved the photograph which Victoria had sent her, smiling at her sister's serious expression as she gazed down at baby Margaret in her arms. Little Cecil, who was almost three years old, was standing beside a footstool on which Walter, aged eighteen months, perched. Staring intently at the camera, he was already the image of his stern father hovering in the background.

Margaret pressed a kiss to the baby's brow, wiping a tear hurriedly from her cheek before it could damage the print. She had sent Walter a jack-in-the-box, and for Cecil and Margaret, she had chosen music boxes. In the trunk, which would accompany

Marion across the Atlantic, there was a music box for Mama, too, and a copy of *Little Women* for Mary. It was signed by the author, whom Margaret had met at one of Mary Louise's salons. She had picked up the new edition of Mary Louise's own book, *A History of the City of New York*, in Appleton's, thinking that her father might enjoy it, forgetting just long enough for it to hurt when she remembered that he would not welcome any gift from her. Replacing the book on the shelf, telling herself he didn't deserve it anyway, had proven much more difficult that it ought to have. She didn't love him, but neither could she completely cease to care, no matter how badly he treated her.

With a wistful sigh, Margaret carefully set down the photograph of Victoria's family and began to pack the last of her gifts into the trunk. There was a spangled silk scarf for Julia in her favourite cornflower blue and a pair of rather risqué black silk stockings. Another copy of *Little Women* was destined for Breda, and there were gifts for all her brothers and sisters and her mother, too. Jacob's ladders; jack-in-the-boxes, and a small mountain of candy including peppermint sticks, liquorice whips, Whitman's sugar plums, Necco Wafers, and peanut candy were earmarked for the Enniskerry schoolchildren. The trunk was so full she had to sit on the lid to force it shut.

It was snowing outside, a fresh, soft fall on top of the crisp frozen blanket already covering Washington Square. Margaret traced the path of the snowflakes as they landed gently on the windowpane before they melted. Was it only three years ago when she had stood in the orangery at Dalkeith doing the same thing? Three years, since she tried so desperately hard to stifle her feelings and do what was expected of her. Her first exile, and her first Christmas apart from her family. Would she ever share another Christmas with them? It seemed unlikely.

Louise would be at Osborne for Christmas, as usual. She was, according to Mr. McAllister, who took a great interest in the latest

London society gossip, fast becoming the darling of the British public, a very glamorous alternative to the queen. Louise, like Margaret, loved to give presents at Christmas, priding herself on her idiosyncratic choices. Margaret had sent her an album of lithographs which she had cut from magazines, depicting some of New York's most famous scenes, annotating each. *Battery and Castle Garden where Marion and I first set foot on American soil; the view from the upper terrace in Central Park towards the boating pond where I skate in winter; the traffic on Broadway, which you cross at your peril; the Fifth Avenue Hotel where we stayed on our arrival, following in your brother Bertie's footsteps.* She doubted the gift would be acknowledged. Louise had not written to her for a year. When she saw Margaret's writing on the parcel, would she open it? Would she look through the pages and imagine Margaret walking on the streets, strolling in Central Park? Would Louise pick up her pen on a whim and break her silence? Again, unlikely.

And Donald? Margaret traced a particularly large snowflake's track from the top of the window to the bottom. Julia had informed her that he had been elected to Parliament in November as the member for Inverness-shire, making good on his intention to settle in Scotland. Would the next step be finding a wife? She wanted him to be happy, yet the notion of him marrying anyone else was painful to contemplate.

The snow was falling heavier now, and the wind was getting up, causing a flurry of flakes to coat the window in white. Margaret pulled the curtains. *Look forward*, she reminded herself, *not back*. Tomorrow was her last day with Marion, and she was determined to make it memorable. Then, when she had tearfully waved her off with her best wishes, she would consider her own plans as a new year beckoned. She would, for a start, publish her book of children's stories as Jane had been urging her to do.

And then—who knew? The big difference from before was that she now found the uncertainty exciting rather than frightening.

The Rectory, Lambeth, 15 December 1868

Dear Margaret,

A very large *parcel arrived this morning all the way from New York, causing great excitement here. I have so far resisted opening the one marked with my name, though I am not sure that I will be able to do so for another ten days! As for the rest, your thoughtfulness and generosity touched all of our hearts. After consulting with my Lambeth Ladies, as you call them, we decided that we would hold a party for the children in the church on Christmas Eve when the sweetmeats—or candy, as you adopted Americans say—will be distributed. Aside from the peppermint sticks, we have never seen anything like the selection you have given us, and I am sure the boxes of Santa Claus sugar plums in particular will be treasured. I shall include a full account in this letter of the party, and will defer posting it until after the big event.*

Your letter to me, which came with the parcel, I have now read several times. Your accounts of New York are so vivid, the life you are leading there so filled with excitement, I almost feel that I am there. Please do continue to send me the Demorest's *Magazine if it is not too much trouble. I read your monthly column out to the Ladies, who take such pride in being acquainted with the author—yes, even Sally, I promise you.*

The door-bell is being rung most impatiently, and our housekeeper is out for the afternoon. I shall abandon this letter for now, and continue it as promised after the party.

It is with enormous sorrow and a very heavy heart that I resume this letter to impart the most dreadful news imaginable. It turns out that the door-bell was being rung by two policemen. Dear Margaret, I hardly know how to say this. ~~Even now, a week later, I cannot believe he~~

I shall try to be succinct. They came to inform me that Sebastian had been ~~murdered~~ *fatally wounded. It appears that he was stabbed when attempting to prevent a moneylender from beating a defaulting customer. The debtor fled when Sebastian stepped in, and the moneylender, fearful of being detained, wielded a knife. The only witness to this dreadful event refused to make an official statement for fear of reprisals.*

I am told by the police to expect no further action. The altercation took place in a neighbouring parish. Had it been closer to home, I fervently believe someone would have gone to Sebastian's assistance, or at least borne witness. ~~As it is, my brother's murderer will never be brought to justice.~~ *The Bible preaches forgiveness. I confess that I am finding it almost impossible to comply. I pray that in time I will find it in my heart to do so* ~~but at this point I am too consumed with anger and grief~~

We laid my dear brother to rest yesterday. As you can imagine, the church was packed to the rafters, with many having to stand outside in the rain. It is some comfort to know just how valued and highly thought of Sebastian was. The funeral service was delivered by his curate, Mr. Glass, who will now take responsibility for the parish. The archbishop wished to lead the mourning, but I felt certain Sebastian would demur. I fear I have offended the archbishop, but I refuse to feel guilty about upholding Sebastian's values to the end.

As to my own future, though Mr. Glass has assured me there is no urgent need for me to quit the rectory, my staying here without Sebastian is quite improper. My parents would welcome my return, for they are both extremely infirm, but I am loathe to leave Lambeth, and will make use of Sebastian's modest bequest to find alternative accommodation. The one consolation for my loss is knowing that by continuing with my work here, I am honouring my brother's memory. Sebastian would wish me to stay here. If I can do so, then I am determined that I will. I owe it to him to protect his legacy.

Margaret, I am deeply sorry to have to impart such dreadful news, and at a time of year which should be filled with joy. Your letters will continue to reach me through the good offices of Mr. Glass, wherever I may be. You are in my thoughts and prayers as ever.

God bless,
Susannah

Chapter Thirty-Six

New York, January 1869

I T WAS A MISERABLE, COLD day and the snow had turned to sleet. Pulling her scarf up over her mouth, Margaret set out across Washington Square. Two weeks had passed since Susannah's letter had reached her. She had settled down happily to read her account of the Christmas party, and could not, at first, take in the contents of that terrible addendum. It took some moments, gazing at the tear-stained paper, before the awful news sank in.

Even now, she could scarcely believe that Sebastian was gone. The initial shock had given way to a deep sadness that was not only grief for the man she had once imagined herself in love with but also a profound sense of sympathy for Susannah and all the men, women, and children of Lambeth whose lives he had touched and improved. How could Sebastian, who had been so full of life and so filled with love for his God and his flock, have been so cruelly and so casually struck down? Why had he been so foolish as to intervene? A silly question, for Sebastian would have been incapable of turning a blind eye, even though he'd be perfectly aware he was taking a risk.

Poor, dear Sebastian. Margaret's days at Lambeth seemed so long ago. Recalling the naive young woman she had been then was like remembering someone else entirely. She had long ago ceased to believe she and Sebastian could ever have been happy as man and wife, but he held a place in her heart as one of the few people to value her. Poor Susannah, though, must have been utterly bereft.

It was her words which had led Margaret to undertake the mission she was embarking upon today. *The one consolation for my loss is knowing that by continuing with my work here, I am honouring my brother's memory.*

Sebastian would not wish anyone to grieve for him, but he would be delighted to know that his life's work was being continued. By Susannah and Mr. Glass in Lambeth. And now hopefully here in New York, too, where Margaret was determined to pay her own practical tribute. Today she had an appointment at the Ladies' Five Points Mission. A Methodist institution, which had been established in downtown New York almost twenty years ago, it was a day school and more importantly a lifeline for a large number of the poorest children, providing the neediest with food and clothing as well as an education.

Its practical efforts being made to relieve suffering reminded Margaret so much of Sebastian, when she had heard of them from Bina and Mouse, that she had taken it for a sign and written, offering her services. The sisters were appalled when she told them what she had done. Five Points had a dreadful reputation, an area where only the completely destitute or those without hope or prospects would live, but her maids' protests only made Margaret more determined, thinking that Five Points was precisely the sort of parish Sebastian would choose, were he in New York.

Knowing that the sisters would do everything to dissuade her, Margaret had left this morning after breakfast without telling them where she was headed. Emerging from the park onto Broadway, she swung herself on board the white-topped streetcar; paid the driver for her ticket; and took her seat, taking shallow breaths while her oversensitive nose adjusted to the raw odour of humanity.

Outside, New York rushed past at its usual heady pace, and Margaret felt a surge of excitement knowing that she, like everyone else, had her own destination, her own part to play in this vast, continual performance. The streetcar rumbled along on its tracks, with private carriages, hansom cabs, horses and carts, and men with barrows all jostling for space. To the rattle of horses' hooves on the cobbles and the clang of carriage wheels was added the thump and clatter of building works. There was the usual constant bustle, an air of excitement, as if something significant was just about to happen. There were men in drab brown and black attire, labourers in leather aprons, working women in starched aprons. Crippled veterans from the Civil War sat on street corners, reminding her of Fraser Scott, which in turn reminded her to check that her purse was secure in her petticoat pocket.

As they headed farther south, the sidewalks became busier still, the roads more clogged, the noise deafening. At a wide intersection very far downtown, the impressive building of white marble which was City Hall loomed into view and Margaret, realising she had missed her stop, hurried to join the other passengers in disembarking. Looking around her, she could see few signs of poverty, but her experience in London and Dublin had taught her it took but a few steps from the wealthiest sections of a city to find the poorest. Her excitement faded a little, giving way to unease. In Dublin, she'd had Breda by her side. In Lambeth, she'd had Donald. Ought she to have brought Mouse or Bina with her after all?

Undoubtedly, but it was too late now, and it wasn't that she was unfamiliar with such environments. It was broad daylight. A combination of confidence and wariness were all that were required, Margaret told herself. A man hawking newspapers looked like a good candidate for providing her with directions, but he was on the opposite side of street. Spotting a fleeting gap in the traffic, she picked up her skirts and ran as fast as she could across the road, feeling the hot breath of a cart-horse on her neck, hearing the angry yell of its driver. Heart pounding, she reached the other side. "Pardon me," she said to the newspaper seller, "I'm looking for the Mission at Five Points."

The man frowned. "There's two of them, you know which one you're after? The Ladies' Mission is on Park Street, and the House of Industry is on Worth. You need to go back up Broadway four blocks and then onto Worth. You can't miss them, one is diagonally opposite the other."

"Thank you."

"You watch your step now, miss."

"I will."

Margaret walked quickly away in the direction the man indicated, trying to maintain the confident expression of a woman who knew perfectly well where she was going. Turning onto Worth Street, the thoroughfare narrowed and very quickly became down at heel, the brick buildings interspersed with wooden shacks. She could still hear the roar of the traffic on Broadway, but it was clear she was entering another world entirely. The cobbles gave way to mud from which horse manure was the prevalent but far from the only smell. Water dripped from stand-pipes into the gutter. The traffic consisted largely of carts and rusty wagons. The shops were dingy: a grocer's, a second-hand clothing shop, a shop that sold single boots and shoes. The houses had sagging roofs and cracked walls, brown paper holding broken windowpanes together. Rickety stairs led up the outside of some of the tenements, and washing hung limply in the cold, sooty, stagnant air, reminding her of the very poorest parts of Sebastian's parish.

Irish brogue, Italian, and German voices mingled with the New York twang and the heavily accented drawl of the American South. Black-skinned men and women were very far from being a noticeable minority, as they were farther up-town. It was she who stood out here, despite her shop-bought woollen gown and plain winter cloak. It wasn't the colour of her skin, or even her red hair, but the lack of darns and patches on her clothes, the lack of holes in her boots. She was sure that even the pristine fur lining of her mittens was visible.

In Lambeth and in Dublin, people had eyed her covertly as an obvious stranger. Here, they stared openly at her as she passed. Finally seeing her destination, Margaret gave a huge sigh of relief. The substantial angular edifice loomed high into the grey sky, its identity proclaimed in block capitals fixed under the roof and painted on the side of the building. Diagonally opposite were two large brick buildings which must be the House of Industry. The sidewalk in front of the mission was paved; the front door, offset on the left, was imposing. Margaret stood before it, beset with nerves. They might reject her. They might think her a fraud, coming here with no testimonials, for it had not occurred to her until now to try to obtain any. She had never applied for work before, had never had to justify her experience or her credentials.

From behind the high fence came a squeal, then a peal of laughter. "Race you to the wall," a small child cried out.

These were the children she hoped to help teach. She had conquered the formidable Lambeth Ladies. She had won over the Enniskerry infants and their schoolmaster. She was here to honour Sebastian, and she was determined to do him proud. And Donald, too, though he would never know it. His continual bolstering of her confidence had given her belief in herself.

Ignoring the familiar pang the thought of him evoked, Margaret squared her shoulders. "First things first, M.," she said to herself. "You've still to persuade them to take you on." Stepping up to the door, she rapped the knocker.

A Redoubtable Irishman Bids a
Fond Farewell to the Metropolis

Yesterday evening, Mr. Patrick Valentine bid a grandiose farewell to New York by hosting—rather appropriately— a party on St. Patrick's Day. Warm of heart and hard of head, Mr. Valentine is not everyone's cup of tea, nor does he aspire to be. His guests were an eclectic mix, representative of their host's most egalitarian outlook on life, and needless to say did not include many from Mr. McAllister's infamous list. While Irish porter and soda bread were served, all tastes were catered for spanning the gourmand (lobster in aspic) to the common man (a hearty concoction of barley and mutton called Irish stew), and so the appetites of all guests were thus sated. The celebrations continued well into the night, with several Irish reels being danced and a rendition of traditional songs bringing a tear to every eye.

Mr. Valentine, who left Ireland during the years of the Great Famine, has embraced every opportunity offered to him by our Great Country, making his extremely large fortune in many and diverse ways, from iron to copper, timber to the railroads. Mr. Valentine likes to say that he enjoys a flutter, though the weight of his fortune indicates, we venture, that his fluttering takes place on the stock market rather than the track.

However, it is to the Sport of Kings back in the Old Country that his thoughts have of late turned. At the celebrations last night, Mr. Valentine announced that he had recently acquired a large tract of land in County Kildare, where he was establishing a thoroughbred stud farm and training stables. This is to be a charitable endeavour, providing much-needed employment in a rural area blighted by poverty. Readers might be surprised to learn that he has entrusted Mrs. Marion Scrymgeour, Lady Margaret Scott's eccentric companion, to oversee the endeavour. Though perhaps we should not be too surprised, given the growing speculation amongst their acquaintances of a closer alliance forming between Mrs. Scrymgeour and Mr. Valentine.

That speculation is now at an end—for the present, at least. Though Mr. Valentine assures us that a regular excursion across the Atlantic will be very much on his future agenda, for now he is headed to the other side of our country to explore new opportunities in California. Bidding him a very fond farewell last night was Lady Margaret Scott, whose charming presence in society has been much rationed this season. Lady Margaret, whose regular diary in *Demorest's* delights thousands of readers, is proving herself an authoress of varied talents. To her journalistic endeavours, she is about to add the release of a book of children's stories entitled *Tall Tales and Wagging Tails*.

It seems, however, that writing and socializing are not sufficient to keep the irrepressible peeress occupied, for she has taken on yet another occupation, that of assisting the teaching of ragamuffin children in a mission in the somewhat insalubrious surroundings of Five Points. It is of course expected that every young society miss take an interest in charitable works—knitting socks, prettily stitching children's caps, selling jelly and preserves to raise funds for charity—but few of these hothouse flowers mingle directly with those they aim to aid.

Will the Scottish peeress, or novice New Yorker as she

has come to be known, set a new trend? We can but hope she doesn't follow Mrs. Scrymgeour's example and return from whence she came. She would be sorely missed here, for all sorts of reasons!

Chapter Thirty-Seven

New York, April 1869

RETURNING FROM HER AFTERNOON STINT at the mission, Margaret bathed and changed. The fashion for a bustle with skirts drawn back and pinned like a pair of drapes continued to reign in New York society, forcing the wearer in the most extreme cases to lean forward in order to prevent herself toppling backwards on her heels. The posture, known as the Grecian bend, was subject to much ridicule in the press for giving rise to physical discomfort. Margaret eschewed this particular trend, having no intention of replacing her hated crinoline with another instrument of torture unless it was absolutely necessary. Gone were the days of requiring a maid to help her to dress or of having her corset laced to a specified circumference. For her occasional forays into polite society, heeding Marion's advice to keep every door open, she wore a small bustle and perched fashionably sideways when she sat down, but on all other occasions she kept her undergarments to a minimum of petticoats and sat squarely and comfortably on her chair to write. She would never be willow-like, but she had grown accustomed to her natural curves and much preferred them to anything enhanced by bustles, crinolines, or corsets.

Arrayed in a gown in her favourite turquoise with a dark-blue jacket, she set out for Delmonico's, where she had arranged to meet Mary Louise and Jane for dinner. The restaurant, on Fourteenth and Fifth, near Union Square, was a ten-minute walk away. Last year Jane had, despite her best efforts, failed to persuade the Press Club to invite any female writers to the dinner given in honour of Charles Dickens unless they stayed hidden behind a curtain. Defiantly, she had, with Mary Louise and several other like-minded businesswomen, formed the Sorosis Club. Lorenzo Delmonico has offered them the use of the private dining room for their inaugural meeting, the first restaurant in New York to admit a ladies' only club, and since then Jane and Mary Louise had become regular customers.

Tonight was not a club event, with just the three of them for dinner, which meant waiting in line with the rest of the diners, for Delmonico's policy was to offer tables on a first-come, first-served basis. When Margaret had first explained this in a letter last year, Julia had been outraged, not only by the notion of ladies actually queuing up to eat but by the idea of ladies dining in public. Victoria, in contrast, made no secret in her letters that she envied the various freedoms Margaret enjoyed and relished reading every detail of her shopping trips as well as the delights of Delmonico's extremely expensive menu. In fact, Margaret found the atmosphere of hushed reverence in the luxurious restaurant rather overpowering, and the food too rich for her taste—though Marion had revelled in it—but she was looking forward to catching up with Jane and Mary Louise.

She arrived early, and having ascertained that neither of them were in front of her, she took her place. Her friends had still not arrived by the time she reached the head of the line, and she was in the process of informing the maître d'hôtel that she was expecting two friends, when a stranger approached her. Dressed in an expensive brown wool suit, he looked to be around thirty. With short dark hair and brown eyes, he had the kind of frank, open expression that made him neither classically handsome nor memorable but genially attractive.

"Excuse me, miss. I wonder, if you are still waiting on your friends to arrive, would you mind giving your position up?" he asked, indicating three older men standing some way back in the queue.

"I beg your pardon?"

"Ah, you are English. A visitor to New York, no doubt. I hope you are enjoying your stay in our fine city. Now, if you could oblige me, I would very much appreciate—"

"I am Scottish actually," Margaret interrupted, irked by his smooth, urbane manner, "and I am not a visitor but a resident with no requirement to oblige you. The policy, as every New Yorker knows, is that you wait in line at Delmonico's no matter who you are."

"I am aware of the policy," the man replied equably, his smile remaining annoyingly fixed in place. "I dine here regularly. If you could see your way to accommodating my request, I would be happy to pay for your meal—and for your friends, too, for I assume you are not dining alone."

"Whether I am or not," Margaret said, her hackles rising, "is frankly none of your business."

"Your dining companions are late, or you are early," the man persisted. "Why take up a table when you could—"

"Surrender it to someone who can't be bothered waiting?" Margaret snapped, by now thoroughly rattled.

"Do a fellow a good turn, will you not, miss? I wouldn't normally ask, but we are running late, and are expected at another engagement in just over an hour, so—"

"Then you will have to choose between arriving late or arriving hungry. And here are my friends," Margaret said, waving to Mary Louise and Jane. "If you will excuse us. Come, ladies," she said, turning her back and following a waiter into the dining room.

"What on earth was that all about?" Mary Louise asked, as they sat down. "You look quite flustered."

"Some entitled fellow in a suit tried to bribe me into giving up our place in the line. The gall of him!"

"Who was he?"

"I have absolutely no idea."

"Oh my, we are in exalted company tonight!" Jane nodded over at the doorway, where a party of four were being ushered in. "The one with the whiskers is Cornelius Vanderbilt. I'm surprised you don't recognise him—he's the richest man in New York."

"And the one on his right is his eldest son, William," Mary Louise informed her. "I think that's Goelet on his left, the founder of the Chemical Bank."

"The young man with them, raising his glass and smiling over at us, is the man who accosted me. Clearly the people next in line had no qualms about accepting a free dinner," Margaret said, glowering.

"That's Randolph Mueller," Jane said. "He's an attorney, a well-known deal maker. He creates trust funds, ties up property acquisitions, that sort of thing. Makes sure the rich stay rich and no doubt amasses a small fortune for himself in the process."

"There's nothing wrong with earning an honest crust," Mary Louise said.

"If it *is* honest," Jane said darkly, before shaking her head. "No, that's not fair. One of the reasons he's so successful is that Randolph Mueller is said to be clean as a whistle and sharp as a needle. Did he really try to bribe you with a free dinner, Margaret?"

"Three free dinners," Margaret said contemptuously.

"We could have run up an enormous bill, and those four wouldn't have batted an eye," Mary Louise said. "Champagne, a couple of bottles of good burgundy. And I could have had the woodcock. I've never had the woodcock here, for it is hideously expensive."

"Mary Louise! You are surely not suggesting I should have accepted that man's offer?"

"No, no, of course not. Goodness, Margaret, that man has got right under your skin."

"He most certainly has not!" Margaret picked up her menu. "I probably wouldn't even recognise him again if I passed him in the street."

Chapter Thirty-Eight

New York, May 1869

WHEN MARGARET WAS FIRST ACCEPTED as a volunteer at the mission, her offer to help out "in any capacity" was treated with some scepticism. Despite her previous experience in Lambeth and Enniskerry, the board found it difficult to believe that the daughter of a duke would be happy to assist in the most menial of tasks and willing to mingle with the dirtiest and most bedraggled of the children. Realising that she had to prove herself, she determined to do so. By the second month of working there, she was no longer greeted with mild surprise when she turned up on time every morning, nor did she suffer an embarrassed silence when she entered the staff room.

She had grown to relish the variety of the tasks and the excitement of not knowing what each day would bring. Today, she had been helping out with new admissions, which tended to be both harrowing and heartwarming. There could be as many as four hundred and fifty children of all ages attending the school on any given day; and at times they were forced to turn children away because they had reached capacity, though they did everything to avoid doing so. The first day could be daunting for the mothers as well as the children, for they were essentially handing their little ones into the care of strangers, sometimes against the wishes of their family. The Irish and Italian communities in particular had to overcome the resistance of their church to having the children educated by Methodists. Some mothers, deeply ashamed of the ragged and filthy condition of their children, would nudge them over the threshold and hurry off, while others were defiant, aggressive, and demanding.

Not even Lambeth had prepared Margaret for the condition of some of the poor souls she helped to treat: their clothes and hair alive with lice and fleas, their feet caked in mud, all of them under-nourished. Once the children were cleaned up, fed, and clothed, Margaret was on very familiar ground with them—the naughty ones and the shy ones and the clever ones and the sullen ones alike, each a challenge and a reward. Kindness, she had been told, was the watchword of the mission, and it was that which brought the children back each day.

Having completed the admissions, Margaret had gone on to her storytelling hour with the infants class, and was descending from the schoolroom when the door to the superintendent's office on the third floor opened, and none other than the man who had tried to buy her place in the line at Delmonico's stepped into the corridor. Unremarkable is how she would have described him if asked, yet she recognised Randolph Mueller instantly. And it seemed, from the way he was smiling at her, that she was not alone.

"Well, well," he said, "we meet again, Lady Margaret."

"How do you know my name?"

"Titian-haired, Scottish accent, and feisty. Your reputation preceded you."

"No it didn't. You had no idea who I was when you tried to bribe me."

"I offered to buy you dinner in return for a small favour, hardly a capital offence," Mr. Mueller said, holding up his hands in surrender. "You're right. I didn't know who you were when I very politely asked you to switch places, but it wasn't too difficult to find out. What *are* you doing here, may I ask? You're a long way from your natural habitat."

"As are you. I help out here four days a week. What's your excuse?"

"I guess you could say I'm helping out, too. Look, I know we got off on the wrong foot, but do you think we could start over?"

"Does that mean you are going to offer to buy me dinner again?"

"What an excellent suggestion."

"I assume you're joking!"

"I wasn't. Why not?"

"Dinner, just the two of us? In London that would be tantamount to a proposal."

"I don't have any designs on you other than to get to know you, but when you put it like that, maybe it's a bad idea. Though this isn't London."

"Very true." Margaret was tempted. Though she had no shortage of friends and acquaintances, since Marion had left she'd had no confidante, and even Marion had been no substitute for the one person she had always confided in. In Donald she had found a kindred spirit and it was that closeness that was lacking in her life. She had no idea whether the man still smiling encouragingly at her was the solution, but she was drawn to him, and she'd never find out if she snubbed him.

"I'll tell you what, Mr. Mueller. I think dinner is a step too far, but if you are free now, you could take me to lunch."

She saw with quiet satisfaction that her answer had both surprised and pleased him. "How long do you have?"

"I'm finished for the day, actually, but if you were thinking of Delmonico's . . ."

"I know it's sacrilege to say so, but I only dine at Delmonico's when I'm doing business. Personally, my taste is for something a bit less formal."

"Really?"

He laughed. "Don't judge me by the company you've seen me keep. There's more to me than that, I promise."

"Where are we going?" Margaret asked ten minutes later.

"There's a place on Canal Street. It's not too far if you don't mind walking. Just watch your purse, though I guess you know to do that if you've been working here for a while."

"Since the start of the year, though to be honest, aside from my route from the streetcar stop to the mission, I don't venture far. I've never been on this street, for example."

"This is Bowery. Don't worry, you'll be safe enough in daylight. It's been cleaned up quite a bit in the last twenty years. It's where people come to shop who can't afford Broadway prices."

"Like the market in Lambeth." Margaret eyed the plethora of small stores, stalls, street vendors. "Only on a huge scale."

"Lambeth?"

"It's a district near London. Poor but hard-working."

"Yeah, same here by day, but you'd encounter a very different atmosphere if you came here after dark. Which I wouldn't recommend."

"You seem to know it well."

"I was raised not far from here, in the Kleindeutschland—the district known as Little Germany. I'm a second-generation immigrant."

"Oh. I had no idea."

"You thought I was born with a silver spoon in my mouth? My father was a clerk. I'm an only child, which is why he could afford to put me through college and then law school. I told you not to judge me too hastily. Although I'm guessing that you get judged regularly yourself, being a member of the aristocracy and all."

"A little, though not nearly so much as back home."

"What brought you here in the first place?"

"Lots of reasons."

"In other words, it's none of my business."

"To be fair, Mr. Mueller, we have only just met."

"True, but I have a good feeling about you. I reckon we're going to be friends, don't you?"

He smiled down at her, a frank smile that met his eyes, making them crinkle at the corners, and her planned equivocal response died on her lips. "Do you know," she said, "I think you might be right."

"I usually am, Lady Margaret. So if we're to be friends, do you think we can dispense with the formalities. Could you call me Randolph?"

"I could if you will call me plain Margaret."

"Plain Margaret! That's a misnomer if ever I heard one. Now, let's eat."

"Here? Isn't this a theatre?"

"Yes, the Old Bowery, and next door is the Atlantic Garden beer hall, but we're going here, to the lunch counter. Or wait, did I read you wrong?" Randolph asked, for the first time looking uncertain. "I thought you'd enjoy something a bit different, but if you'd prefer . . ."

"No, different is good. After you."

It was clear from the way he was greeted with a warm handshake and a slap on the back that her new friend was a regular here. Though he spoke in German to the waiter who showed them to a small booth at the back of the room, Margaret could hear any number of other accents and languages. The table was bare wood but scrubbed clean. A number of men were dining alone with quiet concentration at the counter, but at the tables there was a variety of customers, mostly though not all men, several families, and one group of women.

The food, served on large platters, was copious, fragrant, and completely alien: ham knuckles smothered in red cabbage; sausages of every size, shape, and colour, served with mashed potato and pickled white cabbage; cold roasts; boiled onions; black bread, rye bread, and bread with the texture of a biscuit twisted into an elaborate shape.

"I wouldn't know where to begin," Margaret said, when the

waiter appeared with a jug of foaming beer and two glasses, and asked her what she would like to eat. "Please, will you order for me?"

"Happily," Randolph answered. "Would you like to try the lager?"

"Oh yes! I developed a fondness for a glass of porter when I lived in Ireland, but I've never had this kind of beer. What shall we drink to?"

"*Freundschaft.*"

"Friendship?" When he nodded, she raised her glass. "Cheers."

"*Prost.*"

MARGARET SET DOWN HER CUTLERY with a happy sigh. "That was absolutely delicious. I am going to ask Mouse to buy some of those smoked sausages."

"Mouse?"

"Her real name is Mary. She cooks and keeps house for me, along with her sister, Bina. I rent a place on Washington Square."

"I'm on Bleecker."

"Goodness, really? But that's just on the other side of the square. It's a very unusual choice for a lawyer of your standing, isn't it? Oh no!" Margaret laughed. "Please, I beg you don't tell me again not to judge."

"My parents would agree with you. They think I should live uptown, nearer my clients, but I see enough of them during the day—though that's only one of the reasons I live on Bleecker. I guess what I like most about it is that it's such a mix. Not uptown and not down. Not poor and not smart. There's all sorts, from writers and artists to families, and I guess there are also some whose morals wouldn't stand up to scrutiny, but it's a decent place all the same. People look out for each other, but they don't—" Randolph broke off, looking sheepish.

"They don't pass judgement?"

"I know, I know, but it's true. You can dress and live as you please. You're thinking it all sounds very Bohemian and not at all suitable for a slick attorney who makes his money from the Vanderbilts and their ilk, but that doesn't mean I want to live cheek by jowl with them. Quite the opposite."

"No more than would I wish to, even if I could afford to, which I can't," Margaret said. "How strange that we've been living just a few yards apart and yet we've never bumped into each other." She drained the last of her beer. "I like it, but I think I still prefer porter. Tell me, what business did you have at the mission this morning? Surely they can't afford to hire you to represent them?"

"I wasn't acting for them. My client is the mother of one of the kids they've had adopted."

"From Five Points? How can she possibly—"

"Because I don't charge for that kind of work."

"Oh. No, of course you don't. I really did get you all wrong, didn't I?" Margaret frowned down at her empty glass, embarrassed. "I don't understand, though. The Mission Board have children adopted into good homes, where they will have a far better life than they would have done if they'd remained in Five Points."

"It's a bit awkward talking about it, since you work there, but I guess if I maintain client anonymity it would be allowable. I don't doubt they mean well at the mission, but sometimes there's another side to the story."

"So tell me the other." Realising how defensive she sounded, Margaret uncrossed her arms. "Please."

"Okay. So there is a woman, let's call her Jane . . ."

She listened in growing horror as the tale unfolded. Jane had arrived in New York with her parents and two brothers five years ago. They were a hard-working family, and all quickly found respectable jobs. Jane was a seamstress at A. T. Stewart when she met a man Randolph called John, unable to hide the contempt in his voice when he said the name. John was a carpenter. Within a year they were married, and a year after that, John was out of work and had taken to drinking heavily in taverns. Meanwhile, Jane had a baby boy.

"Things were bad," Randolph continued, staring down at his empty coffee cup, "but they got worse. Turned out that John was already married, and his wife wanted him back."

"So he left Jane in the lurch?"

"He sure did. Jane's family were appalled when they found out she wasn't really married and the child was illegitimate. They wanted her to give the child up, but she refused. She had no money though, so she needed to work, and so . . ."

"She put the little one into the school."

"From the mission's perspective, she was in no position to look after him properly, and the kid would have better prospects with a new family, without the stain of being born on the wrong side of the blanket, as they say in polite circles. So they had him adopted."

"No! Regardless of the fact that it wasn't the mother's fault and she was doing her level best by the child!" Margaret exclaimed, horrified. "That is so wrong."

"It's not so straightforward. Really, no one is to blame other than that cur of a bigamist," Randolph said. "Everyone else is doing their best in difficult circumstances. Jane is hoping that her mother—the child's grandmother—will take them both in. Apparently she would happily do so, but she's having a problem persuading her husband—the child's grandfather—to be reconciled with his daughter."

Margaret refrained from commenting, but she couldn't help thinking of her own situation. "If she does move back with her parents, will she get her baby back?"

"I'll certainly have a much better chance of persuading the mission to reverse their decision. The adoption isn't finalised yet." Randolph checked his watch and groaned. "I had no idea it was so late. I'm afraid I need to go. I've a meeting uptown. A client that pays," he added with a wry smile, signalling for the check.

"Do you do a lot of work downtown, for free?"

"As much as I can. I want to give something back, you know? I was one of the lucky ones—I've made something of myself, but I'm no blind crusader, Margaret. I've only got so much to give, so I put my weight behind those cases I can win." Randolph paid the check and stood up. "Are you headed back home? I need to catch a cab, but I can drop you off."

"Thank you." Looking around her with some surprise Margaret saw that they were the only people left in the room. "And for lunch, too, I really enjoyed it."

"They are good people—at the mission, I mean. It was clear from my meeting this morning: they truly do believe that they were acting for the best. The work they do—that you help with—it's vital."

"Yes, I know."

But bidding the waiter goodbye, following Randolph back out onto Bowery, Margaret was unsettled and pensive as they made their way uptown. "I think I need to broaden my horizons," she said, when the hansom cab drew up at Washington Square. "I don't mean give up my work in the mission, but I'd like to see what it is we are saving people from. The other side of the story," she added, with a sad smile.

"You're welcome to come with me to see Emily—that's Jane's real name," Randolph said.

"Thank you." She touched his arm lightly before descending from the hansom cab. "For trusting me, I mean."

"That's what friends are for." Smiling warmly, he pulled the cab doors closed. "I'll be in touch."

Chapter Thirty-Nine

M ARGARET HAD RETURNED EARLY TO the city from upstate, where she had been staying with the Astors once again. Finding herself surrounded by fellow guests with well-established philanthropic credentials, she had been unable to resist trying to interest them in the plight of the Five Points children. She had abjectly failed. Frustrated, against her better judgement, she had made a final, fatal attempt at the dinner table two nights ago, demanding to know if there was anyone present interested in her views on the scandal going on downtown in their own city, rather than her inside knowledge of the relationship between a widowed queen and her Scottish ghillie. The result had been a startled, embarrassed silence, followed by a hum of conversation in which she was pointedly ignored. Though her ostracization was temporary, by the end of the evening Margaret had made her excuses and left first thing the next morning.

Randolph, who had remained in town on business, was sympathetic but pragmatic when she poured her heart out to him over dinner on her return. "These socialites pride themselves on their charitable largesse, but they prefer projects where they can see their name above the door, like the library William Astor built. You should have known better, Margaret. They're never going to be interested in something hidden away in a part of town they barely acknowledge exists."

He had suggested that they take a day out, forget all about the world for once, and simply enjoy themselves; and when she woke this morning, Margaret already felt considerably better. It was a beautiful summer's day and the sun was blazing down from a cloudless sky as they arrived at Peck Slip, paid their fifty-cent fare, and boarded the little side-wheeled steamer headed for Coney Island.

"It's not too late to take a cruise on the Day Line instead," Randolph said, as they jostled for space on the crowded deck.

"A sedate cruise in comfort and elegance, with views of the Hudson Highlands," Margaret quipped.

He grinned. "Yeah, boring. I know."

"But lovely, I did it last year. They're nothing like the real Highlands, though."

"You feeling homesick?"

"Not really, a little emotionally battered and bruised after the debacle at the Astors'. For some reason," she added sardonically, "failure always makes me think of home."

Randolph, who knew most of her history by now, smiled sympathetically as he edged them both towards a seat on the port side of the deck. "Is this okay, or do you want me to check and see if there's space in the saloon?"

"On a day like this! Don't be daft!"

"Don't be daft," he repeated, laughing. "I love your accent. Come on then—let's grab this space before someone else does. It's been a few years since I did this trip. I'd forgotten how busy it gets."

She sat as comfortably as she could in her new polonaise-style gown of turquoise-and-cream-striped cotton trimmed with a deep ruffle of plain turquoise, for it had to be worn with a bustle. With a frivolous hat of lace and ribbons and cotton gloves, she had thought herself suitably dressed for a holiday outing, but her toilette was almost plain compared to some of the other women in their elaborate gowns with demi-trains and outsize bustles, festooned with layers of ruffles, flounces, frills, and sashes.

Randolph, looking cool and elegant in a cream linen sack coat and trousers, sat down beside her. "We'll be glad of the breeze during the sail. The city's been unbearable this last couple of weeks. I was beginning to wish I'd joined my parents on vacation in the Catskills after all. It's a shame you had to come back early—though a bonus for me."

"Did you win your lawsuit against the landlord of the Bed House on Mott Street? Though to credit him with the title of landlord is being overly generous. Exploiter of the poor more like," Margaret said grimly. "Charging those desperate people twenty dollars a month for a hovel because they have no choice, when so-called respectable people can rent a room in a decent tenement just a few blocks north for half that sum."

"Calm down," Randolph said, putting his hand on her arm, "I won."

"Oh, excellent. Though I wonder what will happen to the poor wretches who were the man's tenants now. Do you think—"

"I think that we should stop talking shop."

"Sorry. Only I was wondering, Randolph, given that Bina is getting married next month, whether one of the women from the Bed House could replace her."

"What will Mouse make of that?"

"She'll be happy to train someone up. I may even take two on, have them both trained, and then they can find work uptown, when they don't smell of Five Points anymore," Margaret said sardonically. "Do you know, that was what one of the Astors' guests actually said to me after my little outburst at dinner."

Randolph sighed. "I can imagine, sadly."

"You think that I should have saved my breath to cool my porridge."

"One of Molly's sayings?" He patted her arm again. "You know what that crowd are like. I told you last night: they like to support good causes, to donate their bucks and their names to any number of worthy initiatives, but they don't want to know about Five Points, especially not when they're on vacation."

"I know, I know," Margaret said despondently, "but there are so many little ones in such desperate need of food and clothing. Sebastian used to say you can't improve your mind if your stomach is empty. He also said there was no such thing as the *un*deserving poor, and he was right about that, too. Why can't more people understand that?"

"But some people do. Like you."

"And you."

"Yeah, but I know when to give up on a lost cause," Randolph said, his expression momentarily darkening as he recalled— Margaret had no doubt—his failure to return poor Emily's little boy to her.

"There are always other causes to pick up, though," she said.

"And always will be. Now, let's enjoy our day out, shall we?"

A blast of the horn signalled the ship's beginning to make her ponderous way onto the Hudson, and a cheer went up from the crowd of people on board.

"I'm really glad you came back early," Randolph said. "I missed you."

He had taken off his hat. The wind ruffled his hair, which he had allowed to grow longer on top than usual. There were shadows under his eyes, testament to the hours he put in to keep up with his work, not to mention the humid summer nights which made it impossible to sleep in the city. He had proved himself the kindred spirit she had hoped for, the friend she had needed and come to rely on more and more. As their eyes met, there was for the first time the prospect of something more than friendship flourishing between them. "I missed you, too," Margaret said.

"I hoped you would." And then before she could even begin to feel awkward, he quickly looked away.

416

JUST OVER AN HOUR LATER, the steamer berthed at Norton's Point and the passengers surged ashore, armed with parasols and picnic baskets, small children holding on to their mother's hands, older children running and shouting ahead.

"Headed for the beach," Randolph said. "It's just five minutes from here, though there's actually three beaches. West Brighton is the nearest; then there's Brighton, where the railway terminus is, and I guess it's the most respectable; and then Manhattan is the farthest away. We can catch one of the conveyances if you want to do the full tour, but I reckon you'd rather walk?"

"Correct," Margaret said, tucking her arm into his. "What are all these people sitting at tables dotted around the pavilion doing?"

"Sharking, mostly. Skin games—you know, taking money from greenhorns. Thimblerig, where they hide a pea under one of three cups—you must have seen that on Broadway? Three-card monte, which you might know as find the lady. Chuck-a-luck, which is a dice game."

Margaret giggled. "It sounds like a character in a children's story. Cluckaluck, the noisy hen."

"Maybe you should write that one."

"Maybe I shall."

"During college vacation, I'd meet up with my old gang in the Lower East and we'd come down on the steamer and make a day of it. I was never dumb enough to bet on any of those games, though. We drank beer. Watched the girls. Went sea-bathing."

"Sea-bathing! I would love to try that. I almost did once in Ireland, at Bray which is a little seaside resort near Dublin, but it was October and Lewis was appalled."

"Lewis?"

"Julia's brother-in-law. An actor and an artist, too, amongst other things. Haven't I mentioned him before? Julia told me in her last letter that he was talking of going to Paris to help tend to the wounded from the war with Prussia. I haven't heard if he did, but it wouldn't surprise me. Lewis," Margaret said, "is a butterfly. Once he masters something, he moves on. It was actually he who first planted the idea of coming to America in my head."

"Then I'm grateful to him. Here we are. What do you think of the beach?"

"It goes on forever!" she exclaimed, delightedly eyeing the long, narrow stretch of sand which shelved steeply below the path, the waves rolling gently in. "And it smells so fresh here, so very different from the city. I am so glad we came."

"Will we stroll on a bit?"

"Yes, please. Are those bathing huts?" Margaret pointed to a row of little whitewashed cabins perched on the sands. "Do you think they would provide us with suits?"

Randolph burst out laughing. "Dear lord, you're serious?"

"Aren't ladies permitted in the water?"

"There's no rule against it, so far as I know, though whether it's something respectable ladies do . . ."

"Is that a gauntlet being thrown down?"

"Lady Margaret Montagu Douglas Scott, sea-bathing." Randolph shook his head mock-disapprovingly.

"Come on, Randolph, surely you're not *feart*, as Molly would say?"

"Certainly not, but I think we'll head farther along. As I said, Brighton Beach is a bit more respectable. We can hire a couple of huts from the Tilyou's Surf House, which I have frequented many times because he sells proper German lager."

"Excellent, something refreshing to look forward to after our swim."

The Surf House was a large wooden shack with a rickety veranda built on the sand. The boarding advertised Bavarian lager at five cents a glass on one side, and fancy flannel bathing suits on the other. For a modest sum of twenty-five cents apiece, Margaret and Randolph rented a hut, each complete with a suit and a towel, and were informed that they would qualify for a bowl of homemade chowder after their swim.

"'Bathing without full suits is positively prohibited by law,'" Margaret read, as she clutched her suit and towel outside the hut allotted to her. "There don't seem to be very many people in the water."

"Having second thoughts?"

"Yes," she said frankly, gazing at the sea. It had seemed so blue and benign and inviting a few moments ago. Now it looked much colder and somehow wetter.

"We could just go and have lunch in a hotel instead."

"Certainly not. Last in the water buys the beer," Margaret declared, darting inside her hut.

It was small and very basic, with a few pegs on the wall and a chamber pot, but no other furnishings. With every passing moment as she struggled out of her clothes, bumping against the walls as she wriggled and hopped, her courage seeped away. The hut smelled of sand and sea and wet wool. The boards beneath her feet were gritty. The maroon bathing suit was so large, with cumbersome buttons, that she had to roll up the sleeves and the legs. It was clean enough, but she was acutely conscious of the fact that it had been worn against someone else's skin, and wondered if she should have kept her own undergarments on beneath it. But then they'd be wet, and she'd have to either abandon them in the hut or roll them into a bundle and carry them, and either prospect was embarrassing.

Cautiously peering out of the door of the hut, Margaret saw that Randolph, in his blue suit, had preceded her, and was already standing waist-deep in the water. So the beer would be on her! Feeling decidedly indecent, her instinct was the close the door and get dressed again; but as if he read her mind, he turned his back on her, dove into the water, and began to swim parallel to the shore. It was obvious that he was no novice.

"At least if I get into difficulty, Randolph will save me," Margaret muttered to herself, "which would be marginally less embarrassing than drowning." Stepping onto the damp sand she began tentatively to make her way towards the water's edge. It was so very strange, being outside with her ankles and shins exposed, wearing only this huge, flapping woollen garment. It was this thought which spurred her on, gasping as her bare skin met water which wasn't as cold as she had expected. It was nothing like the icy shock of a loch, for example, which instantly turned one's feet into blocks of ice. The salty water made her skin tingle, and the contrast of the hot sun blazing down on her head and the sea lapping at her bare skin was rather delicious.

In the bathing hut there had been instructions for men to "enter the water briskly until it reaches the waist," which Randolph had obviously followed. Women were exhorted to proceed with caution lest they be overcome with hysteria. Intent on immersing herself, Margaret waded out as steadily as she could. Forgetting to be embarrassed, she concentrated on keeping her balance, for the sand underfoot was soft; the waves not quite so gentle as they looked; and more importantly the flannel swimsuit was like a huge sponge, soaking up the water and dragging her down.

By the time the water was the required waist-deep, her suit was soaked, her hair was escaping and flying about her face, and her skin was tingling with salt. Yet she was imbued with a feeling of fierce, wild happiness, the joy of being alive and of being only just in control and not quite out of her depth.

"You did it!" Randolph swam smoothly to within a couple of yards of her and stood up. "I'm impressed. Seriously."

His bathing suit had short sleeves. His forearms were faintly tanned and surprisingly sinewy. The neckline of the suit had stretched, exposing his throat and a smattering of dark hair on his chest. The wet fabric clung to his lean body, making her acutely aware of him not as her friend but as a man. And a very attractive one at that, with his wet hair falling over his brow.

Meeting his gaze, Margaret saw her awareness reflected in his eyes. Abruptly conscious of her own suit clinging to her, she turned away just a fraction too late. "It's cold," she said unconvincingly, wrapping her arms around herself.

"It is," he agreed, though she knew she had not fooled him. "Let's go claim our free chowder, and you can buy me a beer."

Ever the gentleman, Randolph headed for the huts, leaving her to wade in unobserved, though he did not, Margaret noted, go into his own hut until she had safely set foot on the sand.

THEY CAUGHT THE LAST, CROWDED STEAMER back to the city and shared a hansom cab to Washington Square. "My nose is burnt," Margaret said, watching the cab head uptown. "I'm afraid my hat isn't very practical."

"It's cute, though," Randolph said.

"It's supposed to be elegant!"

He laughed. "Whatever you say. Did you have a good day?"

They had reached her stoop. The day had cooled, and it was that quiet time after sundown but before dark had fully fallen, when the city seemed to pause for breath. The square felt deserted. "I did." Margaret smiled up at him, and her breath caught and her heart fluttered as their eyes met; and the awareness that had flickered between them all day took a more decided hold in the pit of her stomach. "It was perfect."

"Almost perfect," he corrected her softly, taking a step closer.

She could have stepped back, but instead she lifted her face, and when his lips met hers, she closed her eyes. His kiss was soft, not quite chaste but the kind of kiss which could easily be passed off as belonging to a friend, if she chose. For a second, just a tiny second, she recalled the last time she had been kissed, so very differently, and then she closed her mind to it, and put her arm around Randolph's neck.

He needed no encouraging, but he took no liberties, pressing her close but not too close, his kiss gentle but no longer soft. Though not particularly passionate either, she thought as it ended, vaguely puzzled by her own lack of response.

"I guess we need to get used to being more than friends," Randolph said wryly, proving himself as attuned as ever to her thoughts. "Only I didn't think you'd imagined me as anything *other* than a friend, until today."

"I hadn't. Had you?"

He shrugged. "For a while, but I didn't want to risk wrecking our friendship. I hope I haven't now."

"No—oh, no."

"I'm aware," Randolph said, with a crooked smile, "that there was someone, once. It's the one subject you've carefully avoided. I'm not asking you to tell me about it, but you're over him, yes?"

Donald hugging her tightly. Donald saying goodbye, mounting the grey stallion, and riding off, and herself sinking to the ground, dropping her head into her hands. "Yes," Margaret said, "it's over."

"Look, I don't know where this might lead, but I hope—only you should know you're not the only one who—I mean . . ."

She put a finger to his lips, shaking her head. "You're thirty-one years old, Randolph. I don't imagine you've lived like a monk—but, like you, I don't need to know the details."

"We think alike on this as everything."

He slid his arm around her waist, pulling her close again. There was nothing platonic about this kiss, yet as she stood on the stoop watching him head in the direction of Bleecker Street, her pulses had already slowed, her quickened breath returned to normal.

"The question is, M.," she asked herself as she put her key in the door, "would you do it again?" And, though there was considerable room for improvement, the answer was undoubtedly yes.

CHARLOTTE, DUCHESS OF BUCCLEUCH, TO LADY MARGARET

Montagu House, 10 October 1869

My dearest Margaret,

I have decided to break my silence on this, your twenty-third birthday. I enclose a small gift, a gold locket which you may recognise as one given to me by my own mother. It once contained miniature portraits of your grandparents. I have replaced these with photographs of myself and your sister Mary, and it comes with our love.

My decision to write was not lightly taken, but having made it and taken up my pen at last, I already know it is the right course of action.

Let me explain. Two months ago, I received a parcel from Lady Julia containing a number of American publications which she suggested, in her customary understated way, might be of interest to me. Imagine my astonishment when I discovered that my daughter had become a writer—and a popular one at that, judging by the volume and variety of articles Julia enclosed. I have read your work, Margaret, and am inordinately proud. Your dear and very distinct voice comes through so clearly on the page that I confess I was moved to tears, even when at times I was also moved to laughter. I have always known that you have a talent for storytelling, of course, and I cherish my copy of Tall Tales and Wagging Tails *(which Lady Julia tells me has now been published in America!), but these pieces represent a real departure.*

I will be frank and admit that I was alarmed to see your name attached to them. I feared that if the duke saw your work, he would treat it as a breach of his terms and cease your allowance, thus threatening your hard-won independence. I was in a quandary, more desperate than ever to write to you, more afraid than ever of the consequences. I owe it to Mrs. Scrymgeour for deciding me. She paid me a visit. Margaret—what loyal and true friends you have, and how ashamed I am that I have not been one of them. Mrs. Scrymgeour was much franker than Lady Julia. Through her I came to understand your life in New York more clearly. Your desire to earn your own living, to be free from any requirement to placate the duke or indeed anyone else (what she told me you refer to as your "golden handcuffs") and your sensitive understanding of my own situation—Margaret, when Mrs. Scrymgeour left, I felt very small but quite determined to take action.

I spoke to your father the very next day. It was one of the most difficult conversations I have ever had with him, but the outcome of it is that I am free to write and your allowance is not under threat. I cannot lie and tell you that he is as proud as he ought to be of his daughter, but he did not condemn you. Mary, too, is free to write to you now and I believe has done so. She shows a great deal of independent spirit, and no more inclination than you did to marry young. The duke, I am relieved to say, has learned his lesson in that regard, and as yet has made no moves in that direction.

It would seem that Princess Louise is another young lady determined to avoid matrimony. The speculation that she was to marry Princess Alexandra's brother has proved false, and while Her Majesty's preference for a German who would be happy to live in England is well-established, your friend has made it clear that she will only marry a British subject. Very patriotic, some would say, but the dearth of suitably titled candidates leads me to believe that it is simply a tactic to avoid nuptials. Princess Louise is much more interested in her sculpting, and has been taking private lessons most recently from a Mr. Boehm. He is working on a statue of John Brown for Her Majesty which has caused some controversy within the Family.

I will update you on my own news separately. Though I do not deserve it, I know that you will be pleased to hear from me and trust that we can recover lost ground in our re-established correspondence.

With the greatest of love,
Mama

Powerscourt, County Wicklow, 1 January 1870

Dearest Margaret,

It is the beginning of a new year, and I find myself in a reflective mood. It is two years now since you boldly set sail for New York in search of pastures new, a prospect I would have found terrifying. Yet I have come to admire and envy your courage. You must know from the frequency of my letters how much I value you as a friend, yet I have never said so candidly. I will never forget the day you arrived at Powerscourt, broken but unbowed by your cruel exile. Even in those dark early days, the flame of your courageous heart flickered defiantly. You brought hope into my drab life, and to the lives of the many friends you made here.

Your letters and your wonderful writing have been a balm to me in some of my darkest days, but I am resolved to stop living vicariously. I have had enough of enduring and making do. I am going to follow your example, listen to my heart, and trust my instincts. I have no idea what that means yet, and, reading it over, I can imagine your surprise, for the words sound so very unlike me! I may do nothing more than escape Powerscourt for a while. ~~It is as much a prison for me as it was for you.~~

What has become clear to me is that I cannot waste my years waiting for an event which may never happen. In April I will have been married seven years. I am twenty-seven years old, and must accept that the chances of my having a child now are receding. My sister Gertrude is expecting her first child in the spring after five years of marriage, but she is three years younger than me. Your dear mother has invited me *to join her at Drumlanrig for the summer, or Montagu House for the Season. I may do one or even both!*

And that is quite enough about me! On a much more positive note, I will turn to dear Marion, who has made a great success of the stud farm and provided work for so many disadvantaged young people. It truly is a wonderful venture, and much talked about from County Kildare to Wicklow, Dublin, and beyond. Imagine the excitement then, when Patrick Valentine himself turned up just before Christmas. I have never seen Marion so animated, and so very coy when I teased her about her beau. Mr. Valentine is just as you described, larger than life. Wingfield thought him frightfully vulgar, but I liked him very much. He and Marion seem to me a very well-suited couple, though they both insist that they do not intend to formalise their arrangements. Absence, Marion told me when I asked her (for I did ask—wasn't that bold of me!) will most decidedly continue to make the heart grow fonder.

I have written far more than I intended and will end now with one piece of news which I hope, knowing your generous heart, you will be pleased to hear. Cameron of Lochiel is to be married, Margaret. The betrothal has not been announced yet, but according to Wingfield, who met Lochiel in London, it is imminent. The young lady is a Miss Helen Blair and, from what little I know of her, is a very kind and good-natured young woman and a fellow Scot. Lochiel will now have a chatelaine for his Achnacarry estate and, God willing, the heir which I am sure he desires.

Now I really must finish. Please write soon.

With much love,
Julia

P.S. How remiss of me not to thank you for my Christmas present. The scarf is exactly the shade of cornflower blue which matches my eyes—and the towels which you sent last year are so lovely I can hardly bring myself to use them!

THE QUALITY OF KINDNESS IS NOT STRAINED
BY LADY MARGARET MONTAGU DOUGLAS
SCOTT

The district of Five Points lies just a stone's throw from City Hall. Busy shoppers on Broadway can glimpse it if they care to look beyond the marble and glass retail palaces towards the East River. They'll see a place where the currency is misery, not dollars, where commerce quickly gives way to wretchedness. The very air here is thick with want and suffering. Even in the height of summer, the sun struggles to break through the grey cloud of hopelessness. No-one chooses to live in Five Points. Those lucky few who scrabble and clamber their way out never look back, never mind return. But for the unlucky majority of its residents, it is a life sentence.

Children who are born here all too often die here. The missions work tirelessly to provide succour, feeding, clothing, and schooling them, but for every child they take in, an untold number start the day on an empty stomach picking rags and go to bed even hungrier. The street urchins of Five Points are not an edifying sight. They are clad in rags, barefoot, caked in mud, and crawling with lice, their eyes huge in their heads, their bodies stick-thin. They are not attractive candidates for wealthy benefactors in search of a charitable cause. Confined to their slums, they are the undeserving poor, and easy to ignore.

They are unfairly maligned and often vilified, these Five Points children. They are not born criminals, though their life often forces them down that path. They are innocent, though they do not remain so for long. They are not stupid, but without schooling they will grow up ignorant. They are children who deserve a chance, every one of them, legitimate or fatherless, regardless of their religion, the country of their birth, their parents' occupation or disposition.

The children of Five Points have nothing, but their needs are simple and few: food, clothing, warmth, a roof over their heads. Though first and foremost what these children deserve is to be treated as children; to be given a place to play, a place where they can be safe, free from judgement, treated as equals. A place where they can learn what happiness is.

We cannot continue to ignore what is going on under our very noses. We cannot continue to pretend these children don't exist. In London, the children of the Rookeries are reviled and condemned; but this is the New World, the Land of Opportunity, where all men, women, *and* children have equal status.

Kindness benefits both the giver and the recipient. The children of Five Points deserve to be shown kindness. Who will offer it? Will it be you?

Chapter Forty

"I T's AN EXCELLENT ARTICLE, MARGARET, very powerful and clearly spoken from the heart," Randolph said, setting the copy of the *Revolution* newspaper down on her desk, "but how many people read this publication? A thousand?"

"Three thousand."

"And I guess from your expression that there's not been much of a response?"

"A few letters of support and that's it. I don't know what else to do," Margaret said despondently. "I've tried to interest the wealthy people I know, to the point where I'm in danger of being ostracized from society, but to no avail. I tried to have that article published in a magazine with a significant readership, also to no avail. *Demorest's* wouldn't touch it, nor *Harper's*. It was Mary Louise who introduced me to Mrs. Cady Stanton, who is one of the founders and editors of the *Revolution* and a member of the Sorosis Club. Even with Jane's help, I couldn't persuade any of the other dailies to take it."

"I'm not surprised. You're holding up a mirror to a part of the city their readership prefer to ignore."

"Those who could do something about it aren't sympathetic; those who are sympathetic don't have the means to help."

"The real problem is that we tend to accuse people who fail to make something of themselves of being lazy or no good." Randolph joined her on the window seat and put his arm around her. "Don't look so down. You already do more than enough, helping at the mission. I know you use your own money to buy things for those kids, not to mention finding their mothers work when you can, including positions in your own home. There's a limit to what one person can do."

"But there's no limit to what needs to be done, and my contribution is a drop in the ocean. These children need somewhere they feel safe, Randolph, a sanctuary they can go to anytime."

"Somewhere they won't be judged." He smiled sadly. "I'm flattered you've taken that idea so much to heart but, like I said, maybe it's time to stop berating yourself for what you've not achieved and pat yourself on the back for what you have."

"It's not enough. I need to find a way to reach more people. New Yorkers need to know what is going in their back garden."

"And then what? Even if you persuaded the *New York Times* to publish that piece, what difference would it make? A few more people shaking their heads and muttering about how dreadful it all is before they forget about it and get on with their lives."

"You're right," Margaret said grimly after a moment. "Words are not enough. What we need is action. I need to raise the funds myself, but how? I have signally failed to interest a single one of my philanthropically minded acquaintances that this is a worthy cause."

"You're really set on this? No, that's a stupid question. You want my advice?"

"Always."

"Start small, with what you know. That's how I tackle my cases, the complicated ones, I mean, a step at a time."

"Or a brick at a time, in my case. Start with what I know? But the only thing I know is that I need money, and the only way I know to earn money is by writing, and—oh! Randolph, I think you might be a genius."

"You only think!" he said indignantly.

"I could write a book of stories for children set in Five Points, with all profits being ploughed back in. I would have to paint a slightly sanitized picture, but actually children like gruesome tales. It won't raise very much, but it will be a start, and the publicity can only help make more people aware of the true situation."

"Will you include the noisy hen story?"

"What? Oh, Cluckalot! I shall write that one especially for you."

"Wow! You really are serious!"

"I am indeed." Margaret smiled suddenly. "I'm going to do it, because if I don't, then no-one else will."

"It could take years."

"So be it."

"Don't let it become all-consuming. Leave room for other things."

"I will continue with my writing and work at the mission."

"I was referring to more personal commitments."

She stared at him for a moment, and then the penny dropped. Appalled, Margaret sat abruptly down at her desk. The very last thing she wanted was for Randolph to propose. She had already rejected three proposals, and the memory of the last one still made her heart ache. The love Donald had declared so passionately had died, and now Miss Helen Blair held Margaret's place in his heart. Reading the news back in January, her first reaction had been very far from the delight Julia had predicted. On the contrary, she distinctly recalled crying out *no!* It was wrong, impossible, for Donald to marry someone else, for Donald to love someone else. When her shock had subsided, she had set about rationally persuading herself that she *was* happy for him, but it had taken her much more time than it should have to accustom herself to the fact, and longer still for her to truly and honestly believe what she told herself she ought to feel.

Donald would probably be married now. Miss Helen Blair would be Mrs. Donald Cameron, a position Margaret had rejected and probably would again. Probably? Almost certainly. But it wasn't Donald who was on the brink of proposing, it was Randolph.

Perhaps she had mistaken him? "Didn't you tell me that you wanted to give yourself at least until you were thirty-five before you made any changes to your life? I distinctly remember you saying that there weren't enough hours in the day as it is without—without any other distractions."

He didn't answer her for a moment, staring down at his hands and then out the window at Washington Square. Then he shrugged. "It's a nice day out there. Maybe even the first proper day of spring. Shall we take the streetcar up to Central Park, join the other Sunday strollers?"

In other words, Margaret thought, *I know you don't want to talk about it, so I won't push it*. She was so relieved she almost agreed, but another horrible realisation prevented her. Whether they talked now or in a month's time or in six months, she wouldn't feel any different. "No, wait."

Randolph had half got to his feet, but now he sank back down onto the window seat, not saying anything but watching her. What was wrong with her! They were best friends. They respected each other; they had an instinctive understanding of each other that meant their occasional differences never turned into arguments. She was unlikely to meet another man who seemed such a perfect match, and now that Donald was married—but, no, she would *not* compare Randolph to Donald: that would be quite unfair to both of them.

Though wasn't that the root of the problem? Randolph wasn't Donald. Sadly, Margaret recalled Marion saying something similar about Patrick not being Alexander. If Donald was her ideal, then Randolph was doomed to come up short in comparison. The kisses they shared were delightful, but they had never stirred her to the passionate heights of Donald's kisses. Randolph made her laugh, she thoroughly enjoyed his company, he made her feel *comfortable*.

Oh no! Oh, M.! She did love him, but as a friend, and far too much to hurt him. Rejoining him on the window seat, she angled herself to face him. "I have to be painfully honest with you—it's the least you deserve. You are my best friend, Randolph. I don't want that to change."

"Yeah! That's the problem, isn't it? We haven't really been able to move *beyond* being friends."

"Oh!"

"You thought it was only you?" He shook his head. "Don't get me wrong, there have been times when I could happily persuade myself—because logically we're perfect for each other."

"We are!" Margaret said fervently. "That's what I don't understand."

"I guess love isn't logical."

"Perhaps that's a good thing." Giddy with relief, Margaret took his hand. "Why didn't you say something?"

"Why didn't you?"

"I haven't allowed myself to think about it until just a moment ago, and when I did—" She broke off, for there was a lump in her throat. "I *should* have spoken up earlier. It was wrong of me to kiss you when I knew—though I didn't know, or I wasn't sure. Oh, Randolph . . ."

He hugged her briefly. "Don't blame yourself. I wanted this to work, I kept hoping it would, but I'm glad we've sorted it out now. That was brave of you, to force the issue. I wouldn't have pushed you."

Margaret sat up. "No, but then it would have been there all the time between us, wouldn't it?"

He sighed. "You're right, but all the same, it was brave of you."

It would be the most natural thing in the world for their lips to meet, but what passion they had nurtured between them had dissipated. Margaret moved away, blushing. "Can we remain friends, do you think? I would hate this to come between us."

Randolph got up. "I don't want to lose you either. I think I'll take that walk in Central Park by myself, though, if you don't mind. I need a little time to adjust."

"We'll find a way, won't we?"

"You bet."

She heard him call goodbye to Johanna, the newest recruit from Five Points. Standing by the window to watch him descend the steps, Margaret was relieved when he looked up to wave as usual before he headed for Broadway. Turning away, tears stung her eyes and doubts crowded her mind. Would love eventually have blossomed between them, given time? Was she misremembering her feelings for Donald, creating a false ideal that no man could live up to?

It didn't matter. The point was that she still wasn't ready to marry. She would have to accept that she might never be ready to marry; and until she was, there could be no more romances. She'd had a narrow escape with Randolph, provided their friendship was not a casualty. She would not risk misleading another man.

"And in the meantime," Margaret said, scrubbing at her eyes and giving herself a mental shake, "there is the small matter of raising funds to build a Five Points children's sanctuary." Had she finally bitten off more than she could chew? Sitting down at her desk, she selected a fresh notebook bound in her favourite turquoise leather. Pulling the inkstand towards her, she dipped a newly sharpened pen and began to write.

~~Cluckaluck~~ *Cluckalot was a very noisy hen. The noisiest hen in the henhouse in fact, and that was saying something . . .*

Chapter Forty-One

New York, 8 August 1870

MARGARET KNEW NEXT TO NOTHING about sailing. In her first disastrous London Season she had been invited to Cowes, but by August, when the regatta took place, she had already been exiled to Dalkeith. When Randolph informed her that he had an invitation to the New York Yacht Club on the morning of the Queen's Cup challenge, she had been ambivalent about accompanying him. He had laughed when she queried his sudden interest in a pastime he had never before mentioned, telling her that it was likely to prove quite a spectacle and, besides, he hoped to seal an important bit of business which she might be able to assist him with.

And so this morning Margaret had donned one of her most elegant gowns in emerald silk trimmed with cream lace, and prepared to enjoy the experience. It was a beautiful summer's day, bright and sunny, the heat tempered by a gentle breeze. To her astonishment, the harbour was alive with people competing to board the ferries and steamers from where they would watch the race.

"It looks like every single person in New York is trying to get out onto the water," she said to Randolph. "My goodness, there are even people in rowing boats."

"Luckily we have a reserved place on a steamer to take us to Staten Island, courtesy of our host. It's this one, I think," he answered, putting a protective arm around her. "We'll get a view of the competitors if we're lucky. They've been in the Narrows overnight, and won't head up to the starting point at the yacht club until just before the race gets underway."

The steamer on which they were settled was significantly less crowded. "Who is our host?" Margaret asked, looking around her at the well-dressed guests, some of whom she recognised as Randolph's richer clients.

"James Gordon Bennett Junior."

"You mean the editor of the *Herald*?"

"And a mad keen yachtsman. He won the first transatlantic race back in sixty-six on the *Henrietta*, and he's commodore of the New York Yacht Club."

"He's not your usual type of client."

"It's his father I've been doing a bit of business with. Trust funds, the usual stuff. It's him I want you to meet. No, don't ask me any more questions; you'll find out why in due course. For now, let's just enjoy the spectacle."

Spectacle was certainly the right word. Their steamer began to ease away from the dock and out into the bay, where it joined the flotilla, all crowded with people, women and children as well as men, dressed to the nines. Horns blared, sails flapped, and steam billowed into the clear blue sky. In the Narrows, the strait between Brooklyn and Staten Island, Margaret and Randolph stood at the rail to view the schooners that would take part in the race later that morning.

"That's *Cambria*, the British challenger," Randolph said, pointing at a yacht that looked almost exactly like the others. "She's from the Royal Thames Yacht Club. You might even spot a few familiar faces in her entourage."

"I doubt it very much. Is there only one challenger? Isn't that rather unfair? It makes it very unlikely that they will win, doesn't it?"

"Dear lord, Margaret, don't go saying that—you'll have us ejected from the club."

She giggled. "I can't tell one of these boats—I mean schooners—from the other, so you'll need to tell me when to cheer."

"Which side are you on?"

"Oh, if the challenger was from Leith—that's Edinburgh's port—then I might have a dilemma, but they're English, so there's no question but that I'll be cheering for our team."

"That's my girl! Come over to the other side and take a look at the crowds. Fort Richmond over there is the most popular viewpoint, because you can see both the start and the finish of the race."

"There must be tens of thousands here!"

"Some of them will have been here since dawn. Maybe earlier."

Randolph leaned on the rail, his elbows brushing hers. Back in April, she had worried that their friendship would falter, but after an initial awkwardness they had established a new, easy camaraderie, leaving neither with doubts or regrets. He was formally dressed today, in an expensive black suit, though he was holding his hat, for the breeze had got up, ruffling his hair over his forehead. When she reached out to push it back, he grinned. "I guess I need a haircut. We'll be docking in five minutes. The race is due to start at eleven thirty, so we'll join Gordon Bennett and his party when we arrive."

She listened with half an ear as he ran through a list of people she may or may not bump into, surprised to hear that it included both the Astors and the Vanderbilts. "You still haven't told me how I am to help you."

"Have a little patience. Come on, let's see if we can get you a cup of tea before the race starts."

They disembarked and walked up the short hill to Rosebank. The club-house was built in the Swiss-Italian style with a broad front porch and situated just above the shore with a commanding view of the harbour.

"Gordon Bennett Junior acquired this place for the club about two years ago," Randolph said as they joined the line of people waiting to be received. "That's our host there."

Mr. Gordon Bennett looked to be about the same age as Randolph. His sparse hair was cropped very short in the military style, and this combined with the vigorous moustache and hawk-like nose made him look rather forbidding.

"Mueller," he said, thumping Randolph on the back, "glad you could make it."

"Allow me to introduce you to Lady Margaret Scott. Margaret, Mr. James Gordon Bennett Junior."

"Well! How do you do?" Mr. Gordon Bennett took her gloved hand, surprising her by bowing over and kissing it. "A Scott from Scotland. Now that's a good joke! Do you like sailing? Of course you do, coming from an island and all, eh? My father will be delighted to meet you. Not sure where he is at the moment, but I'm sure—anyway, you'll need to excuse me. I have to go and make sure we're set for the off. Good to meet you, Lady Margaret. There's champagne—or maybe you prefer a wee dram? Ha! Enjoy the day."

Nodding absently at the line of guests waiting behind them, Mr. Gordon Bennett picked up a cap from the table behind him and made his way out.

"I can't see the old man," Randolph said. "We'll go and watch the start, then I'll track him down."

"I still don't understand—" She broke off, shaking her head ruefully. "Patience is not one of my virtues, is it?"

Despite her scant interest in sailing, Margaret couldn't help but get caught up in the excitement as she stood among the crowd on the veranda, watching the tugs pull the schooners, in full sail, into position. Flags were being unfurled on the shore and on the yachts. Then just before eleven thirty, a gunshot cracked, making her jump; the cheering and whooping became a crescendo; and the race was on. The schooners very quickly picked up the breeze and headed out into the bay.

"What happens now?" Margaret asked.

"The course is about forty miles, I'm told. We should know the winner in four hours, maybe a bit longer, but before that, you and I have work to do."

"At last!" She followed him back into the now empty clubhouse. "What do I have to do?"

"Make a pitch," Randolph said. "Sell your idea for Five Points Children's Sanctuary. James Gordon Bennett is not your typical philanthropist, but he's agreed to hear you out. I've opened the door for you; it's up to you now to persuade him."

"Randolph! *This* is the bit of business you wanted my help with? You might have warned me."

"If I had, you'd have prepared a speech. Much better to speak from the heart, Margaret—it's what you do best. There he is. Mr. Gordon Bennett, sir," Randolph said, hailing an elderly man who was seated partially obscured in an alcove, "allow me to introduce Lady Margaret Scott to you. Go on," he whispered as he pushed her forward, "work your magic on him."

Mr. James Gordon Bennett Senior got to his feet. He was dressed in an old-fashioned coat with a high cravat, was very tall, and had a thick head of white hair and a beard trimmed in a Newgate frill. His features were large. He was distinctly cross-eyed under a pair of fierce, shaggy brows, giving him the look of a battle-hardened general rather than a partially retired newspaperman.

"Lady Margaret," he said, his voice belying his appearance for he had the soft accent of the north-east of Scotland, "a pleasure to meet you. Won't you take a seat?"

She did so, her heart beating wildly, vaguely aware of Randolph disappearing into the background. She had, as he would say, one chance at this. "I understand you might be interested in helping set up the sanctuary I want to build in Five Points."

"I'm interested to hear what you have to say, Lady Margaret, especially in that accent which reminds me of the old country.

You've made an unusual choice, in the people you wish to help."

"Someone has to help them, Mr. Gordon Bennett. They deserve a chance, the same as every other child in this city."

He smiled, gently shaking his head. "When Randolph was trying to persuade me to meet you, he gave me that piece you wrote for the *Revolution*, so there's no need to cover old ground. Don't tell me what I should be feeling; tell me what difference you want to make."

"I can't promise anything," Margaret said, regrouping her thoughts, "because as far as I'm aware nothing like it exists, but I want to build a safe space where children can escape the drudgery and the misery of their lives."

"The missions—"

"Do a wonderful job," Margaret said, interrupting him. "I have been a volunteer at the Ladies' Mission for the last eighteen months, but they have limited resources and must therefore spend them on the causes which they deem worthiest. It is the same with the House of Industry, and the Howard Mission, too—they *judge* the children by their parents—or their lack of parents. I want to help the ones who fall through the cracks, so to speak. It is not a child's fault, Mr. Gordon Bennett, if their father is a drunkard or their mother a streetwalker. I hope I have not shocked you."

He laughed gruffly. "I'm an old hack, Lady Margaret. I don't shock easily. What I find interesting is that *you* don't shock easily."

"Oh, I never fail to be shocked by what I see in Five Points, but it doesn't make me want to close my eyes and pretend I haven't seen it," Margaret said earnestly. "Besides, Five Points is sadly not unique. In London . . ."

"I think I've heard enough," Mr. Gordon Bennett said sometime later.

"I'm so sorry. Randolph warned me not to make a speech, but I fear I have let my enthusiasm get the better of me."

"It's certainly not like any appeal for funds I've ever heard." Mr. Gordon Bennett pulled out his gold watch, frowning. "I have to get back to Fifth Avenue. My wife is expecting me."

Her heart sank. "You're not staying to see the end of the race?"

"I don't share my son's passion for sailing. Now, to practicalities. Have you a location in mind? Have you estimated the building cost, the upkeep? How many places—"

"Wait!" Margaret involuntarily clutched his hand, then immediately let him go. "I beg your pardon. You mean you're going to help me?"

"I like the cut of your jib, to use an apposite nautical phrase. I'll tell you something, Lady Margaret. When I first dreamed of launching my own newspaper, I made all sorts of rookie mistakes. I lost a lot of money, even after I launched the *Herald*. I nearly went out of business, but I kept my dream alive, and I fought for it, doing everything save actually turning the presses, and eventually I made it. Listening to you, I don't doubt your enthusiasm or your commitment. Randolph told me you're writing a book . . ."

"*Tales of the City* is what it will be called. It is to be published in September, and all the proceeds will go towards the sanctuary."

"Are they likely to be significant?"

"Every dollar counts."

"Then I'll see what I can do to provide you with the rest. You're well in, as they say, with the Astors and the like; I'm wondering why you haven't gone to them."

"I tried, and failed miserably. My cause isn't considered worthy enough."

"Maybe they don't understand, as I do, what it's like to have to scrabble up the greasy pole." Mr. Gordon Bennett held out his hand, shaking hers warmly before getting to his feet. "Now here is Randolph come to rescue you. I'll be in touch, Lady Margaret. I'm very glad to have met you."

"Well?" Randolph said a few moments later, having seen the old man down to the pier.

"He's agreed to help me, and it's all thanks to you." Margaret threw her arms around him.

Laughing, he disentangled himself. "Like I said, I opened the door, but you walked through it."

"I can't believe it. Oh, Randolph, thank you!"

"It's what friends are for, isn't it. Now why don't we— Hey, who's that over there?"

"Who?" Margaret looked in the direction Randolph was pointing. "The man is—"

"No, not the man, the woman. My lord, isn't she striking?"

"It's Geraldine Haight. Her father owns the St. Nicholas Hotel on Broadway."

"You know her! Please tell me she's not married."

"No, she's not married," Margaret said, eyeing Randolph in astonishment for he looked quite—smitten, was the only word she could think of. "She's a friend of Jane's. A suffragist. I think she's a member of the Sorosis Club. I take it you'd like me to introduce you?"

He quickly smoothed his hair back and straightened his jacket. "You bet!"

PRINCESS LOUISE TO LADY MARGARET

Balmoral Castle, Scotland, 10 October 1870

Dear Margaret,

I am writing to solicit your congratulations, for I am engaged to be married. Six days ago, on the banks of Loch Muick where the queen's little widow's house sits, Lord Lorne declared himself. Such was the strength of his feelings that he did so without first obtaining Her Majesty's consent, though we both felt certain that she would approve of the match, and we have already been proved right. Lorne's father, the Duke of Argyll, is similarly delighted, and the formal announcement is to be made today.

And so, M., you may send me your felicitations, and tell me how delighted you are for me, for I am very satisfied to have achieved my aim of not marrying a foreigner; and though he is a commoner, I have found in Lorne a most amenable *husband who will be happy for me to indulge my artistic pursuits after we are married. (Having taken up residence on the other side of the world, you will not be aware of the acclaim I have been receiving for my sculptures and I, being ever inclined to hide my light under a bushel, have chosen not to enlighten you. However, I can with all due modesty point to some very high praise indeed for my latest efforts from* those qualified to comment.*)*

The wedding will be next year, most likely in the spring, and will be a very grand *occasion, for my humble attempts to stand in for the queen in the years since you deserted us have been* exceedingly well *received by the Great British Public. My marriage has been much anticipated by them—some (though not I!) would call it the match of* the decade—and we wish to reward them for their loyalty with a great spectacle.

I shall design my dress myself, for no-one knows better than I just what flatters my figure—not even Alix, whose taste has of late become much praised. (I, of course, have always thought her understatedly elegant.)

I am sure you have a great deal of your own news to share. As you can imagine, I will have scant time for tittle-tattle, but I would be happy to receive word from you. I was obliged to ascertain your whereabouts from the duchess, an odd state of affairs, Margaret, considering the length of our friendship. Your mother forwarded me a selection of your writing from various American periodicals. It was very strange to see them attributed to you. I must assume social mores in the New World are very different from here. Your mother seems to be very enamoured of your talent. I am afraid I do not feel qualified to comment.

I must dash; the queen requires my services! I am so much in demand, and likely to be more so every day when the announcement is made later. Such a whirlwind of activity lies ahead regarding the arrangements. ~~Oh, M., remember how we always promised that whichever of us married first would have the other as her bridesmaid?~~

I look forward to receiving your well wishes on the day, since you will not be able to attend the ceremony, and will end with my own felicitations for your birthday which is today. What a coincidence! You will forgive the absence of a gift.

With best wishes,
Louise

Lambeth, 15 December 1870

Dear Margaret,

    I write to you on the second anniversary of Sebastian's death knowing that you, too, will be remembering my brother on this day. How very proud he would be if he knew of the wonderful work you are doing in Five Points. Though it was his loss that inspired you to seek work in the Ladies' Mission, it is your own kind heart that led you to battle so hard for your children's sanctuary. I am absolutely delighted to hear that you have finally found a suitable site. The bureaucracy and the corruption you encountered did not shock me, though it should have—I fear every big city is blighted by self-interest. What a wise benefactor you have in Mr. Gordon Bennett, whose experience in both foreseeing and surmounting these obstacles has proven invaluable. You play down your own role, but I know you too well to imagine it was in any way minor. I look forward to hearing that the foundations are being laid, and this time next year perhaps you will have opened the doors of your sanctuary to the first intake of children.

    Your generous parcel of candy and toys for our own Lambeth children arrived safely, and in plenty of time to be distributed at our Christmas Eve party. I could not resist taking a peek at your new book. The stories are very dark, very different from your last set of tales (or should that be tails!), but you have somehow managed to make them hopeful, too, without being mawkish.

    The news of your friend Mr. Mueller's whirlwind engagement did, I must admit, astonish me. I confess that I had nurtured hopes that you and he might make each other happy. I know you well enough, though we have not met face-to-face for far too many years now, to believe that when you say you are delighted for him, you truly are.

I will end this missive with news of another match—my own! (Oh, how I wish I could see your reaction to that news!) You may recall my mentioning the priest who came to Lambeth from a neighbouring parish to help Mr. Glass? His name is Martin Poll Wright. He was a great support to me in those dark days, and in our case friendship has blossomed into love. He proposed today, the dear man wishing to endow this saddest of dates with a much happier significance, and I was delighted to accept.

I am, I assure you, very happy. My beloved Frederick will always have a place in my heart, but I have discovered that there is room there for another. My love for Martin is very different in nature from my feelings for Frederick, but no less true. I never believed I would marry again, and if Sebastian had lived, I may never have considered it, but the loss of my brother forced me to re-evaluate my own life. I have been lonely, Margaret. An odd thing to say, perhaps, for a woman who never lacks for company or occupation, but it is true nonetheless. In Martin I have found real and much-needed companionship as well as love.

My future husband has been posted to a new parish in Cornwall, and so this will be my last letter from the little cottage in Lambeth I have called home for the last two years. We will be married in his church on the fourteenth of January and commence our new life there immediately. It could not be more different from Lambeth, which I will miss terribly, but is an exciting change nonetheless. Who could have imagined, only a few short years ago, me in Cornwall and you in New York. Isn't life wonderfully unpredictable?

I will write from my new address as soon as I can, and look forward to hearing every step of your journey to build your sanctuary. Think of me on the day, dear Margaret, and send us your blessing.

With love,
Susannah

A Very Worthy Cause Opens its Doors on Worth Street

The new Worth Street Children's Sanctuary was officially opened yesterday by Lady Margaret Montagu Douglas Scott. The Sanctuary, as it is already known by the Five Points residents, is a new-built three-story brownstone on a site with ample room for expansion.

A great deal of thought has gone into making the building both inviting and enlightening for its diminutive clientele. There is a playground fenced off at the back, with a fairy fountain and several benches which, when the newly planted trees mature, will be pleasantly shady in the summer. On the lintel of each of the arched windows the letters of the alphabet are carved in the shape of fantastical animals. Inside, the floors are hard-wearing wood, the walls plastered and brightly painted with alphabets and numerals. The rooms are spacious and bright; the chairs and sofas strewn around are comfortable though upholstered in durable fabric with mounds of cushions; and enticing little corners, too, for those in search of solitude. The bookshelves are consciously pitched at child-friendly heights, with the simplest texts on the bottom shelves. There are practical amenities, too, where the children can bathe, eat heartily, and even take a nap.

The Sanctuary is open to every and any child. No questions are asked, no judgments made. The only rule is that kindness is to be both dispensed and received. The primary aim of the Sanctuary is not to educate or improve morals, but to provide first, much needed relief and second hope. Such aims, New Yorkers may think, sound laudable, yet Lady Margaret, the champion of this excellent cause, struggled to interest any of our great Metropolis's philanthropists in it. A true Scotswoman, she stubbornly refused to give up the fight, and her grit and determination eventually won her the sympathetic ear of an anonymous donor.

Many hundreds of people amassed yesterday in the bright morning sunshine for the opening of the facility. They were mostly children and their mothers, but there were some fathers, too. While the *Herald* was given privileged access to the Sanctuary before opening day, reporters from other newspapers and journals were forced to jostle for position with their cameras on the sidewalk. Two notable exceptions were made in Mrs. Jane Croly, better known as the writer Jenny June, and Miss Mary Louise Booth, editor of *Harper's Bazar*. Both ladies enjoy long-standing friendship with Lady Margaret, an author of some note herself. Having seen the completed Sanctuary, these ladies of the press have sworn to laud it lavishly in their journals in the hope of engaging their hitherto uninterested readers.

The ceremony itself was brief, with Lady Margaret doing little more than warmly thanking her benefactor and declaring the facility open. There was a great deal of cheering and applause when she cut the ribbon, and a spontaneous chorus of "Happy birthday, Lady Margaret," it being, serendipitously, twenty-five years since the day of her birth. Then without any more ado, the double doors were thrown wide and the children stampeded through, some laughing and shouting, others glancing over their shoulders to their parents for permission, still others hanging back until Lady Margaret coaxed them in with her generous smile and the offer of cake.

Yesterday was a real turning point for the neglected and ignored children of Five Points. It took a titled immigrant to force us native New Yorkers to look and see what was going on in our own city and to remind us that here in this land, all men, women, and children should be considered equal. We thank the day this charming, self-effacing, and determined young woman chose to make her home in our great Metropolis. There is no need for us to wish her Sanctuary every success, for it was assured the moment the doors were opened. We can only hope it acts as an example, that more places where kindness and hope are distributed without judgment may now spring up for those in need of it most.

Bravo, Lady Margaret!

Chapter Forty-Two

New York, Wednesday, Christmas Day, 1872

MARGARET GAZED DOWN IN AWE at the tiny bundle sleeping in her arms. Little Margherita Mueller, known affectionately as Petite Rita, was only three weeks old, and already she had her parents and her honorary aunt wrapped around her tiny dimpled fingers. She smelled of milk, and when Margaret buried her nose in the silky-soft mass of her hair, that particular baby scent that made her so fiercely protective and at the same time filled with a wondrous love. Though she was accustomed to children, she knew little about infants and had, the first time she had held Rita, been terrified of breaking her.

"She's so perfect," she said now to Randolph, who was leaning over her shoulder with the stunned expression he had worn ever since his daughter was born.

"You won't get any argument from me on that front. I still can't believe she's here."

"Happy first Christmas," Margaret said, kissing the baby's impossibly soft cheek before handing her back reluctantly to Geraldine. "And thank you for inviting me to share it with you. I know that both sets of grandparents were vying for the honour of having you to stay."

Geraldine snuggled her daughter close, kissing the top of her head. "The very idea of having to get dressed up and endure one of my parents' gargantuan formal dinners is exhausting."

"And though my parents promised they'd only invite a few of

the neighbours and just our closest family to dinner—well," Randolph said ruefully, "you can imagine."

"Then I'm even more honoured to have been your guest, but it's getting late, so I'll let you put little Rita to bed," Margaret said, getting to her feet.

"It's only just after seven, but I must confess I'm exhausted," Geraldine said. "Thank you for coming, and for Rita's beautiful christening gown. We'll see you at the ceremony next Sunday. Randolph will walk you home."

"Good idea," he said, jumping to his feet. "I could use the fresh air; otherwise I'll fall asleep in front of the fire."

Outside, it had stopped snowing and the sky had cleared. Randolph had moved only a couple of doors down to a larger town house on Bleecker when he married, and now he and Margaret walked the well-trodden path to Thompson in companionable silence. It was bitterly cold. The sidewalks crunched under their feet; the air was painfully sharp to breathe; but as they reached the entrance to Washington Square and the street lights dimmed, the stars brightened in the clear sky. The park had a magical quality, carpeted with snow, icicles dangling from the trees like Christmas decorations, the noises of the city muffled. Pausing to lift her face to the sky, Margaret was transported back to Dalkeith, as she always was during the festive season when there was snow, but this time when she opened her eyes, the longing that engulfed her refused to dissipate.

"What is it?" Randolph asked. "Are you worried that Rita is going to come between us?" he joked, though his smile faded when he saw she was close to tears. "Just because I'm a father now doesn't change our friendship, Margaret, anymore than my becoming a husband did."

"Don't be daft! I couldn't be happier for you and Geraldine. My goodness, I remember that first time you saw her, on the day of the Queen's Cup. You looked as if you'd been struck by a thunderbolt."

"An arrow straight to the heart." He grinned sheepishly. "One look and I simply knew, though if you'd told me that could happen, I'd have laughed in your face."

"I saw it with my own eyes, remember?" Margaret squeezed his arm. "You're my best friend, Randolph. I want you to be happy, and you very obviously are."

"So what's bothering you all of a sudden? And don't try and deny it—you can't fool me."

"Seeing you with your new family makes me think of mine, I guess." She started walking towards the lights of the town houses on Washington Square, forcing him to follow. "It's five years in January since I landed at Castle Garden, but it's always more difficult to be so far away from home at this time of year. More so, since Mama started writing to me again. I feel I'm missing out on so much. My niece Margaret, my first little namesake was four in the summer, and now my sister, little Margaret's mama, is expecting her sixth child this month—can you believe that!—and I've not set eyes on any of them save in the photographs she sends. In fact I have a brood of nieces and nephews I've never met and— oh, ignore me, Randolph, it's like I said, I'm a little homesick, that's all. Now here we are, back at my little town house. I won't invite you in—Geraldine will be expecting you."

"You sure you're all right on your own? I know you've given your help the day off."

"I'll be fine. I've had a lovely day, but now I'd rather be alone." Margaret stood on tiptoe to kiss his cheek. "See you at the christening, if not before."

Randolph waited until she had let herself in, then bounded off down the steps, understandably anxious to be home. She locked the door behind her, turning up the lamp which had been left low, shedding her outer clothing before climbing the stairs to her study, where she set a taper to the logs in the fireplace.

Curling up on the hearthrug, she picked up her bundle of

Christmas letters, shuffling through the well-read pages. Susannah was happily established in Cornwall, and as busy as ever with her mothers' groups. Victoria looked decidedly matronly with her ever-growing brood in her annual photograph, and Kerr, now the Marquess of Lothian, with his grizzled beard, looked much older than his years. Marion had written in eager expectation of what had become Patrick's annual pilgrimage to County Kildare, and Julia was spending her Christmas with her sister's family while Wingfield remained at Powerscourt.

He made no effort to dissuade me and appears perfectly content to spend Christmas without me, Julia wrote, *and I find I, too, am perfectly content without him.* Which for Julia, Margaret thought, folding the letter back up, was akin to a declaration of independence.

Louise's brief note informed Margaret that she would be spending Christmas with the Argylls at Inveraray Castle. As usual, she gave no indication of her state of mind and made no mention of the possibility of motherhood. The photograph she enclosed was not of her husband's family home but of the pretty fishing village by the same name on the banks of Loch Fyne, *which I thought you would like, for I know how much you enjoy the Highland scenery,* Louise had written. It *was* a very beautiful scene, with heather-clad hills in the background beyond the still waters of the loch, but the image Margaret saw as she looked at it was of another castle on the eastern side of the country, set in more familiar gently rolling countryside.

A tear tracked down Margaret's cheek as she picked up Mama's letter, knowing in her current mood that it would be a mistake to read it again, yet unable to resist. July 1866 was the last time they had been together, at Princess Helena's wedding. Lenchen had four children now and, according to Mama, was very happy with her unprepossessing prince.

You always assure me that you want to know who will be spending Christmas with us, Mama wrote, *but I always worry, even as I accede to your request, that I am causing you pain. I hang your stars on the tree each year, those bright jewel colours so distinct even after all these years, and I say a little prayer that you are happy, Margaret. You seem so. You have achieved so much already in your young life that I find it difficult sometimes to reconcile the impetuous, impulsive child with the sensible businesswoman.*

Margaret sniffed, rubbing her eyes with her sleeve. What she would give if she could be with Mama for just a few minutes! But it wouldn't be nearly enough. She would almost rather do without than have one snatched moment. She wanted to linger among familiar accents, and to have her own pass unremarked. She wanted to take a walk in the countryside under a driech, mizzling sky, her feet soaked through, the soft rain falling like mist and the smell of peat smoke wafting lazily through the air. She wanted to meet all her nephews and nieces, to hug them, to tell them stories. And she wanted to take tea and cake with her sisters and Mama, to chat about nothing of consequence knowing that there would always be more time and yet more to talk together.

What she wanted was to go home.

But this was her home, wasn't it? This little town house in this extraordinary metropolis, the place where she had truly grown up, become a woman she barely recognised. She'd had no idea when she sailed from Ireland what path her life might take, but now there was ample proof on her desk of her achievements. The Sanctuary was being expanded and, thanks to the bequest dear Mr. Gordon Bennett had left in his will, would be secure for years to come. Between her work there, her writing, and the few social engagements she continued to keep, her days were full.

Yet watching Randolph revelling in domestic bliss had unsettled her. He would always be her friend, but his marriage had changed things between them. Naturally, Geraldine and now Rita came first with him. It wasn't that Margaret wanted what he had, but it reminded her that she, too, had a family and that they were very far away.

She loved New York and all the people from every walk of life who had allowed her into their lives. She would never have had the freedom to achieve what she had done here back home, nor even have gained the confidence to try. She loved the fact that every day she could prove herself useful; but as she stared down at her latest turquoise notebook, open on her blotter, Margaret wondered, wasn't there room for more?

Her heart ached for home. Her inconvenient heart, she thought wryly, always pulling her in another direction whenever she was in danger of becoming too settled. But already her tears were drying on her cheeks, her spirits lifting.

Could she go home? She could not possibly make such a momentous decision on the spur of the moment. How would she live? She would breach her father's terms the moment she set foot on Scottish soil, and though she no longer relied upon her allowance in New York, she had no idea whether she would be able to earn enough to live on in Scotland.

She would find a way. She always did, didn't she? She could continue to wield her pen. Another book of stories? Perhaps *Demorest's* would be interested in the *Journal of a New Yorker in Scotland*? And there was that Englishwoman, the rather terrifying suffragist she had met at one of Mary Louise's soirées, who had offered her work. Emily Faithfull, that was her name, and the magazine she edited was the *Victoria*.

Would that be sufficient? Margaret had no idea, but she knew without a quiver of a doubt that she was determined to find out. As to where she would live, that was easy, for she would go to Edinburgh. A city like every other, no doubt, in having children in need of sanctuary.

Because if I can do it here, then why should I not succeed on my home turf! she thought, smiling to herself and picking up Mama's letter once more, this time taking out the photograph. Staring back at her, his hand on her mother's shoulder, was the one large obstacle to her plans, the duke. She forced herself to study him, trying to understand her feelings for him, which she had not done for a very long time. She was unable to conjure any trace of love, but there was pity, for he never would be able to understand her while she understood him very well. Was she going to let this bully who had never cared for her continue to dictate her actions and mitigate her happiness?

Absolutely not! Propping the photograph up on the desk, she picked up her pen. In the act of pulling a fresh sheet of writing paper towards her she caught her father's eye. No, she didn't love him, but he was her flesh and blood. Surely, eventually, even for him, that would count for something?

Your Grace, Margaret wrote, *you will no doubt be surprised to hear from me after all this time. . . .*

Jenny June Bids Farewell to Our Favorite Novice New Yorker

Last week, I waved Lady Margaret Montagu Douglas Scott off on the voyage across the Atlantic which would take her back to Scotland. Having graced us with her presence for five years, she is now returning to her ancestral home. I am sure that I am not the only one who will miss her.

Lady Margaret delighted readers with her monthly journal in this periodical. While many incomers to the Metropolis insist that they intend to immerse themselves in the city, what they actually mean is that they intend to play the tourist and see all the sights. They consider themselves true New Yorkers if they have waited in line at Delmonico's or braved a ride on a streetcar, but they do not seek out the Gotham beyond their guide-books, which is precisely what Lady Margaret did—and more! Not content with joining the crowds on the ferry to Coney Island in the heat of August, she went sea-bathing in a hired suit. Though she never managed to prefer coffee to tea in the morning, she was happy to sample the many and varied cuisines this city offers, from baked beans and succotash to pumpkin pie; oyster stew; and her favorite, beer with sauerkraut and smoked German sausage.

Lady Margaret's desire to explore all aspects of the city took her to places where few people venture, tourists or residents alike, and it is in the infamous Five Points district where she has left her most enduring legacy. The Children's Sanctuary which she worked so tirelessly to establish has been extended several times since it was opened almost two years ago, and the model is now being replicated in other needy areas of the city.

"I would do almost anything to make a child smile," Lady Margaret told me not once but several times, when the battle to fund her Sanctuary looked to be lost. It is to her great credit that she fought on, and the battle was eventually won against the odds.

On a personal note, I will miss my friend and her sparkling company very much. She will be a huge loss to the Sanctuary, and to Five Points, but she will also be missed in the mansions of Fifth Avenue. I do not doubt that her natural curiosity, her innate kindness, and her irrepressible spirit will lead her to fight new causes in her homeland.

Will she triumph? Readers will be delighted to know that Lady Margaret is not entirely lost to us. Her "Journal of a New Yorker Returning to Her Roots" will debut in next month's issue. I am sure I am not alone in looking forward to it immensely.

Chapter Forty-Three

Y OUR FATHER IS MOST PUT-OUT to be marooned in London, and concerned Her Majesty will take offence at his absence," the duchess said. "But since the queen only informed Lochiel yesterday that she planned to call on him tomorrow, she cannot possibly imagine he will have been able to conjure a significant welcoming party at such short notice."

Or that the party would include me, Margaret thought, gazing out at the view as the train puffed towards their destination after a somewhat complicated journey into the Highlands. Though Donald would know by now that she was coming, for Mama had sent a telegram. When she had proposed that Margaret deputise for the duke, it had seemed like an excellent opportunity for her to lay the ghosts of their past, but the closer she got to their destination, the more she wondered if she was ready for this encounter.

Her mother knew nothing of their friendship and would have been astounded if she knew how close it had come to marriage. Margaret had consciously refrained from asking any questions, anxious not to arouse her suspicions. Was Donald looking forward to seeing her? After all this time, he was most likely indifferent, especially if he was happily married, which she truly hoped he was. She hoped he loved his Helen, and was loved in return, and that when she saw them together it would put paid to any of her own residual feelings for him, once and for all. She had to knock him off the pedestal she had created for him and clear the way for the possibility of finding love herself, a possibility she finally felt ready to consider. She didn't want to spend the rest of her life alone. But first she had to prove to herself that Donald was not an obstacle to her future happiness.

"You are eerily quiet," Mama said, as the train began to slow for the approach to the station.

Roused from her reverie, Margaret smiled apologetically. "The view is so beautiful, I was quite distracted," she said, which was partially true. "I wonder what my father's reaction will be when he discovers that I have taken his place?"

"He is in no position to object," the duchess said dryly. "Besides, I am sure the queen will be very pleased to see you again. The royal party are to drive from Inverlochy Castle tomorrow, where they are on a little sketching holiday. Poor Lochiel has no idea when they will arrive or for how long they plan to stay. You know how it is with Her Majesty when she is in Scotland. She will say that she wishes the call to be quite informal with no ceremony, and has no notion of the amount of preparation it takes to receive her, informally or otherwise. Thank heavens I had a decent plaid gown to bring with me."

"And thank heavens that Mary's tartan dress fitted me."

"Your younger sister is very like you in figure and in temperament."

"Oh, poor Mary."

Mama laughed. "You know perfectly well I meant it as a compliment. It is a shame that Louise isn't with the queen, but I believe she will only have Princess Beatrice with her."

"Oh, Louise is far too busy for jaunts to Scotland. She is redecorating the private apartment in Kensington Palace she has been granted, and so excited to finally to have space to create a sculpting studio of her own. Her letters are full of her designs and plans. She is absolutely determined to have it reflect her personal taste, which I suppose is no surprise, after having endured the queen's more sombre preferences for so long."

"She and Lorne seem to spend an inordinate amount of time apart." The duchess pursed her lips. "I am assuming that there is no substance to the latest round of speculation in the press, that she will shortly be making an addition to the house of Argyll?"

"Not that I am aware, though she does not confide in me as she once did, and even if she did . . ."

"You would not break her confidence. Quite right. You are a very loyal friend. It is a pity that you have managed to see her only the once since your return."

"She has a very full calendar, but I am delighted she made the effort to come to Edinburgh especially to see me. It was wonderful to finally meet face-to-face again. It's been such a long time."

"How does being married suit her?"

"Louise has never been one to give much away." Her friend had been vivacious, garrulous almost, over the dinner they had shared in Edinburgh last month, but when Margaret attempted to steer their conversation onto a more personal level, the drawbridge was hoisted up. "It was bound to be a little awkward, given the gap, but by the end, it was just like old times."

"Did she find you much changed? What does she make of your Sanctuary in Five Points?"

"We didn't talk much about New York. Louise is involved with so many charitable endeavours herself . . ."

"And she never could bear to be outshone."

"Mama!"

"Yes, I know, that is unkind but perfectly true nonetheless. She is one of your oldest friends, and she ought to be proud of you. I know I am."

"And you tell me so, at every opportunity. There really is no need . . ."

"There is every need." Mama took her hand, squeezing it tightly.

"I know I also say this every time we meet, but I am so very pleased to have you home."

"And I am very, very pleased to be here."

"You don't regret leaving New York?"

"Oh no, not a bit of it. I miss it and my friends there; but really, the world is not such a vast place as it seemed when I first crossed the Atlantic. I know I'll visit one day. For now, I am very happy to be back in Scotland. I knew the moment the train started to pull in at Waverley station back in March that this is where I belong. We came through the tunnel, and I saw the big grey bulk of the castle looming over me. When I stepped onto the platform, I was surrounded by Scottish voices; and even though it had been seven long years since I'd set foot here—" Margaret broke off, smiling sheepishly. "You've read my first piece for *Demorest's*, I don't need to repeat it verbatim."

Her mother smiled warmly. "I am so relieved that the closeness we established in our correspondence continues to thrive. Your father . . ."

"Oh, let us not spoil things by talking of him."

"He will never admit it, but he is astonished by what you have achieved, Margaret. The fact that he has not once mentioned stopping your allowance should have told you at least that he no longer opposes the choices you have made."

"Though he cannot endorse them!"

"No, that would be quite beyond him, but he makes no objection to my visiting you and even staying overnight in that little town house you have rented on Heriot Row, though Dalkeith is only seven miles from the city. What's more, when I suggested that I could help raise funds for your Edinburgh sanctuary, he said he expected no less."

"I'm delighted that we will be working together."

"As am I. I wish I could spare you more time, but I have so many other commitments and spend far less time in Edinburgh

464

than I would like. Ah, here we are. I believe Lochiel has arranged a carriage for us. All we need to do is find a porter for our luggage."

A mere twenty minutes later they were on their way, following a sinuous road along the banks of a river. The nerves which Margaret had quelled now set her stomach roiling, making her wish that she had eschewed her boiled egg at breakfast. It was less than fifteen miles to their destination. In two hours, perhaps less, she would see Donald again.

My home is the Achnacarry Estate in Invernesshire, near the little village of Spean Bridge, and just north of the town of Fort William. The land is rugged, with some fine woods, and the castle itself sits low on the terrain, not far from Loch Arkaig, where I am thinking of building a new pier to allow a steamer to berth. She still had the letter he had written to her in Ireland. She still had all his letters. *I think you would like it, Margaret. I know that I would very much like to show it to you one day.*

And now that day had arrived, but she would not be arriving as the estate's future mistress, only as additional ballast to the guests he and his wife had assembled to greet the queen. She smoothed an imaginary crease out of the olive-green travelling gown that Mama had been astonished to learn she had bought ready-made. It was quite plain, a pleated hem and cuffs and a row of pearl buttons on the bodice the only trimmings, but she had long ago given up any attempt to be fashionable and the colour suited her. Would Donald think her much changed? Perhaps she would find him much altered? What would Helen look like? And goodness, would they have children? It hadn't even occurred to her until now. Mama had made no mention of children, but then Mama had no notion at all that Margaret and Donald were anything other than acquaintances. Which they were not, now.

"This must be Loch Lochy," the duchess said, leaning out of the window. "Isn't it lovely?"

"Beautiful," Margaret agreed, gazing out at the wooded banks of the loch, the hills behind looking blue rather than green. The road turned away from the loch to follow the banks of another river and the terrain became much more lush, the mountains more rugged. They had left Dalkeith in mizzle. As they journeyed north the skies had darkened and the rain had fallen with determined ferocity, but now the skies were clear, with only a few harmless puffy clouds drifting on the horizon. Through the open window of the carriage came the scent of spruce trees and bracken, the rush of the river, and the rumble of the coach wheels on the rutted road.

And then came Margaret's first glimpse of Achnacarry, sitting low in the land just as Donald had described it, surrounded by a riot of oak trees which were green against the grey stone, the conifers on the steeply rising hill behind in hues of purple and teal. Donald's home was not so much a castle as a country house with baronial aspirations, with a lower wing, obviously a late addition, spoiling the symmetry of the central block, and a balustraded roof adorned with an assortment of turrets. It was a solid house with a commanding view over some pretty fields full of contentedly grazing sheep to the front, and presumably the river to the rear, but it was neither imposing nor intimidating.

Margaret banished the thought that this could have been hers, reminding herself sternly of the purpose of the visit; but as the carriage came to a halt in front of a white portico and the coachman opened the door and pulled down the steps, a man appeared in the doorway to greet them and her legs turned to jelly.

"Your Grace," she heard him say to her mother, "it is a great pleasure to welcome you to Achnacarry. I am very much obliged to you for making the effort at such short notice."

To hear his voice was so very different from remembering it. To have him actually standing only a few feet away was unnerving. She wasn't at all certain she could get herself out of the carriage, but she could not remain inside indefinitely. Taking herself in hand, reminding herself that it was dear Donald she was about to face, not some hostile tyrant, Margaret gathered up her skirts, pinned a smile to her face, and climbed out of the carriage.

"Margaret, you remember Lochiel, of course," Mama said.

"Margaret!" He stared at her, utterly confounded.

"Didn't you get my telegram? I am afraid the duke is in London," Mama explained, "and so I brought my second daughter. Her Majesty will be pleased to meet her again. The last time was at Princess Helena's wedding, which would be— Oh, goodness, how long ago was that?"

"Seven years," Margaret said, holding out her hand, pleased to see it was not shaking. "How do you do, Lochiel?"

"Margaret." He clasped his hands around hers, staring at her as if she was an apparition. "I thought you were in America."

"I returned in March."

"March? You are paying an extended visit, then?"

Gently she disentangled her hands from his. "I am home for good. I have taken a town house in Edinburgh."

"A house? In Edinburgh? So you are married, then?"

"No. Oh no, I live alone," she said, swallowing hard, for a lump had risen in her throat. That couldn't possibly be anything other than surprise in his voice, and the way he'd clung to her fingers could only be attributable to shock. He was older. There were more lines at the corners of his eyes and just a hint of grey at his temples; but he was still clean-shaven, still handsome in that plain, unassuming way of his, and the smile which was dawning on him still reached his eyes.

"Your wife," Margaret said, taking an unnecessary step back. "I am looking forward to meeting her."

"My wife?"

"Lochiel is not married, Margaret. Whatever gave you that idea?"

"Julia." Margaret looked from Donald to Mama and then back

to Donald. "Julia told me you were engaged. A Miss Helen Blair. She said . . ."

"In the end we agreed we did not suit."

"Oh! I'm so sorry," Margaret said, appalled and confused, staring at him helplessly. "I thought—I had no idea."

"Why should you? It's not as if—I mean—" Donald broke off, making a visible effort to smile at her mother. "You've had a long journey; you'll be wanting to wash your hands. Your Grace, I have allotted you the state rooms. Margaret—Lady Margaret—you must have the Blue Room. When you are ready, perhaps you would like to join my cousins, Susan and Camilla, in the drawing-room for tea? Fortunately for me, they both live nearby. They arrived yesterday and have been working tirelessly with my housekeeper to prepare for every eventuality. I'm afraid I have no idea even of the time of day Her Majesty plans to arrive. She insists that the visit will be informal but . . ."

"I understand, but you should not worry. Your house is in a lovely setting, surrounded by exactly the kind of hills and lochs Her Majesty adores," the duchess said. "And here is your good lady housekeeper come to show us to our rooms, if I am not mistaken. If you will excuse us." She took Margaret's arm again, saying softly, "I do hope that when you resolve whatever issue exists between you and Lochiel you will see fit to inform me what on earth is going on."

DONALD LISTENED AS CAMILLA AND SUSAN explained the arrangements they had made for dinner that night and the many options they had prepared for tomorrow, though he didn't actually hear a word of what they said.

Margaret was here.

Margaret was not in New York; she was here at Achnacarry.

He had never been able to convince himself that he didn't love her, but he had long ago given up any hope of seeing her again.

Yet what difference did it make? She wasn't married, but didn't he know better than anyone that was most likely because she never would? He would be a fool to imagine that the outcome would be different if he asked her a second time. Misguided to imagine that she was here for any other reason than to accompany her mother. An idiot to read anything into the look they had exchanged as he took her hand.

Yet there *had* been something in that look.

Abruptly informing his cousins that the duchess would be joining them for tea, Donald cut short the conversation, heading to the front terrace. Somehow he was not surprised to see Margaret leaning out the window of the Blue Chamber with her chin cupped in her hands. Whatever she had been doing in New York, it suited her. She had always been lovely, but now she wore her more mature beauty with a quiet, understated confidence that he found extremely attractive.

He beckoned her to join him, and in a few short moments she was with him, still in her travelling gown but without her hat and gloves.

"I thought we could take a walk along the path by the river."

"I can think of nothing I'd like more," she answered, hesitating only a moment before slipping her hand into the crook of his arm. "You don't mind my being here? I'm sorry it was such a shock."

"It was, but a very nice one. I thought it was perfectly obvious that I was pleased to see you."

"I'm so sorry if I embarrassed you by mentioning Miss Blair. For the last three years, you see, I've laboured under the misapprehension that you were married. I was glad when Julia wrote of it—well, I was glad eventually, once I had recovered from the shock—for I wanted so much for you to be happy."

"I tried to be. We had a great deal in common, Helen and I. I thought if I could make her happy, then I would be happy, too, but it doesn't work that way. Fortunately we both realised it in time." Donald grimaced, recalling that painful conversation. "The betrothal was never formalised, but it was wrong of me, very wrong, to have allowed matters to have progressed as far as they did."

"Sometimes it's much easier to go along with a situation than to call a halt," Margaret said. "Especially when you think it's what you want. In New York there was a gentleman, a good friend, and I wanted him to mean more to me, but as you said it doesn't work that way." She smiled wryly. "Randolph and I are still friends. He's very happily married now and has a little girl."

"Helen is married, too."

They paused by the banks of the river, where the clear water tumbled over the pebbled bed. Donald picked up a flat stone and skimmed it down river.

"Five," Margaret counted. "That's impressive." She picked up a stone, but her own attempt sank after one bounce.

"Here." He picked up another stone and gave it to her. "Now hold it like this, and pull your arm back—let me show you." He stood behind her, adjusting her arm. She still used the same perfume. Her hair tickled his chin.

She cast the stone, laughing as it sank again, whirling around, and whatever she had been about to say died on her lips as their eyes met. The urge to take her in his arms and to kiss her was almost overwhelming. She wanted him to—he could see it in her eyes. But if he kissed her now, and it led him nowhere—no, he couldn't go through that again.

Stooping, he picked up another stone and handed it to her. "Perseverance is the key."

Chapter Forty-Four

T HE MORNING OF QUEEN VICTORIA'S visit to Achnacarry was bright and sunny. Margaret, perched by the window staring out at the River Arkaig, was enjoying the luxury of a breakfast of tea and bread and butter in her bedchamber. Despite her reservations, yesterday had turned out to be most wonderful of days. Though there had been the occasional awkward moments between Donald and herself, the sympathy that had always existed between them had been rapidly re-established. They had sat up talking long into the night. Some of the conversation was expended on filling in the gaps in their respective histories, but they had also talked of other, inconsequential things, the sort they used to discuss in their letters. Only as dawn was fast approaching had the mood changed. Donald had turned to her to say good night, and the easiness between them became charged with a desire for a different kind of closeness.

Margaret had lain in bed wide awake watching the sun come up, disturbed and confused by the emotions swirling around in her head, and making no progress. Less than twenty-four hours ago, she had arrived here, hoping to prove to herself that her feelings for Donald were a distant memory. Frowning deeply, she poured the last of her tea into the pretty cup painted with forget-me-nots. The moment she heard his voice, the moment their hands touched, their eyes met, she knew that her feelings were no figment of her imagination. There was no doubt in her mind: she still loved him, and not only as a friend. She wanted more from him than that.

Dear lord, M., what are you saying? More to the point, what are you imagining you might do about it?

Dumbfounded, she gazed into the dregs of her tea-cup, as if they would provide her with inspiration. She didn't even know if Donald felt as she did. Was she too late? This was far too momentous a decision to do anything other than wait, consider things rationally. Yes, but if she did nothing, she might never get the chance again.

A soft tap at the door saved her from descending into complete panic.

"I came to tell you that Her Majesty has finally sent word of her plans," Mama said, breezing into the room. "She is expected this afternoon, so there is no rush to dress, though if you are expecting to monopolise Lochiel for the rest of the morning, you are out of luck, for he has gone down to the pier to make sure his little boat is ship-shape for the royal party."

Queen Victoria and her entourage arrived in the late afternoon, and drove straight to the pier Donald had built at the head of Loch Arkaig. Margaret and the duchess, Camilla and Susan were waiting to greet them, decked out in the various forms of tartan that the queen seemed to expect everyone in the Highlands to wear no matter the weather or the occasion. While the other three ladies wore cotton and silk, Margaret's gown, borrowed from Mary, was wool, which in the unseasonable heat of the early-autumn sun, made for uncomfortable wearing.

If Donald was suffering from the heat in his full Highland regalia, he did not show it. As he made the final arrangements for the sail with his captain, Margaret guiltily availed herself of the opportunity to admire the picture he presented, the broad plaid draped over his body, the gleaming buckle of the belt that held his tightly pleated kilt in place, the shapely calves, and the tanta-lising glimpses above his knitted stockings which the gentle breeze granted her. Her cheeks grew hot as her thoughts turned shockingly carnal, and even hotter still when Donald glanced over his shoulder and caught her staring at him. Could he read her mind? She discovered that she was brazen enough to want him to, and had the satisfaction of seeing her desire momentarily reflected before a shout went up that the royal carriages were approaching.

The screw steamer *Scarba* was too small to accommodate everyone, and so the honour of accompanying Queen Victoria, Princess Beatrice, Baroness Churchill, and the two gentlemen escorts was confined to Donald and the duchess. The plan to sail the full fourteen miles of Loch Arkaig had to be curtailed, for the queen had arrived late and did not wish to endure the return trip back to Inverlochy Castle in the dark.

"But she very much enjoyed her tea on board and admired the scenery," Mama said later, back at Achnacarry over dinner. "Though Lochiel was disappointed not to be able to show her the most rugged of views at the far end of the loch, Her Majesty was delighted to hear of his connection with Bonnie Prince Charlie."

Donald rolled his eyes. "And equally delighted with the screeching of young Gordon's bagpipes from the pier when we returned."

Margaret giggled. "It's a treasonable offence, Donald Cameron, not to love the skirl of the pipes."

He grinned. "I loathe them every bit as much as you do, and you know that fine and well. I remember you saying in one of your letters—" He broke off, remembering too late that they were not alone.

"It's getting very late," Camilla said, breaking the pointed silence, though it was not much after nine.

"Aye, I'm very tired," Susan said, smothering a theatrical yawn.

"All that fresh air out on the loch has made me long for an early night. If you'll excuse me," Mama said, getting to her feet and causing a minor stampede as the other two ladies followed her.

Donald heaved a sigh as the dining room door closed. "That's our skeleton well and truly out of the cupboard."

"My mother guessed straightaway that we were more than mere acquaintances, though I have told her nothing of our history."

The mood had changed now that they were alone. Donald twisted his wine-glass, staring down at its almost untouched contents. "Do you ever regret refusing my hand in marriage?"

Would he prefer her to lie? But she'd never lied to him, and just as important, she had long since stopped deluding herself. "I don't," Margaret said. "I regret hurting you, but not turning you down. It was the right thing to do at the time."

He looked up, smiling crookedly. "Do you know, that's what I thought you'd say." He pushed back his chair, getting to his feet.

"No, wait!"

"I thought we could go for a walk down to the loch side. It's a beautiful evening—it would be a shame to waste it."

"Oh. I thought you were—I thought . . ." To her horror, Margaret found herself on the brink of tears.

"You thought that I was about to storm off in a sulk?"

She laughed weakly. "I'm not sure you know how to sulk. I thought you still hadn't forgiven me."

"Oh, Margaret, don't be daft. There was never anything to forgive. Come on, let's take that walk, shall we?"

"Please." She sniffed, dabbing her eyes with her linen napkin.

"Do you want to fetch a jacket or a shawl?"

"Oh no. This blasted tartan gown of Mary's is wool, but there was no time to change for dinner. I was so hot earlier in the sunshine, I felt like a boiled lobster. How you managed to look so cool in all that regalia, I don't know, though I must agree with the queen on this one point, Donald, you looked very handsome in it."

"It was heavier than a suit of armour, but if it pleased you, then I'm sorry I discarded most of it the first chance I got."

They had reached the terrace at the rear of the house, where a path led down to the river. Above them, the moon was bright in the dark-blue sky, making mere twinkling points of the stars. Donald was still wearing his jacket, kilt, and sporran, though he had lost the plaid and the various belts, buckles, and ceremonial swords and daggers. Margaret wondered at her younger self taking so long to see how attractive he was and to understand that he felt the same about her. "I am sorry," she said gently, "for hurting you all those years ago."

"You'd have hurt the pair of us a great deal more if you'd accepted my proposal when you weren't ready. I told you at the time, remember—I didn't want a half-hearted bride. I still don't." He took one of her hands, kissing the fingertips. "Shall we let the past be?"

"Yes." She caught his hand, lifting it to her cheek, and couldn't resist pressing a kiss in return to his fingertips. "Please."

They made their way down to the river in silence, both lost in their thoughts, turning to follow the tumbling water to the pier at the head of the loch, where the *Scarba* was berthed.

"We'll take a seat on the deck, shall we?" Donald jumped on board, holding out a hand to help her. The boat rocked gently, then settled as they sat on one of the wooden benches. The air was still unseasonably warm, though there was a faint trace of autumn in the freshness of it, and the leaves on the trees which hugged the shores of the loch were just beginning to turn.

"In New York in the fall, the leaves hang on until the very first frost. One day the trees are golden, the next day they're quite bare. I prefer the way they take their time to modestly undress here."

"That's a very literary turn of phrase."

"I've been commissioned to write a journal-style series for the *English Woman's Domestic Magazine*, comparing life here and in New York, I might use it for that."

"What else are you writing, apart from the journal for—is it *Demorest's*?"

"Mary Louise Booth, the editor of *Harper's Bazar*, has some ideas she wants me to think about, and then there's the *Victoria*, which I think I told you about last night. Oh, and I have been asked by another publication to serve as their dispenser of wise words and sage counsel—you know the kind of thing, never share an umbrella with a man unless you are betrothed."

Donald burst out laughing. "No, I don't know the kind of thing. Did you invent that?"

"Unfortunately not."

"Will all of this work be published under your own name?"

"Most of it. Are you wondering what my father will make of it? My mother says that provided I don't become a journalist for *The Times*, he will simply ignore my journalistic efforts."

Silence descended between them once more, but it was becoming tense again. Tomorrow she would return to Edinburgh, and what then? Margaret didn't want to leave Achnacarry without an inkling of what the future held for them—if anything. She had to speak, to say something, no matter how difficult it was.

"I'm twenty-seven next month, Donald," she began, pausing to clear her throat. "I've been living on my own now for almost four years. I am no longer the impulsive young woman who ran away from her own betrothal party with no thought of the consequences."

"It's obvious to me how much you have changed."

"Yes, but I'm going to sound as if I'm being impulsive again. We've only just become reacquainted, and we are *both* older and wiser, in some respects much changed, too. But I *know* how I feel, and I'd rather we—because if I'm wrong and you don't feel the same way, then it would be better for both of us if we said so now, don't you think?"

He angled himself more towards her. "I am not sure what you're about to say, but I think it might be pretty much along the lines of what I was planning to say myself."

Her heart began to race. That smile of his, she wasn't imagining the tenderness in it. Despite earlier exhorting herself to exercise caution, Margaret had plunged headlong into this declaration without any preparation, but she was sure it had been the right thing to do. "A wise friend once told me, when I was appealing for funds, to always speak from the heart," she said. "I love you. I have never stopped loving you, but I thought you married and thought nothing could come of it."

Donald let out a long sigh, taking her hands, edging closer to her. "You must know that I still love you. I tried, but I haven't managed to find anyone who came close to taking your place."

"Oh! You put it so much better than I can." His hands tightened on hers, but he made no move to kiss her. "You want to know what has changed, don't you?" Margaret said. "I suppose the simple answer is that I have. I know that it would be a huge step for both of us. We would both have to adapt, but I don't see that as a compromise anymore." She was conscious of his gaze fixed on her, their hands twined, their knees touching. "I want to share my life with you and be part of yours," Margaret said, with every word becoming more certain. "I could carry on as I am alone and be perfectly content, but with you by my side I would be so much happier and I think—I hope—that you feel the same?"

For a terrifying moment he said nothing, and then he pulled her into his arms. "Oh, Margaret, I feel exactly the same. I love you so much."

At last, their lips met and clung and then opened into a kiss that was tentative and just a little strange. They stopped, smiled at each other, then kissed again, more deeply this time. Donald murmured her name, and this set her body alight, urging her to close any gap there was between them, wanting and caring for nothing save more kisses, and more of him.

She wasn't sure if it was the world which was rocking on its axis or the boat on the waves when Donald gently eased her away, shifting uncomfortably on the seat, adjusting his kilt, swearing under his breath. "We need to talk about what we're going to do."

"Get married?"

He laughed raggedly. "We are definitely getting married. The question is, when? I really don't think it would be a good idea to make our vows anytime soon. No, don't look at me like that, listen to me a moment, Margaret. It's what you've already acknowledged, in essence. We've both got lives we're happy with, but which are very different. I've got my work as an MP and the Achnacarry estate to care for; you've got your writing and charity work in Edinburgh."

"We can make it work, though, can't we?"

"Of course we will, and it will be worth it." He kissed her tenderly. "But the adjustments required will be significant. Simply trying to decide where we will live and how, for example. Then what if we are blessed with children—which I dearly hope we will be? It may be selfish, but after waiting so long I'd like to have you to myself for a while first. What do you think?"

She forced herself to consider, though she already knew what he said made perfect sense. "How long do you think we should wait?"

"A year? Maybe even two? Time for you to establish yourself, to build this Edinburgh Children's Sanctuary you're so set on, and time for me to decide if I'll continue in politics."

"I know you're right, but it seems a very long time." She was still struggling to get her breathing under control, her body still heated and clamouring for something other than rational, logical discussion.

"When you're sitting next to me like this, it seems an impossibly long time," Donald agreed. "To be perfectly honest, I don't want to wait another minute, but I'm trying to be sensible."

As a wicked idea popped into her head, Margaret once more edged closer to him. "We'll wait two years for the ceremony, and we'll decide how we'll live and where, and all the other practical details in a sensible and considered manner." She kissed him. "But in the meantime, provided we're careful . . ."

"Are you suggesting what I think you are?"

"Are you shocked?"

Donald laughed, sweeping her up into his arms and kissing her deeply. "I'm delighted," he said, making for the intimacy of the cabin.

Local Benefactress Weds Highland
Chieftain

Yesterday in St. Mary's Church, Dalkeith, Lady Margaret Elizabeth Montagu Douglas Scott was married to Donald Cameron, MP, 24th Lochiel of Clan Cameron. The ceremony was a private affair, witnessed by a small gathering of close family which included the bride's parents, the Duke and Duchess of Buccleuch; and her eldest sister, Lady Victoria Kerr, Marchioness of Lothian. Lady Mary Montagu Douglas Scott served as the chief bridesmaid, while the bride's close friend, Her Royal Highness Princess Louise, was her matron of honour.

The public service record of the Duke and Duchess of Buccleuch is well-documented and most laudable. Both have held prominent positions within Her Majesty's Court in the past, and continue to serve on countless Committees and Boards, and to provide patronage to numerous charitable institutions. While their second daughter has inherited this same public spiritedness, she has chosen to demonstrate it in a very different manner. The Edinburgh Children's Sanctuary, which Lady Margaret opened last year, was built on a model she had previously established in the slums of New York city. The Sanctuary is, unusually, open to every and any child, regardless of their circumstances or parentage. The success of the Edinburgh institution has been such that Lady Margaret is now overseeing the establishment of another in Glasgow.

We are delighted to report the newlyweds intend to

remain in Scotland and will set up home in the Clan seat of Achnacarry. We await with interest further developments, both domestic and professional, in the lives of this well-matched and intriguing duo who are a credit to their homeland.

Epilogue

THIS YEAR, THE TREE, WHICH had been set up in the entrance hallway at Dalkeith, was so tall that Mary had had to climb to the top of the stairs to fix the topmost star in place. Every room was filled with the scent of pine from both the tree and the garlands which festooned the bannisters and adorned every fireplace.

This morning the household had processed from the house to attend the Christmas service at St. Mary's. After church, Mama, Victoria, Margaret, and Mary had handed out presents to all the children on the estate, and Margaret had read them a new story she had written specially.

In a break from tradition, Mama had arranged for the usual array of aunts and cousins to be invited elsewhere, much to their disappointment. "I want us to enjoy an intimate family gathering at Dalkeith, this year of all years," Mama had explained, pressing Margaret's hand. And so every one of Margaret's six brothers and two sisters and their children had made a special effort to be there. The dining table had to be extended to its limit to accommodate the adults, and now that dinner was over and only the remains of Mrs. Mack's famous clootie dumplings were left, the rabble of children had joined them from the nursery for party games. Margaret, seated in the middle of the table, gazed around at her extended family, smiling with quiet contentment. Mama had left the table and was seated on the hearthrug helping several of her

481

grandsons to assemble a toy train track. The eldest two of Margaret's brothers were gathered around the side table, where the huge silver punch bowl was set out, arguing over which of the array of bottles, oranges, lemons, and selection of spices were to be pressed into service. Victoria was seated at the far end of the table, which had been cleared, umpiring a game of spillikins, and on the other side of the hearth from Mama, Mary was allowing little Meg, Margaret's namesake, to tie a multitude of coloured ribbons in her hair.

The duke, who had retired to the smoking room after dinner with Margaret's youngest brother, returned and gazed around the crowded, noisy room before electing to resume his seat at the head of the table. As usual, his only acknowledgement of her presence was a curt nod.

Little Meg abandoned Mary and crept over to her side with a storybook, demanding that her aunt listen to her reading, but as Margaret prompted and turned the pages, she was aware, once again of her father gazing at her over his gold-rimmed pince-nez, his expression slightly baffled, though there was also a hint of grudging respect. He had done his level best to rid himself of her, he seemed to be thinking, yet here she was. Having made her mark on America, she now had the nerve to use the name he had given her to promote her causes in Scotland. Her extremely happy marriage to someone the duke considered to be a friend should have met with his approval, but that he, too, considered to be inexplicable, for why should she choose to do now what he had tried and failed to force her to do all those years before?

Margaret smiled quietly to herself. Because *she* chose to. Because she refused to know when she was beaten. Because she was stronger than she looked, as Molly had reminded her when she had been on her way to spend her first Christmas alone right here at Dalkeith Palace all those years ago.

A small but defiant shriek coming from the doorway caused all eyes in the room to look in that direction. Smiling, already on her feet and holding out her arms, Margaret was astonished to see a hint of a smile on the duke's face as the newest addition to the family entered in his papa's arms. Donald Walter Cameron was just six weeks old. Earlier that day he had tolerated being handed from pillar to post around his many relatives, enduring the outpouring of cooing and cuddles and kisses with remarkable equanimity.

With a thatch of dark-brown hair and brown eyes, Margaret's son was the image of his doting papa. "I had to rescue him from your Mrs. Mack," Donald explained as he carefully handed the precious bundle over. "She was most reluctant to let him go. It seems his only flaw is that his hair is not the same colour as yours. It's long past his bedtime."

"We'll take him up in a minute, but there's something we need to do first."

Snuggling her son on her shoulder, Margaret took Donald by the hand, leading him out to the entrance hall where the tree stood. The baby snuffled then sighed, his eyes heavy.

"See here, this is the first ornament your mama ever made," she said, pointing out the emerald one. Reaching into her pocket she pulled out a tiny little gold star. "And this is your first star, which Papa will hang on the tree for you." Margaret planted a kiss on his downy-soft hair, drinking in the special newborn baby scent of him. "Then next year, little one, you can help Papa and Mama make the first star of many to hang in our own tree in Achnacarry."

Author's Note

Dear Reader,

Her Heart for a Compass has been fifteen years in the making. It interweaves two journeys through life: Lady Margaret's and my own.

It was when I began to research my own ancestry, discovering to my astonishment that my great-great-great-grandparents were the Duke and Duchess of Buccleuch, that I first encountered their second daughter, Lady Margaret Montagu Douglas Scott. She and I share a given name, our birthdays are within a few days of each other, and we are both redheads. I felt an immediate affinity with her and wanted to know more about her. When very little could be found, my imagination began to take over. Lady Margaret, the heroine of this book, is a courageous woman who fights for her voice to be heard and has the confidence to follow her heart. She is strong and resilient, determined to live her life on her own terms, to empower herself against all odds.

Bringing Lady Margaret to life, I have been transported in my imagination to Scotland, London, Ireland, and New York, learning so much about my ancestry and the history of each of these locations along the way. Writing through the COVID-19 pandemic, it has been a relief to escape into Lady Margaret's world and the huge cast of characters who share the book with her, some real, some wholly fictional. The Buccleuch family are not my only ancestors in this book. The Seventh Viscount and Viscountess Powerscourt (Wingfield), who also feature, are my great-great-grandparents.

I am delighted to finally be able to bring my version of Lady Margaret to life. I hope that you can lose yourself in her journey as I have. I hope she inspires you, Dear Reader, to have the confidence to follow your heart as I have learned to do.

Of course, every successful journey requires a helping hand. Mine was provided by Marguerite Kaye, my co-author, the mentor who guided me along the peregrinations of this literary journey. Together, we have forged a new, collaborative method of working, and become close friends in the process. Thank you, Marguerite, for teaching me how to translate the story that was in my head and my heart onto the page, and for helping me to realize my dream of becoming a novelist.

This journey would not have been possible without Rachel Kahan, an outstanding editor. She believed in me and in Lady Margaret from the very beginning and encouraged us both to be stronger and more courageous. Thank you, Rachel, for your attentive eye and insights, and for allowing Lady Margaret the page space she needed to grow into the feisty, fulfilled woman she becomes at the end of her journey.

Thank you to Lisa Milton and all the team at Mills & Boon for your abundant support and enthusiasm for this book. You introduced me to Marguerite and you gave us the fabulous Flo Nicholl to help steer us through the writing process and Becky Slorach, who devised the wonderful cover concept.

Many thanks to Jennifer Hart, Kelly Rudolph, Imani Grady, Kaitlin Harri, Naureen Nashid, Brittani Hiles, Alivia Lopez, and Mumtaz Mustafa at William Morrow for their diligence and professional savvy in bringing Lady Margaret's story to readers in America.

Thank you to Susan Lovejoy, my walking library who has diligently carried out an enormous amount of the research for this story. Aside from devouring and digesting a raft of books and delving into countless archives, she has an eye for historical detail and arcane facts that has been invaluable in bringing the Victorian world to life and making it as historically accurate as possible.

Camilla Gordon-Lennox also contributed enormously to the research, particularly when our heroine travels across the Atlantic and immerses herself in New York life. Thank you, Camilla, for the American ambiance and for the New Yorkers you found to share the page with Lady Margaret.

Thank you to Jan Miller and Lacy Lalene Lynch from my literary agents, Duprec Miller, in Dallas. You have never, ever stopped believing in my dream of becoming a novelist.

Thanks to everyone at the Royal Lodge, to my own office team and my publicists. Steadfast supporters, who have been pillars of strength for all these years, thank you all. I couldn't have done it without you.

And finally thank you to my wonderful sister, Jane, whose impressive memory has helped to refresh my mind regarding all our ancestors.

Sarah,
The Duchess of York

Historical Note

Her Heart for a Compass is populated by a mixture of real-life historical characters and those entirely of our own invention, and set, as far as possible, against a background of real events and locations.

Lady Margaret Montagu Douglas Scott was the second daughter of Walter, the 5th Duke of Buccleuch, and his wife, Charlotte, who were the Duchess of York's great-great-great-grandparents. The scant information we have been able to glean about Margaret, we have woven into this story: her age, her appearance as a bridesmaid at the wedding of Princess Helena and Prince Christian of Schleswig Holstein, and the date of her marriage to Donald Cameron, 24th Lochiel, which was comparatively late (she was twenty-nine, he was forty). The remainder of Margaret's journey, save for these salient facts, is entirely fictional, though we have tried to be true to the prevailing culture of Victorian society in which she and her family would have lived, especially in the London scenes.

All Margaret's relationships with real people, including the troubled one she has with her parents and her romance with Donald, are entirely imagined. While there is evidence that she was friendly with Princess Helena, not only from her appearance in the wedding photos but from a reference to "Helena Letters" in Donald Cameron of Lochiel's personal papers in the Highland Council Archives, there is no evidence that Margaret and Princess Louise were friends, though they would certainly have been acquaintances. Where possible, we have tried to place Louise in the right place at the right time, primarily using Queen Victoria's journals, with one notable exception: there is no evidence that she attended Margaret and Donald's wedding. Princess Louise continued to sculpt and exhibit after her marriage to the Marquis of Lorne, who later became the Duke of Argyll. The couple had no children.

Mervyn, 7th Viscount Powerscourt, and Lady Julia, Viscountess Powerscourt, are coincidentally another set of the Duchess of York's great-great-grandparents. It is from Viscount Powerscourt's own work, *A Description and History of Powerscourt*, that much of the detail of the house is taken, including his obsession with stags' heads. Interestingly, while there's nothing to associate Lady Margaret with Powerscourt, there is an oil painting of the forest at Achnacarry with Ben Nevis in the background recorded as hanging in one of the bedroom passages, so it is just possible that Lord Powerscourt and Donald Cameron were acquainted.

Lady Julia's desire for children was eventually fulfilled, though not until she had been married for sixteen years, after which she had five in rapid succession. Lord Powerscourt, however, had long before given up hope of having an heir and apparently set out to spend his considerable wealth in order to prevent his brother Lewis from inheriting, which meant, sadly, that his son's inheritance was much depleted.

As for Lewis Strange Wingfield—it would be impossible for a novelist to invent a more colourful life than the one he lived. The third and youngest son of the 6th Viscount and Lady Elizabeth, some believed his father to be the 4th Marquess of Londonderry, his mother's second husband. Lewis was variously a traveller, actor, critic, playwright, theatrical costume designer, novelist, and painter (his work was exhibited at the Royal Academy) with a penchant for role playing, spending nights in workhouses and pauper lodgings, and becoming an attendant in a madhouse and a prison. He travelled to Paris as a war correspondent during the Franco-

German War (1870–71), where he trained as a surgeon. Though rumoured to be gay, he did marry in 1868, though he had no children.

The New York section of our book is also peppered with real historical characters. While their interactions with Lady Margaret are entirely imagined, every effort has been made to be true to the real person's character and history—with apologies for any mistakes, oversights, or omissions.

Mrs. William Astor was still climbing the social ladder when Margaret arrived in New York, just ahead of the Gilded Age and the legendary "Four Hundred" defined by Samuel Ward McAllister, but they were already assuming their roles as gatekeepers to society, and the competition to gain an invitation to "the" party of the Season was fierce.

Jane Cunningham Croly, who wrote a number of hugely popular articles and a cookbook as Jenny June, was a founding member of the Sorosis Club, whose first meeting took place in 1868 in Delmonico's. Mary Louise Booth, also a founding member, became the first editor of *Harper's Bazar* the same year. Both were advocates of a woman's right to earn a living and were closely involved with the women's suffrage movement.

James Gordon Bennett had retired from editing the *New York Herald* by the time we had him meet Margaret and had handed the reins over to his sports-mad son, who became the youngest-ever Commodore of the New York Yacht Club.

The lives of two of our main fictional characters have been inspired by real people. The Reverend Arthur Osborne Jay's work in the Shoreditch parish of London is to a degree the model for Father Sebastian's work in Lambeth. Reverend Jay, like Sebastian, believed that his parishioners' material well-being was as important as their spiritual health, and established a social club and gymnasium in his parish.

Marion Scrymgeour's experiences in the lower echelons of the diplomatic service have their roots in the lives of several diplomatic wives, travellers, and explorers, including Lady Mary Sheil, Isabella Bird, Lady Hester Stanhope, and Isabel Burton. It was Lady Anne Blunt who actually first established a stud with imported thoroughbred Arabian horses, rather later than our doughty Marion.

As for all the other main characters in our story, including Killin, Randolph Mueller, Susannah Elmhirst, Patrick Valentine, and Fraser Scott, their appearance, characters, and traits are entirely the fruit of our imagination.

The locations, however, are all real, and many can still be visited.

Sadly, Montagu House, which was the Buccleuch London residence until 1917, was converted to offices, and then demolished in 1949. The site is now occupied by the Ministry of Defence building. However, the other main Buccleuch residences still exist. Dalkeith Palace, just outside Edinburgh, is currently leased by the University of Wisconsin, but you can visit the surrounding park and enjoy a meal in the beautifully restored stables that were once home to Spider, Margaret's beloved pony. Drumlanrig Castle near Dumfries can also be visited.

Donald's home, Achnacarry Castle, was used as a base for training commandos during World War II. It still exists, and though it isn't open to the public, you can visit the nearby Clan Cameron museum.

Inveraray Castle, principal seat of the Duke and Duchess of Argyll, is still a private residence but also open to the public. The writing desk which Queen Victoria gave to Louise as a wedding present is one of the exhibits.

The world-renowned Powerscourt Gardens continued to be developed by Mervyn, Julia, and their heirs. Though they have been much enhanced since Margaret's time, all of her favourite areas in the grounds still exist and can be visited, including of course the spectacular waterfall where Donald first proposed. Unfortunately, in 1974 a fire swept through Powerscourt House, leaving only a shell. It was twenty-two years before it was renovated, and it is now one of the Autograph Collection of hotels.

New York in the early 1870s was being built and rebuilt at a bewildering rate. We have tried to be as accurate as we could with who stayed where, and what had been built or not, using contemporary guide-books and the epic *Light and Shadows of New York*. Five Points in New York was the junction where Worth Street, Mott Street, Park Row, and Bowery met, just south of Columbus Park. In Margaret's time, the area was a notorious slum, though it was not the den of iniquity and crime it later became. The two missions were located exactly as described in our book, but Margaret's Children's Sanctuary, sadly, never existed.

We have endeavoured to be as historically accurate as possible in all respects, but as this is a work of fiction, any inaccuracies, oversights, or errors are entirely our own.

Sarah and *Marguerite*

Lady Margaret: The Story Behind the Story

Lady Margaret Montagu Douglas Scott in her bridesmaid's dress for the
wedding of HRH Princess Helena, 10 March 1863.

(Used by kind permission of Donald Cameron, 27th Lochiel)

I'll let you into a little secret. The journey of Lady Margaret, which you have just read (and hopefully enjoyed!), was originally intended to follow a very different path indeed. Long before I sat down to write *Her Heart for a Compass*, I carried a vivid image of Lady Margaret in my head. I pictured her—dressed in breeches and a waistcoat with a man's white shirt and tall black riding boots, her red hair flowing out behind her—astride a white cob called Pasha, galloping over a bleak Scottish moor. She had stayed out too long, and was trying to sneak back unnoticed into a Palladian mansion, when she heard a pistol shot through the open French window. Rushing to investigate, she found her father lying dead. She picked up the gun and was holding it when her brother came on the scene and assumed that it was she who fired it. "Duke's Daughter Accused of Murder" would be the banner headline in the *Illustrated London News*. I imagined sending my fledgling heroine off on a journey that would take her to the slums of London, to Bedlam hospital, and journeying half-way across the world in order to clear her name.

Of course, as any writer knows, your characters have minds of their own—capricious Lady Margaret was never going to do what she was told—but in essence her character has changed very little from the person I first imagined: a woman with great personal charm and strength, with the courage and conviction to break with convention to live her life on her own terms.

As the daughter of one of the most influential aristocratic families in the court of Queen Victoria, it's difficult to overstate just how strictly controlled Lady Margaret's life was. Her sole purpose was to make a prestigious marriage and to start popping out the offspring required to continue the line and extend the dynasty's web of influence. Queen Victoria herself set the benchmark with her nine children. Her eldest daughter, Princess Victoria (Vicky), had eight. Margaret herself was one of seven; and her elder sister, another Victoria, matched the queen by having nine of her own. But Lady Margaret bucked the trend: she didn't marry until she was twenty-nine. She was a rebel, I realized after encountering her on my family tree.

To get an idea of just how extraordinary the woman I have portrayed must have been, let me give you an insight into what her life might have been like. For a start, the dynasty she was born into was one notch off royalty. Both her parents, the Duke and Duchess of Buccleuch, had held senior positions at court and were intimate with both Queen Victoria and Prince Albert. The royal couple paid them a great honour by visiting Dalkeith Palace in 1842 at the beginning and the end of a royal tour primarily organized by the duke. If you visit the towns of Dalkeith or Dumfries, where two of their stately homes are located, you can see the Buccleuch name everywhere you look—on street signs, over pubs, on plaques, and on civic buildings. The Buccleuchs were a serious power couple of the day.

Margaret was educated at home by governesses, but with minimal emphasis on subjects like maths and literature. She would have been taught embroidery and deportment. She could probably speak French, play the piano or the harp, and paint with watercolours. But the most important aspect of her education would have been preparing her for her future role as the wife of an eminent nobleman, with several great households to run. Though I have chosen to feature Dalkeith Palace as Margaret's main childhood residence, in reality she would probably have shuttled between all of the magnificent family estates in Scotland and England. She wouldn't have a clue how to make a bed or boil an egg, but she'd be able to plan a twelve-course dinner for fifty guests or a light supper for a ball with two hundred attendees. She'd be expected to understand the niceties of court protocol and precedence, as well as politics, in order to ensure that dinner guests were appropriately seated, that the best bedrooms were appropriately allocated, and that the right mix of guests was invited—avoiding political and romantic clashes! Flitting between those various country establishments and Montagu

House, the family's London residence, would have been an almost military exercise carried out several times a year. The family would have moved from town to country and back again, depending on whether Parliament was sitting or whether the grouse season had opened. The family would have moved again at Christmas and Easter, and most importantly to London in the spring when girls made their debuts during the Season.

Margaret would have been raised to command her own grand domestic sphere, with hundreds of servants to carry out her wishes and to tend to her needs. From her birth, she would have been waited on by servants. The complexity of a Victorian lady's dress and toilette would require at least one maid to help her get in and out of her clothes. Servants would be witness to all her tears and her laughter. There was no concept of a private life and very few opportunities for secrets or intimacy in such a privileged milieu. Parenting was very much done by proxy. Servants were an integral part of her life, yet Margaret would have been expected to ignore all but her closest attendants—one did not converse with a maid or footman, or even acknowledge their presence—though of course, Lady Margaret often does, and indeed treats her maids more as friends, which in her world would have been considered eccentric at best.

Ironically, though she would have been given a thorough grounding in the science of running her households, the subject of wedding nights, pregnancy, and giving birth were completely taboo. Many Victorian young women would have had no idea what to expect on their wedding night, and it's possible a number of their husbands had no clue either!

As a young unmarried woman, Lady Margaret would almost never be alone. If she went out riding, she would have had a groom with her, at the very least, even in the country. If she went walking, she'd have been expected to take her maid. When she reached marriageable age, her key asset was a spotless reputation, so her virginity must be protected at all costs. Heaven forbid a young woman was discovered alone with a man—in a park, in a carriage, on a terrace during a ball, or in a drawing-room. The immediate assumption would be that her virtue was compromised. And once the rumour mill began, it was very difficult to stop. The result would have been an agony of public humiliation, for even the most loyal of friends would be forced to shun such a girl for fear their own reputations would be sullied. And if the rumour took hold, the stain also spread to the girl's family. The Victorian court was an extremely exclusive club. The Buccleuchs were established members, but that didn't mean their position was always secure— when you were in, you were in, but when you were out, you were well and truly out. The queen did not forgive or forget whose family had caused a scandal.

For Margaret, though she grew up in such a closeted and constrained world, there must have been any number of occasions when such a free-spirited, irreverent young woman would want to kick over the traces, to make mischief, to say or do something outrageous. Her close friend Princess Louise shared her desire for independence and her exuberant sense of humour. I found it very easy to imagine the two of them at Windsor Castle, their laughter echoing in the corridors as they plotted and schemed to find ways around the strict protocol enforced by an army of courtiers. At a formal dinner, for example, where Margaret, late to the table, was seated by a notoriously tedious courtier, I pictured Princess Louise, more happily ensconced, finding a way to tease her, to make her laugh, while keeping her own expression suitably po-faced.

Princess Louise of course was much more savvy than Lady Margaret, and had a strong sense of self-preservation which my heroine lacked. Louise was ambitious, and adroit at playing the aristocratic game, knowing just how to keep on the right side of court rules and to use them to her advantage if necessary. Margaret was too honest and too straightforward. She did what no lady of breeding should do: she wore her heart on her sleeve. She refused to keep her opinions and her thoughts to herself, and by doing so, she broke some of the implicit rules of court life that still prevail today. At the opening of the book, when she very publicly made her feelings known by refusing to marry the man her parents carefully selected for her, she committed a heinous crime. A woman was the property of her father, until she became the property of her husband. Margaret's father, the duke, had almost no choice but to exile her in order to preserve his own good name. When she dragged that good name through the mud in the press, albeit through no fault of her own, their relationship never recovered. When Margaret was intent on publicly refuting the smears to her reputation, her parents were appalled by her naivete. No comment was the only permitted response in this case, even though a comment or two might have helped enormously. Undaunted, my Lady Margaret bounced back and tried to redeem herself by embracing the business of marriage.

Victorians didn't like to talk about bodily functions, or even admit that they existed. Convention dictated that women were fragile creatures with the appetite of a mouse, who would resort to a deep fainting fit for entertainment—as would you, if you were laced into a steel-boned corset and dress that could weigh between twenty and thirty pounds. Bear in mind that women of the day generally weighed only one hundred pounds themselves! Lady Margaret's full court dress—the corset plus many yards of cloth in her gown and petticoats—would have been so heavy as to almost paralyze her. One poor young woman making her debut in the same year as my heroine actually toppled over backwards when making her curtsy, felled by the sheer weight of her gown. The tradition of court presentations was ended by Her Majesty Queen Elizabeth II, but some of the protocol that Lady Margaret followed still endures. A person doesn't sit down in the presence of the queen, no matter what. In a deleted scene from this book, I had Charlotte, the Duchess of Buccleuch, seven months pregnant (and still corseted and crinolined), forced to stand for hours as one of the privileged guests at the opening ceremony of the Great Exhibition.

Court life was a privilege, but it was often, frankly, incredibly tedious. It became even more so after Prince Albert's death in 1861. Queen Victoria's daughters led a pretty miserable life, permanently dressed in black, forced to keep their mother company, deprived of any fun. They followed the queen in everything. If she didn't wish to talk, no-one conversed. If she wished to converse, she chose the subject. Public shows of affection of any kind were frowned upon—something else that has changed very little in court life. No wonder the Victorians developed a whole language of communicating with their fans. Lady Margaret would have had to endure the endless ceremonies and mindlessly boring rituals of court life when required—as she must have been regularly, in her mother's company. Her role as one of Princess Helena's bridesmaids was testament to her elevated status.

In high society, women may not have had a voice, but they must have had a great deal of stamina. During the London Season, Lady Margaret's day might begin around nine with a ride in the park. The day's invitations would be sorted through after this, and any domestic business taken care of, orders given to servants, menus planned, and the dreaded seating arrangements finalized if a dinner party was in the offing. Another change of clothes and a shopping trip might follow, then another change of clothes for tea, then another change of clothes before the ritual evening promenade at Hyde Park. Life was about seeing and being seen. Another toilette and then dinner, followed perhaps by a ball or three, the amount of time spent at each determined by the prestige of the hosts, and then bed at around three in the morning. Lady Margaret's dance card would have been supervised by her mother, who would also have been instrumental in shepherding suitable men towards her and keeping the unsuitable ones at bay. From Lady Margaret's debut to the announcement of her betrothal, she would have had almost no say in the process. No wonder she rebelled.

Lady Margaret was irrepressible in an age when women from all walks of life had very few legal rights, and almost no say in their destiny. Unfortunately, the stark contrast in Victorian society between the lives of the rich and the poor as depicted in my book was not exaggerated and was all too real. Whether Lady Margaret was in Lambeth, Dublin, or Five Points in New York, the poverty and deprivation she encountered first hand was both shocking and widespread.

She was acutely aware of how privileged she was, but also of the price she was expected to pay to remain in polite society circles. Ultimately, she chose not to pay it. To sticklers like her father, the duke, she was something of a horror. I love the Christmas scene at Dalkeith Palace at the very end of the book, where she catches him looking at her, wondering what on earth he's done to deserve such a daughter who keeps coming back for more, still smiling, still very much her own person.

After an adventurous life, she did indeed find happiness and settled down with Donald Cameron at Achnacarry, where they raised four sons. A conventional outcome? Yes, but one chosen by a very unconventional woman for her own reasons, on her own terms.

I hope you have enjoyed this little peek behind the curtain into the life and times of my heroine and that I've given you an insight into the world she inhabited. Her journey is complete. Mine as an author, I hope, is only just beginning.

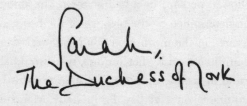

Reading Group Guide

1. What does Princess Louise's early observation that keeping one's thoughts from showing on one's face is "simply something one does" tell us about the world she and Lady Margaret inhabit? Are women still expected to do this today?

2. Margaret's father, the domineering Duke of Buccleuch, describes her at the start of the book as "immature and overly dramatic." Do you agree? Does Margaret's character change significantly over the course of the novel?

3. How do the snippets from the gossipy *Illustrated London News* fit into Margaret's story? How do you compare that paper's reputation-destroying power to the tabloids of today?

4. What do you make of the advice that her sister Victoria and Princess Louise give Margaret, telling her to harden her resolve and marry the Earl of Killin? Would you have married him?

5. What do you think about Victoria's admission that she had "reservations as to our suitability" when she first met her husband, but that with "determined effort" on her part, she had developed "affection and esteem" for him?

6. Was Margaret right to reject Father Sebastian? What kind of future would they have had together if she'd taken a leap of faith and

married him without her parents' permission? Do you think they would have been happy together?

7. The Duchess of Buccleuch, Margaret's mother, tells her, "You are my daughter and you always will be . . . you must never forget that." But she also says, "You understand that what the duke decrees, I must implement. All I can do is attempt to soften the blow." How much freedom does the duchess truly have? Is she also a victim of the strict social rules of the time? Of her autocratic husband?

8. Why does Margaret turn down Lochiel when he comes to see her in Ireland? Did her decision make sense to you? Would marrying him at that point have been a solution to her problems? Why does she accept his proposal years later?

9. What do you make of Margaret's friendships with the women around her? Besides her lifelong friendship with Princess Louise, what about her alliances with her maids Molly and Breda, Susannah Elmhirst, Lady Julia, and her companion, Marion? How do they help guide Margaret's journey?

10. What opportunities does America offer Margaret that simply wouldn't have been available to her in Britain? How is high society different in New York than in London? How is it similar?

11. Has Margaret truly reconciled with her parents at the end of the book? Do you believe the duke and duchess eventually come to accept her as she is?

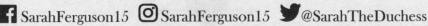

MILLS & BOON

THE HEART OF ROMANCE

LET'S TALK

Romance

Follow us:

f millsandboon

⊙ @millsandboonuk

⊻ @millsandboon

For all the latest titles and special
offers, sign up to our newsletter:

Millsandboon.co.uk